Finding Our Reality

Finding Our Reality

BOOK TWO

HALCIE DAWN

Published by Halcie Dawn
Edited by Elaine York/Allusion Publishing
www.allusionpublishing.com
Cover Design by Stacey Blake/Champagne Book Design, www.champagnebookdesign.com
Formatting by Elaine York/Allusion Publishing
www.allusionpublishing.com

For Kuntry, Boo, Dandy, and Big Deddy
Love isn't a big enough word.

For Granny
You left. But I know where to find you.
"Scratch my back and make me laugh…"

Author's Note

Finding Our Reality is Book Two in *The Reality Duet*. This is not a standalone novel and should not be read until after you devour...

Escaping Our Reality: The Reality Duet Book One

Otherwise, you'll be as lost as a Christmas goose.

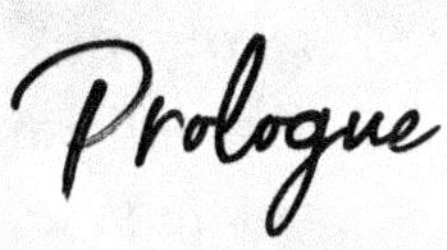

Prologue

Ella

I sit in my SUV, frozen in place, frozen in shock, looking at the place I once called my home. Everything is gone. No furniture, no storage bins, no tent. The only things that remain are the poured concrete patio, the stone firepit, and the wooden dock. And those were only left behind because they are permanent. Hell, if Ry had enough time, he probably would've jackhammered the concrete.

But I guess he was too anxious to get away from me. Too excited.

I tear open the envelope, ignoring the tug of my heartstrings when I see his handwriting.

Hate me.

That's the only way I'll be able to survive.

I don't think I'd be able to live my life knowing that you're spending every day, every waking moment, loving me the way I will love you until the day I die. Don't love me. Stop. Find someone worthy. Someone better. Someone who can give you what you need. Someone who can provide for you.

I'm a burden to you, Lulu. Don't you see that? I'm not the life-jacket; I'm the anchor. I'm drowning you, pulling you under. And I love you too much to do that. So, yes, I made this decision without you. But you have to know that I made this decision for the both of us. I need a higher purpose in life than just trying to survive the shit existence that surrounds me. I refuse to be like my parents or my brother. But I also refuse to have the woman I love give up the life she's been given. A life that's not a shit existence.

Let's face it, being born rich is a privilege. You are the most beautiful woman to ever walk the face of the earth. You are smart and funny and humble and fiery and passionate and... everything. My everything. You deserve every good thing that heads your way. But the truth of the matter is, you will always have more opportunities than those who don't have money.

You're the one who told me not to squander an opportunity. And that's just what you're doing with me. You're tossing away a future of endless possibilities. You deserve happiness now. Not in ten years, when I hopefully have a good job. Not in fifteen years, when I hopefully have some money to call my own. Not in twenty years, when I hopefully have the land to build our dream home.

Now. You deserve happiness right now.

So, hate me. Move on with your life. Find love. Find happiness. Start a career, get married, have babies. Do all the things that Carrie won't be able to do. Make your sister proud. Take what should've been our life and make it your own. I give it to you. I'm giving you the life you deserve. It's the least I can do.

I won't lie and say I wish we had never met. Nothing could be further from the truth. The night I saw you on the back porch was the moment I actually started living. The night I started hoping, dreaming. Don't ever think for one second that I didn't love you, that I don't love you. Because I did. And I do. My heart will beat for you until the heavens cascade to the earth.

Your laugh, your kiss, your touch.

Mine.

You're mine. My Lulu. Never before. Never after.

And I'm content with that.

But I want you to have it all.

The fault lies with me. I made the gravest mistake of all. I told you I wasn't a fan of escaping from reality. And yet, I fell into my own trap. I escaped. With you held captive in my arms.

You're free now, Lulu.

Reality reminds you where you belong.

So, he wants me to hate him.

Well, wish granted, motherfucker.

Nearly Twelve Years Later

Chapter 1

Ella

Holt wraps his arm around my shoulder, tucking me against his side. I don't really need the assistance; he's just trying to save me from the crowd of people who want to gather in my face, expressing their condolences—some be it authentic and some be it fake. Uncle Ray and Aunt Teresa take the brunt, allowing me an escape. We walk across the grounds, weaving around the headstones. My heels keep sinking into the wet dirt.

Figures I would have to bury my parents on a rainy day. They've never made anything easy for me.

When Marcum and Nancy come up to us, Holt untangles my body from his, quickly shaking hands with Marcum, as Nancy pecks my cheek and gives my hand a loving squeeze.

"Come on, Nancy, let's give them some time to talk," Holt says, holding out his elbow. Nancy tucks her arm into his and they head off, bending their heads against the mist falling from the sky.

Marcum pulls me into a hug, kissing my temple. "Been a long time since you've been back home."

"Yeah, things have been really good with the business. Busy."

He nods at the crowd. "Looks like half the city came out for the funeral."

"I know." I shrug, snorting in malcontent. "Social event of the season, I guess."

Marcum doesn't approve of my sarcasm. "Ella," he scolds.

"You're right. I'm sorry. That was a terrible thing to say."

"Did you ever hear any more from the NTSB?"

"Definitely pilot error. Dad only got his pilot's license two years ago. Bad weather came in. He should've turned around, re-routed. But he didn't. They gave me more details, but it doesn't really matter, does it? It doesn't bring them back."

He simply nods and doesn't coddle me. He doesn't spout made-up jargon about how nice and well-loved my parents were and how much they will be missed. Or how much they would've loved to see me grow and flourish in my adulthood. Marcum is one of the few people who really understands the troubled dynamic of the relationship I had with my parents. The struggles, the battles. The reason we only saw each other a handful of times since I left home at the beginning of August after my senior year of high school.

"How long will you be able to stay? It'd be nice to have more than just a day or two with you this time."

I sigh, rolling my shoulders. My low back is throbbing. Standing at attention like a perfect little statue—a perfect little daughter—definitely has its downsides. "It looks like you'll get your wish. It'll take several weeks, if not months, for me to get their affairs in order and close out the estate. I have to deal with Mom's original trust. Dad's business. His share of the medical building. I've already told all my clients that I'll be working from here for the immediate future. So much of what I do can be done remotely, via the laptop, so that's good. And I'm still close enough to my coverage territory to make all the upcoming trips that I need to."

He winks at me. "Well, I'm glad. You've been running from your home and your hometown for so long that you might be surprised to find you actually like it here now. And you know you can always stay with us if you don't wanna stay in that big house by yourself."

I can't help but smile, despite the circumstances. I really got lucky with him. "Thanks, but I'll be fine. I'm gonna stay in the Children's Wing, in my old room." I look around, spy Holt and Nancy talking to Ridge and Cullen, and nod in their direction. "Holt's done with physical therapy. He's heading back to North Carolina to clean out his condo and put it on the market. When he gets back, he's gonna move in with me for a while. I told him he could stay in Carrie's room."

"But you don't let anyone go into Carrie's room."

"I know. But why?" I shake my head. "At this point it's become nothing more than a shrine. It's time... time to let go. Lord knows I've gotten really good at letting go over the years."

He nods, looking up, studying the gray clouds. "We should go before it starts to pour again."

I look around the cemetery, gaining my bearings. I point to the right. "Just a minute. I need to make a quick stop first."

He doesn't ask who. He already knows because he delivered flowers for me. Nine years ago.

Fortunately, only three people stop to talk to me on my way to the headstone. One of them being Kristie. We've not really kept in touch over the years, just a sporadic conversation here and there. She was angry for a really long time when I left town. She was probably angrier that I had the locks to the door changed before I left on my graduation charity trip so she couldn't bust into my house any time she wanted.

And let's just call a spade a spade...she's not exactly the picture-perfect image of aging gracefully. She's thin. Her auburn hair is fried from using curlers and straighteners every day. She looks worn and haggard. But living with and working for her dad—even now, after all these years—can't be easy. And of course, she's still single. I don't guess she's dating anyone, but I'm not really one to call the kettle black in regard to that.

She asks to come over, asks to spend the night with me like she used to when we were young. I tell her no. Politely. But quickly. I'm definitely not starting that trend all over again. I'm a grown-ass woman. I don't need a sucker fish hanging out in my fish tank, sucking the life from everything around it. Especially not when Holt is there. He's got enough women hitting on him as it is. My house should be a safe zone for him. And from what Raylee said, Kristie may be single, and she may not be dating anyone exclusively, but that's only because she sleeps with any man with an easily accessible zipper. Raylee's husband, Will, owns a bar downtown. He's seen Kristie leave with different men, on more than one occasion. More like, fifty or sixty or seventy occasions.

I guess overprotective Phillip can't be cramping her style that bad. It sounds like the no-fly zone finally lifted over the zip code of her crotch and she's taking commercial liners by the dozen.

I read the headstone and run my fingers across the smooth, gray granite. "Hey, Harlan."

A cold burst of wind blows my jacket open and I quickly wrap it around myself, securing the buttons. "You may know this somehow, but I buried my parents today. Plane crash." The wind makes my nose run. "I miss you. I miss talking to you."

I sigh, rubbing my hands together for warmth. True to Alabama weather, the temperature is supposed to be back in the sixties tomorrow.

"Does *he* miss you? Does *he* talk to you? Maybe *he* visits you?" I bite my lip, thinking back to a happier time. To life at the garage. The three of us, sitting around, talking. "I hope wherever he is that he hasn't forgotten about you. Like he's forgotten about me."

All of a sudden, waves of nausea fire in my stomach. An eerie feeling makes the hair on the back of my neck stand up. I look from side to side, studying the people as they leave my parents' gravesite. I'm taken aback when I see a shadow lingering underneath a tree in the distance. My heart hammers in my chest, making me lightheaded.

Someone is watching me.

I take a step forward, but my heel catches in a thicket of wet grass, making me stumble. By the time I look up again, the shadow is gone. And dragging with it my unwanted anxiety.

Creep.

Kissing my fingertips, I touch Harlan's engraved name and walk over to join everyone else. Stepping from the grass, into the parking lot, all of a sudden, I realize that I'm an orphan.

No parents. No sibling. No husband. No children.

And that all fucking sucks.

Chapter 2

Ella

It still looks the way it did when she disappeared.

Clothes still scattered on the floor. Crocs still laying underneath the desk chair.

This coming summer will be thirteen years. Thirteen years since I've heard my sister laugh. Thirteen years since she walked around this house, driving me crazy with her horrible singing voice. Thirteen years since we cuddled under a blanket and watched a movie together.

I sit on her bed. Drained. Exhausted. Depressed.

The past two days have been filled with meetings. The lawyers, the estate planner, the financial advisor. For now, I'm done with the immediate tasks. Probate will be filed next week. I have to wait until I get the paperwork showing me as the executor of the estate before I can proceed with anything else. I emailed all my business contacts and told them that I was settled in and ready to pick back up with work tomorrow. That's the good thing about being self-employed, though. I can make my own hours, as long as the work gets done.

But today? Today, I focus on cleaning out Carrie's room.

Holt moves in on Saturday. He's using all of Carrie's furniture, so I just need to box and store her personal items. And wash the bedding. Despite how much he loved Carrie, I don't want him sleeping on thirteen-year-old sheets with his cousin's DNA all over them. Especially considering, that cousin is most likely dead.

Dead.

Like everyone and everything else in my life.

My parents.

Harlan.

The woman I called Grandma for a few years.

My heart, my soul, my passion, my fervor.

My Reality.

And then there's *him*. He's not dead, but he might as well be.

I hate him. That commandment in his letter was easy to follow. The hate flows from me naturally. Like a freshwater spring, never stopping, never slowing down. He left me. Broken and shattered. And it only got worse. Exponentially worse. And I hate him more every single day. Why? Because I still think about him. And that makes me furious.

I tap my foot against the hard floor, hoping the repetition calms me, but it doesn't. The longer I sit, the angrier I get, the more pissed off, until tears are streaming down my face, and my lips contort into a grimace. Unable to fight the need for destruction any longer, I stand up and scream. Louder than I've ever screamed in my entire life. I scream bloody murder. Reaching out, I sweep my hand across the top of Carrie's dresser, sending everything shattering to the floor. Picture frames, a vase, her jewelry box, a stack of textbooks.

It's loud. And messy.

I stand there, gulping air in and out of my lungs, trying to calm myself. Eventually, my tears dry in sticky streaks to my face and my breathing returns to normal. The destruction scattered across the floor makes me laugh. So, I stand there, amidst the shards of glass and crumpled necklaces, laughing like a damn lunatic.

Then, something catches my eye.

Her large jewelry box is turned upside down, and it looks like an envelope is attached to the bottom of it. It's peeking out from underneath a broken piece of particle board. The wood is a different color, like this bottom to the jewelry box was added as an afterthought, with no one even taking the time to stain it the same cherry wood color as the rest of the box. Carefully navigating the landmine I created, I bend down and grab the box, holding it upside down. I give it a few hard shakes and more earrings and bracelets and necklaces tumble out. One of the drawers even pinches my finger. Sitting back on the bed, I snag my hand under the torn section and give it a quick pull. The paper-thin pressed wood falls apart easily, sending little pieces of sawdust everywhere. I run my fingers across the large envelope taped to the bottom—the *actual* bottom—of the jewelry box. Quickly, I pull my fingers away. Something in the back of my brain tells me this is important. That this isn't just a note that was put here when Carrie was a little girl and this was her top-secret location for hiding the combination to her school locker or something.

Luckily, I know how to handle important things. It's a business hazard.

Taking the jewelry box into the kitchen, I set it on the kitchen counter. I race around to the sink and knock over five-thousand bottles of cleaning supplies before I find the box of clear plastic gloves. Gloving up like I'm about to give a prostate exam, I carefully peel the tape away from the white envelope. I open a plastic baggie and shake the tape from my fingers.

Bile rises from my stomach, coating my throat and mouth. My lips are so dry they crack. What's so important about this envelope that my sister felt the need to hide it away from the world? Hide it away from me, her best friend.

Secretly, I pray that it's nothing more than a bad report card. Or a credit card bill for a maxed-out account that she didn't want me to know about it.

But I also secretly hope that it's more.

A question. An answer. A smoking gun. A clue. A remnant telling me what happened. Telling me where my sister went.

I take a deep breath and tug it open. I peek inside, making sure there isn't anything that could hurt me. It looks like papers and an ink pen or marker. Carefully reaching down, I grab some papers and pull them out.

Correction: Pictures. Not papers.

The first picture slices through my heart with a chainsaw. And it only gets worse from there.

There's a total of six pictures, and unfortunately, the background in these pictures is familiar to me. Why? Because I've seen it before. In the picture tucked snuggly away in my case file on Carrie.

It's Trey's mobile home.

Same couch. Same coffee table. Same tilted framed poster of a stoner movie on the wall.

There's my sister, with her beautiful blonde hair, her beautiful blue eyes, and her timeless grace. She's not high in this picture. She's sober. She's sitting on the couch by herself, perched on the edge, watching someone in the distance, not looking at the camera. It's a candid. There's no smile on her face. No joy in her eyes. She looks serious and impatient.

She looks like she's jonesing for a fix.

The next two pictures show she got what she wanted.

She's high as a damn kite. Her face is contorted in ecstasy and her fingers twitch in front of her, palms wide, knuckles bent at odd angles. She looks lazy and lopsided, like her body is a wet noodle. Trash is sitting by her in one of the pictures. His hand is on her thigh. I have to swallow back my vomit. I haven't seen that repugnant shit's face in so long, I was nearly lucky enough to forget what it looked like. The other picture shows her spread out across the couch, laughing. It also shows half of Trash's body and half of someone else's body, but I can't make out the face.

Pictures four and five have me seriously concerned.

Seriously.

Carrie is passed out cold in both of them. In picture four, she's sitting up on the couch pressed between a guy and a girl I don't know. They are acting like bookends, keeping Carrie's body upright. Her head lobs to the side, and her mouth is slightly ajar. The guy is holding Carrie's hair back so you can see her face. The girl is smiling, like she's posing for a school picture. Next to the girl is Trash. Picture five is the exact same set up, except a new guy has joined the picture. They've laid Carrie's head straight back and, in that position, her mouth has opened wide in automatic reflex. The new guy is standing over her, behind the couch, making an obscene gesture with his hands. His hands are folded in front of his crotch, like he's holding his penis, making it look like Carrie is giving him a blowjob. He looks somewhat familiar. Maybe I've seen him someplace before. In the far corner, you can see Trey, watching and laughing.

Picture six is what kills me.

Kills me.

Makes my heart stop beating.

In fact, I rub my palm against my breastbone, checking for a pain reflex the way paramedics do, praying the panic stays deep down in my body. I would be sobbing uncontrollably if I weren't in such dire shock.

Picture six shows my unconscious sister being raped.

Her unconscious body is folded over the arm of the couch with her bare ass in the air, panties and shorts gathered around her ankles. Her face is smushed against the couch cushion and her hair is tangled across her eyes. One arm lies above her head, and the other arm dangles limply off the couch. A man is standing behind her, gripping her hips, pumping into her. This guy is different. Not one of the guys from the party.

How do I know? The clothes.

Well, what I can see of his clothes, that is.

He doesn't have a shirt on. Because of the angle of the couch's arm, he's having to squat a little bit and bend forward across her back. All I see is skin. He either took his shirt off or lifted it up to his chest, out of the view of the camera. But he did keep clothes on his bottom half. Brown leather belt, khaki pants, black boxer briefs, and brown leather loafers.

This is a guy who doesn't belong in Trey's trailer. Dude is dressed like an investment banker. Like a school principal. Like an accountant. Like a lawyer. Like a store manager. He's dressed like every single man I pass on the street every single day of my life.

And he's raping my sister.

I pull the picture closer to my face, inspecting the man for details. There's something on his upper left leg, on the side of his thigh. A scar? A birthmark? Whatever it is, it looks like the letter J.

I flip through all six pictures again, fingers trembling uncontrollably. They're familiar in one other way too. The bottom corner shows the date and a series of letters. The exact same letters that are on the picture Ry gave me all those years ago. I mentally count out the weeks. That date is about six weeks before Carrie disappeared.

Carefully stacking the pictures to the side, I reach back into the envelope to grab the marker. Except it's not a marker. It's a pregnancy test.

I'm staring at a pregnancy test.

And the two dark pink lines tell me that whoever took this test was pregnant.

My missing sister—my *dead* sister—was pregnant.

I can't even swallow. I feel like I'm going to collapse. Fighting that urge, I place the pictures and the pregnancy test back in the envelope and store them in a separate plastic baggie.

Then, I race back into Carrie's room and rip everything apart, looking for more.

I open the door to the sheriff's department and stalk across to the small reception window. They've remodeled since the last time I was here. Heck, they've probably remodeled a couple of times since I was last here. Don't get me wrong, Marcum and I talk frequently, and I saw him every time I briefly came into town, but we stopped meeting at the station a long time ago. He's... family. Not just for me, but for everyone—Uncle Ray, Aunt Teresa, Holt, Raylee, even Ridge, Cullen, and their parents. I don't need to hide my love for him under the guise that he's only an investigator working on my sister's case. He's so much more than that—him, Nancy, and even Nate, who's not a toothless baby anymore.

A petite brunette greets me. "May I help you?"

"Yes, I need to speak with Detective Marcum, please. Tell him it's Ella."

She taps away on the computer. "I'm sorry. He's out of the building right now. Is there something I can help you with?"

I knew I should've called. "That's okay. I'll try him on his cell."

She smiles. "Most likely, he'll be unable to answer. He's conducting some interviews. Is your visit pertaining to a case?"

"Carrie Hill." Shit. Why did I say that? I meant to keep that to myself. My nerves are just fried. I'm not thinking clearly. She's young. She won't even know who Carrie is.

She immediately starts typing on the computer again, and I try to politely interrupt her. "It's okay, really. I'm friends with Detective Marcum. I'll just leave him a voicemail to call—"

"The detective assigned to that case *is* in the building, though, if you would like to speak with him."

I square my shoulders, hoisting my purse higher. "Pardon? Marcum is the detective assigned to the case. He's primary. Detective Leary is secondary."

She doesn't notice the firm unease in my voice. "Looks like it was reassigned about two years ago."

"Reassigned?"

"Yes. And *that* detective *is* available in the building. I'm showing he has an open block now, if you would like to speak with him?"

I nod, unable to formulate a verbal response.

Why? Why would Marcum not tell me this? How could he? How could he do this to me? To Carrie?

She buzzes me through the locked door, meeting me on the other side. She ushers me to the left, down the hall, and into one of the interview rooms—one of the nicer ones, not reserved for true suspects. I wish I were a suspect, because then, she would've taken me down the right hallway, and I would've passed the small office where Marcum, Leary, Colson, and Peele sit. I need to see what's going on; I need to talk to them.

"I'll let him know you're here, miss. And what is your name?"

I squint my eyes, studying her and her small little body. I bet she was a gymnast in school. "I'm not ready to give that information yet." I'm not giving any information at all until I find out what the hell is going on. I swear, if my sister's case has been reassigned to some idiot, I'm gonna beat Marcum to a bloody pulp.

She nods and shuts the door.

I put my large purse on the table, checking it one last time for the baggies of evidence. The room has a wooden table with four chairs. There's one small window above my head, just big enough to let in a little natural light. There's a clock on the wall and a framed generic print of some woody landscape and waterfall. It's meant to be calming.

It's not doing its job.

I'm not very calm.

And every minute I have to wait for this guy gets worse. Five minutes. Ten minutes. Fifteen minutes.

Twenty-five minutes in and thousands of paces back and forth, I'm one split second away from tearing out of this room when the door opens. But it doesn't open all the way. And I'm not greeted by a full human body. Instead, it opens just a smidge, and I'm greeted by one boot, one cargo pant leg, a file folder, and small sliver of a hand. He hangs his body out the door, talking with someone in the hallway. The voices are muffled, and I can't make out what they're saying.

How freakin' rude can this guy be? I've made up my mind that I'm not telling him shit. And I'm not leaving this station until Marcum is back on the case. Spinning around, I refuse to face him when he walks through the door. He doesn't have time for me? Well, fine, I don't have time for him.

But then, everything changes.

The door opens all the way, and I hear him kick it closed with a boot. "Sorry to keep you waiting, ma'am. I'm told you're wanting to speak with someone regarding the Caroline Hill missing person's case?"

I don't have to turn around to know it's him.

True, his voice has more depth now. More tone. Aged like a fine wine. But I would still know it anywhere.

Because it's the voice that refuses to leave my head. No matter how much I want it to. No matter how much I hate hearing it.

It's the voice I hear when I touch myself, alone in my bed, late at night.

And I despise the fact that it still sends a chill down my spine.

Chapter 3

Crutch

She doesn't have to turn around for me to know it's her. I would know that body anywhere.

As soon as the last syllable leaves my mouth and I glance up from my notepad, I know it's her. That stiff back, those perfectly postured shoulders, that head tilted in the air, wafting the scent of fake arrogance throughout the room.

There's no denying it.

Her mile-long legs have a tighter line to them. Her waist, although still trim, is a little softer. Her hair, although still the color of heated honey, is shorter. It grazes the tops of her shoulders. It's also wavy now, not straight.

Her hips are wider. She's a mature woman. Child-bearing age.

Holy shit. Lulu may be a mom.

Marcum refuses to tell me anything about her. In fact, no one tells me anything about her. And I refuse to do a web search on her. So, it's a great possibility that she may be re-married by now. She may be someone's mom.

But, even if all that wasn't a dead giveaway, the hand rubbing the scar on the back of her neck would be.

She freezes the second she digests my voice. She knows it's me. We can feel each other in this small-ass room. She's literally sucking

21

all the energy from my body, even though she's more than eight feet away.

She doesn't have to take it, though. I'm willing to give it. I'll give every bit of energy I have to this woman… still.

I was always willing to give everything to Lulu. That's why I gave her life back to her. And I've been regretting it every second since.

Lowering her hand, she slowly spins around to face me. I stop breathing the moment I lay eyes on her gorgeous face. Time has been kind to My Lulu. She's only grown more beautiful. Just like the night we first met, her makeup is expertly applied. Her lips shine with gloss, her cheekbones are highlighted pink, and her eyelashes are luxurious and dark, probably painted with mascara that costs more than my bi-weekly paycheck.

Her eyes glitter with more hidden emotions than I ever thought possible. Despite the dilation, I'm pretty sure the overriding emotion is anger. She takes a deep breath, swelling her chest. It looks like her breast size has increased. A half-cup, maybe. A cup?

My dick jumps in my pants and I quickly cover it with my notepad and file folder.

Out of all the things I see that I like, there is one thing that I don't like. It's pretty damn clear that *Lulu* isn't standing in front of me.

Ella is.

She finally breaks the silence, hissing at me. "What are you doing here?"

"I work here. It's called a job."

"You came back to town? You live here?"

"I do. Most people live where they work. Makes life easier, you know."

Why am I being an asshole to her? I'm the one who left her.

She scoffs. "When? Did this just happen? Marcum would've told me."

I toss my folder and notepad on the table and fold my arms across my chest. "I've been back for years. And he has a rule—he doesn't talk to me about you, and he doesn't talk to you about me."

She starts to toss her hands in the air but quickly forces them back to her side, clenching her fists. "What are you talking about? How could he talk to me about you? I didn't even know there was a *you*."

She says the word 'you' with enough disgust that it tears a small hole in my already-empty heart. "There's always been a me."

What I want to say is 'there's always been an us'. But I don't. Because that would make me an idiot. I let her go for a reason, to have a great life, and I bet she's had one.

She bites her lower lip, thinking about those words. She opens her mouth and then closes it. Shaking her head to clear her thoughts, she massages her temples. "I can't even fathom this right now." Snapping her head, she puts back up her Ella wall. "Well, there's definitely gonna be some discussions with Marcum, but nonetheless, you still need to tell me what you're doing here."

"I thought we established that I work here." I run my finger across the sheriff's department emblem on my black polo, and then I tap my weapon. "It's not a water pistol, Lulu."

"Don't call me that."

Harsher words have never been spoken.

"I'm not stupid. Obviously, you are a cop. I mean what are you doing in this room? With me? Why are you the detective on Carrie's case? I need some answers. I *deserve* some answers. Why on earth would Marcum give this case to you?"

"He didn't give it to me. I asked for it. As soon as I made investigator two years ago."

"Why would you want it? Best way to keep an eye on your asshole brother and his merry band of douchebags?"

I'm shocked. "You cussed. You never cuss out loud. Only in your head."

"A lot can change in nearly twelve years, Ry. You can thank yourself for that."

She rips my heart from my chest. I never thought I would hear my nickname fall from her perfect lips ever again. Only one other girl calls me by that name, and it's not the same. Nothing in life has been the same without Lulu. And she's right. A lot can change in twelve years, but some things never change. Ever.

I lick my lips, thinking about her words. Her pain. Her anger. "You're right." I clear my throat and walk to the table, picking up the small file folder with only the highlights of Carrie's case in it. "Did you just come by to get an update on Carrie's case?"

She stares at me, not saying anything. She blinks.

She's hiding something.

I cock my head to the side. "Lulu," I warn.

She folds her arms across her chest, biting back at me. "Stop calling me that."

"You found something, didn't you?"

She snorts. "Maybe."

"Lulu, I'm not playing this game with you."

Wrong choice of words. I didn't mean to say anything that had a sexual connotation to it; it just slipped out. She remembers, though. She remembers the games we used to play. She tries not to blush. Really, she does. But it happens just the same. She pretends to busy herself with straightening the zippers on her large leather bag.

Then, she remembers who she is and stares me down again, trying to bore a hole into my soul. "Well, if I did find something, it would probably be the most activity my sister's case has seen in the past twenty-four months. Two years, Ry. You say you've had it for two years, and I don't remember getting any phone calls telling me you've found Carrie, telling me you've arrested someone."

That burns my ass. I'm a good detective. A fucking great detective. She knows nothing about me. I mean, the new me.

"It's a stone-cold case, and you know that. No new forensics. No new leads. Nothing. I've studied it and re-interviewed everyone that I can. Don't question my abilities or my allegiance to this department. Or my allegiance to your sister. Despite what happened between the two of us, I would never shove this case in a drawer and forget about it. I would never do that to you." I trip over my words, stumbling like a fool. "I mean, I would never do that to Carrie."

She just stands there like a statue, giving me one curt nod when she finally decides that I'm telling the truth. This standing and nodding crap? It's just like the night we first met. She's driving me mad. I drag my hand over my jaw and touch the items on my duty belt in nervous habit. "Now, you plan on telling me what you know? What you found?"

She squints her eyes and straightens her spine. "No."

"Well, I suggest you quickly modify your plans, then," I say, repeating the same phrasing I'd used multiple times on her over a decade ago.

"What will you do with the information?"

"What do you think I'll do with it?" Sarcasm drips from my voice like a leaky faucet. Is she seriously quizzing me on my aptitude right now? "I'll take it, investigate it, and let you know the outcome."

"Yeah, that's not gonna work for me."

A laugh bellows from me before I can stop it. "Excuse me?"

"That's not gonna work for me. I need to be a part of this investigation. I've sat on the sidelines since Carrie disappeared because I was just a kid, and I'm done with that. It obviously hasn't worked, so a fresh approach is needed. That's what I provide. A fresh set of eyes. I'm in this."

"Lulu, have you gone mental? You can't be involved in the investigation. It's a conflict of interest. Plus, you're a civilian."

"You're obviously not too concerned with any type of conflict of interest because you had yourself assigned to the case. And we both know that there is a good chance your brother knows something, or worse, was directly involved in Carrie's disappearance. Open up the dictionary to 'conflict of interest', and your picture would be right there. So do you want to re-evaluate my involvement or not?"

Anger circles in my stomach, rising up in heaps, burning my throat like lava. "I disclosed all possible conflicts in the beginning. It's all been cleared."

"Really? So, you told everyone about the drugs? Finally? You decided to do the right thing? For once..."

Low blow. She added 'for once' as a sucker punch, hitting me below the belt. Doing the right thing is all I ever wanted to do for her. Even at my own sacrifice.

I lower my voice, trying to gain control of my escalating emotions. "I am not having this conversation with you right now, like I owe you some sort of report card on my past work performance." I lean down, pressing my palms against the table, and growl at her. "You *will* tell me what you know."

She mimics my stance, giving it right back to me, bending forward across the table, placing herself in my personal space. *There's My Lulu.* Get her angry enough and she'll show up quick.

"I won't give you shit until you bring me into the investigation."

"Never gonna happen. Watching your crime shows on TV is way different from real life."

"You have no idea who you're dealing with. Do you even know what I do?"

I stand up, shaking my head. "Yeah, you give me a headache is what you do."

Wrong thing to say. She snatches her purse off the table and skates past me, flinging the door wide open. Those long legs and knee-high boots slam across the floor, covering the distance to the reception area door in no time flat. She slaps the unlock button and slams the metal door against the wall.

"I didn't say you could leave."

She spins around. "Oh, I'm sorry. You're the only one who gets to leave without permission, right? How silly of me to forget."

Our exchange quickly piques the interest of Tara, the receptionist, and of the others in the front office. It's hard not to garner their attention, we're not exactly being quiet.

"You're out of your mind to think you can be anywhere near this," I say.

"And you're out of your mind to think I'll leave it alone."

Tara opens the bulletproof glass window and leans out, watching me. "Crutch, do you need me to call for assistance?"

Lulu turns her head to look. Her eyes dart back and forth between me and Tara. Her eyes widen and her jaw slacks. And then... she rolls her eyes. I mean, she *really* rolls her eyes.

It'd be funny, if it didn't drag up some painful memories from the past. Memories from when we were actually happy. It'd also be funny if it weren't true. But it is.

"Are you kidding me? Seriously!" Lulu taps her ring finger, letting me know she saw Tara's wedding ring. "Unbelievable."

Hey, I had sex with Tara before she got married, but I keep my mouth closed because I don't really think Lulu wants an explanation right now.

Turning, she walks out the exit door, hollering behind her. "This isn't over."

Damn right, it isn't over.

I stand at the door, watching which way she walks. Unfortunately, there's about to be someone else getting an even bigger headache than me.

Marcum's loving smile to his de facto daughter dies the second he sees the look on her face. I prop open the door and lean out, eager to eavesdrop on their conversation.

"What the hell, Marcum? Did you ever plan on telling me he was back? How could you keep that from me?"

"I have a rule—I don't talk to him about you, and I don't talk to you about him."

She tosses her hands in the air. "Why does everyone keep saying that? I didn't even know there was a *him* until ten minutes ago!"

Marcum reaches out and rubs his hand on her upper arm. She snatches it away. "And you gave away Carrie's case? All those times I asked you about it, and you just said there was nothing new?"

"That was true. There was nothing new, *is* nothing new. Hasn't been for quite some time." He pulls at his belt. "And while we are on the topic of keeping secrets from each other, you care to explain the drugs to me? Carrie using and selling? You kept that from me. From Ray and Teresa. You've been keeping your fair share of secrets for the past twelve years and we've all sat back twiddling our thumbs waiting on you to speak the truth. To us—your family."

She's taken aback. Her voice lowers. "They know about that? Everyone knows about the drugs? *You* know about that?"

"Of course, I know about it. He's a deputy, Ella. He's sworn to tell the truth. But he told us about the drugs long before he became an officer."

"What are you talking about?"

Marcum shakes his head. "That's not for me to tell you. It's his case. And he's done an excellent job at working with what little information he has. It sounds like you and Crutch have some talking to do."

She shakes her head, slumping her shoulders. "But years, Marcum. He's been back here for what—nearly six years—and you never told me?"

"This past fall was eight years, actually."

"Over eight years! What are you saying? The Marines discharged him early? Why on earth would they do that?"

"It was a medical discharge."

I prickle, growing uncomfortable with the information that Marcum is sharing. I push open the door and step outside, letting him see me, alerting him to my presence. Even from here, I can hear the slight quiver in her voice, and it breaks my empty heart in two, making me feel something that I promised myself I would never feel again.

"Medical discharge? But he's fine. I just saw him." She turns around, expecting to see only the building. She sees me instead, standing sentry on the front walkway.

Hiding her feelings and the need for answers, she pulls her shoulders back and stomps away.

Chapter 4

Ella

It's very stinky.

Is it supposed to smell this bad?

I lift the Long Island Iced Tea to my nose and sniff again. I stifle a cough and place it back down on the sleek wooden bar in front of me. Cullen notices and asks if I need anything. Who knew Ridge's little brother would grow up to be so damn sexy? If only I were a couple of years younger.

I chuckle under my breath. Then what? I would date him? Be with him? Close my eyes and pretend his touch is someone else's? I did that for too many years and it didn't end so well.

I can't believe Ry is here. In town. Working with Marcum. Working on my sister's case. The whole thing is freakin' unbelievable. I can't believe Marcum lied to me. It makes no sense. Why would he do that? I wish I had given in to the urge to web search Ry's name. Multiple times over the years, I started to do it, but each time I quickly deleted his name and tried to wipe his face from my memory. Now, I wish I had done it. At least, I could have been mentally and emotionally prepared for today.

Words can't describe what went through my mind when I heard his voice. Before I got angry, it tickled my senses. Pure euphoria flowed through me. Delicious. Sweet. Orgasmic. Warm life poured into my dead body, and for a brief moment, I forgot all the pain and heartache of being without him, of surviving what I survived, of losing every person in my life so quickly.

But then I remembered.

I remembered the pain. The horror. The trauma. And I remembered that I will never forgive him. For leaving me, for making that decision for the both of us.

I run my fingertips across my lips, spreading my lip gloss, thinking. But, damn, if he didn't look good. Time has morphed the boy into the man. Sensitive parts of my body swell just picturing him. His hair is styled a little shorter now, and the color is a shade darker. His pale green eyes are still the most gorgeous color I've ever seen, almost translucent and trimmed in an almost-black hunter green. His shoulders are broader. His forearms are corded with thicker muscle, making the veins pop and protrude. He's tall and firm and wonderfully glorious. And based on the way that receptionist girl jumped to his rescue, his extra-large dick must still be in fine operating order.

It should be a sin for an asshole to look that good. All assholes should be ugly. They shouldn't be sexy, strapping men. They should be sniveling, little weasels.

I'm caught off guard when the barstool beside me moves. "First, there's the cussing." He reaches out and grabs a lock of my hair, twisting it between his fingers. "Then, there's your hair." He drops it and nods down at my drink. "And now, there's this." He grabs my glass, spinning it around. "Lulu drinking. You're right, a lot of things have changed in nearly twelve years."

I push the drink away from him, careful not to brush my fingers against his. "I'm thirty years old. I don't need to worry about lowered inhibitions anymore. A drink is just a drink."

"You're not thirty yet. One more month."

He remembers my birthday.

He reads my mind. "It's Valentine's Day. Kind of hard to forget."

Bastard.

"Is there something I can help you with?" I smirk, trying to bite back my grin because I know what's coming.

"Well, somehow, I think you already know. But I just got off a conference call with the sheriff, the mayor, and the chief of the city police. Imagine my surprise, when they informed me that the brilliant Ella Hill wants to provide her services to the forgotten case of her missing older sister. Apparently, someone promised them involvement in a TV show if the case gains traction."

"I didn't promise them a TV show; I don't have the power to do that. I simply said that it would make for good TV if the case actually went somewhere, and I have multiple lines of communication with all of the major TV news magazines and crime channels."

He scoffs. "I didn't even know what they were talking about. I had to put them on hold and web search your name."

"You've never googled me before?"

"Nope. And I can only assume by your reaction today that you didn't search for me either."

"Nope." His brow furrows. I can't believe it, but that actually hurt his feelings. I sigh, "Well, you're not good at groveling, that's obvious. You could've just called to give me the news. Why'd you come here?" I tip my chin in the air. "Speaking of, how'd you know where to find me?"

"Your SUV is still in the parking lot at the station. I knew you couldn't have gone far."

I mock him with a bitchy reply. "Well, he *does* know how to investigate." I bring the glass to my lips but lower it before taking an actual drink.

He bypasses my snarky comment. "You still drive the same thing?"

"It was just sitting at my parents' house. It drives perfectly fine. Why would I toss away something good?"

I side glance at him, waiting for him to tire of my catty comments, but he's doing quite well at hiding his feelings, all things considered. Cullen walks over from the opposite end of the bar.

"Crutch, what'll it be?"

"Just a beer. Thanks, Cullen."

Are you kidding me? I sit up straight, holding on tightly to my purse with the evidence bags tucked neatly inside. My eyes dance between the two of them. "You know each other? I mean, of course, you know each other, but..." I turn to Cullen. "You remember him?"

Cullen is completely confused by my reaction. Back in the day, Ridge never got into any specifics about my situation with his younger brother. Cullen just knew Ry was my boyfriend for a while, and then he wasn't. He was just the guy who helped out when the tornado came through their neighborhood. I'm sure they've all shared a little bit more with him, now that we're all older, but he's never come right out and told me that he knows everything about my past.

"Yeah, he comes in here a couple of times a week. Why?"

I bore a hole into the side of Ry's beautiful face.

Look at me, dummy.

His jaw twitches as he takes a long pull from his beer. A more expensive beer than what he used to drink. "You come in here all the time?"

"It's two blocks away from the department. It's a cop bar, Lulu. We all hang out here." He waves his hand back at several of the tables, indicating that other patrons filling the seats must be deputies or cops as well.

I try to swallow, but I can't. Has everyone lied to me? Every person in my life? "If you know Cullen, you must know Will, Raylee's husband."

Right then, Will comes walking around the back of the bar, carrying a case of beer. He freezes the second he sees Ry and me, sitting next to one another like long lost pals. "Oh, shit."

I lean forward, growling at him. "Shit doesn't even begin to describe the mess all of you are in." I twist in my seat, blocking the side of my face with my hand, like that will magically make me disappear from Ry's line of sight. "You knew *he* was in town? All of you knew? For all these years? And *he* comes into the bar! He's actually hanging out with my family! What the hell, Will?"

Will reaches out, covering my hand with his. "Ella, why don't we go in the back and talk about—"

I jump off the bar seat, wrapping my purse around me. "No. I think I've had enough shock for one day from the people I know. Maybe it's time I find a stranger to talk to. Maybe a stranger will be more truthful than my own family." I stalk away to the pool tables, searching for some distance.

Thirty minutes later, I'm in the middle of a game of pool with a younger girl—probably just twenty-one—when a ruckus at the front catches my attention. I nearly laugh when I see Raylee standing in the middle of the front door, legs spread out, eyes scanning the room. She looks like a gunslinger. But I don't laugh. Because I remember I'm mad at her. Pissed, actually. Will is standing behind the bar and he nods in my direction. Ry moved from the bar to a table about fifteen minutes ago, and he's been watching me, making my brain toss and turn like a rolling tumbleweed.

Raylee stops in her path when she sees him. She points her finger in his face, hissing. "Why couldn't you just stay away from the bar for a while?" He at least has the decency to look sheepish.

Her eyes catch mine, and I quickly spin away, pretending to watch the girl's next shot. She misses.

Raylee touches my back. "Ella, I'm so sorry you had to find out this way. Can we talk for a minute?"

"Why? So you can lie to me some more?" I make my shot.

"Don't be like that to me. You know we are always on your side. And we only want what's best for you. Now, you can come with me to the back to talk, or I can have Will and Cullen physically drag you to the back and tie you up, forcing you to listen to me. Your choice."

Dramatic much?

I apologize to the girl for my hasty exit and hand my pool cue to her friend. Pulling my shoulders back, I walk with my head held high to the back room. I turn around, leaning against the crates of booze and liquor. Immediately, the door swings open and Will joins us.

"So, you all knew," I say it as a statement and not a question. "How long have you known?"

Raylee sighs, biting her lip. "Years." She waits to see if I'm going to interrupt her before she continues. "Marcum told us. Well, he called Dad when Crutch discharged from the service and started to talk about joining the sheriff's department."

"And you just welcomed him back with open arms?"

She shakes her head vehemently, and Will reaches around, gently rubbing his wife's back. "Of course not, Dad told Marcum that he best keep Crutch out of his sight. Dad threatened to kill him if he even laid eyes on him. He could never forgive him for what he did to you. What he did to..." Her voice trails off, growing thick with emotion.

I bite my own cheek, using the pain to keep my eyes dry. "But now you're friends with him?"

Will jumps in. "This was already a cop bar when I bought it four years ago. Crutch had already been coming in here. At first, I didn't realize it was him until Cullen pointed it out. By then, I had already had a few conversations with the guy. I just couldn't bring myself to throw him out. I'm sorry."

Raylee turns around, sitting down on a crate. "It looks way worse than it is. Trust me. It's not like we invite the guy over for family dinner and games of charades. We just don't throw him out of the bar. Dad's run into him a few times and let him live. So, we aren't giving him friendship—just booze at a reasonable price and the ability to keep breathing."

"But why not tell me?"

She lowers her voice, trying to soothe me, trying to calm me. She really is a great mom. "You said you didn't wanna know where he was, sweetie. Every time one of us tried to talk to you about it— about *him*—you shut us down. You said you never wanted to hear his name, never wanted to think about him again. You said you didn't care where he was."

I purse my lips. "I know what I said, Raylee. But I didn't actually think he was drinking beer with my cousin-in-law and working ten-hour days with my adoptive father." I straighten the zipper on my purse, looking down. "Did you tell him? Did you tell him about what happened?"

"Of course, not! Never."

I glance at Will. He reaches out, grabbing my hand. "I know what we did was wrong. Keeping this from you. But Crutch and I never talked about you. I promise. He knows better. As soon as I found out who he was, I told him that you were off topic. He didn't even know I was your cousin until Cullen told him."

I nod, trying to give them the benefit of the doubt. That's hard to do. Even with my own family, it's hard to do.

Raylee stands up, stretching her back. "For what it's worth, he seems to be a decent guy. Marcum speaks highly of him. The newspaper has done a few articles about crimes he's worked. I think he regrets leaving you. Not that it makes up for anything, I just thought you should know."

"Well, he should regret it. I hope he tosses and turns every night, just thinking about the way he walked away from me, away from what we had." I snort. "Besides, he can't be *that* decent of a guy. He's only been back in my life for a few hours, and I've already run into a girl he's had sex with. He works with her. And she's freakin' married. Can you believe that?"

Will and Raylee share a look. The kind of look that married couples give one another. "What? What was that look for?"

"Nothing."

"No more lies, no more secrets. Tell me. Tell me right now."

Raylee takes a step closer to Will. "Well, it's just... he's still a very attractive man. Probably more so now than when you were involved with him. And, well, when you're attractive and single..."

Fury covers my body like a raging case of the hives. It makes me want to charge out there and punch him in the face. Punch him until he bleeds. Until he can't walk. Until he can't even function. "You're telling me he's a man-whore."

Will tries to defend him. Somewhat. "No, it's not that bad. He just leaves the bar. With women. On occasion."

"Maybe he's just trying to forget you the only way he knows how."

I clench my fists. "It's been nearly twelve years, Raylee. He forgot me a long time ago. That's plain as day. You can't tell me he's sticking it in any woman with a hole between her legs because his heart was broken over a decade ago. He was a sex fiend before we met, and he was probably just counting down the seconds until he could start his dick taste-testing again." I click my heels, walking away from Will and Raylee and saying on my way out, "Well, let's just give him a taste of his own medicine, huh? Game on."

Before the back-room door slams, I hear a confused Will ask, "What the hell does that mean?"

Chapter 5

Crutch

Six hours.

She's been back in my life for six hours and she's already driving me bat-shit crazy.

I down the rest of my beer in fuming silence. I want another one, but I can't; I'm driving. DUIs are kind of frowned upon when you wear a badge and carry a gun. She's been flirting with the same guy for about an hour—but she was never particularly good at flirting. She gave off too much of a bitch vibe. Although, based on what I'm seeing, she's gotten a little better at it over the years. Of course, this guy is too wrapped up in himself to notice the way her laugh fades the second he turns around, the way her smile falters the second he looks somewhere else, the way her spine stiffens, almost painfully, every time he tries to put a hand around her shoulder.

She emerged from the back room, after talking with Raylee and Will, with a newfound fire to her eyes. She refused to even look in my direction, heading straight for the bar where she began talking with one of the patrol officers for the city police. I don't really know him, but we've run into each other a few times. The city police and the sheriff's department do a lot of joint work together. He touched her back. Twice. I followed him to the restroom and promptly told him to keep his fucking hands to himself. Respecting the uniform we both wear, he obeyed, immediately sitting with a group of friends at a table and avoiding Lulu at the bar.

That's when she set her sights on this guy. It's Friday night, so the bar is full of willing participants. I don't know him so I can't threaten him. Shame.

How am I supposed to function with her back in my life? It took years before I could sleep a full night without dreaming about her. And I still can't get off without closing my eyes and thinking about her. Whether I'm balls deep in some random girl, or in the shower with my hand wrapped around myself, I still think about her.

Professionally and financially, I'm finally in a good place in life. Finally in a place where I can give her everything she wants. And she hates me. Of course, she hates me. I told her to do that very thing.

I left her.

It makes me sick to my stomach every time I think about it.

When I finally got a chance to talk to Harlan after MCRT, when I was in SOI, he told me everything that she had said. She was willing to drop out of school, follow me, be with me. At the time, I thought it proved my point—I was ruining her life. And I thought that every single day.

Until today.

Until I saw her face to face. Until I was close enough to reach out and touch her. And it turned my brain into scrambled mush. It makes me think what could've been. If I just called her. Told her to wait on me, told her to follow me, told her to love me.

I touched her hair today. That's the only part of her I've touched, and it stirred more passion in me than my last twenty sexual encounters.

What does that say about me? Either I'm still in love with her, or I just choose really boring sexual partners. I'd like to think I choose really boring sexual partners. Because loving her is not an option. Even if she'd allow me, I gave up that right twelve years ago.

I rake my hand over my face, turn my ballcap around backward, and scratch my forehead. I did the right thing, right? I must have. She apparently has some amazing career as a crime genius. I can't believe I didn't know anything about that. Sure, her family and Marcum refused to talk about her, but it definitely sounds like they should have bragging rights. It looks like Lulu is very accomplished. If she were mine, I would brag to every single person I saw. Strangers on the street would know about My Lulu.

Of course, the web search I did today only gave me professional highlights, nothing personal. She has a business website, and that's it. No social media. Lulu always did hate social media, though… just like me. But it would be nice to know something before we start working together. I grit my teeth, thinking about her marriage. Unable to control my anger, I push away from the bar with such force, I nearly topple my barstool to the ground. Cullen hollers over the music and TVs, asking me if I need another beer.

What the hell. Fuck it. I might as well. Because I'm definitely not leaving the bar while Lulu is here, acting like some kind of cat in heat.

Grabbing the beer, I head over to the room to the right of the main bar, where Will is helping tonight's band set up. "Need any help?"

Will looks over, studying me. "Nope. Just finished. They're about to tune up. Should be a good show. You sticking around?"

I glance over my shoulder, watching Lulu. I shrug. "Not sure. Depends."

"You know I'll watch out for her. Make sure nothing happens to her."

I believe him; I do. But that doesn't mean I'm going to leave. I nod over at her. "That's the second Long Island Iced Tea I've seen her with, but she's not had one single sip."

"Yeah, Ella doesn't drink. I mean, she had half a glass of wine one Christmas. And maybe one beer at our wedding years ago. I'm not sure why she's carrying that thing around. But after the trouble I got in tonight, I'm not about to question her on it. I did tell Cullen to make her drinks weak. Just in case she does decide to drink them."

"Yeah, man, I'm sorry about that. I guess I was fooling myself to think I could come here, hang out, talk with you, and she'd never find out. I'm sorry I put you in that position." I raise my eyebrows and take a swig of my beer. "Despite my good intentions, nothing involving her has ever gone according to my plan."

Will slaps me on the shoulder. "Then, maybe you should stop planning."

I follow him back over to the main room, unsure of how to even respond, when someone reaches out, snatching me by the bicep and pulling me to the side.

Oh. Fuck. My. Life. Why does this day just keep getting better and better?

Lynn leans forward, tracing her finger across the chest of my blue long-sleeve T-shirt. She sucks in a breath when her nail crosses over my nipple. "Crutch, you're not wearing your polo?"

I grab her hand, quickly removing it from my chest. I can feel a fiery burn scalding the side of my face. Stealing a glance at Lulu, my heart stops beating when I see her watching me. Her eyes flare in anger and her jaw clenches. She squares her shoulders and turns her full attention back to the guy at her side. Sighing, I let go of Lynn's hand. "Lynn, you know I don't wear department-issued clothes when I'm in the bar. When I'm drinking, relaxing."

Lynn has a thing for guys in uniform. She's young. Twenty-five, maybe. She works in the tax assessor's office at the county court-house. That's where we ran into each other. Of course, we hooked up. She flirted. I asked her out. We wound up at her place, having sex. I think her bedspread was a pink leopard print.

She's a nice girl, don't get me wrong, but she's also one of the many poor life choices I have stacked against me. I can remember her bedspread, but I don't remember her kiss. Don't remember her touch. Don't remember her scent.

I'm a complete and total asshole. And now I'm starting to think that my main goal in life was proving I was king of the assholes instead of being what I should've been. Lulu's champion. Lulu's lover. Lulu's partner.

Lulu's husband.

I'm surprised when I hear her behind me, clearing her throat. "Well, see you on Monday, bright and early. We have a lot of work to do," she pauses for a split second before choking on her sarcasm, "partner."

The guy beside her wraps his hand around the small of her back, leading her away. She grimaces, but she doesn't stop him. He's smiling like he just won the damn lottery.

She's not drunk.

She's sober.

She's sober, and she's leaving the bar with a one-night stand.

She's doing the very thing I've been guilty of on more than one occasion.

And what's worse, somehow, I bet she'll remember more about him than just his bedspread color.

Chapter 6

Crutch

She's following me down the hallway, hauling her purse and a large computer work bag on her shoulder. I offered to take it from her, but she refused. On our way to the conference room, we pass by the large bullpen office I share with the other investigators—Marcum, Leary, Colson, and the new guy, Wilson.

She pauses, staring at Marcum's desk. "Where is everyone?"

"Marcum is in a lieutenant's meeting. Leary and Colson are out of the building, and the new guy, Wilson, is actually on loan for a couple of weeks to a department in South Alabama. He did some undercover work when he was on patrol, and he's on loan doing the same thing for a different department."

She walks into the office, not asking for permission, acting like this is a second home to her. And I don't stop her. I should, but I don't. I always do what I shouldn't, and that hasn't changed. She opens one of Marcum's desk drawers and smiles to herself, quickly shoving it closed. I don't know why a drawer full of protein bars make her happy, but I'm glad they do. That little smile is the best thing I've seen in days.

She stops for a moment at my desk. There's nothing personal on it. No framed photos. No mementos. Nothing. At least, there's nothing on *top* of my desk. If she opened a drawer, she would see the dog-eared copy of *Silas Marner*, the last book we read together before I left her.

Reaching across to Colson's desk, she quickly rearranges his framed photographs and shoves his stapler and tape roll into the wicker basket of the large potted plant between his and Wilson's desks. She breezes past me, wafting the scent of her shampoo in my direction. "Let's go."

"You know he's gonna blame me for that."

She shrugs and makes a huh sound, quickly filing her fun side away and bringing Ella back to the forefront.

I unlock the conference room door and step aside, giving her wide berth. I reserved the room for the foreseeable future so we can leave our paperwork here and I can lock the room each time we leave. I've already brought in my case files on Carrie and stocked the room with office materials, a dry erase board, and a thumbtack board. I even bought the kind of ink pens and highlighters she likes. Well, used to like. She wastes no time pulling out her laptop and getting hooked up.

I pull up a seat, adjusting my weapon as I sit down. "So, what exactly is this business of yours? What do you do? Why did the mayor fall all over himself and break protocol to have you work on this case?"

She glares at me with those honey and copper eyes, blinking her black eyelashes. She's seriously considering not answering my question. If she's not even going to communicate with me, this will be one hell of a long investigation. It's already long considering I spent the entire weekend obsessing about what might have happened when she left the bar with that guy.

I know what happened. I've left the bar with my fair share of women, and I know the outcome. And it's driving me into the insane asylum. Driving me into an early grave.

Eventually, she concedes. "LMC Forensic Consulting. That's my company."

"LMC? What's that stand for?"

"It doesn't stand for anything."

"It's an acronym, Lulu. It obviously stands for something."

She stalls, chewing on her lip. Then she rubs the scar on her neck. "Love My Career."

Bullshit. She's lying. I toss the letters around in my head. LMC. I wish it stood for Luella Margaret Crutchfield. Wishful thinking, I know. Giving her this win, I move on. "So, what does a forensic consultant do?"

"I do a little bit of everything."

I grab an ink pen and flick it back and forth on the table, annoying her. "Care to elaborate?" She scowls like I just asked her to explain quantum physics to a toddler.

"A lot of what I do is the tedious searching that others don't want to do or have the manpower to do. Say an attorney is needing to comb through two years of bank and credit card statements to search for specific transactions that occurred at only one particular gas station. I search for that. Take it a step further and say those transactions then need to be categorized with cell phone activity that occurred at the exact same time. I do that." She just named the exact things she did with Carrie's case twelve years ago, and she's turned it into her profession. "I do independent review of police case files to give my opinions. Maybe ask the questions that others might have forgotten. Or say a prosecuting or defense team needs a certain expert witness in a field, but they don't have the time to research each possible expert's credentials and expertise to determine who may be a good fit. I do that. For instance, a surgery malpractice suit may need a witness physician who's specialized in a very specific field of study. Maybe there's only ten doctors in the United States who know this kind of technique. I search out who would be the best fit for the case."

I can't believe it. She's a detective. She may not carry a badge or interrogate people, but she definitely does the analysis part of the job. And it sounds like she does it well. "What about the TV stuff?"

"I was in the courthouse in Mobile one day, consulting for a prosecutor. It was a pretty high-profile case in the fact that it had a lot of news coverage. A prominent councilman was accused of killing his pregnant mistress and dumping her body in the bay. An assistant producer was there doing coverage for one of the major cable channels—one of the all-crime channels. The two of us got to talking, built a rapport. The channel was looking for a scouting and researching correspondent to cover and run down possible true crime events for coverage. It started with them. Others heard about my work, and I begin consulting for some of the major TV news magazines as well. I cover all of Alabama, Georgia, Mississippi, and the Florida Panhandle. I do preliminary interviews so they can plan accordingly for any coverage they may want to give a certain case."

"So, watching all those crime shows and documentaries actually led to something. Unbelievable. What about being an architect?"

She straightens her shoulders and pulls a notebook with green flowers on it from her large bag. "I'm here for Carrie's case, Ry. That's it. Not to rehash my life. We should get to work, shouldn't we?"

She doesn't want to talk about the past. Especially if it involves me. Can I blame her?

When I don't answer, she forges forward. "So, I was thinking we really need to start at the beginning. Go through everything with a fine-tooth comb before conducting any new interviews."

New interviews? How can I take her on new interviews? There's always a risk with any interview, no matter how benign it may seem. She really thinks I'll put her in harm's way? Is she in harm's way when she does interviews for the TV people? I shake my head, trying to clear myself of the binding cobwebs of worry. I can't allow myself to get distracted with that. Not now. I need to do my job. "We're not starting anything until you tell me what brought you in on Friday. You found something or heard something or discovered something. I need to know what it is, and I need to know right now. You may be used to leading the show, Lulu, to being your own boss. But make no mistake, this is my investigation. If you try to hide something from me, I'll toss you out on your ass. Mayor, sheriff, and city police chief be damned."

Ice cold blood courses through her veins. It's like I can actually see it through her winter-tanned skin. I'm such an idiot. Why do I keep sticking my foot in my mouth? We both know I already tossed her out on her ass once before.

Oh well, I guess she knows my words are no idle threat, then.

With about as much emotion as a carrot stick, she reaches into her bag and lays a small plastic baggie in my hand. I hold it up in the light. "Tape?"

"From the envelope. It will need to be tested for fingerprints, DNA. I touched the tape holding the envelope to the underside of Carrie's jewelry box so my trace will be on some of the tape."

"Envelope?"

She produces another plastic baggie with an envelope inside of it. My heart rumbles against my ribcage like thunder. Something tells me that once I see what's inside this envelope, my world will never be the same again. "Let me grab some gloves," I mumble.

Lulu beats me to the punch, pulling a small box of latex gloves from her large work bag. "Here."

She impresses me more every single second.

I have to shake my hands before reaching inside. They are trembling. I don't want Lulu to see me as weak. I can't help but wonder if she thinks I left her because I was weak or strong. Selfish or selfless?

Carefully, I grab a small stack of pictures. Wordlessly, I flip through them. As an investigator, I'm trained to keep my feelings in check, to keep things close to the vest. And I'm having a very difficult time with that right now. I want to scream. I want to break shit. I want to scoop Lulu in my arms and kiss away the pain I know she's feeling inside.

I'm furious. Disgusted. Horrified. Gutted.

Carrie is high. Unconscious. And being raped.

Lulu's whisper is choked. "There's more." She nods at the envelope.

My fingers wrap around something plastic. I've not had any one-on-one experience with a pregnancy test before. But I know enough to know that the two lines mean one thing.

I look over at Lulu.

I'm a fool. A damn fool.

I'm about to get myself into trouble. So much trouble.

We're told to never make any promises. Ever. Never make a promise in this line of work.

Yet, here I am. All I want in this world is to make her feel better. So, I'll promise her the moon and the stars. Why?

Because I shouldn't. And I always do what I shouldn't.

Chapter 7

Ella

He better not say he's sorry.

I don't want his sympathy.

I want his fire, his anger, his determination. I want him to help me find my sister. I want to bring this chapter of my life to a close. I want to bury her, give her peace, give her justice.

Justice. I really want justice.

His lips part, and I close my eyes, not able to look at him. Please, please don't give me empty condolences.

"Let's catch the fucking bastard."

My eyes shoot open. I'm transported back to nearly twelve years ago. Ry knows just what I need, and I'm so glad he's giving it to me. Reading my mind, calming my worry. Feeding me what I need on a plate of defiance and rebellion. Us against the world. He always makes—made—it feel like it's us against the world.

Reaching across, he wraps his gloved hand around mine. "I promise we'll catch him. We'll catch him, Lulu. And I'll never let him come up for air."

Relief chokes my throat, making it hard to swallow. I sigh, nodding in agreement. It doesn't take long for the warmth of his hand to penetrate the latex of his glove. Glancing down, the sight of his fingers brushing against my skin sends a familiar, yet frustrating, tingle through my low belly.

A completely *wanted* and *unwanted* tingle.

I yank my hand from his grasp and rub my knuckles to fend off the lingering heat of his touch. He tries to act like I didn't just hurt his feelings.

Asshat left me.

He doesn't deserve the courtesy of having me worry about his injured little feelings. Boo freakin' hoo.

He flips open his own notebook and prepares to make notes. "I agree we should start at the beginning, but we need to talk about these pictures first. And the pregnancy test. Where did you find these?"

"In Carrie's room, last Thursday. I decided it was finally time to clean out her room. The envelope was taped to the bottom of her jewelry box, hidden underneath a thin piece of pressed wood—she made her own false bottom."

He lifts his eyebrows in surprise. "And you have never seen the pictures or the pregnancy test before?"

I narrow my eyes. "Ry..."

"I'm just asking. I know the answer, Lulu, but I still have to ask."

I inhale, trying to center myself. "I know you do. I know the protocol." I wet my lips. "No. I've never seen the pictures, the pregnancy test, or the envelope before. Assuming the pregnancy test is Carrie's, I had no idea that she was pregnant."

"Do you have reason to believe that the envelope was hidden underneath the jewelry box this whole time? Since before Carrie went missing?"

"I really do. Marcum, Leary, and some uniforms searched Carrie's room. But it wasn't some rushed and messy search warrant toss. At the time, everyone thought there was a real possibility for Carrie to come home so they were gentle with their search. They searched everything—the drawers, the closet, the desk—but they didn't turn everything upside down, shatter jewelry boxes, nothing like that. Which is the only way I found this. All of her jewelry was still inside. Why would anyone think something was stuck to the bottom? Under a false bottom, at that? Carrie had to take all the jewelry out, stick this to the bottom, glue the false bottom on, and then put all of her jewelry back in. I just don't see someone else doing that. I feel confident that it was her."

"Why would you shatter her jewelry box? That's how you found this, you broke it?"

"I don't think that's relevant. It's a hard story to explain."

He nods, giving me some latitude. "But what about other people who were in your house after her disappearance?"

"Who, Ry? You?"

His jaw twitches.

I count off the people on my fingers. "My parents. Marcum. Leary. Uniformed police. Uncle Ray. Aunt Teresa. Raylee. Holt. Ridge. Cullen. Their parents. Janine. Caleb. Kristie. Hudson just a time or two. And you. That's it."

"Hudson was in your house?" His words are bitter and deadly.

So, he knows. I don't know why I thought he wouldn't. Marcum and my family may not have talked about me, but it's highly doubtful that he would live in this town and not know. "Yes, Hudson."

This time the muscle in his forearm twitches. He stretches his fingers to stop the renegade movement. "What about the news people? All of those interviews your parents did?"

"They did all the interviews from the Big House. No one ever came into our section of the house. Even when they had visitors or parties, the Children's Wing was off limits. How could they play the part of the doting, overprotective parents if they showed the world that they blocked their children off with a long hallway and a locked door."

Bypassing that comment, he goes back to my list. "Janine? Your old nanny?"

I grab a bottle of water from the small, glass-door cooler in the corner of the room. "May I?"

"Everything in this room is ours. For the foreseeable future."

I take several swallows to cool my flaming throat. "She came back from Arizona for a few weeks to help with the search. It was devastating to her. We were basically her daughters."

"And what about Kristie?"

"What about her?"

"I never liked her."

I tilt my head. I figured as much. He made a few comments in the past. He didn't like her coming and going as she pleased. "She wouldn't have put the pictures in Carrie's room. She doesn't know any of the people in these pictures."

He sits back in his chair, eyeing me. "I caught her high once."

"You what?" Did I hear him right? "You mean when she showed up drunk?"

"No, before that. She was high as a damn kite. I could tell in her eyes."

I blink. "High on what? Weed?"

"I'm pretty sure it was pills."

I clench my teeth. "And you didn't feel the need to tell me that? She was in my house."

"I didn't wanna upset you."

I snort. "My, how the tables have turned."

He lowers his voice. There's a tremble to his whisper that hurts my soul worse than it should. "I upset you? Now?"

Be a bitch. Protect yourself. Wrap your armor around your heart. "Just being in the same zip code with you upsets me." His eyes widen at my honesty. "Can we please get back to the pictures? Focus on our job."

Using his gloved hands, he spreads the pictures out between the two of us. "Fine. Read them. Tell me what you see."

I don't even look down. "I see your brother. That's what I see."

"This is what they pay you the big bucks for? The obvious?"

I slap my hand on the table. "They pay me because I'm good. Excellent. Better than most. You asked me what I see. I see Trash. Glaring at me like a damn spotlight in the dark. He's a lying, filthy bastard." I point at his brother's picture with the tip of my ink pen. "And he will be the first person we question. Do you understand?"

If I thought my outburst would disturb him, I was wrong. If I thought he would defend his brother, I was wrong. If I thought he would take me seriously, I was apparently wrong. He tries to hide the smirk on his face, but he fails miserably. "So help me, Ryland Joseph Crutchfield, if you don't wipe that smirk from your face, I will claw it off permanently with my fingernails. How can you think anything pertaining to your brother is entertaining?"

"It's not that. I can't get used to you cussing. It's unnatural."

Are you kidding me? I'm trying to find my sister and he's concerned about my potty mouth. He's comparing the new me to the old me. I can't be the old me, ever again. Too much has changed. Too much happiness has been ripped away.

I can't help it; I have to rub my scar before I collapse. As soon as my fingers find it, my mind starts to calm.

He clears his throat, frowning to wipe the smile from his mouth. "Sorry, I agree; Trash should be our first interview. Please continue. What else do you see?"

I take a deep breath, studying the horrible images. "They seem to be sequential. Same night. I think she's dying to get high in the first one and then she's high in pictures two and three." My thoughts race around, trying to connect all the dots. "It's Trey's house. The furnishings are the same as the picture you gave me years ago. The date at the bottom shows that it's about six weeks before Carrie disappeared. In addition, the letters in the digital timestamp are the same on these pictures as the one you gave me. So, my question would be: did Christina take these pictures? Was she there? Was this her camera? Did she have the pictures developed? Did she give the pictures to Carrie?"

He nods, eagerly watching me. "That's perfect. Give me more, tell me more."

"I think everyone left the room. Most likely, they left the trailer. I don't think all these people were present when Carrie was getting raped. I think it was just Carrie, the rapist, the cameraman—or woman—and..."

"And?"

"Trey. I think he was watching. I don't think he would leave his own house. He wouldn't let someone have that kind of control over him."

Ry seems completely mesmerized. He's watching me, just casting a glance downward every so often to make sure his notes stay on the notebook page. He seems almost... proud.

Is Ry proud of me?

"Keep going. Don't slow the momentum," he says, encouraging me.

"Why is the rapist dressed like that? Like a businessman? Was he there buying drugs? Trying to buy a hooker? Or was it something more? Is he the supplier? If Trey always made everyone leave when the supplier was showing up, that would answer the question of who all was present during the rape. Everyone left, but Carrie couldn't move; she was passed out. Maybe Trey took the picture. Maybe Trey took the picture, and Christina found it and gave it to Carrie."

I tap my fingers on the table. "But why take the picture in the first place? If Trey wouldn't even let Christina take a picture with some pills in the background, why take a picture of a felony sex crime taking place in your house? Blackmail? Sexual arousal, maybe?" That thought churns a violent spasm of disgust in my stomach, making me want to throw up.

"He has a scar or something on his upper left thigh, shaped like the letter J. We need to run that through all the databases. We need to find out if there is anything special about his clothes. Can we tell what kind of belt that is? Pants, shoes? Even underwear?"

I bite my lip. "We need to look at the date. Were there any police calls in the area on that night? What about speeding tickets near Trey's mobile home? Was that night anything special for me? Where was I when my sister was getting raped? And what about the pregnancy test? Did Carrie take the pregnancy test after she received the pictures? Or did she already know she was pregnant? And is there any possibility that the pregnancy isn't related to the rape? When's the last time Carrie and Caleb were intimate?" Rolling my shoulders to ease the tension, I take another drink of water.

Ry raises his eyebrows. He bites the corner of his lip, trying to stop his smile, but he can't. It's a sweet smile, a proud smile...a smile that lovers share.

I don't smile back. I can't. I wasn't lying when I said being in the same zip code with him was upsetting. It's terribly upsetting. Because just looking at him makes me *want*. Makes me need, makes me desire. It makes my body betray my mind. And just when I get my body under control, my mind decides to double-cross me as well.

I can't even look at him and hold onto my sanity. I'm going crazy.

Why on earth did I think I could work with him?

He slowly removes the gloves from his hands and reaches across, grabbing my bottle of water. Tipping it to his perfect lips, he downs the rest in one gulp. He nods at the notebook page filled with his handwritten notes. "Is that all?"

"Isn't that enough?"

Seriously, Ry, isn't that enough?

Chapter 8

Crutch

I*sn't that enough?*

Why do all her questions seem so loaded?

Am I making myself crazy by reading more into her words? I'm losing my sanity. Quickly. And the sad part is, I don't even know if I want to save myself from it. Hell knows, I don't deserve saving.

I toss the empty bottle into the recycling bin in the corner. "That's enough."

She scoots around in her seat, sitting straighter and grabbing an ink pen. "Your turn. Tell me what you see. Do you know these other people?"

Careful not to touch the pictures, I point. "That guy is Tyler. Holly," I point to the girl next to Carrie, "was his on-again/off-again girlfriend. They were older than all of us, closer to Trey's age. And the douchebag standing behind the couch is James. I knew him better than Tyler and Holly. He came over to Trash's house more than they did."

I study the images. "Just like you, I think Christina took the first five pictures. But I just don't see her taking the last picture. No matter how high she was, I don't think she would stand by and watch someone be sexually assaulted. She was already a mom, by then. She had kids, you know?" I look at Lulu for affirmation, but she doesn't acknowledge me. "Either way, all the pictures were taken with her camera. Those letters, *CAJ*, after the date? Those are her initials. Christina Ann Janas."

Her forehead wrinkles in thought. "You didn't tell me that when you gave me the first picture."

"You didn't ask."

She sits back, folding her arms across her chest. She's not amused.

Tough crowd.

"Anyway, have you made copies of these pictures? I need to log them and get them over to a crime tech."

"I don't wanna use the state lab. The backlog is too heavy. I'll pay for everything to go to a private lab."

"We'll have to get permission for that from the sheriff and the county prosecutor."

She pulls her laptop in front of her, clicking around. "They responded to my request first thing this morning. You should have the paperwork on that approval by the end of the week."

Who is this woman? My Lulu always loved to bust my balls. Now, she's busting balls in a professional setting. It's amazing, really.

She's amazing.

And gorgeous. And sexy.

I clear my throat, shifting in my seat before my dick gets me into trouble. I pick up my discarded glove and wrap it around the palm of my hand, gently packing up the pictures and pregnancy test. "I'll be back in just a minute. We can start going over the old case file when I get back."

"What about the other evidence?"

"What about it?"

Her face softens for a moment. "You still have it, right? I mean, in evidence lock up? I've worked cases before where the evidence has randomly and inexplicably disappeared. That hasn't happened with the stuff from Carrie's car, right? I know it wasn't much, but still."

"Everything is safe. It's right where it should be at the evidence warehouse. I promise." I keep my mouth shut, not divulging more.

I know for a fact it's safe. Because once a week, I drive down to that warehouse and check on it myself. But I won't tell her that. How do I explain that to her? That I've thought about her so damn much over the years, that the only way I know how to express my concern is to watch over some receipts, soda cups, and a purse that belong to her missing, and presumed dead, sister.

As soon as I'm back in the conference room, we get to work, researching and discussing the day of Carrie's disappearance and the first police report. It seems Lulu likes to take the same approach as me—look at the specific event in question, then dissect everything from the past that led up to the event, and then examine the aftermath. After working in chronological order, go back and review the evidence from the whole chain, segment by segment.

Eventually, my stomach starts to growl and muscles ache from sitting. I flip over my phone, checking the time. "We need to break for lunch. It's two p.m. already. I'm starving." I press the phone to my ear, hitting the command to listen to a voicemail someone left me a bit ago.

She peeks at me beneath heavy eyelids, scanning me from top to bottom. She doesn't think I'm paying attention. She thinks I'm listening to my phone. Well, I can do two things at once, and I nearly wet myself when she mumbles underneath her breath. "Looks far from it."

Kill me now.

My Lulu just checked me out.

I'm a thirty-three-year-old man. But having her eyes on me? It makes me feel like a young schoolboy having his first crush.

I stand up, pocketing my phone and straightening my duty belt. "Let's grab some lunch. Come on."

"I'm fine. I'll eat a protein bar."

"A protein bar? You need something more than that."

She stares at me. Hard. "I know what I need."

"It's food, Lulu. We've made it all day without breaking into a fist fight. I think we can survive a thirty-minute lunch."

She's about to say no. I know she is. But her stomach picks that precise moment to growl. Loudly. Her cheeks pink in embarrassment, but she pretends it doesn't faze her. "Fine. Whatever."

I hide my smile. No need to gloat over this small victory. I quickly lock the conference room door and we head out. It takes all of my effort not to guide her down the hall by placing my hand on the small of her back.

But I like my hand. And based on the way she stares at Tara when we walk through the reception area, Lulu would probably bite my fingers off one by one if I dared to touch her right now.

Fortunately, she lets me choose the restaurant. There are several downtown, around the station. That's the problem, though. In the past, a late night of work meant a quick bite to eat at someplace close, which may or may not have resulted in a quickie hook-up a time or two. I diplomatically choose a restaurant where I haven't banged any of the waitresses. Well, at least that I know of. I also diplomatically choose a restaurant that has Philly cheesesteaks on the menu. They're really good ones too. Greasy. Just the way she likes them.

Since we missed the lunch crowd, we don't have to wait for a table. Lulu takes a few minutes to study the menu before the waiter comes to the table, setting glasses of ice water in front us.

"Can I get either of you something else to drink?"

We both shake our heads. "No, water's fine," I answer.

The kid grabs a pen and notepad from his apron. "Will this be on one ticket or two?"

Lulu and I speak at the exact same time with me saying 'one' and her saying 'two'. The waiter darts his eyes between the two of us, waiting for confirmation on how to proceed.

Her chin juts in the air and she leans forward, getting the server's attention. "This is a business meal. Two tickets. No further discussion." Taking the lead from her tone, he nods, and quickly asks what she'd like to order. She flicks her head in my direction. "You go first."

"I'll have the Philly cheesesteak. Add cheese to my fries." I'll be working my ass off later tonight in the gym, but it's worth it just to see the look on her face.

"And you, ma'am?"

She holds the menu out in her hand. "I'll have the grilled chicken Caesar salad."

That little minx. I know she wants a cheesesteak. I know her like I know the back of my own hand.

Well, I used to know her.

This Lulu cusses and has one-night stands.

As soon as the waiter leaves, an uncomfortable silence engulfs us, swallowing us whole like Jonah inside of the whale. I unfold my napkin, laying it across my knee. "I haven't given you my condolences yet, about your parents. I hate that you are going through that."

She reads me, narrowing her eyes. "Were you at the funeral?"

I scrub my hand across my face. "I was there. Yes."

"But you kept your distance?"

"I didn't think you'd wanna see me."

"How perceptive of you."

I ignore that comment, even though it stings like hell. "What happened? Was something wrong with the plane?"

She takes a sip of water. "Dad only had his pilot's license for about two years. The plane was part of a rental pool between him and some other guys. It was meticulously inspected on a regular basis. Nothing was wrong with it. It's simple, he hit bad weather, should have turned around and modified his flight plan, but didn't. Pilot error. He wasn't equipped to handle something of that magnitude."

"They were flying to Chicago for vacation? On New Year's?" I ask.

She smirks in angered disbelief. "From what I gather, Mom caught him with a new mistress, and flying her to Chicago for a shopping trip was penance."

"Lulu, that's terrible." I reach across the table, wanting to wrap my fingers around hers, but she quickly draws her hands onto her lap. Once again, it stings like hell. "I know you had a shitty childhood with them, but I still wouldn't wish that on anyone. I was really hoping that you'd grow closer to them over the years, as you got older. Did you?"

What I mean *is* that I hoped she'd grow closer to them once I was out of the picture.

She straightens in her seat. "I saw my parents four times since the day I left this town. That's it."

What? Is she serious? I've seen my parents more than that. And they are both in jail right now. "Are you serious?" She tilts her head, not even gracing me with an answer. Of course, she's serious. "Why?"

"Let's just say we didn't leave things on the best of terms when I left."

When she left.

I may not have searched for information on Lulu, her family may not have talked to me about her, but you can't live in this county and not know *this* about her.

"Yeah..." Don't ask. I chant the mantra to myself, over and over and over. Don't ask. Don't ask. Don't ask. Of course, I ask. "I heard that you got married right before leaving town?"

"Then, you obviously heard I got divorced too."

I did.

Drops of sweat run down my back. "Hudson?"

"You already know the answer to that."

I can't even form a response. I do know the answer and it makes me want to projectile vomit. "So, how long have you and Hudson been divorced?"

She reaches around, rubbing the scar on the back of her neck. "This is really what you wanna talk about? You know most people talk about the weather or the news or sports when they are on a business lunch."

"We're not most people."

She tosses her hands up. "Fine. This coming August—the very beginning of August— will be three years."

I quickly do the math in my head. "So, you were married for nine years?"

"Yes, the judge signed our final divorce decree the day before our ninth anniversary."

I click my tongue against my teeth. "So, you got married when you were eighteen? In August? After you graduated high school in May?"

What I really mean *is* you got married two-and-a-half months after I left you? The ink was barely dry on our break-up letter, and you married someone else. Someone you swore was just a friend. While I was off at MCRT, learning to defend our country, some other guy was sticking his cock inside of you, on your wedding night, on your honeymoon.

She's rubbing her neck so hard she's probably giving herself a rash. "Yep."

The server's voice catches us by surprise. "I have a salad for the lady and a cheesesteak for the man."

Chapter 9

Ella

"You've had your nose buried in that computer for two days straight."

I glance up, watching Holt drink straight from the milk jug. Turning back to my screen, I insult him. "It's called having a job, Holt. I can't help it if you're an unemployed lazy bum."

I'm trying hard not to laugh, but when he throws a cheese cracker in my direction and it bounces off my forehead, it's a moot point. Giggling, I pluck the cracker from the countertop and pop it in my mouth.

"What have you been working on anyway? Carrie's case?" he asks.

"No, these past two days, I had to catch up on work from some of my clients." I sit back, scooting the barstool away from the counter so I can stretch my arms without knocking anything over. "Since lunch, I've been working my way through twelve months of text messages between two college-age kids—boyfriend and girlfriend. You wouldn't believe how many text messages young people send. It blows my mind. There's no way I sent a quarter of the messages that these kids do."

He puts the milk back in the fridge and seals the box of crackers. "Why are you having to go through their text messages?"

"They are accused of credit card skimming. She's saying he did it all on his own. He's saying it was all her idea. I'm in charge of reading through the thousands of text messages to compile the ones that have any possibility of having something to do with the case. I then have to index everything, chronologically and by reference to certain aspects of the case."

"So, you're basically reading every single thing these people thought about for a whole year."

"Pretty much."

He cocks his head, flopping his wavy blond hair. "Find anything good?"

I chuckle. "I always find good stuff. And boring stuff. And shocking stuff. And disgusting stuff. You'd be surprised."

He leans forward, stretching his arms across the island countertop. The muscles in his shoulders pop. "Tell me something scandalous."

I lean forward, acting like I'm about to share a huge secret. I whisper, "It's confidential, asshole."

Laughing, he grabs his chest, acting like I shot him. "You're so cruel!"

Moving my finger across the screen to bypass my screensaver, I pick up my ink pen and start taking notes again.

He clears his throat and then sucks air between his teeth. "You haven't said much. How are things going with Crutch?"

I scowl. "Fine, I suppose. He had other work to do as well. The two-day hiatus was probably needed on both sides."

"Are you still mad at us? For not telling you he lived here? For not telling you he was a cop?"

I look up, studying his innocent and handsome face. "Yes, I'm still mad at you. And a big part of me feels betrayed. Y'all should have told me. You know how I feel about him. I hate him."

He nods and then states the obvious. "But you still love us."

"Of course, I still love you. It doesn't mean I can't be angry with you, though."

"What if your hate for him isn't really hate? What if it's just anger?"

His words catch me off guard. What do I say to that? Sometimes, my rage for Ry is so blinding I want to scream and break the world in two. Other times, I cry so hard, longing and wishing for his touch so much, that I would sell my soul to the devil just to feel his lips on mine again. But even those feelings eventually leave me barren and empty and irritated. How can I even think about wanting someone who doesn't want me? He couldn't wait to get away from me, couldn't wait to leave.

He left me. With one single letter.

And that's why I have to hate him.

I have no other choice.

His stunning good looks and sexy southern charm can't sway me this time. I'm older. Smarter. Jaded.

Holt reaches over, pushing the lid of my laptop with his finger. "You should come with me to the bar tonight. I told Cullen I'd come over for a bit to watch some of the game."

"What game? Who's playing?"

Holt lifts an eyebrow. "Do you even care? The only team name you know is mine."

Sometimes, he talks about the team as if he's still on it.

"Well, that's the only one I'm supposed to cheer for, right?"

He mumbles underneath his breath. "I guess it doesn't really matter now, does it?" Walking around the island, he heads for Carrie's bedroom. *His bedroom.* "I'm getting dressed. Come with me. It'll do you some good to recharge your brain."

"Tomorrow's a workday. I can't be staying out all hours of the night."

"I'm not talking about all hours of the night, I'm talking about two hours during the early part of the night. It's not like you're tying one on and then having to fight a hangover the next day. You don't drink."

"I'll have you know that I had a Long Island Iced Tea the last time I went to the bar."

"Correction: You *carried around* a Long Island Iced Tea. Will said you didn't drink it."

"Will needs to mind his own business. He's already on my shit list."

"Ella, nearly every single person in the world is on your shit list. Now go put on some clothes before I drag you to the bar in your sleep shirt."

Neither Cullen nor Holt say anything when I order a Long Island Iced Tea. They know better.

That's how I find myself sitting at the bar, playing the sniff test with it again.

I spin on my barstool, checking the crowd. We sat down and ordered the second we came in, so I didn't even check the place out yet. There's a decent crowd tonight. I'm really glad Will's business is doing well. He's a good guy. More importantly, he treats Raylee and the kids like gold.

I pause for a second when I see familiar-looking auburn hair. Her back is to me, but I can clearly tell it's Kristie. She's standing in front of a table toward the back, talking to two guys. One guy looks to be in his early twenties. I can't see who the other guy is because she's leaning forward in front of him, blocking my view. Her dress is much, much shorter than she ever used to wear when we were kids. She's shifting her legs back and forth, trying to draw attention to her pale, bare skin. There's a winter chill in the air. Plus, Will likes to keep the bar cool. I'm surprised she's not cold.

I guess she's prowling for a one-night stand.

An overwhelming sadness tugs at my heart. I can't believe Ry said he saw her high. Maybe I should go talk to her. Distract her. I can't save her from every poor choice she's obviously making, but I can at least save her from tonight's poor choice.

I tap Holt on the ribcage. "I'll be right back. I see Kristie. I'm gonna go say hi."

Cullen leans across the bar, whisper-shouting as I walk away. "I don't know if I would do that, Ella."

I shoo him away. "I'll be fine."

Wiping the condensation from my glass, I adjust my grip on it as I come up behind Kristie. I call out to her before I get too close as I don't want to scare her. "Kristie?"

She spins around, wobbling on her feet. It looks like she's already had one drink too many. Good thing Will and Cullen always force her to take a ride share or cab home.

"Ella!" Rushing forward, she throws her arms around me, assaulting me with her fake cleavage and knocking the glass from my hand. It flies underneath the table, shattering into several pieces.

And then I see *him*.

He springs up from the table, quick as lightning, trying to avoid any glass shards that are scattering around his boots.

"Oh no! Let me get something to clean this up. I'm so sorry, Ella. I'm just so excited to see you." Kristie scurries off to the bar.

I'm left standing there like a moron. Staring into his infuriatingly beautiful pale green eyes.

Just me and him.

Well, and this other guy, whoever he is.

Ry's eyes don't leave mine. "Hank, we can finish talking later."

Hank tosses a look to me and back to Ry. Silently nodding, he walks away.

We stand there, not moving.

So, Kristie was hitting on Ry. Rubbing her legs together like her crotch was made of 16-grit sandpaper, and flopping her make-believe boobs all around in his face—because trust me, I've seen her in a bikini top and I know what God gave her. And maybe this isn't the first time. In fact, I'd bet my bottom dollar this isn't the first time. Apparently, both Ry and Kristie are sluts, so it stands to reason they would have hooked up before.

"Ella, are you okay?" Cullen bends, looking underneath the table. "Let me go get something to clean this up."

"No, I'll get it," I offer. "I know where everything is in the back. You've got it by yourself tonight, keep an eye on the bar. I'll get this."

Ry steps around, slapping Cullen on the shoulder. "I'll help her. It's fine."

Cullen doesn't hide his skepticism in leaving us alone, in the same vicinity as one another. But, alas, someone calls his name from the bar. Reluctantly, he nods and heads back up front.

Grunting, I push past Ry and head into the back room, swinging the door behind me. "You'll help me? I'm quite capable of cleaning up broken glass by myself, you know? I'm not helpless. I've done just fine by myself all these years. Even cleaned up a broken plate a time or two. Imagine that."

He's walking so close, he's basically on my heels. "What are you doing here?"

"Me? I should be asking you the same question. It's a work night. Are you always here? Are you an alcoholic?" Grabbing the broom and dustpan, I spin around. He's so close, I actually have to take a step back or else we would be touching.

He snorts. "Did you even see me with a beer? I'm not drinking tonight."

That answers that. "Oh, so you just came in for the other thing then? To pick someone up? You feeling horny tonight, Ry?"

He takes a step forward. Despite my best efforts to weave out of his way, I get trapped by a cabinet, and his chest grazes against mine. All the air is immediately sucked from my lungs, rendering me motionless and breathless. My nipples peak.

I curse my body. Curse it to holy hell.

He bends his face down, breathing against the shell of my ear. "Why? You offering?"

A scalding hot shiver runs down my spine and curls low in my groin. I close my eyes, forcing my pain to the surface. Forcing all my negativity to take the reins and bring me back to life. My trauma fills my lungs with fresh air, giving me power behind my words. "I will never offer myself to you again. Get away from me. Now."

His jaw clenches and his eyes flare, but he does as he's told.

Shifting to the side, he reaches behind me and grabs the mop. Wordlessly, he nods to the door. Shaking in emotion, I make my way back to the table.

I'm starting to sweep, when Ry reaches out and gently grabs the broom handle. I can barely hear his whisper above the noise of the bar. "I'm sorry, Lulu. I shouldn't have said that. Please let me get this. I really couldn't stand it if you cut yourself."

I'm about to yank the broom from his hands and tell him to stuff his apology where the sun doesn't shine, but I stop. The look on his face gives me pause. Suddenly, I'm not staring at the confident, accomplished man whom I've been working with the past several days. I'm staring at the boy from twelve years ago. The boy who thought he was nothing but poor white trash. The boy who didn't want anyone to see the real him. The boy I loved.

I let go of the broom and stumble back. Needing to escape, I head to the bar, leaving him behind to clean up the mess, for once.

Chapter 10

Crutch

"So, help me Lulu, if you grunt one more time, I'm gonna flip my shit."

She scrunches her nose, not even looking at me. "Am I supposed to be blamed because your notes are put together like chicken scratch? No wonder your interviews didn't get very far."

This ink pen sucks. I flick it across the room and it bounces off the wall and falls into the trash can below. "That's not what this attitude is about and we both know it. It's about last night."

She shrugs and then straightens her shoulders back into their normal stiff position. "I don't know what you're talking about."

Bullshit. "Go ahead and ask me. I know you want to."

"What?"

"Don't beat around the bush, Lulu. I like you when you get to the point." I had to remind her of that, in case she forgot.

She folds her arms across her ample chest. "Fine. How many times have you slept with Kristie? Is that the real reason you said you never liked her?"

I lean forward, across the table, spreading my hands into her personal space. "I have never slept with Kristie. Never. And it wouldn't have happened last night, so you can wipe that thought from your mind." I stand up, and pace back and forth across the conference room. "Kristie's at Will's bar. A lot. And she hits on me. A lot. But I would never have sex with her, not in a million years."

She reaches around, tracing her scar with her fingertips. "Why?"

I stop pacing. Cocking my hand on my hips, I debate how much truth to give her. I might as well lay it out there. "Well, besides the obvious fact that I'm not attracted to her in the least little bit, it would hurt you. And I think I've done enough of that to last for a while, don't you?"

She nods. Just once. But that's all I need. I know I hurt her. But watching her confirm it tears the heart from my chest.

She clears her throat and goes back to reading the notes from my prior interviews. Around midday, she surprises me, being the first one of us to mention lunch. "I'm getting hungry. It's warm outside today. Feel like walking over to the park? There should be some food trucks down there."

"Yeah, that sounds good."

Locking the conference room door, I slide the extra key off the key ring and hold it out for her. "There may be some days you wanna come in and work on Carrie's case and I'll be tied up on other things or out of the building. Like I said, this conference room is reserved indefinitely, so feel free to use it, even when I'm not available."

"Thank you."

We walk down to the park, enjoying the winter sunshine, and settle on the gourmet sandwich food truck. We each get a chicken salad sandwich and some pasta salad. We eat most of the meal in silence. At least it's a comfortable silence today. Depending on our moods, our silences can either be comforting or completely annoying and disturbing.

She didn't ask for no tomato on her sandwich. She picked it off and it's laying on the side of her plate. "Why didn't you say 'no tomato'?"

"I guess some old habits die hard."

A cool breeze blows, warning of the cold front about to come through. Her hair tangles in her mouth, and she giggles, trying to pull it away.

Kill me now.

"I like your hair. When did you decide to start curling it?"

She shakes her head. "I don't curl it. It does this all by itself."

I wipe my mouth with my napkin. "Your hair changed from straight to wavy? All on its own?"

She rubs her neck. "That happens with women sometimes. We get older, our hormones change."

"Huh." I didn't know that. But I'm not a hairdresser. Or a woman. She licks some pasta dressing from her fork, drawing attention to her perfectly pink lips. The lips I used to kiss. The lips that used to wrap around me. Needing a distraction, I decide to ask a question that's been gnawing at me since we started working together. "Tell me somethi—" I quickly rephrase my question. "Tell me about your career? How did you get started in this? I assume you didn't pursue an architecture degree."

"I didn't. You know that's never what I wanted."

"Yeah, I know."

She surprises me by relaxing her shoulders just a little bit. "I did one semester online with the University of Virginia. Then, I attended Michigan State University. I received two Bachelor's. One in Criminal Justice and one in Journalism. Did my Master's in Forensic Science with the University of Florida. Moved to Mobile and started my consulting business."

Pain and anger grip my stomach, making me lose my appetite. "You moved to Michigan?"

Her stare is blank and void of emotion. "Yes, that's where Hudson was attending college. We moved to Michigan, and I just did my first semester online with UVA before my enrollment at MSU started."

"Two degrees. That's impressive. How long did it take?"

"Just the normal four years. I had to complete everything before the move to Florida."

"Shit, Lulu. Did you even have time for a life?"

"I did twenty-one hours per semester during my sophomore, junior, and senior years. Plus, I took summer classes."

"That's a lot of school." I'm glad we're sitting at a picnic table so she can't see my leg shaking uncontrollably underneath the table. "Must have been hard, socially. Especially for a newlywed."

Her eyes flare and her back arches forward. "I was there for an education. Not for a party. Hudson didn't suffer. He had his own friends."

"And Florida?"

"That's where Hudson attended law school. I moved to Mobile before he finished. His father's law firm was opening an office there to service the Alabama and Florida Panhandle. I moved there early to establish my business. His father helped set me up with some initial clients. My work spoke for itself. I was fortunate enough to be filling a void right when it was needed." She piles her trash on her plate. "That's how the business started."

She's absolutely perfect.

Except for the fact she married that tool, Hudson.

"Those are fascinating accomplishments. Achievement looks really good on you." I clear my throat, rubbing my hand over my face. I'm afraid to say what I'm thinking, so I whisper my words instead. "That's all I ever wanted for you."

The color drains from her face. I didn't mean to upset her. I guess no matter what I say or do, I will always upset her. It must be my destiny.

She nods. Just once. "And what about you? After the service? Marcum said you discharged early?"

I don't have a chance to answer her questions. My cell phone rings, abruptly ending our conversation. I guess she can tell by my one-sided responses that it's time to go. She grabs both of our plates and tosses them in the trash. "I'm sorry about that. I have to run out on a call. I need to head back."

She walks away, not waiting on me. "That's fine. We were done anyway."

I don't know if I'll ever be done when it comes to Lulu.

Tired of crossing the enemy line to the neutral zone, she doesn't elaborate when I try to ask her more questions on our walk back to the station. So, instead, I make small talk about another case I have going on—a robbery. She's making some intriguing comments, giving me cause to think, when she immediately stops walking. Clenching her jaw, her palms curl into fists. I follow her line of sight to an older woman who just stepped outside one of the expensive downtown boutiques with bags in hand. She looks familiar.

The woman suddenly notices Lulu. "Ella! Darling." She trots over to us, clicking her heels on the sidewalk. Bending forward, she brushes an air kiss in the direction of Lulu's cheek. She's shorter than Lulu so she has to bounce on her toes to even come close to her cheek. "It's wonderful to see you. We didn't get a chance to chat after the funeral services. I wanted to tell you how sorry I am that your parents are gone. Susan was such an amazing woman and an amazing best friend. I cry every day just thinking about her and Robert."

Lulu plants a saccharine smile on her face. "Thank you, Noreen."

The woman turns her sights on me. Now I know who she is. And after all these years, she still looks at me like I'm some kind of boy toy. She takes a deep breath, trying to minimize her waist and maximize her chest. I wonder how many times over the years that has worked. How many times she's cheated on her husband? "And who is your dashing friend? A member of law enforcement?"

Lulu doesn't speak. Her eyes grow wide as saucers. She actually looks scared to talk. It's freaking weird. Lulu is many things, but scared speechless isn't typically one of them. She may not talk at times, but that's her choice, her choice to usually piss people off and act like a bitch. But that's not what's happening now. Now, she actually looks afraid.

I hold out my hand. "Sergeant Ryland Crutchfield, ma'am."

The smile disappears from the woman's face. It's quickly replaced with a look of utter disgust. Well, that didn't take long. I guess she *does* remember me from twelve years ago. I guess the badge and gun don't hide the trashy DNA roaming around inside my body.

She slowly turns to Lulu. "*Him*? That didn't take long, did it?"

My Lulu finds her voice. "Be careful what you say, Noreen. I wouldn't want you to say something you'd regret."

Hudson's mother spits words of hate in Lulu's direction. "You're the one who should have regrets. Not me. You have a life full of poor decisions." Her eyes dart back to me. "And it looks like you haven't even learned from your past mistakes."

Screw that. I slice my way between their bodies, blocking their standoff. My back rubs against Lulu's shoulder. "That's enough."

Taking a step back, Noreen rearranges the bags in her hand. "Quite right. Some of us are too sophisticated for petty arguments." She turns, walking away. Before she rounds the corner, she peeks over her shoulder. "Oh, and Hudson sends his regards. He couldn't attend the funeral. He's on a major trial right now, couldn't break away. Plus, Celeste is due any day. He wants her to avoid all possible stress. Meeting her was the best thing that ever happened to him. A healthy birth is his number one focus."

As soon as the nasty woman is out of sight and earshot, I turn around. Lulu has completely locked herself away, deep inside of her own mind. My fingers ache to shake her, break her, bring her back to life. That last sentence tells me all I need to know. Hudson is with someone new, and they are about to have a baby. Is that why Lulu is so upset? Does she miss Hudson? Miss their life? That thought makes me want to lock myself away in my own mind, but I won't give her that satisfaction so I say the only thing I can think of saying to neutralize the situation, "So, Hudson's mom is just as pleasurable as I remember."

"Yeah, she's a fucking bitch."

Chapter 11

Ella

"**N**ancy needs to buy you some new socks. How can you stand to walk around with holes in your socks?" Leary frowns, pointing at Marcum's dress socks, where a hole shows the pale skin of his ankle beneath the cuff of his dress slacks.

"Well, hopefully, the crowd will be looking at my face when I give the presentation, not my ankles. And if you're really that concerned about it, come with me tonight. They'll be too busy looking at the stain on your shirt to notice the hole in my sock."

I bite my lip, trying not laugh. They act more and more like an old married couple, every single day.

Leary scoffs, "It's Friday night, I have a life. Watching you give a speech at the assisted living facility is not my idea of a good time."

"You're forgetting the Bingo. It's a speech, followed by Bingo."

I doodle on a notepad, drawing a house. "Why did you even wear a suit? I didn't know Bingo had a dress code."

He pouts, looking down at his tie. "Nancy made me dress me up."

Leary and I break out into stitches, laughing until my side hurts. After we calm down, Leary says goodbye, leaving me alone with Marcum. Colson is in the file room, finishing up some paperwork with a patrol deputy, and Ry is over in the gym.

Marcum leans back, rocking in his chair. "So, how are things going?"

Tossing my doodle to him, I cross my legs. "Meaning, personally? Professionally? Or both?"

"Both. All of it. But I'm more curious about how things are going with Carrie's case. And Crutch?"

"Well, I haven't killed him yet. That should tell you something."

He raises his eyebrows. "I do find that promising, especially considering the line of work he's in."

"I don't know what you want me to say. I never thought I would see him again. And here I am spending hours a day with him a couple of days a week. I honestly don't know how I feel about it all. Don't get me wrong, I still hate him for what he did to me, but every once in a while, I find myself not completely disgusted to be working with him. I'd never admit that to him, though."

He chuckles. "Of course, you wouldn't. You've never made it easy on me."

"Easy on you? You really think I should take it easy on you? I know Nancy told you on more than one occasion to tell me that Ry was your new work boyfriend these past few years."

He grumbles. "I'm gonna drown Nancy's cell phone in the toilet."

Now it's my turn to chuckle. "You're the one who wanted me to branch out, make more friends now that I'm back in town."

"Friends your own age, Ella. Not a bunch of geriatrics like me and Nancy."

"I'll be sure to tell her you called her geriatric. Maybe I should call and tell her to meet you for Bingo."

"Alright. It's time to stop aggravating me. I have to go to this thing. Seriously, what's happening on the case?"

"I think it's time to start interviewing, but it feels like Ry is delaying it. I don't like it. I hope he isn't trying to protect Trash."

Marcum shakes his head. "Trust me, he's not protecting his brother."

"How do you know?"

"Just ask him. Let him tell you."

I stand, grabbing my purse and work bag. "Fine. I'll go find him and talk to him before I leave. I'm supposed to meet Holt and Uncle Ray at the bar for a drink."

He snickers, knowing I don't drink. He graciously keeps his comment to himself.

I meander down the halls, making my way to the state-of-the-art gym. You need key card entry to get in, and I don't have one of those. Fortunately, I'm not standing there for too long when some-one walks out. The deputy smiles, silently flirting with me. I quickly dart inside, waving goodbye.

I scan the mountain of machines trying to find Ry. There are not too many people in here—just five or six. It's the start of the week-end, everybody is out, doing something fun, not working on their physiques. Although I must say, memories of Ry's own hard body have gotten me through many cold winter nights over the years.

I finally spot him against the far wall, running on an elliptical machine.

And of course, he's shirtless.

I should do this another time. I turn to walk away, but quickly change my mind. I tell myself that it all has to do with work. But re-ally, I want to remind myself what he looks like.

Shirtless.

Naked from the waist up.

Sweaty.

Twelve years later.

His wireless earbuds are in his ears so he doesn't hear me ap-proach from behind. I turn, walking up the row of treadmills and ellipticals to his right. My mouth turns dry and a century-old heat stirs low in my stomach. My breath quickens. His body glistens with sweat. His muscles are larger, firmer than they were twelve years ago. He's thick with masculinity and maturity. The taut muscles of his waist are even more defined, etched into the stone of his body.

The curve of his back is delicious. My tongue tingles, wanting to reach out and trace the beads of sweat along his spine, licking him clean.

And then, I walk close enough to see his left side.

His scarred left side.

His mutilated left side.

The area all around his shoulder blade is tainted with deep, jagged scars. Not long scars like cuts, but circles, holes, and divots. Some skin is white, some is pink, some is tan like him. And other parts of his skin look almost burnt. Singed, stained. I take a step to the side, watching the flex of his arm. The movement makes the large circle of fresh, waxy pink skin on the ball of his shoulder stretch and scream. It's larger than a silver dollar. Smaller scars run down his bicep, just a couple of inches. Not far enough to be seen, even when wearing a short-sleeve shirt.

I can't breathe. My vision blurs, blackening around the edges. My heart isn't even beating any more. It feels like one long continuous rattle in my chest, like a never-ending roll of thunder during a summer storm.

What the hell happened to him?

It looks like someone tried to kill him. With a thousand ice picks.

Marcum's words play in my mind. *Medical discharge.* Someone did try to kill him. They tried to kill My Ry. Take him away from me.

For twelve years, he's been *away* from me. But not *gone.* Not gone from this world. I've already lost too much, and the world nearly snatched the life away from him too? And I had no idea. Why does everyone I love get taken away from me? I can't even bear the thought of it.

My purse and work bag slip from my limp arm, drawing his attention. He turns his head, ready to ignore the possible distraction at his side when he sees me. I'm too upset to even dissect the small smile that tugs at the corner of his mouth. Yanking his earbuds out, he turns off the machine and carefully steps down.

"I thought you left already. What's going..." His voice immediately trails off when we lock eyes. Swooping in front of me, his massive frame shadows my own. He grabs my upper arms. Firmly. Almost too firmly. Just like how he used to hug me. Nearly too firmly.

"Lulu, what's wrong. Did something happen? Is it Marcum? Ray or Teresa? What's wrong?"

My gaze falls to his chest. His perfectly unscathed, beautiful, strong chest. From the front, you'd never know anything was wrong. But all you have to do is look at his upper left shoulder to see the damage. Knowing it's there is almost too much to bear. It has me closing my eyes, begging my tears to stay in. I hate crying in front of people.

"Okay, Lulu, now you're scaring the shit out of me. Talk to me."

Taking several deep breaths, I open my eyes and swallow against the basketball-size lump in my throat. I make some kind of weird gulping noise. He follows my line of sight to his upper arm and the nasty scar that's on display. "You're hurt. Someone tried to kill you, didn't they? How could you do that to me?"

His face falls into a look of utter despair. His heart is breaking because mine is breaking. Well, I mean, if he still had a heart, that is. "Oh, Lulu. It's okay. I'm okay." His hands travel to my face, cupping my cheeks. "It doesn't hurt that much anymore, I promise. Don't worry about me."

Don't worry about him? Has he lost his mind?

I have despised him ever since I got that letter, but that doesn't mean I didn't worry about him. I've worried about him and his welfare every single day since then. Hell, he's probably the reason I had to start using anti-wrinkle cream at the age of twenty.

Visions of him lying in a street somewhere covered in blood consume my mind. I feel like I'm about to have convulsions. And he wants me to chill out? Not worry? Pretend like the entire half of his upper back doesn't look like a shark tried to eat him as an appetizer?

I press my hand into my sternum. Hard.

He is utterly insane.

I need to get out of here before I burst into sobs. And on top of everything, he's still got his hands planted lovingly against my cheeks. Like we're still 'Ry and Lulu' and nothing has changed. Well, we aren't them anymore, despite the names that fall from our lips. "You have to stop touching me. I can't think."

"What if I don't wanna stop touching you?"

I bore a hole into his pale green eyes. "But you did. Nearly twelve years ago you wanted to stop. And instead, you went and got..." What did he get? Shot? Blown up? Chopped up with a samurai sword? I don't even know how to describe his injury, so I just nod at it, jiggling his fingers against my skin. I add a layer of disgust to my voice. "Now, get your hands off me."

He doesn't like to be reminded of the rights he gave up all those years ago. He drops his hands and steps to the side.

I scoop up my purse and work bag and race from the gym. I'm fast, but not fast enough to escape my tears. Not fast enough to escape my anger. Not fast enough to escape the pain of Ry leaving me behind.

Not fast enough to escape that reality.

Chapter 12

Ella

I'm staring at the brown liquid of my Long Island Iced Tea when Will places a plate of bright orange cantaloupe in front of me.

"Ahh, trying to ease the bad mood with fruit." Holt nods in appreciation at Will. "Smart move."

I ignore their banter, popping a juicy piece of fruit in my mouth. Cullen's been making some sort of fancy cantaloupe and mint cocktail for the past few weeks, so this won't be the first time I've had one my favorite foods as a bar time snack.

Will tosses me a napkin. "I wish you would tell us what's wrong."

"Nothing is wrong."

Will cocks his head. "Your eyes are bloodshot, and your eye makeup is smudged. I could be wrong, but I don't think that smoky eye was specially applied for your night out with your uncle and cousins."

Uncle Ray clicks his tongue. "Leave the girl alone. She'll tell us when she's good and ready. Besides, if we think about it real hard, I'm sure we can solve some of the puzzle. We might not guess the *what*, but somehow, I don't think the *who* will be all that hard."

I swing my foot back and forth against my barstool. "I'm glad my life provides so much amusement for you."

Holt steals a cantaloupe ball from my plate. "Hey, we all have our spot in the sun for a while. Just think back a few months ago.

You couldn't turn on any news channel without seeing my face and hearing some dumbass commentator say my life was over because I couldn't play football anymore." He thumps his chest, smiling. "Now, look at me."

I snort. "Unemployed and drinking at the bar."

Holt chuckles. "Hey, I'm just weighing my options." He turns to Will. "On a side note, may I say how disturbing it is that you even know what a 'smoky eye' is?"

Will flips him the bird before turning to help a customer.

Just a couple of minutes later, the front door flings open so loudly, it catches all of our attention. Anxiety and tension quickly drown out the noise of the music and bustling crowd. Ry's standing in the doorway, scanning the room. Unfortunately, the bastard looks drop dead sexy. I guess he showered. His hair is wet, and small beads of water are rolling down his neck. He hasn't shaved the past couple of days, and the brown stubble on his face and jawline make him look absolutely dangerous.

He's wearing a green T-shirt with a gray hoodie jacket and jeans. The green really draws attention to his eyes.

And the muscles around his collar bone.

And his firm chest.

Damn that green T-shirt.

Ry takes a breath when he sees me. Rolling his shoulders, he charges across the barroom like an elephant thundering across the savanna. Holt immediately jumps from his barstool and presses the palm of his hand against Ry's chest. "Whoa, there. She's upset. She hasn't told us what happened, but I'm pretty damn positive you have something to do with it. It might be best if you turn around. None of us bought a ticket to the shit show tonight."

Ry narrows his eyes and stares down at Holt's hand. Ry definitely doesn't like someone's hand being on him. In confrontation. In challenge. A fight between the two of them would probably be the brawl of the century.

I should step in. I should intervene. Oh well, I always do what I shouldn't do. This should be no exception. I turn my head back to my drink, listening to them talk about me like I'm not even here.

Uncle Ray clears his throat and calmly takes a drink of his beer. "Holt, take your hand off him, son."

Respecting his father's wishes, Holt does as he's told. He doesn't sit back down, though. He stands sentry in front of me, blocking Ry from part of my view.

Uncle Ray leans across the bar, grabbing Cullen's attention since Will is busy with other customers. "C, get Crutch a beer, will you?"

Cullen slides a cold beer bottle into Ry's hand and Uncle Ray nods, urging him to take a drink. I'm glad no one's getting thirsty in this standoff. Come on, people! Can't you see I'm falling apart over here!

I just found out the love of my life nearly died.

I mean, I just found out the ex-love of my life nearly died.

"So," Uncle Ray places his empty bottle on the counter, "you wanna tell us what happened?"

Ry looks at me, trying to gauge my feelings. I put my hand up, shielding my face from his prying eyes. About this time, Will walks up to join the guys. Sighing, Ry glances around at the men of my family. "I didn't tell her about my service injuries. She caught me in the gym. She saw it."

Uncle Ray nods. "Oh. I see."

Holt clears his throat, shifting his weight from leg to leg.

"I just need to talk to her." Ry's voice cuts like a knife, slicing through a small layer of my steel armor. "Lulu, please. Can we just talk for a minute?"

I ignore him.

Will tosses his hand in the air. "Hey, a table just opened up in the back. Why don't you take a load off? Maybe Ella will feel like talking in a little while."

Ry licks his lips. Chugging the rest of his beer, he slaps the bottle on the shiny wood countertop and walks off toward the back of the bar.

Holt sits back down and Will tosses my empty fruit plate in the trash. No one says anything for a long time. We just sit, listening to the Aerosmith song pumping through the speakers.

"If you hate him so much, why are you so upset?"

"Holt, did you really just ask me that? You know why. No matter where I go, no matter what I do, Ry will always be a part of me. There's nothing I can do about that. Just because I hate him, doesn't mean that I wish him harm." I twist my glass around in a circle. "He joined the military to get away from me, to run away. And it nearly cost him his life, by the looks of it. How am I supposed to deal with that? He ran to danger because of me."

Will shakes his head. "There's a million different ways for someone to run away. Not every guy running away from his hometown joins the military. You may think he joined the service just to get away from you, but he joined because he felt a higher calling, a need to serve, a duty to his country. More importantly, a desire to grow into a man he could respect. We've talked about his time in the military. And I can tell you right now, that there are only three things in life that Crutch seems truly passionate about. And two of them are being a Marine and being a cop."

Don't ask. Don't ask. Don't ask. My voice croaks, "What's the third?"

Will shrugs. "You."

Dagger. To the heart. "I thought none of you talked to Ry about me."

"We haven't. We don't. But I don't need to have a conversation with him, Ella, to know that he's explosively passionate about you. The way he looks at you? It's the same way I feel about Raylee."

And what do I say to that? I have no choice but to hear him out. I peek back at the table. Ry's leaning forward clutching his head in his hands. Growling, I snap at Will. "Hand me a beer, dum-dum."

Wrapping my purse around me, I weave my way through the crowd, balancing the beer bottle in one hand and my Long Island Iced Tea in the other. His head snaps up when he hears the chair scrape across the floor. Wordlessly, I slide the fresh drink across the table to him. I don't say anything. No one said I had to make this easy for him. It sure as hell isn't easy for me.

"I didn't tell you about my injuries."

Obviously.

"I wanted to." He tosses his head back and forth. "Then again, I didn't want to. It's hard to explain."

I raise my glass, rubbing my lips back and forth across the rim. There must be a drop of alcohol there because my bottom lip starts burning.

Ry chuckles, leaning back and lacing his fingers behind his head. "You always have to bust my balls, don't you?"

"Do you expect any different?"

"No, I guess not." He sighs. "I wanted to tell you because it was a big part of my life. It *is* a big part of my life. But I couldn't bring myself to do it. I was worried. I was worried you wouldn't care. After what happened twelve years ago, it wouldn't surprise me if you wanted to see me get run over by a bus. But I was also worried that you *would* care. Care too much. How can I let you care about me when I left? When I did what I did? I don't deserve your compassion, your worry, or your thoughts."

I lick my lips, praying for patience. "You've always been very good at trying to tell me what to think about you. Don't you think it's time you left that up to me?"

"I guess so." He leans forward, hooking his calloused finger around mine. "So, what do you think of me?"

I pull my hand away, folding it in my lap. His touch, no matter how small, stirs passion. And that's not something I need to feel about him.

Not now.

Not ever.

I ignore his question. "Tell me what happened."

"It happened in South Sudan."

"Not Afghanistan or Iraq?"

He shakes his head. "I was deployed to Afghanistan for a while. Then, I was sent to South Sudan to help guard the US Embassy. We were driving in a convoy, taking the ambassador to a meeting at the Presidential Palace. There was an IED. We had to abandon the vehicles." He shrugs. "And then, there was another IED. I got a little too close for comfort on that one."

He's so nonchalant. It's like he just told me he burnt his finger on the hot stove. "Who did it? Who set the IEDs?"

"Doesn't matter...this group or that group. There are always people out there who wanna hurt other people."

My voice sounds shaky. "Did anyone die?"

He rubs his fingers across his lips. "Yes. Some really good people."

My chest feels heavy, like a ton of bricks is sitting on top of me. I can't help it; I reach around and fondle my scar. "Did you nearly die?"

"No. It was bad, but not life threatening." He smiles, lifting his left arm in the air and pumping it like he's lifting weights. "See. I'm fine. Completely fine."

"Well, it's pretty damn obvious you weren't fine. Or else you wouldn't look like an eighteen-wheeler drug you across the interstate. What damage was done?"

"Shrapnel. That was the worst of it. It basically imbedded metal and plastic along the back of my shoulder blade and top of my bicep. A larger piece of metal sliced part of my upper arm away," he points to the area where I saw the large circular scar. "When I went down, I tore my rotator cuff and a ligament. It could've been a lot worse. I'm actually pretty lucky."

I cough, clearing my throat. "Lucky?"

"Yes, Lulu. I made it out alive."

I stare at him. "They sent you home after that?"

"Yeah. It was a long recovery."

"How did you become a deputy? Doesn't the injury rule you out?"

"Nope. I just had to pass their physical fitness test and receive clearance from a doctor. And trust me, their physical fitness test is nothing compared to the Marines."

There are so many questions. I furrow my brow in thought. "When?"

"Our convoy was hit the day before my twenty-fifth birthday. I was sent home. Received a medical honorable discharge. I spent that whole year rehabbing and working out like some kind of damn steroid addict. Took the first deputy test on my twenty-sixth birthday."

No wonder his body looks so good. Apparently, he's kept up with the regimen.

"You don't have any lingering problems?"

"The shoulder surgery went perfect. But you can't have shrapnel injuries and not have some lingering problems," he says, with a glance at his shoulder.

My hand flies to my mouth in horror. "Oh my god. It's still coming out of you, isn't it?"

He sighs softly, "The body knows what should be there and what shouldn't be there. So, yeah, it works its way to the surface, just small pieces. But, it's fine."

"It's fine?" My voice raises. "You have pieces of debris coming out of your body, and you say it's just fine? Are you delusional?"

His jaw clenches and his hands ball into fists. I've pissed him off. "No, Lulu. I'm realistic. I've got it good. I can see. I can hear. I can walk. I can talk. I can work and provide for myself. I can wipe my own ass. All major accomplishments in my book. Especially if you had seen what I've seen."

My heart pounds against my ribcage, snuffing the fight right out of me. "I didn't mean it like that. I apologize."

He drags his hand across his stubbled jaw. "I know."

"You must have seen some terrible things."

He sits back, spreading his legs in front of him. He studies me, long and hard. Smirking, he takes a long drink of the beer, downing half of it in one swallow. "Go ahead and ask me. I know you want to."

"I don't know what you're talking about."

"Don't beat around the bush, Lulu. I like you when you get to the point."

He can be so arrogant sometimes. "Fine. Do you suffer from PTSD? You say you're fine physically, but you went through a major trauma. Are you doing okay?"

He leans forward, preparing to tell me a secret. "Listen to me, Luella Margaret Hill, I saw a lot of fucked-up shit when I was in the service. People blowing themselves up just to a make a point. Terrorists shooting little kids just because they happened to be in the vicinity of us troops. Men beating their women just because they walked more than a quarter mile away from their home. But none of that gives me nightmares. None of that keeps me awake at night. The only thing that makes me toss and turn is you."

He slams his chair back. Swinging the beer bottle from the table, he stalks away to the bar.

Well. What am I supposed to say to that?

Chapter 13

Crutch

It's a busy Friday night. The only available spot at the bar is next to Holt. It looks like Ray has already headed home for the night.

"Surprised to see you stomp away from the table mad. I thought for sure it would be her."

"You and me both." I sit down and wave my empty bottle in Will's direction, signaling I need another. He breaks away from the crowd and quickly hands me one. I gulp it down, letting the cold liquid quench the burn in my stomach. I'm already ready for another one. Looks like I may be taking an Uber over to Marcum's house and crashing on his couch. Maybe one day, service will eventually make it out to my house. I doubt it. Highly.

Holt and I sit for a while, watching a sports show on one of the big screen TVs behind the bar. The volume is muted so it doesn't interfere with the music piping from the speakers. The band for tonight is setting up, but they haven't started playing yet.

I chance a sideways glance at Holt when a story about Sunday's big game flashes across the screen. "So, Sunday is February 1st."

"Yep."

"Super Bowl Sunday."

"Yep."

"I'm surprised you didn't go."

He shrugs. "NFL asked me to go. I said no."

"Why?"

"Because I would be sitting there, just watching the game and enjoying myself, and before you know it, they would flash my picture on the screen and spend the next few minutes talking about my injuries and what could have been. No, thank you. I'm fucking over that."

I check the time on my phone, making sure I haven't missed any important work calls. "Everything I read before the season started said that your team could've done it again this year."

He pops his knuckles, laughing. "They could've. Too bad their dumbass quarterback injured himself before even stepping out onto the field."

"From what I hear, that dumbass quarterback saved his niece's life."

Holt narrows his eyes, scowling at Will's back. "Will sure has a big mouth." He spins on his barstool, facing me. "You sure he didn't tell you anything about Ella?"

I hold up my hands. "Promise. Lulu's been a tight-lipped secret with all of y'all. Just the way we both wanted it, I guess." Cullen sets a fresh beer in front of both me and Holt. "Out of curiosity, though, why did you lie about how you got hurt?"

"I already told you—the media. They're relentless. I couldn't put Anna through that. She's only five. If they found out what happened, they would be talking about her, trying to interview her. I love that little girl too much to put that burden on her. Or Raylee."

I nod, it's all making sense now. "I never got a chance to give my condolences for your injuries. I know a couple of guys who had the same surgery. Recovery is brutal. Damn brutal. Are you doing good with it?"

"It's been six months. I'm getting better, stronger each and every day. I rehab and work out like crazy, more now than I did when I was training."

"Well, what's next for you?"

Holt waggles his eyebrows and spins his bottle around and around. "Didn't you hear? My career is completely over."

His sarcastic humor nearly has me spitting my drink all over the floor. "Bullshit. I hate when people say that about you. You're what? Twenty-nine? You have your whole damn life ahead of you. You can have five more careers if you want. You just have to find *what* you want."

Holt smiles, his sarcasm flipping to sincerity. "I'm glad someone else finally gets it. I was beginning to worry that me and my family were the only normal ones in the northern hemisphere. People keep acting like I should be wallowing around in self-pity on my death bed because I can't play football professionally anymore. What they never understood was, that for me, it was just a game. A game I was really good at. A game I loved playing. I'd play from morning till night if I could. But it's not *who* I am. I'm still me. I just finally have to grow up now, be an adult. No more getting paid to play on a big green field."

I laugh and pound his shoulder with my fist. "Well, you're definitely not NFL material. They'd pull that Super Bowl ring right off your finger if they heard that."

"Let's keep it to ourselves."

I toss my head in Will's direction. "Better not tell big-mouth Will then," I joke.

Lulu's voice makes the hair on the back of my neck stand. "What's so funny? What are y'all laughing about?"

Holt smiles. "Nothing."

She frowns. "You're lying."

"Yes." He doesn't elaborate. He just turns back to watching TV. And ignoring the girls at the end of the bar who have been trying to hit on him all night long.

I glance to the side, seeing that no other barstools are available, I get up, offering mine to Lulu.

"No, it's fine. I didn't come up here to steal your seat."

"Lulu, sit down."

She licks her lips and nods. Hopping her fine ass on the cushioned leather, she places her still-full Long Island Iced Tea on a paper coaster in front of her. It's like she's carrying around a security blanket. She crosses her legs, drawing my attention to the tight leggings covering her skin. She rubs the scar on her neck. "So, I wanted to talk to you about next week. I think it's time we start conducting interviews."

"You're gonna completely ignore the conversation we just had." I flip my arm back in the direction of the table we had been sitting at.

She bores a hole into me with her honey-glazed eyes. "Yes."

The redness in them is finally gone, which is good. When I saw she had been crying, I wanted to crawl across glass and beg her for her forgiveness. That was, until she made me mad. Her earlier emotions left her eye makeup smudged and her hair lightly tangled. She looks like she just got fucked. Hard.

And it's driving me into delirium.

"So, do you agree? We start interviews next week? Monday? I'll be out of town Tuesday and Wednesday. I can work on the case Monday, Thursday, and Friday, though. You?"

I think of my upcoming schedule. "Monday, Thursday, and Friday are fine with me."

She lifts her chin in the air. "Good."

She's about to say something else when someone taps my right shoulder. Lulu's eyes darken to small beads and her lips thin. I turn sideways, feasting my eyes on a buxom blonde. She's pretty. Looks a little too flashy for me, but attractive, nonetheless. She flashes a bright smile and cocks her head to the side.

"I'm sorry to bother you, but you look so familiar. Do we know each other?"

Holy shit. Did I sleep with this woman? I flip through my mental little black book, trying to place her. No. No, I definitely have never seen this woman before. "No, I don't think so." I chug my beer in relief. I sure as hell don't need that kind of drama with Lulu sitting right here.

"Oh well, I guess you just have one of those faces." She reaches out and touches my bicep, fondling me through my hoodie. "A kind face, you know?"

Lulu rolls her eyes so hard I worry she'll fall right off the barstool. I try to hide my laugh with a fake cough. It doesn't work. Scowling, Lulu spins around, pretending to watch the TV like Holt.

The girl giggles. "Would you like to get a fresh drink? Find somewhere quiet to talk?"

"I appreciate the offer, but I'm just gonna hang out with my friends tonight."

Biting her lip, trying to be seductive, she slips away. "Let me know if you change your mind."

Lulu looks over her shoulder. "Friends? Is that what we are?"

"I don't know, you tell me. You said you were tired of me telling you what to think about me."

She lifts her drink to her mouth, sniffs it, and then puts it back down. She turns her head. She tries not to smile. Really, she does. She'd be furious if she knew I saw her smile. "Not yet. Maybe one day."

Holt slaps me across the chest. "C'mon, best buddy. Buy me a drink. You have a tab, right?"

Surprisingly, the three of us fall into an easy conversation, chatting about nothing, everything. I drink a few more beers, letting the buzz of the alcohol settle over me like a comforting blanket. Its warmth gives me promise, promise of things yet to come.

Maybe she's right.

Maybe one day we can be friends again.

And who knows, maybe that will take us back to where we were. Her lips on mine. Her heart in mine. Take me back to the place I was a fool to leave.

But... I always do what I shouldn't do. And I always mess things up.

I shouldn't turn around when I hear the high-pitch squeal of my name. I shouldn't turn around. But I do.

"Crutch!"

I barely have time to process the little fireball of energy in a tight halter top, leather leggings, and a tiara that says 'Happy Birthday'. And I definitely don't have time to react before she jumps up, wrapping her arms around my neck. It throws me off balance so I'm completely unprepared for when she crashes her lips to mine, forcing her tongue into my mouth.

So much for avoiding drama with Lulu sitting right here.

I force my beer bottle into Holt's side and he quickly grabs it. With gentle force, I pull Brittany off my body, peeling her away like a sticker.

"What the hell, Brittany?"

She jumps up and down and points to the plastic tiara on her brown hair. "It's my birthday!" A gaggle of girls surrounding her whoop and holler. "The girls asked me what I wanted for my birthday, and I said another night with you! I remembered you said you liked coming to this bar. I can't believe you're actually here. We just took a shot in the dark that you'd be here." She lowers her voice to an exaggerated whisper and leans close, breathing her vodka breath on me. "You know a lot of college kids don't like to come here because there's always cops around."

I drag my hand across my jaw, scratching my stubble. So much for having a buzz.

I steal a glance at Lulu. Her mouth gapes open in shock. Brittany's little scene has stolen the vocabulary right from My Lulu's brain.

Brittany leans forward, grabbing the sides of my hoodie. "Kiss the birthday girl. You know you want to."

I untangle myself from her again. "Brittany, I think you've had too much to drink. How about we get you a water?"

She shoos her friends away and they file to the other end of the bar, shouting drink orders at Cullen. "No water for me. I was sober as a judge when we got together last time." She winks. "Don't you wanna try me drunk? I like to experiment when I'm drunk."

Are you kidding me? Could it get any worse? "Brittany, stop."

"Don't be a prude, Crutch. Experimenting is what college is for. Last time was explosive, just think about how good it could be."

Lulu jumps down from her barstool. I don't think I've ever seen her look so lethal. She scares the piss right out of me. She's looking at me like I'm the scum of the earth. And I am. I am scum. She shoves her own water glass into Brittany's hand. "Happy birthday."

"Thanks." Brittany takes a sip and makes a sour face. "Water. Yuck. I thought it was something good."

"You said college? How old are you today?" Lulu asks and I'm slowly dying inside watching this exchange.

Brittany raises her hand high in the air, dancing around on her stilettos. "Twenty-one, bitches!" Hearing her warrior cry, all of the girls scream and jump.

Kill. Me. Now.

Lulu turns, leaning so close to me that her nose nearly touches mine. She growls, "Twenty-one, bitches." Elbowing past me, she marches across the bar, flinging open the door to the back room, hiding herself away.

Holt laughs uncontrollably. "I guess I did buy a ticket to the shit show after all."

Chapter 14

Crutch

I stare at her for the umpteenth time today. She's the most gorgeous thing to walk the face of the planet, so it's fair to assume that I want to stare at her. All the time. But I'm also staring because I'm mad.

Furious. Boiling.

She went home with someone again.

Friday night after my little reunion with Brittany, she wandered the bar and found a guy she deemed worthy of her one-night affection. I sent Brittany away. She and her friends left the bar after thirty minutes. After she hit on both Holt and Cullen. Hell, she even hit on Will.

But that didn't matter. Lulu still wanted to make me pay. And she did. She kept touching the guy's arm, whispering in his ear, laughing at things that probably weren't even funny. And then she left the bar with him. My Lulu snuck away so some stranger could put his lips on her body. So some stranger could be inside of her, in the place that was meant for only me. The place I broke. The place I explored.

Why does she keep giving pieces of herself away? I've given away enough for both of us.

She glances up from her work. When she sees the look on my

face, her spine stiffens even more. "So, we are meeting him at three today?"

"That's what I said, isn't it?"

She lifts an eyebrow, but turns a deaf ear to my attitude. "How do you know he'll be home?"

"Trash is supposed to meet with his parole officer. I know the guy. I called and he was more than happy to turn the reins of the meeting over to me."

She flips a few pages in her notebook. "He's been out of prison for a little over seven years, right?"

When Lulu first found out my brother went to prison, when reading over Carrie's updated case file, she was unable to hide the gleam in her eye. You would've thought it was Christmas morning and she just saw presents from Santa stacked underneath the tree.

"Yeah." I answer quickly, hoping my one-word response doesn't garner her attention.

"And he was arrested for the drug charges in September, after we both left town?"

"Yeah."

She flaps her hand in the air. "Care to elaborate? I haven't searched all the records on Trash yet."

"Anonymous tip." I glance down, pretending to busy myself with some emails on my work laptop. "Marcum received an anonymous tip regarding the drug activity at the gas station. It happened right after you left town."

She doesn't say anything for a long time. A *really* long time. Eventually, the anticipation forces me to look up.

She knows I'm hiding something. She's rubbing the back of her neck and eyeballing me with suspicion. "You're hiding something, Ry. What aren't you telling me?"

I have to tell her. Her investigative skills are pretty stellar, she'll piece it together sooner or later. "I called. I turned them in."

She gasps, not expecting that. "What?"

"I called Marcum. I told him everything I knew about the drugs, who was involved, the system for buying, everything. Officially, the tip was listed as anonymous, but it was me."

"You turned your own brother in?"

I snort. "You know how I felt about my brother. How I *feel* about him. He's always been a piece of shit."

"So that's what Marcum meant when he said you told him about the drugs before you were on the force." She shakes her head, dumfounded. "But why? You wouldn't let me say anything. You wouldn't let me go after them. You said the risk of danger was too great. What changed?"

"What changed was you. You were gone. Safe."

She scoffs. "Safe. Right."

I don't like the sound of that. "What's that supposed to mean?"

She stares at me, quickly avoiding the question with her glare. "Nothing. How did you know I was gone? How'd you find out?"

"Harlan. He said you came by and saw him before you left town. Said you married Hudson and moved far away for college. I didn't get a chance to talk to him until I was in SOI for a couple of weeks. You were already gone by then. I called Marcum the day after I talked to Harlan."

She lowers her head, for once not looking me in the eyes. It's unnerving. That's not the Lulu I know. "I asked him not to tell you... not to tell you that I married."

Bile rises in my throat. I'm not sure if I prefer my own vomit or my own anger when it comes to thinking about Lulu being married to Hudson. "Yeah, he told me that you didn't want me to know."

I'll never forget that conversation. Never. For as long as I live. For the first half of it, he told me everything she said when she came back from her charity trip. He told me she wanted to follow me, be with me, do anything to make our relationship work. She was ready to drop out of college. For me. My stupid brain went into overdrive, thinking my point was proved—I was ruining her life.

And then he dropped the bomb. The second half of the conversation had My Lulu getting married and leaving our world behind.

"Did he tell you other things too?" she asks.

"Meaning?"

"Well, Marcum and my family say they didn't talk to you about me. What about Harlan? Did he?"

"I mean, we talked about the past. Nearly every time I called him when I was in the service, he wanted to rehash some old story about the fun times the three of us had. Is that what you're asking?"

She cocks her head, gauging my reaction. "Yeah, sure."

She's lying. "Lulu," I warn. My growl comes out harsher than I intend.

"We talked."

"Who talked?"

"Me and Harlan."

"You and Harlan talked?"

"I called him every Sunday night."

I feel dizzy. Like I just got off a spinning roller coaster. "You're telling me that you and Harlan talked once a week, every week, after you moved away?"

She nods.

"But you weren't even at his funeral," I say.

The mention of Harlan's death has tears brimming in her eyes, but she keeps them in check, rapidly blinking and sniffling. "I talked to his son. He told me they were postponing the funeral a couple of days because you were granted leave to come home. So, I didn't come back for it."

"You didn't come to Harlan's funeral because you knew I would be there?"

She nods, just once, biting her lip.

She hated me that much. She would miss the funeral of a man she loved, a man she apparently kept in touch with even after I left her, simply because my ugly asshole self would be present. Harlan died during my third year of service, about eight months before my injury. Massive heart attack. I was terrified I wouldn't be granted leave. My commanding officer was very understanding when I explained my relationship to Harlan. Plus, I didn't take my ten-day leave in between MCRT and SOI, so I still had that. I came home and helped bury the man I loved like my own blood.

I drag my hand across my stubble. I should've shaved this morning, but I didn't. "I'm sorry, Lulu. I would've stayed away if I knew you wanted to be there."

"No. He was like a grandfather to you. Like a father. It was only right for you to be there." Her hand slides across the table, reaching out to mine, but she quickly pulls it back.

I wish she would touch me.

I cough, trying not to choke on emotion. "No, he didn't tell me that you guys talked. He didn't tell me anything about you."

She smiles, thinking fondly of Harlan. "Good. He was a man of his word."

"He loved you." I stare into her caramel-colored eyes. She nervously dabs at the edge of her eye with her pinky finger, making sure her perfectly applied eye makeup hasn't smudged.

He loved you.

I loved you.

She clears her throat. Picking up her ink pen, she pretends to read through her notes. "What about your safety? Weren't you worried about Trey?"

"I knew I would most likely be on a different continent by the time he figured out it was me. Trey had connections, but not *those* kinds of connections. I mean, we aren't talking about a Mexican drug cartel or anything."

"And then he died."

"Yep. Pissed off the wrong people in prison. He was stabbed in the cafeteria one day about four years ago. It was before I made investigator, so I never got to interview him. Marcum went out there a couple of times but never got anywhere with specifically tying him to Carrie's disappearance."

"Yeah, I read the transcripts." She licks her lips in thought. "If only we had the pictures back then. Everything could've gone so differently."

Yes, but if the police had found the pictures in the beginning, then Lulu might not have ever come searching for answers at the gas station on her own. Might never have gone to the party my brother invited her to. Might never have met me. She's probably wishing she never met me. But meeting her was the highlight of my damn life. Being with her, loving her, it gave me purpose and strength. Strength to make the hardest decision of my existence—to leave her. I wasn't lying when I said there would be no one after her. All these years later, she's still the love of my life.

And that thought scares me shitless.

Her cell phone beeps with an incoming text message. "Ry, I just got notice that I need to do a web call meeting with an attorney's office in Macon, Georgia." She waves her phone in the air. "I'm doing some work for them, and it looks like they just came across a ton of other paperwork they need me to sort through. Do you mind if I use the conference room in private for a little bit?"

I close the lid on my laptop and grab my phone. "No, I have some other work I need to do. I also have to walk over to the courthouse for something." I glance at the watch on my wrist. "It's one now. What do you say we just meet in the parking lot at two-thirty?"

"Okay."

Then I hold her gaze a split second too long. And because she's My Lulu, she doesn't turn away.

I'm standing in front of the station, watching the cars drive out of the parking lot, when Lulu pushes open the door. Sashaying her hips left and right, she struts over to me. I'm too stunned to even speak. My eyes drop to the pavement and start their slow perusal up her body. She's been in black ankle pants all day long. Except now, she's in a short black skirt. Still long enough to be considered business attire, but when you have legs as long as Lulu's, it doesn't take much for something to be considered short. And her legs are completely bare.

They look even better than I remember.

Firm and lean.

Her skin always has a soft glow to it, even in the wintertime, and it makes her whole body look like a butter toffee treat, ready to be eaten. She watches me checking her out. I don't even hide what I'm doing; I'm not ashamed one bit. She tries not to blush, but pink tints her face regardless.

As much as her bare legs make my dick super happy, it makes my brain and heart a little pissed off to know that my idiot brother is going to see her this way. It's cold out today, no Alabama winter making us sweat. Why did she change?

"What happened? Did you spill something on you?"

She looks down at her blouse, tugging it out to inspect it. "Why? Do I have something on me?"

"No, it's just... you changed clothes."

She props a leg in front of me. "Yeah. Trash always made a big deal about my legs, so I changed into a skirt."

Rage blinds me. Makes me stupid. It makes me say asinine things. "So, you're whoring yourself out for him?"

Wrong thing to say. I am a total and complete asshole.

Lulu agrees.

Her eyes widen in shock and her mouth falls open. The shock wears off in about two seconds and she hauls back, slapping me across the face. The noise rings out across the parking lot. My face tingles with burning heat and my jaw buzzes with pins and needles.

I completely and totally deserved that.

She spins away, shaking the stinging pain from her fingers. Stomping across the parking lot, she comes to a complete stop when she realizes that she has no idea what I drive. I quickly hit the un-lock button on my key fob several times. My taillights flash and my horn honks. Lulu doesn't say anything. She just makes her way to the large black pickup and climbs into the passenger's seat. My truck is pretty damn tall, so I can only imagine what body parts she flashed when trying to climb in.

A couple of guys pour out of the station door, waving to me. I really hope they don't see the red mark of a palm print on my face. Then again, I deserve to be embarrassed by that. I can't believe I basically called My Lulu a whore.

No wonder she hates me.

Shaking my head in disgust, I climb in the driver's side. Instead of starting the engine, I lean my head back against the supple leather, close my eyes, and take several deep breaths, trying to calm my nerves. Eventually, I lean up. She's not looking at me. She's just staring out the passenger-side window, rubbing the hem of her skirt between her fingers. In the enclosed space, her coconut and mint smell invades my nostrils, making me think all sorts of things I shouldn't be thinking. "I'm sorry, Lulu. That was an absolutely horrible thing to say. I don't even know where that came from."

She doesn't make any noise.

I sigh. "That's a lie. I know where it comes from. You're right. Trash has always had a thing for you. For your legs. For your body. And I can't stand the thought of him looking at you. I know that's none of my concern anymore—that I have no right to be concerned by that. But it doesn't mean I don't think about it."

"Can we just go, please? We're gonna be late."

Late to see my druggie, pathetic, worthless, felon of a brother? We can't have that, can we?

Chapter 15

Ella

The trailer hasn't changed much—except for looking shittier now than it did twelve years ago. At least some of the vegetation has grown, giving it a little bit more of a residential appearance. The ride out here was tense, to say the least, especially when we passed the road that leads to the old homestead.

I did my best to keep my memories locked up tight, but some still seeped out, like a leaky faucet that drips water no matter how many times you tighten it. Visions of floating water lanterns, blue-flamed fire, and mismatched patio furniture tugged at my heartstrings.

Reading books together late in the night underneath the shelter of our tent. Splashing in the cool creek water beneath the bright afternoon sun. Screaming his name into the night sky as I came all over his cock.

Ry was thinking about it too. I know he was. He stopped breathing.

When we passed the gas station and body shop, he spoke for the first time since he apologized. "Different name. Harlan's son sold it about a year after he died. It's had a couple of different owners since then."

And now here we are, at the place where we first met.

"I'll come around and help you," he offers.

"I'm climbing down from a truck, not scaling down the side of the Grand Canyon. I don't need help." I step on his running board and hop down. My heel does catch on a divot on the uneven packed dirt driveway, twisting my ankle just a bit. I don't care if the damn thing were to break, I would keep my mouth glued shut. I rummage around in my work bag, grabbing my notebook and pen. Walking around to Ry's side, I see him standing at the back driver-side door, pulling on a bullet-proof vest.

"Shit, Ry. You think he'll react that badly to seeing you?"

A small smile tugs at the corner of his mouth. I'm still furious he basically called me a whore. I shouldn't be happy to see him smile, but for some reason, my heart still leaps out of my chest every single time Ryland Joseph Crutchfield smiles. It always has, and I guess it always will. It has to be my hormones. A nostalgic and biologic reaction.

"My body cam is on my vest. I record all of my interviews."

I plant my free hand on my hip. "That would've been nice to know when I was trying to decode and reconcile your scribbled notes with the typed transcripts."

He shrugs. "You didn't ask." He attaches the last strap in place, nodding at my notebook. "Besides, I have you to take notes now, don't I?" He pushes past me, leading the way.

He pounds on the door and I quickly rub my scar, trying to gain the courage to see the monster again. Trash is completely taken aback when he opens the door and sees his own brother standing in front of him. He basically looks the same, just older. Tired and weary. I guess on the Richter scale of aging drug addicts, he's doing fairly well.

"Well, if it isn't my brother, the cop. Something tells me my PO won't be coming by today, huh?"

Ry fiddles with his utility belt, lightly running his fingers across his weapon, badge, phone, and walkie. "He's trusting me to give him a full report. Can we come in?"

"Do I have a choice?" Trash walks away, leaving his door wide open. He bends down, stubbing his cigarette out in the ash tray on the coffee table before turning around. When he does, he blinks several times before realizing that it's me he's staring at. "Holy shit, Ella Hill, is that you?" He chokes on a laugh before stumbling forward, pulling me against him in a hug.

Ry's eyes immediately flare and he reaches out to grab his brother by the collar, ready to fling him across the room. I put my hand up, stopping him in his tracks. I don't hug Trash back, but I don't step out of his embrace either. The smell of cigarette smoke, bad breath, and dirty clothes assaults my nose. It takes all my strength not to gag. His body feels so fragile against mine. His bones feel light and airy, like those of a baby bird.

He meanders away, stumbling back to sit in his stained and dingy recliner. "What the hell are you doing here?"

"I had to come to town to take care of some family business. I decided to stay for a little while. I'm doing some consultant work for the sheriff's department."

Trash looks over at Ry and bursts out laughing. "Damn, brother, must be your lucky day. Never thought you'd get over this one," he flicks a thumb in my direction. "Now, here she is. The gods just keep shining on you, Crutch, don't they?"

"Don't start playing that woe-is-me card, Trash. We come from the exact same circumstances. You chose your path, and I chose mine."

He flings a leg across the arm of his chair. "Speaking of those *circumstances* we come from, Dad called the other day from lockup, said you weren't putting in a good word for him or Mom."

"They don't deserve a good word. They were caught using stolen credit cards. Again. We're talking prison this time, not just county or city jail. There's nothing I can do for them."

Ry didn't tell me his parents are currently sitting in a jail cell.

Trash swings his leg. "You mean nothing you *want* to do for them."

There's no emotion on Ry's face. "Semantics," he says simply.

Trash snorts and folds his arms across his chest. He doesn't say anything, but I think it's just because he doesn't know what the word semantics means.

Ry changes the topic. "We've come to ask some more questions about Carrie's case. We've come across some new information. Okay if we talk?"

"Do I have a choice?"

"I'm giving you the choice to do it here or at the station. Your call."

Trash sweeps his arm in the direction of his couch. "I don't feel like driving anywhere so you might as well have a seat."

I glance at the couch. It's a different one from the last time I was here, but it looks just as old. I'm definitely not interested in sitting on the nasty thing, but I don't have much of a choice. Alienating the subject right off the bat by refusing hospitality is never a good start to an interview.

Ry steps to the side, placing his hand on the small of my back as I maneuver around the coffee table. My spine stiffens like an electric shock just paralyzed me. Feeling it, he immediately removes his hand. I'm grateful he removed it when he did... before that old and familiar tingle poured through my body. I perch myself on the edge of the couch and prepare to take notes. Trash snickers like a child in trouble, garnering my attention.

"Shit, Ella. The last decade has been good to you. I nearly forgot how good those legs of yours look." He leans forward, scrunching his nose, baring his yellow and brown stained teeth. "I bet they'd look even better wrapped around my waist."

Oh crap. Normally, my reflexes aren't that quick. I mean, they're quick, but not supersonic speed or anything. So, how I react so quickly this time can only be described as a miracle. Ry growls, shifting to pounce from the couch and beat the snot out of his brother. Before he can move more than a centimeter, my hand slides across his leg, pinning him to the couch in stunned silence. We both look down at my hand, splayed across his upper thigh. I can feel the tight band of his muscles contract beneath the fabric of his jeans. Slowly, his head lifts, his eyes meeting mine.

I should move my hand. I should move my hand.

But I don't.

I always do what I shouldn't.

My heartbeat pounds through my fingertips, playing a rhythm against his body. Suddenly, his calloused hand covers mine, holding me to him.

Was I mad at Ry? I can't remember.

Our moment is interrupted by the squeal of his obnoxious, parolee brother. "She's still got you on a leash, Crutch. After all these years, huh? Can't do anything without the little lady's approval? You tell her about that house—."

"Enough!" Ry's yell startles me and I yank my hand away. The discord tumbles me back into reality. Blinking rapidly and breathing a sigh of relief, I remember *that's* a good thing. Reality reminds you where you belong. And according to Ry, we don't belong together. That's the reality I have lived with for nearly twelve years, and I need to remember that.

"Geez. Settle down, brother."

Ry peeks over at me. I can't even read his expression. What's the point in trying to decipher what just happened? I nod, urging him to move on. "Let's just get started."

He turns on his body cam and states the date and time. "I will be recording this session with audio and visual. Please state your name."

"The amazing Daniel Crutchfield. Everyone calls me Trash."

Ry spends the next twenty minutes going over things we already know. General background information, things that we knew back then, duplicate questions from the last two times he interviewed Trash. None of this is uncommon. We can take the answers and comments to this benign stuff and compare it to previous conversations to see if anything has changed, if anything raises a red flag.

"A couple of weeks ago, we came across some new evidence that is most likely tied to the disappearance of Carrie."

This part intrigues Trash. It's what he's been waiting to hear since we started. "What evidence?"

"Some photographs."

"Photographs of what?"

I hand Ry the blown-up copies of the photos from my notebook. "We wanna show you some of these photos. See what explanations you may have for what's going on in them."

"Where'd you get them?"

"We're keeping that information confidential for now," Ry says, handing the first picture to him.

To my surprise, Trash actually sits up straight and really focuses on the picture. "Carrie."

Duh.

Ry tries to corral his brother's thoughts. "Can you tell me anything about the picture? Location? Who took it? Anything based on the date stamp?"

"This is at Trey's. I guess Christina took the picture. She always had that fancy camera with her. Don't know why, she could've just used her phone."

"Anything with the date?"

Trash rolls his eyes. "How am I supposed to know what I was doing on a particular date? I was either partying or working."

"What about Carrie's appearance? Do you remember seeing her in clothes like that? Anything?"

"I know she looks fucking fine with a capital F. That girl was like a model." He flaps the picture back and forth in his hand. "In this picture, she looks like she really needs some bananas."

He's talking about hydrocodone.

Ry gives him the next two pictures. "Hey, it's me!"

Duh.

"What can you tell me about these pictures?"

"Well, that's me. Carrie's probably laughing at something I said.

She was always real fond of me, you know." He glances up and winks at me. "Not sure who that other person is. Can't see his face."

We figured out it was that Tyler guy based on the color of his shirt.

"Your hand is on her thigh."

"Yeah, I've told you a hundred times, we were friendly. Touching someone's leg isn't a crime." He looks over at me. "Is it, Ella?"

Ry grinds his teeth so hard I can actually hear the sound. "Keep your answers on topic and address only the interviewer, please."

Trash chuckles. "Testy, testy."

"So, despite this display of affection, things were never sexual between you and Carrie? No kissing, no sexual activity?"

"No, she didn't want me like that. It's fine, though. I had my fair share of women to pick from." He narrows his eyes and points at his brother. "But, if I remember correctly, she did have a thing for you. Didn't she make a pass at you once? Didn't things get *sexual* between the two of you?"

Ry ignores the question and hands pictures four and five to Trash. He laughs and kicks his legs up on the coffee table. "Well, there's some faces I haven't seen in a while."

"Can you detail that picture?"

"Well, that's Tyler and Holly and James. And of course, there's Trey."

"Tell me about them. Last names, jobs, what did they do, do you still see them, where are they now?"

We know a lot already, but we want to see what we may have missed.

"Tyler Spangler and Holly Yates. They had this on-again, off-again thing. They partied with us quite a bit. They were hardcore. He was some kind of welder, and she was on disability for something. Her back, maybe? Got into a car accident when she was little. I haven't seen them in years. Last I heard, they weren't together anymore. I think they still live in the area, but I don't know for sure. They were mostly Trey's friends.

"And this other guy, his name is James. I don't know his last name. He was a tool. Tried too hard to be funny. He just wanted a good party and a pretty woman by his side. He was more of a drinker, anyway. I heard he got scared shitless when the rest of us got busted. Cleaned up his act and moved away."

"Do you remember this night?" Ry asks. "Now, that you've seen who all was present?"

"Yeah. We partied good that night. Trey was waiting on his supplier to show up, so he let us clean out the rest of the old inventory he had on hand. Carrie paid for everything. That rich chick always had money on her."

Bastard. He talks about Carrie like she wasn't even a person. She was *my* person. My sister.

"None of you are concerned that Carrie is unconscious?"

He snorts, "You can't get concerned every time someone passes out. That happens all the time. There's a big difference between a 'normal' pass out and an 'OD' pass out. We were all pretty good at telling the difference. Carrie just got some really good shit that night."

Ry presses him, "What happened when the supplier came? You all stayed at Trey's? Kept partying?"

"We kept partying alright, but down here. You know Trey never let anyone meet his supplier."

"So, everyone left before the supplier got there, including Carrie?"

"No, Carrie was out like a light. We couldn't get her to move, she stayed. But there's no way she saw the supplier. She took enough meds to be in dream world for hours. Trey knew that. That's why he let her stay. The rest of us were too wasted to pick her up."

"And what about Christina? Did she stay?"

Trash rolls his eyes. "Of course not. Trey never let her stay. Doesn't matter they were together. Rules are rules."

Glancing at me, begging silent forgiveness for the trauma he's about to put me through, Ry hands the modified last picture copy to

Trash. Carrie's body is blurred for a small modicum of decency. The only thing you can see are her hands, arms, and face. Her gorgeous, beautiful face, with her twisted and knotted hair draped across it.

"Holy shit. Is she getting boned?"

My voice is firm and steady. "Raped. Unconscious women can't give consent, Trash. Perhaps you should remember that for future reference."

He drops the picture in his lap and holds up his hands. At least he has the common decency to act surprised. "Hey, Ella, I had no idea that Carrie was raped, okay."

Ry interjects, "You had no clue that this happened that same night? No one said anything to you? After the fact?"

"No, Trey kept a lot of things close to the vest. He called us his friends, but we were his pushers, his ticket to money. You know that. It's why I flipped on him to get reduced time. He didn't give a shit about me. Hired some big, fancy lawyer. Left me with the acne-faced, dick-in-hand public defender."

I point to the picture. "Do you know him?"

"No."

"Look again," I beg. "Is he the supplier? Is there anything familiar about him? The clothes? The scar on his leg?"

"I don't know him." He scoffs, "I don't look at naked men. How am I supposed to know about a scar on his leg? And his clothes? He's dressed like a professor."

Closing my eyes, I reach back, rubbing the scar on my neck. I take several deep breaths trying to calm myself while Ry wraps up the interview. Feeling defeated, I tuck the toxic pictures back into my notebook while Ry turns off his body cam.

"Do you mind waiting for me in the truck? I need to talk to Trash about a couple of personal things before we go." Ry hands me his truck keys.

Nodding, I make my way out of the room, trying to escape before Trash lights up another cigarette. "Ella, don't I get a goodbye hug?"

I turn and flip him the bird.

It's not meant to be funny, but for some reason, he laughs like a hyena. "That's okay. I have a feeling we'll be seeing each other again. Now that you're back, you think my brother's gonna let you leave? Think again."

I slam the door, which is hard to do when it's made of warped aluminum. So, I kick it for extra measure.

The winter sun has already set, coating the earth in darkness. Chill bumps immediately break out on my bare legs. I jump in the truck and start the engine, cranking up the heat. It's a really nice truck. Leather seats, all the fancy buttons, moonroof. My eyes meander to the glove box.

Huh. The glove box.

Ignoring the urge to snoop, I pull out my phone and listen to the two voicemails I received while we were interviewing Trash. One is from Aunt Teresa telling me to be careful on my work trip tomorrow. The other call is from an assistant producer, telling me she emailed some specific questions she wants answered with the first-round interview tomorrow afternoon. I check my emails, but quickly decide it will be easier to work from the laptop when I get back home.

I slip my phone back in my purse and find myself staring at the glove box. Again.

Little tendrils of curiosity climb from my stomach to my throat, weaving through my body like a suffocating kudzu.

Screw it.

Before I can change my mind, I flick the button, and the lid of the glove box bounces open. There, sitting obnoxiously among the car title and insurance cards, is a red box of condoms. Not only that, but there are several loose condom foil packets floating haphazardly around the compartment. The loose condoms are a different brand from the condoms still in the box. How many different kinds of condoms does one man need? I pick up a black foil packet.

XXL. Ultra-Thin. Ribbed.

Well, it's ribbed for her pleasure. Whoever the hell *her* is. But I already know the answer to that. There isn't just one her, there's a million. Ry is having sex with every Susie, Jane, and Jill in the county.

And it makes me furious.

Absolutely furious.

Like cut off his dick and run it through a blender furious.

For me, sex with Ry was indescribable. I closed my eyes and pictured him every single time Hudson laid a hand on me. I thought what Ry and I had was more than just sex—I thought it was making love. And to know that he's still chasing that feeling with every vagina in town breaks my heart. He must really love sex. Was I just another hole to stick it in?

Because for me, it was more.

He was mine. He was supposed to be all mine, forever.

And then, he threw us away. Threw me away. Threw Reality away.

I'm engrossed in my own thoughts when the driver-side door opens. It scares the crap out of me, and the condom flies from my hand, landing somewhere on the floorboard. I slam the glove box closed and stare out the window, pretending like I wasn't snooping through his truck.

He climbs in without saying a word. I wait for him to drive off, but nothing happens. I'm too chicken to turn around and face him, so I just keep staring out the window.

He leans over, picks up the condom, and holds it underneath my nose. "Need to borrow something? You could've just asked." The edge of the foil wrapper tickles my nostril, making me squirm and sniffle.

I tsk through my teeth. "You don't need to worry about me. I can make my own purchases. Besides, from what I've seen over the past few weeks, you need every little packet in your glove box arsenal."

"Me? I'm not the one who went home with a stranger Friday night."

Now, *that* has me turning around. "That's what's wrong? Your piss-poor attitude today? It's because I left the bar with a guy on Friday night?"

He grunts, not saying anything.

"That's rich coming from you. I'm surprised your dick hasn't rotted off over the past twelve years. And I'm not even talking about disease. I'm simply talking about over-use. A twig can only bend so many times before it breaks."

His jaw clenches. He does not like that analogy.

I forge forward, hot in anger. "I'm thirty years old, Ry. If I wanna leave the bar with ten men at one time, I can do that. It's nobody's business but mine. Why do you even care?"

"First of all, you're not thirty yet. Second of all, *why do I even care*? That's like asking someone why the sky is blue. You know why I care."

"Do I?" He doesn't say anything. He just scowls. So, I turn the spotlight on him instead. "Tell me, when's the last time you had sex?"

He shakes his head. "I'm not answering that."

"Oh yes, you are. You're the one who started this conversation. When is the last time you had sex?"

His eyes flicker down my body, from my mouth to my legs and back again. I don't like the way he looks at me when I say the word sex, like he's thinking of me. Because I know he's not.

"So help me, Ryland Joseph Crutchfield, you *will* answer this question. Tell me. Now."

His eyes soften, the fire in them dying. "New Year's Day."

Of course. Of course, it was. That's just great. "So, while my parents were dying in a plane crash, you were sticking your cock in some perky teenager?" I snort in sarcastic disgust. "And you wanna chastise me for trying to connect with someone? Trying to feel something?"

I fold my arms across my chest. "You gave up the right to monitor what happens to my crotch twelve years ago when you left. Now, start this truck and drive, or else I'm going back inside and asking Trash for a ride."

He starts the truck and drives.

Chapter 16

Ella

I crawl across the floor on my hands and knees. Grazing my nose across the bare skin of his torso, I playfully nibble on his stomach.

He squeals in delight, pumping his hands and feet in the air.

Anna bends over her baby brother, tickling his nose with her hair. "Ty, is Smelly Ellie tickling you?" He immediately wraps a tiny fist around her damp hair and tries to pull it into his mouth. "No, no." She gingerly pulls her hair from his grasp and runs back over to Uncle Ray, crawling onto his lap and secretly stealing a sip of his soda. Ray and Teresa already gave her a bath and had her brush her teeth, so Raylee would reprimand them if she saw her daughter drinking a Coke.

Raylee rounds the corner. "Mom, I threw Ty's onesie in the washer. I have no idea how that kid manages to pee on everything he wears. No one told me that changing a little boy's diaper is like a fireman trying to wrangle a hose."

Holt props his feet on the coffee table. "Just wait until he's a teenager."

Raylee smacks her brother upside the head. "Shut up."

Anna gasps, tattle-telling to Aunt Teresa. "Mimi..."

Smiling, she fake scolds her children. "Raylee, don't tell your brother to shut up. Holt, don't aggravate your sister."

Tyson grunts and wiggles around on the soft blanket I spread out across the living room rug. "Come on, Ty. Let's work those muscles." I roll him onto his stomach, encouraging him to push up with his arms.

Will joins us, sitting next to Raylee on the couch. He offered to do clean-up duty from tonight's family dinner. Flopping onto my back, I pick up Ty and lay him across my chest. I smile, watching his little face contort into a gummy grin as he tries to bite my chin. Instead, he drools all over my face.

When Aunt Teresa called me last night to say she wanted to have a family dinner, I was worried I wouldn't make it back in time from my out-of-town work. But they waited on me. My wonderful and sweet family—whom I am still completely mad at—waited on me. Dinner was supposed to be at six. I didn't pull up into the driveway until seven and found them all sitting around the kitchen table, waiting on me.

"Where'd you go, Ella?"

I peer around Ty's head, looking at Will. "Huntsville. It was a pre-interview for a television show."

"What happened?"

"This woman had two sisters. Twenty years ago, one sister killed the other. Poisoned her. She did it slowly over a year's time. Then, when she was in prison, she was so distraught, she hung herself. I met with the surviving sister, asked her some questions. I have to make an interview format for the producers."

Raylee tosses me a spit rag so I can wipe my face. "Plus, she's older so they wanted to make sure her house would be a suitable filming location. Then, I met with some others—the defense attorney, the prosecutor, some of the police, family friends. The local university there has a really nice conference room in their library. They should be able to film all the other interviews there."

Holt cocks his head. "Interview formats. I had people do those on me before I had to give big interviews."

"Yeah, it just helps the flow."

Will shrugs. "What do you mean?"

"Well, everyone talks in a different manner. When you ask someone to tell a story, some people start in the beginning, some people start at the end, and some people start in the middle. When you watch these crime shows on TV, they usually start with a little information about the crime itself. You know, what makes it so horrific to human nature, and then they have to wind back around and tell the story from start to finish. If I can figure out how the subject talks, tells her story, how she likes to answer questions, how much information she elaborates on, then I can come up with a plan for what all the producers need to ask and in what order they need to ask it. It definitely makes the editing process easier in the end."

"Honey, that's so amazing. I must say, when you became obsessed with all that true crime stuff after Carrie disappeared, I became more than a little concerned. I can't believe you've actually turned it into a career."

I smile upside down at Aunt Teresa. "I can't believe it either. I love what I do. Just think, if I followed Mom and Dad's path, I would've been an architect. Don't get me wrong, that's an amazing profession, just not for me."

Uncle Ray clears his throat. Anna is still sitting on his lap, but she's curled up against his chest, losing the battle to keep her eyes open as he softly scratches her back. "Speaking of Carrie, how are things going? I heard you went to interview Crutch's brother on Monday before you left town."

"And which little spy did you hear that from? Marcum or Holt?"

"Crutch."

My ears snap to attention. "Excuse me? For someone who said he didn't hardly see or speak to the man, you sure seem to be talking to him a lot lately."

A small shred of shame slices away at my heart, knowing that I shouldn't make such comments. If anyone deserves to be spied on, I guess it should be me. I did keep the fact that Carrie was selling and using drugs from my family. We haven't really talked about it, but I knew I had to apologize. I barely had the words, 'I'm sorry' out of my mouth before they all forgave me.

I guess I should take a lesson from my own family.

Unfazed by my attitude, Uncle Ray answers, "A couple of cars got broken into at the factory. Crutch and Leary stopped by when they heard it over the radio."

"And?" I wrap my arms around Ty and clamber into a sitting position.

"And...I asked him how things were going between the two of you."

I narrow my eyes. "Why not just ask me?"

Holt snorts. "Some could say you're a little defensive when it comes to questions about Crutch. Or offensive, depending on how you look at it, I guess."

I blow air from my mouth, which makes Ty grunt in excitement. "I only call it like I see it when it comes to him."

Raylee leans forward. "And how do you see it? After all these years?"

I could lie. Tell them that everything between me and Ry is completely dead. That we're consummate professionals and nothing more, but this is my family we're talking about. Not my parents. Not my in-laws. Not my stuck-up society peers. My *real* family. They deserve the truth.

Especially after what I already hid from them.

"It's complicated to see past the cobwebs. I'm so angry with him. I don't know if I'll ever stop being angry. Sometimes just being in the same room with him makes me wanna scream and cry and punch him in the face."

"And other times?"

"Other times..." My voice trails off in thought. I close my eyes, picturing Ry's sexy smile, imagining what it would feel like to have his muscular arms wrap me in a hug. His frame is larger now than it was back then. Firmer. Solid. Masculine and mature. What would it feel like to be pressed against him? With nothing separating us but a thin sheen of sweat. "Other times, and don't get me wrong, it's only a small—very small—portion of the time, but I feel like I finally found my best friend again, the person who makes living life better."

"Have you gotten any closure, any clarity?" she asks.

I kiss my baby cousin's nose, making him yawn. "I don't think I'll ever get closure."

"Well, you definitely won't if you never tell him."

"So, Caleb's secretary refused to give me his cell phone number or personal email address. But she did talk to him, told him I was trying to get ahold of him. He told her to schedule me on his calendar for the first day he's back in the office."

Ry opens a fresh bottle of water and sets it in front of me. "So, he's working a six-month stint out of the country?"

I nod. "Sweden. He and his family left mid-December. They'll be back in Atlanta in June. He's taking a week off work and then he'll be starting back at the local office. We can meet with him then. He doesn't do social media, his wife does. I could reach out to him that way, but I really think we need to have the conversation with him in person and not over the phone, from half a world away."

I wait for him to ask if I'll even be around in June. He completely bypasses that comment. "Yeah, asking someone if they got their ex-girlfriend pregnant before she mysteriously disappeared is probably something best to do in person. What did you tell the secretary?"

"Just that he and my sister were best friends for many years, and I am working on a book about her and wanted to interview him. See him again."

Ry licks his perfectly brown-pink lips, causing a flutter in my stomach. "A book? Is that part real?"

"Maybe one day." I shrug. "I'd love to write in-depth about a case. They say to write about what you know. There's nothing I know more about than my sister. Plus, it's not like I can write about one of my hired cases. I have standard language in my contract that says I will not pursue any outside activity from anything I'm hired to work on."

He stares into my eyes, causing me to sit up straighter. "Well," his voice purrs over his words, "let's hope we can give the book a proper ending. Closure."

Closure. There's that damn word again.

Focusing back on my computer screen, I ask, "Any luck in finding Tyler, Holly, or James."

"I've got the information on Holly, figured we could meet with her tomorrow. Based on what I've read, I'm thinking a surprise visit while her kids are at school may be the best route. I'm still waiting on address information for Tyler and a contact phone number for James. He lives in Dallas now, works in accounting at a big oil office."

"And Christina knows we're coming today?"

"Yeah, she seems to be in a really good place. Turned her life around. She married several years ago, and her husband owns an insurance company."

"That's good. Let's just hope she's willing to be forthcoming."

Ry leans back in his chair. "Meaning?"

I stare into his pale green eyes. "Maybe she hasn't told her husband all the gory details about her past. Most husbands don't exactly enjoy hearing about their wife's past indiscretions."

His voice lowers to a whisper. "Did Hudson hear about yours?"

The blood stops circulating in my body. Even at my angriest, I would never refer to Ry as an indiscretion. He used to be my everything. Making love to him was never a poor choice. I had no choice. If I wanted to keep breathing, I had to be with him.

At least, that's the way it felt.

Hindsight could call it misguided, I guess. He left me. Obviously, I was freakin' misguided.

My voice chokes in my throat. "I never talked to Hudson about you."

"Never? He didn't ask?"

I nearly burst out laughing. "Oh, he asked." Every single time we fought. Every single time I acted indifferent. Every single time I refused to let him touch me. Every single time I reacted nonchalantly to the news he had a new mistress. "I just didn't comply."

Ry sucks in a breath. "Why?"

Lie. Lie. Lie. Like an idiot, I tell the truth. "Because he didn't deserve to hear about us."

"Just like he didn't deserve to see the real you? Did you keep hiding from him? Even after you married him?" Ry leans forward, dragging his hand across his clean-shaven jaw. "Lulu, how the hell could you marry that asshole?"

Fortunately, I don't have to answer. There's a knock on the conference room door, and Colson peeks his head around the corner. "Hey, Ella, sorry to interrupt." He nods his head to Ry. "We're up, Crutch. Have to respond to a call."

A low growl rumbles in his chest. He grabs his cell phone and slams his laptop shut. "I'll be back to pick you up about one." Pausing in the doorway, he looks over his shoulder. "Christina never talked about your legs, right? I don't have a mini skirt to worry about?"

I bite my lip. "No. She's always been a breast woman."

Chuckling, Ry closes the door, and I swear I hear him mumble something like, "Yeah, me too."

Chapter 17

Crutch

Fortunately, Lulu was kidding about the breast part. Knowing My Lulu is full of piss and vinegar, I half expected her to be wearing a crop top when I picked her up. We're going through a two-week cold snap right now, and it's freezing outside. I really don't think I'd be strong enough to see her cleavage and frozen nipples. And wasn't looking forward to it.

Well, I was.

But you know what I mean. Thinking of her body only makes functioning like a normal human being more difficult.

We pull up in front of the brick office building, and I reach around in the back seat, grabbing my vest. Jumping out of the truck, I quickly put it on while making my way over to the passenger's side, hoping Lulu will let me help her for once. I'm not quick enough, and she bounces down from the seat with her notebook, pen, folder, and phone in tow.

"Chivalry isn't dead, you know? I can still help you out of the truck. You used to let me do it all the time."

She raises her eyebrows. "Well, if that's the rule…" Her voice trails off, laden with sexual innuendo. Quickly realizing that she's supposed to hate me, she wipes the playful smile from her face and leaves me standing there.

Damn if I don't miss playful Lulu. She was always a hell of a lot of fun.

Jogging to the door, I quickly open it for her. Stepping to the side, she politely lets me take the lead. The lobby is filled with some workers, but thankfully, it looks to be customer-free. The receptionist does a double take when she notices me and the phone drops from her hand, clattering across the desk. I side glance at Lulu, watching in amusement as she rolls her eyes.

"How may I assist you?" The lady stands, playing with the beads of her necklace.

"Ma'am," I nod, folding my hands in front of me. "We have an appointment to see Chris—"

"Crutch!"

Our attention immediately turns to the left, where Christina emerges from an open office. At least I think it's Christina. She looks like a completely different person. I pulled up her DMV photo before our meeting so I knew she looked better than twelve years ago, but seeing her in person is completely surprising. And refreshing. She's dressed in nice clothes with gold bracelets that jingle when she walks. Her hair is clean and styled, her makeup perfect. She's a healthy weight, maybe even a little on the plump side. She actually seems happy to see me. Before I know what's happening, she's wrapping me in a hug. When she pulls away, I can see some of the small scars that still dot her face, but the makeup does a good job at hiding most of it.

"It's so good to see you. I've actually thought about you a lot over the years. Especially when I heard you became a detective. I always wanted to reach out. Just never did."

"Christina, you look phenomenal."

She smiles and her smile widens even more when she catches a glimpse of the man walking out of the office that's next to hers. "Crutch, I'd like you to meet my husband, Donnie Poland. Donnie, this is Ryland Crutchfield." She turns back to me. "I'm sorry, do we need to call you Detective or something?"

"We've known each other since I started kindergarten. Crutch is fine." I turn, holding out my hand to Lulu.

"Ella Hill," she introduces herself. "Nice to see you again, Christina."

Christina's eyes cloud with confusion. "Again?"

Lulu shifts on her feet but holds her back stiff and straight. "We met once. A long time ago. At a party."

Christina looks over to me, questioning, "Trash's?"

I nod in confirmation before she turns back to Lulu. "I wish I could say it was nice to meet you again, but there's a lot from those days I don't remember. So, I'll just say it's nice to meet you now."

Lulu smiles and nods. "Sounds good to me."

Donnie wraps an arm around Christina. "We cleared out the conference room. Shall we?"

"Ella Hill? That name sounds familiar. Are you related to Carrie? Is that why you're here? Are you with the sheriff's department too?"

I hold out a rolling chair for Lulu. She stares at me, debating whether or not to accept my help, before she finally sits down. "I'm Carrie's sister. I'm working a consulting assignment with the department regarding my sister's case."

"Carrie's sister." Christina's eyes dart back and forth between the two of us, as she tries to pull her memories to the forefront of her brain. "Wait, didn't the two of you date?"

Hell yeah, we did.

I don't answer, leaving that ball in Lulu's ballpark.

She rubs the back of her neck. "We dated briefly, many years ago, before Ryland joined the service."

Christina nods, smiling like she knows a secret. "All the girls were furious you got snatched up, Crutch." She turns to Lulu, laughing. "Rumor had it, he was head over heels for you."

Hell yeah, I was.

Reaching over, Donnie laces his fingers with Christina's. "Sweetie."

"Sorry. I talk when I get nervous."

I try to calm her. "That's okay. There's nothing to be nervous about. We're just here to ask some questions about what all was happening in your life around the time Carrie went missing. We've run across some new evidence, so we're just following up on information. Sometimes, a little bit of time helps everyone put things into perspective, allows them to revisit events that might not have seemed significant back then."

"I'm ready to help in any way possible."

I lean forward, spreading my hands across the table. "Some of the questions we ask may be a little sensitive in nature. Perhaps some privacy will provide a level of comfort." I nod at Donnie.

Christina squeezes her husband's hand. "I appreciate the concern, but Donnie knows all about my past. He pulled me from the brink of hell, knows every dirty little detail. Unless you have a rule against him staying, I would like for him to be here."

"Okay." I gain permission to record the interview and start with all of Christina's background questions. We talk about her childhood, where she grew up, her descent into drug use, her partying with my brother and Trey, her run-ins with Carrie. "So, think back to the summer when Carrie went missing. Did anything strike you as unusual about that time?"

"Well, the beginning of that year is when I had my third child. By the start of the summer, he was already in the system, living in a foster home. I'm just thankful the same family took him in as my other boys. They were all together, so that's one small blessing. Other than that, I was just in the throes of addiction. Using every day. Working one meager job after another, trying to make money to score. Partying with Trey, day and night. Sleeping with him, begging for product when I was too broke to buy anything on my own."

"You don't remember anything unusual about Trey during that time?"

She scoffs. "Trey was always unusual. He was a drug dealer."

I glance over at Donnie, hoping he's prepared himself. "Was Trey the father of any of your children?"

Christina shifts in her seat. "Yes. He was the biological originator of my third son."

Well, I've never heard that terminology used before.

"Is there any sense of connection there? That you would keep something from the police, anything that involved Trey, because he was the father of your son?"

Her face grows serious. "Trey was never a father. Donnie is the father to my three boys, in every single way that matters."

Donnie wraps his arm around Christina again. "Our family counselor encouraged us to use the word 'originator' because our son couldn't bring himself to call Trey his father. I can assure you that there is no sense of allegiance between Christina and Trey. Or anyone from her past, for that matter."

I nod. "He never mentioned what he thought happened to Carrie?"

"He just said that she probably had a bad trip, wandered off in the woods, and died." She glances over at Lulu. "I'm sorry to be so blunt. It must be painful to hear."

Lulu looks up from her notebook, smiling sadly. "Please continue."

"They found her car in a parking lot by some woods, right? I guess that's why the explanation seemed plausible. All I know is that you didn't talk about it...ever. Trey didn't like anyone talking about Carrie or asking questions about her."

"Why is that?"

"Because the police came around asking about her. Because of the gas station thing. The gas station drew police attention to Carrie and that drew attention to Trey and the whole operation. And that made him nervous. He thought the gas station was becoming a liability. He thought Trash wasn't taking his role seriously, that he wasn't screening his customers closely enough. They couldn't stop the video feed, the owner of the station refused to do away with the video cameras. He didn't know about the drugs, you know? Anyway, Trey thought Trash was being reckless. At first, he was happy when

Trash brought Carrie around. He was excited to have a girl pushing on the university campus. He only had a few fraternity guys pushing back then. When Carrie went missing, he told Trash that he never should've brought her into the mix."

"And that went for everyone? No one talked to Trey about Carrie?"

Christina shudders. "You remember how he was. He killed that one guy. Sure, they called it self-defense, but we all knew it was murder. No one wanted to go against Trey's wishes. He didn't want anyone to talk about Carrie, so we didn't."

"What about Trash? Did he ever tell you what he thought happened to Carrie?"

She shakes her head. "He just said the same thing as Trey—that Carrie went off on her own. He said she probably ran away."

"What can you tell us about Carrie?"

She nervously looks over at Lulu, seeking permission. "It's fine, Christina. Tell the truth. You won't offend me," Lulu says.

"Well, she was beautiful, of course. All the guys wanted to be with her. She was refined, mature, confident. She was in deep, sure, but she was still a newborn compared to most of us. She hadn't crossed that line yet, where the drug use was all-consuming. She still functioned, lived that part of her life in secret. I'm assuming you didn't even know she had a problem, right?"

Lulu nods. Just once. "You're right, I didn't."

"We all start out that way. A little here, a little there. Some people can live that way for years and years before it becomes the complete DNA of your life, ruling every single second of every single day. Carrie wasn't there yet. She was on a runaway train, headed in that direction, but she wasn't there yet." She reaches out, grabbing Lulu's hand. "I think she could've been saved. Before she reached that point, I mean."

Lulu lifts her chin in the air, politely nodding before sliding her hand from Christina's grasp. She never liked to be touched by strangers.

I change the subject. "Do you still take pictures, Christina?"

Donnie smiles proudly. "She's a wonderful photographer. Started a little side business a few years ago. Wedding pictures, Christmas cards. Her work is beautiful."

Time to get down to business. We pull out the photograph copies and go through them one by one. Christina quickly confirms they came from her camera, that she was the one behind the lens. She even remembers the night. We pause before we get to the last picture.

"Do you remember what happened after this picture?"

"Oddly enough, I do remember that. Trey's supplier was coming over so we all had to leave. We went over to Trash's trailer. I realized I forgot my camera, and I wanted to go back to get it. I thought I could make it there before the supplier showed up. I took Trash's car and drove back. The door was locked so I had to knock. Trey didn't like that. Not one bit. The supplier was already there. When I asked for my camera, Trey punched me in the face and pushed me down the stairs. I twisted my ankle. Went back to Trash's and got completely wasted to help with the pain."

Donnie clenches his jaw, thinking about his wife getting hit.

I sit forward in my seat. "You were there when the supplier was there? And you're sure it was the supplier and not someone else?"

"Trey wouldn't have cared if someone else was there. It was only the supplier he protected that much."

"Did you actually see the supplier?"

She shakes her head. "No, of course not."

"What about a car? Anything like that?"

"No, I'm sorry, I've never been good with cars. But I also wasn't the most observant person back then, as you can imagine."

I look over at Lulu, getting her silent permission to proceed with the last picture. She blinks. Sometimes I can easily read her mind. Other times, it's like she's hidden behind an impenetrable curtain.

"Okay, Christina, this is the last picture we have to show you. I warn you. It's explicit."

Her eyes widen in fear. "Okay." Both she and Donnie lean forward, looking at the picture. Shock and horror etch across their faces. It's clear as day that Christina has never seen this picture before. Donnie leans back, refusing to look at the horrible image.

Christina wipes tears from her eyes and stutters over her question. "Is... is Carrie being... raped?"

"Yes." I point at the perpetrator. "Do you know who that is, Christina? Is there anything familiar about him?"

She reluctantly looks back at the picture. Even blurred, the scene is graphic. I hate showing it to people. I hate putting Lulu through that.

"No, I have no idea who that is. I can't believe that happened to Carrie. I had hope for her, hope that she would avoid what so many of us went through."

Lulu's eyes dart to mine. Her face grows long and serious, her voice full of concern and question. "So many of you? What are you saying, Christina? Were you sexually assaulted?"

Donnie reaches over, firmly holding his wife's hand. The sad smile on Christina's face tells me everything I need to know. I'm sure Lulu's seen that same face before. "I was an addict for over five years. You can't put yourself in those circumstances and not have something like that happen to you."

Anger swirls in my stomach, fucking pissing me off. "Trey and who? Trash?" I swear on all that's holy, if my brother raped this woman—any woman—he won't be able to walk by nightfall.

"No, not Trash. He always talked crap about women, their bodies. But he was more concerned with getting high than chasing women. He was always ready for a roll in the sack, don't get me wrong, but he waited for the women to come to him. Willingly." She tries to make light of the situation. "You know your brother never liked to work all that hard."

"Who then?"

She cocks her head to the side, speaking to me slowly and softly, like a child. "Crutch, it's nothing to chase after. Trey is already gone. And the others? I don't even know who they are. I remember the faces of some, but don't know their names. I know nothing about them.

Others are just shadows, blurs. Leaving nothing in their wake but a sore feeling between my legs."

I look over at Donnie. He's handling this better than me. I guess Christina wasn't lying when she said he knew everything about her past. I sigh, sitting back in my chair. "That doesn't mean they should get away with it."

"No, it doesn't. But what's more important to me now is making sure that no one else goes through what I went through. Addiction can be prevented. If you never start, you never have to worry about stopping."

I try to calm myself, absorbing her words. When I don't say anything, Lulu takes over, bringing the interview back on course.

"So, going back to the picture, you weren't present when this picture was taken?"

"No."

"Did Trey know how to operate your camera?"

"Well, he saw me use it plenty of times, but I never saw him even pick it up. It simply didn't interest him."

I nod at Lulu, wordlessly thanking her for taking over, before I ask the next question. "In your opinion, did Trey take this picture?"

"No."

"Do you have any idea who might have been there that night besides the supplier and Trey?"

"The only person who was there when we left was Carrie. She was passed out." Tears fall from her eyes. "Ella, I'm so sorry I left her behind."

Donnie reaches over to a side table, grabbing a box of tissues. I give Christina a few moments to compose herself. "Carrie was in possession of these pictures. Why did you develop them and give them to her? I'm not understanding how you never saw the assault picture before. Did you just forget about seeing it?"

"Not just that picture. I've never seen any of these pictures before."

"What?"

"I didn't develop these pictures. When I went back the next day to get my camera, the memory card was gone. I was furious because I had just put a new one in." She takes a deep breath. "I had a huge bruise on my face from where Trey hit me. I guess he felt bad about it because he bought me a new card. I'm guessing whoever took the memory card developed the pictures."

"And was Carrie there? The next day?"

"No, she was already gone."

Who the hell took the memory card and developed these pictures?

We all sit in silence for a minute, absorbing that information.

Lulu has stopped taking notes. She's just sitting back, studying Christina, and rubbing the scar on her neck. "What happened? How did you go from there to here?"

"Well, after the raid, when Trey was arrested, I was sent to court-ordered rehab. Long term. Six months. Fortunately, it stuck with me that time. Afterward, I got a waitressing job, and that's where I met Donnie."

He chuckles. "I asked her out and she said no. I went there for lunch every single day for two months straight. Finally, she caved."

"I was completely forthcoming on our very first date. I basically gave him my complete life story. I never expected to hear from him again. But he showed up at the restaurant the next day, asking me out again. A couple of months later, I came to work for him at the insurance company. He helped me get my boys out of foster care."

She smiles at her husband. "The rest is history. We married. He adopted all three of my boys. They are sixteen, fifteen, and thirteen now. And we have a little girl. She just turned eight."

She smiles at me, genuinely happy. "Everything I went through led me right to this place, Crutch. As crazy as it sounds, I wouldn't change a thing." She sighs in contentment. "I go to regular counseling sessions, twice a week. One by myself, and then we attend a family session, all of us. It was really important for me to give the boys a way to come to grips with all I put them through. I was a horrible mother for many years, and I wanted to give them a safe environment in which to discuss that. I didn't want them to turn to drugs and alcohol like I did. I do outreach through our church, talking to others about addiction. In fact, I'm speaking at a juvenile detention center in South Alabama next week, giving my testimony." Christina smiles, wiping the leftover tears from her eyes. "Once a month we have dinner with the foster parents who took my boys in when I was unfit. I'm even a classroom volunteer at my daughter's school. *Me.* It's all a dream come true."

We end the interview with Christina, and I know that Lulu is reeling from all the information because she actually lets me open the truck door for her. She's not in the mood to talk so we don't. If quiet is what My Lulu needs, then quiet is what she can have.

We're parked back at the station before she breaks the silence. "Why didn't you tell me your parents were in jail?"

I shrug. "I didn't know it was important. Didn't think it mattered."

She turns in her seat, facing me. "Are they still on drugs?"

"They were up until they got arrested. They're in the city jail right now. They run a pretty tight ship over there so I can't imagine they have access to any contraband substances. I know the nursing staff had to give them some medication to help with withdrawals."

"And what about Trash? Obviously, he's not supposed to drink or use drugs while on probation."

I scoff. "Laws never stopped him before; trust me, they aren't stopping him now. He's just being a little more discreet. But I can guarantee you he still uses. I don't ever see an end in sight for him."

She braces her arms on the console, pinning me in place with her penetrating stare. "If you stayed, do you think you would have turned to drugs? Become an addict? Is that the real reason you left me?"

Kill. Me. Now.

My voice catches in my throat, making me gag and choke. I have to cough twice to even get a word to come out. "Oh, Lulu." I reach across, stroking the side of her face with my calloused thumb. "My letter was true. I left *for you*. Because it was the right thing to do *for you*. I was nothing but dead weight, dragging you down. Back then, I was nothing. Just some worthless kid with no idea of how to support a woman."

Don't say it. Don't say it. Don't say it. And because I always do what I shouldn't, I say it. "No idea how to support a wife."

She pulls away from my hand. Her body shudders. "You'll never understand, will you?"

"Understand what?"

"You weren't worthless to me."

Chapter 18

Ella

"I just don't understand how you can be okay with what we just saw?"

His jaw clenches, and his grip tightens on the steering wheel. "Did I say I was okay with it?"

I rub my hands together, trying to warm them against the frigid weather. Not asking permission, I reach over and crank the truck heater to full strength. "No. You're not saying anything, and it's driving me absolutely crazy. That was a horror show back there. That woman is completely cracked out. And that house? The thought that those children actually sleep there? My god, Ry, Protective Services should be there right now. Right this minute."

He pulls the truck off the road and slams it into park. "Damn it, woman, you should know me well enough by now to know that I can't talk about it without getting angrier. And the angrier I get, the more I wanna turn this truck around, grab that lady by the throat, rub her face in that pile of dog shit, burn her house to the ground, and steal those kids. Run away with them to a tropical island where the only thing they'll ever have to worry about is building sandcastles and jumping waves."

I sit back in my seat, watching him. His broad chest heaves with every staggered breath. The muscles in his shoulders bunch with pounds of tension. A strand of his hair is cowlicked from where he took off his ballcap. I want to reach over and straighten it. I sit on my fingers instead. "You never struck me as the tropical island type."

He licks his lips, smirking. Slowly, his breathing returns to normal. "Oh yeah, and what do I strike you as, Lulu?"

"The mountain type. With woods and creeks. Like the homestead."

His eyes flare with a familiar desire, causing me to rub my thighs together, and I quickly switch topics. "Why didn't you arrest her? What we saw was more than enough physical evidence to show negligence and endangerment, at the very least."

"Because the kids came home. Because CPS is more equipped to handle a domestic situation like this. When domestic situations are involved, there's a protocol to follow. It's for the safety of everyone involved. What if I tried to arrest her today? She could've hurt one of the children. I wasn't equipped today."

"So, what will we do?"

"Well, *I*," he points to himself, emphasizing the word I, "will contact all of the proper people. CPS will probably gather the kids while they're at school. That would be the easiest and safest transition. And you can bet your fine ass that I will request to be on the arresting detail for taking Holly into custody."

The interview with Holly was not an afternoon filled with sunshine and rainbows, as you can imagine. She was high. The complete and total opposite of Christina. Christina crawled her way out of the shit of her past. Holly decided to keep crapping and then roll around in it for good measure. Her arms were full of track marks. Her hair looked like it hadn't been washed in months, her clothes were filthy, and her face was covered in scabs from drug-induced picking. Even her nails were stained with the black smoke from whatever she cooks up.

The outside of the house was bad but not horrible, dilapidated but not a total dump site. So, I had high hopes when we knocked on the door. Those hopes came crashing to the ground the second we stepped over threshold. In fact, my hopes crashed to the ground, spontaneously combusted, and then the ash blew in my face, making me vomit.

Her house was covered in trash—rotten food, empty beer cans, soiled clothes, piles of dog shit from the little puppy whimpering in the corner. The smell was so bad, I had to spend most of the time with my fingers underneath my nose, trying to suck the last little bit of scent from my cherry almond lotion into my nasal cavity.

And then... the kids got off the school bus.

A little boy and a little girl.

We didn't realize there was only a half day of school today. The boy said he was nine, and the girl said she was seven. While Ry was interviewing Holly, I attempted to keep the children occupied. I was glad for the distraction; I couldn't stand to be in her presence anymore.

Well, I thought I was glad for the distraction.

Until the kids showed me their bedroom.

One half of the room looked like the rest of the house, meaning it was completely filthy. The other half of the room is what the kids actually considered 'their bedroom'. There were two bare mattresses lined up against the wall, both stained brown and yellow.

But what really broke my heart was their few meager personal belongings, neatly stacked by their makeshift beds. Stacked and organized to display everything, the way only a child would do. The little girl told me that her brother has a rule that they have to keep their part of the house very clean. They each had a small pile of folded laundry, a few books, and a few toys.

When Ry finally came to get me, he froze in the doorway, watching me as I played with the children. Even the little boy was so happy to have someone to play with him, he allowed his sister to choose a game of dolls. She owned three small plastic dolls. We each got one.

As soon as we got in the truck, I started crying. And I absolutely hate crying in front of people. That's probably what added to my anger. When the tears finally subsided, I decided the best thing to do would be to lash out at Ry.

Taking a deep breath, I nod. "Okay, I understand. I'll let you handle it. But you *will* handle it? Today?"

"Lulu, I promise you, no one will be laying a head on their pillow tonight until they know about this situation. I can swear to you, shit will happen. It may be Monday. But I will make sure it happens."

"Okay." I reach for my bottled water, eager to wet my dry throat. I look down and see Ry already drank his. Offering him my bottle, he takes it, tipping it up to his mouth. While he's drinking, I turn the heat back down. It's suddenly very hot in here. "So, how did the interview go? Did you get anything useful?"

"No, her brain is complete mush. She barely remembers her own name."

"Not surprising."

"I taste you."

My head whips around and my face blushes beet red. "Excuse me?"

He nods at the water bottle. "Your lip stuff. It tastes like oranges." Placing the bottle back in the cup holder, he leans against his door, narrowing his eyes in amusement. "Why? What did you think I meant?"

The bastard always liked it when I was tongue-tied and embarrassed. "Nothing. I just didn't hear what you said."

"Yeah. Sure."

I nod my head at the windshield. "Do you plan on driving anytime soon?"

Chuckling under his breath, he pulls back onto the road. He's making me furious. And horny. Leaning my head against the cold window, I close my eyes, rubbing my scar to calm my nerves. Visions of Ry burying his head between my thighs makes the breath hitch in my chest.

I taste you.

He sure tasted me alright. Moisture drips down my leg just thinking about it.

And that makes me even angrier.

"You're a grown woman, now. Do you think it's appropriate to have your feet up on my desk?"

"You're a grown man. Do you think it's appropriate to keep secrets from your best friend?" I retort, still guilt-tripping him about keeping Ry a secret all these years.

Marcum twirls his ink pen in his hand like a baton. "Who said you were my best friend."

"Well, I have to be more fun than Colson. And we all know I'm better to look at than Leary."

He snorts on his laugh. "You've got me there." He tosses the pen down on his desk and laces his fingers behind his head. "Didn't go good today, huh?"

"Did Ry tell you?"

"He did."

"It was devasting. Traumatic. Those poor kids. To live through that?"

He nods in empathy. "I know your parents left a lot to be desired in the way of love, affection, and attention, but at least they supplied for your basic needs. Food, clean clothes, a safe place to live. Up until that summer, I mean."

"I'm not delusional enough to compare the struggles of my upbringing with what those kids are going through." I look over at Ry's empty desk. "Or even what he went through as a little boy."

"Yeah, from what I gather, his plight was pretty damn rough before his grandparents took him away."

I think back to all the stories Ry told me.

Marcum cocks his head. "But just so you know, your struggles after leaving here were pretty damn significant. Catastrophic. I'm not bypassing that. Have you ever thought about sharing those with him?"

I shrug.

Marcum leans across his desk, knocking my feet to the ground. "Ella."

"Okay, yes, I've thought about it. But I always come back to the same conclusion... no. Hell, no. He left me. He chose not to be a part of my life. He chose to wash his hands of any problems—any feelings—for me. I can't put myself out there like that. What good will it do? He probably wouldn't even care."

"Ella Hill, that's a damn boldface lie, and you know it."

"All I know is that I can't open myself up to him again. Even if he wanted me to. Even if *I* wanted to. I barely survived the last go round. I'm not strong enough to make it."

Marcum smiles. "You're the strongest person I know."

I snort. There's no point in rebutting his compliment. Marcum likes to shower them on me like a spring rain. I learned a long time ago to keep my mouth shut. I decide to switch topics instead. "You should've told me about his injuries. I wasn't prepared."

"Yeah, I heard."

"He told you?"

"No, Ray called. He wanted me to know how upset you were in case you reached out to me."

"Ry was bombed, Marcum. Someone tried to kill him."

"Sweetie, you can't think of it like that. That kind of danger comes with being a soldier. That bombing would have happened with him there or without him there. At least, him being there kept some people alive."

I shake my head in question. "What do you mean?"

Marcum's brow furrows in confusion. "He saved lives, Ella."

My hand flings to my mouth in shock. "What? Who?"

"Well, the US ambassador for one."

"He didn't tell me that."

"Of course, he didn't." Marcum glances over at Ry's desk, puffing his chest outward like a proud papa. "Crutch received awards for his bravery."

I swallow, trying to digest that information. It sticks in my throat like dry oatmeal. "How do you know all that? He told you?"

"Well, some information came from him. Some from his commanding officer."

"You talked to his commanding officer? When I went to the recruiting office, after he enlisted, they wouldn't tell me anything."

"I was his POA."

Now, I'm really blown away. "What?"

"He came to me after Harlan's funeral. Harlan had been his power of attorney. He couldn't ask his parents or his brother to do it. He said I was the only person he could think of. One of the few people he respected. He said that if you trusted me, then he trusted me too. It was either me or Ray, and he knew Ray wouldn't do it, not considering how he'd left you." Marcum clears his throat. "A power of attorney was even more important in his situation because of his grandmother and the decisions regarding her care that had to be made on a regular basis with the nursing home. He left me in control of all his finances, all decisions about his grandmother, everything. Of course, I didn't do anything without consulting him, but there were a couple of times that I had to act first and ask him about it later. Being overseas, he was sometimes out of pocket for days or weeks. I was his medical POA too, and listed as his next of kin contact. They contacted me after the IED explosion."

I shake my head, rattling my brain from one side to the next. "How could you not tell me he nearly died?"

Marcum leans forward, wrapping his hand over mine. "The same way I didn't tell him that you nearly died."

Chapter 19

Ella

I'm completely caught off guard when my headlights flash across Ry's body as he sits on the small front stoop of my house. Well, the small front stoop of the Children's Wing, I mean. He quickly stands, pushing his hands in the pockets of his jeans. My heart jumps in my chest and nerves tickle the back of my throat. I wish my physical attraction to him would fizzle out, go away.

But it doesn't.

He's wearing jeans and a button-up blue checkered shirt with the sleeves rolled up to the elbow. The cold snap finally broke so he doesn't need a jacket. Which sucks. Because his forearms are sexy enough to drive me to the edge of madness. The gray baseball cap on his head shadows his face in danger and seduction.

I climb out of the car and grab my work bag, purse, and overnight bag from the back seat. He rushes to my side when he sees the load I'm trying to carry.

"What are you doing here?" I ask, my curiosity piqued.

He slips the overnight duffle and work bag from my shoulder. I don't argue; I know it's a moot point to protest his chivalry.

I changed into flats before the drive back to town, so he towers over me, reminding me of his power and strength. I always loved it when he picked me up. When I wrapped my legs around his waist. When I—

"No hello?"

I snort, walking ahead of him. "Hello. Now, what are you doing here?"

"You didn't tell me you were going out of town."

I dig in my purse for my house key. "I told you I wouldn't be going to the station yesterday."

"True, but you didn't tell me you would be in a completely different state."

"I didn't realize I had to clear my schedule with you, Detective." The door swings open, and I lean in, dropping my purse on the floor. I refuse to invite him inside. The last time he was in my house—in the Children's Wing—we were happy, we were together. Seeing him in these familiar surroundings would undo me. I spin around, holding my hands out for my bags.

"I can put these inside for you."

Staring into his pale green eyes, I nearly lose myself... nearly invite him in. "I can handle it."

He smirks but stops resisting and hands me the bags. I gently set them next to my purse. "You didn't answer my question, Ry. What are you doing here? Did you need something?"

"Happy birthday."

Oh my god. "You remembered."

"It's Valentine's Day, Lulu. I do own a calendar."

I giggle, trying to disguise my emotions. "Yeah, I think you've mentioned that before."

"I went to the bar. Will said you weren't coming out. They wanted to take you to dinner, but you said no?"

I shrug. "You know how crowded every place is on Valentine's Day. Not to mention, it's a Saturday. Besides, I haven't ever really celebrated my birthday since leaving town; it's just another day."

There's no point in reminding him that my only true birthday celebration was with him—twelve years ago. He knows that Carrie had to remind my parents about it every single year.

Then, Carrie was gone.

And then he was gone.

What was left to celebrate?

He takes a step closer to me, making me hold my breath. "It's not just another day to me."

I can't do this.

I can't be here. With him. This close to me.

I clear my throat. "Well...umm, thanks for stopping by. I'll see you on Monday."

His large hand slaps against the door, preventing me from closing it. "You forgot your present."

"What present?"

He holds out his hand. "Come on."

I stare at it. Is he kidding me right now? He wants to hold my hand? No. Definitely not. Not doing that.

Holy shit. He's holding my hand.

My body turned Benedict Arnold and grabbed onto him without my brain even giving consent. Our palms fit together like melted butter, and his thumb slowly rubs against my soft skin, stroking back and forth like he's done a hundred times before.

Although, those hundred times were over a decade ago. When we were young, when we were just kids.

Liquid heat boils in my body, gathering in a soft pool, low in my stomach. I'm about to ask where we're going when he turns down the sidewalk and leads me through the wrought-iron fence and into the backyard.

Kill. Me. Now.

The swimming pool twinkles and shines with the soft glow from the floating water lanterns that I love so much. The paper lanterns that I dream about. The paper lanterns that filled the pond of the homestead on this very same night exactly twelve years ago. The night my parents forgot about me. The night he gave me vital information about Carrie's case. The night he claimed me as his own, with his mouth, underneath the stars of the night sky.

"Thirty of them. Happy thirtieth birthday, Lulu."

I can't think. I can't speak. I can't even function. He's sucked the dead existence from my soul and dared to ignite it, trying to stoke it to life. I pull my hand from his and rub the back of my neck. It hurts to even whisper. "Why are you doing this to me?"

"Don't overthink it. It's just a birthday present, just something nice."

I turn to him. The light cascades off his body in waves, soaking him in highlights of white and yellow. "Is that all it is?" Because it feels like the love of my life is trying to break me. Trying to shatter my hate into little pieces. Pieces that will dissolve into the ground, leaving the past in the past, allowing us to carve a new future for ourselves.

He smiles softly. "For tonight it is." He then sighs, dramatically. "Besides, it's getting cold. And cold grease isn't good for anybody." He points over to the patio table where it's set with plates and napkins and a cooler. Sitting in the middle of the table is a familiar paper bag dotted with grease stains.

My eyebrows raise into my hairline. "Philly cheesesteaks?"

"With cheese fries and sour gummy worms for dessert."

My stomach instantly growls. Laughing, he sets the food out for us, giving me a Diet Coke and opening up a beer for himself. Ry doesn't talk. He lets me eat in peace. Correction: he lets me stuff my face in peace. It's frustrating that he knows me so well. He knows I've been craving a sandwich like this and denying myself just because I wanted to prove a point to him. Now, I can't get it in my mouth quick enough. I'm surprised I don't choke.

I'm leaned back in my chair, sucking the sugar off a gummy worm before we say more words than *'hand me a fresh napkin'* and *'do you need another drink'* and *'you have cheese on your eyelid'*. By the way, I'm the one who had cheese on her eyelid.

"So, where'd you go?"

"Jackson, Mississippi. I got there Thursday night. I had meetings yesterday and today."

"What for? TV stuff?"

"No, this is consultant work for an upcoming trial. Medical malpractice."

He cracks open another beer. "What are you doing for it?"

"Well, they hired me a while back to do in-depth research to find two medical professionals who would be the best fit for our case. I needed one expert in a particular surgery technique and one expert for a particular piece of equipment. We had web meetings with both of them to discuss and prepare. One of them is from Indiana and the other is from California. They also hired me to do a timeline of the three victims' medical histories. The doctor visits, medical histories, and medication logs aren't linear, they're concurrent. So, we need a breakdown to make it easier for a jury to understand. I'll have some visual aids done up for that so we can submit them as evidence."

"You do that too?"

"Not me personally; you know I can only draw buildings. I have an amazing graphic designer I outsource that stuff to. She works with one of the cable networks."

"I still can't believe you turned that morbid obsession of watching true crime documentaries into a successful career." He takes a drink and I watch the muscles in his throat work. "When will the trial be?"

"Most likely in the summer." I toss the bag of gummy worms to the middle of the table. "I'm stuffed. Do *not* let me eat anything else."

He cocks his head to the side, studying me. "That's a tall order. Have I ever been able to control you?"

I bite my lip, thinking about the past. "I guess it depended on the order, didn't it?"

He hasn't shaved in a few days and his fingers scratch against the scruff lining the square set of his jaw. "What did you mean when you said you don't ever celebrate your birthday? Didn't Hudson take you out, make the day special?"

"Of course not. The only thing Hudson celebrated was a legal win." I can't help but mock, "Whenever his dumbass got lucky enough to win, that is."

"Lulu, that's terrible."

"Oh, they only let him be first chair on a few cases. They kept him mostly as second chair—and even that is a very liberal title for him. The wins for the firm still stacked up; it just wasn't because of Hudson. He didn't care, though, as long as he got his big paychecks."

"I'm not talking about his law career. Fuck that. I'm talking about his lack of making sure his wife had a proper birthday."

I hate to hear Ry call me Hudson's wife. "It's no big deal."

His eyes narrow in irritation. "It's a huge deal. I mean, seriously, your birthday's on Valentine's Day. There's no excuse for it. Call a restaurant and make a reservation. It's not hard."

"Oh, he made Valentine's Day reservations, alright. They just weren't for me."

Ry takes a deep breath. "What are you saying?"

Holy hell. I didn't mean to blurt that out. Didn't mean to air my dirty laundry like it's washing day. Now, I'm trapped. No way to back track, no way to escape.

Ry leans back in his chair, studying me with a lethal look on his face. "You plan on telling me what you mean by that comment?"

"No."

"Well, I suggest you quickly modify your plans, then."

I pretend to busy myself wiping imaginary crumbs from the table. Then I remember who I am, straighten my back, and stare straight into his eyes. "I just meant that he spent days like Valentine's Day with whichever poor, unlucky girl happened to be his mistress at the time."

"That asshole cheated on you?"

"Ry, it's fine."

He slams his chair back from the table and stands up. "On what planet is that fine, Lulu?"

I shrug. "Our relationship wasn't like that."

He cocks his hands on his hips. "Relationship? I'm not talking about your dry cleaner, Lulu. I'm talking about your husband. It was a marriage. It was sacred."

His possessiveness stirs unwanted lust in my body, and I shake my head, trying to clear the fog of desire. "Nothing about that situation was sacred."

He shakes his own head, dumbfounded with my answer and attitude. "Let me get this straight, Hudson cheated on you...multiple times. And you let him live? You didn't stand up for yourself? Didn't fight? That doesn't sound like the Lulu I know." He leans down, splaying his hands across the table. "It sounds like your mother."

Now, it's my turn to push away from the table and stand up. I point my finger in his face. "See, that's where you're wrong. My mother *hated* that my father cheated. She wished he wouldn't. She tried to mold herself into this fake little person, just trying to capture his attention. She *wanted* my father's love and affection. I'm nothing like my mother because I actually didn't care if Hudson cheated on me. I didn't want his love and affection. If having mistress after mistress kept his hands off me, then I was completely fine with it. Hell, I nearly wrote some of those women damn thank you cards!"

His mouth slacks open. "I—I don't even know how to respond to that."

"Don't make more of it than it is. After I left the University of Florida and moved to Mobile, we never even lived together again. I have a small house in the country, and he has a huge condo in the middle of downtown. So, when I say it was no big deal, I mean it."

Ry laces his hands behind his head. The movement makes a small corner of his shirt come untucked and a strip of tan skin flashes, making my mouth water. "You cheated on him too?"

"You know I would never do that. That's not me. I kept my vow."

He slowly lowers his hands. His face is confused, bombarded with thought after thought. "You didn't want him to touch you? Does that mean you never had... sex ... with him?"

I try not to blush, but I know I do. Embarrassment, disgust, and resignation must color my face like a fire engine. "I didn't say that. We were married for nine years. Sometimes, I needed intimacy, companionship. And since I wasn't gonna commit adultery myself, I had no other choice than to be with Hudson."

He looks like I just stabbed him in the stomach. He literally doubles over, absorbing the information that he already knew. *I had sex with my husband.*

And why the fuck does he even care?

He broke up with me.

I was free to screw every guy on Holt's football team, if I wanted to.

Except... I didn't want to.

And despite my desire to spew vitriol at him for his reaction, we're kindred spirits in a way. Because I feel his pain. I feel it every time a woman looks in his direction. Every time one of his one-night stands comes around wanting night two. My body shakes in fury just thinking about it.

I grab the trash from the table and toss it into the outside wicker trash can. I zip the lid to his cooler and slide it across the table, placing it right in front of him. "Thank you for the dinner. And the beautiful lanterns. It's been a long couple of days. I need to rest. You can show yourself out."

Ry reaches out, snatching my hand in his. Bending his head, his hot breath skims the side of my face.

Why? How? How can I hate him and love him all at the same time?

His whisper cracks with emotion. "Why did you marry him, Lulu?"

I shrug. "Why not? No one else was standing in line, Ry."

I pull from his grasp and leave him there before any more of his words can bury me in my grave.

Chapter 20

Crutch

I toss my sunglasses on the dashboard and grab my wallet. The mid-March sun is shining down, quickly evaporating the morning dew. I've become one of *those* people. Those people who go at least one time a week, if not more, to buy an insanely overpriced cup of coffee.

A lasting impression from the Lulu of twelve years ago.

She's come into the station a few times with a cup, letting me know she still goes to *our* coffee shop. But for some stupid reason, I've never piped up and told her that I still go to *our* coffee shop too.

I place my order and stand there checking the email on my phone when the heated scorch of her voice races down my spine.

"I don't think Peyton works here anymore. You'll have to make googly eyes with someone else. I hear the drive-thru barista is nineteen. I know you like them young."

Fuck me.

Her smirk is just what I needed to see this morning. Really, it's what I need to see every morning.

"Pipe up a little louder, won't you? I don't think the old lady in the corner heard you."

She hides her smile behind her coffee cup. "Oh, I beg to differ." Her eyes flicker to a corner table, near the front door, where two white-haired women are giving me the evil eye. Lulu laughs, choking on her drink. Some spittle flies out of her mouth, and she quickly wipes her face with the back of her hand.

She missed some. I step closer, reaching out with my thumb to wipe the brown drop from her stubborn little chin. The electricity from her body sizzles through my fingertips and into my chest.

"Crutch?" The girl behind the counter holds my cup out to me. Reluctantly, I pull away and grab it.

"You didn't tell me you still come here." She plants a hand on her curvy, luscious hip, drawing attention to her bare legs.

Spring weather means bare legs. Which means trouble for me. "Nope."

"Don't wanna be known as a coffee snob? Marcum's brew at the station not cutting it anymore?"

"We all know his coffee tastes like burnt tobacco. I have no idea how he even messes it up. Coffee is pretty self-explanatory."

She reaches around me and grabs a napkin. "That's why I stick to water at the station."

"Speaking of, are you heading that way now? I'll walk you out."

"No, I've got a few things to finish here first," she says weakly. Her fingers tangle through her hair, fondling her scar.

I didn't like the sound of that. "Lulu, are you here by yourself?"

"No."

"No?" My voice cracks like a teenager going through puberty. Instinctively, I glance back to *our* table and see the back of a guy's head. "Who's that?"

She shrugs. "Just a friend."

"A friend?"

"Why are you repeating everything I'm saying?"

My jaw works back and forth. Damn, I can't help myself, I wanna rip this guy's head off. "Why are you being so elusive? Who the hell is that?"

"I told you. A friend."

"Well, I consider myself your friend. Let's have an introduction, shall we?"

Her mouth falls open. I'm already five paces closer to the table when my cell phone rings. Gritting my teeth, I glance at the caller ID—Colson. I can't ignore it; I have to answer.

Sure enough, we have a call.

I guess I'll have to host my pissing match some other time.

Although, there better not be another time. I don't know who this friend is, but I can tell from the back of his head that it's not Holt, Will, Cullen, Ray, or Marcum.

And I don't like this stranger sitting at *our* table.

I spin around, planting my body right in front of Lulu. My chest grazes against hers. She tries not to react. But she does. I see it. I feel it. "We have that interview with Tyler today. Say goodbye to your little friend and get your fine ass to the station."

Exaggerated sarcasm drips through her voice like the slow coffee drip behind the counter. "Why, Ryland Joseph Crutchfield, if I didn't know better, I'd say you were jealous."

"Says the girl who rolls her eyes."

"I do not roll my eyes."

"Why don't we find Peyton and ask her if that's true or not?"

Lulu leans forward, whispering in my ear. She knows I love it when her hot breath sends a chill down my spine. "Fuck Peyton."

Clearing her throat, she walks away, joining her friend at *our* table.

"I'll meet you outside. I just have to get something from my car before we go."

I nod, grabbing my stuff. "I'll lock up, get us some waters for the road." Five minutes later, I'm walking out the station door when I see Lulu trotting across the parking lot. Except she's not heading to her own SUV, but an idling red pickup truck. I can't make out who's behind the wheel, but it's definitely a guy.

The truck doesn't look familiar either. It doesn't belong to any of the guys in her life.

And what strikes me as odd is her behavior, her demeanor. Her stiff shoulders and straight back are gone. Gone is the imaginary hanger in her shirt, pulling her upright like a marionette. She leans through the open driver-side window, completely relaxed, completely at ease. Suddenly, she tosses back her head and laughs. Loudly.

It's the laugh I can't wait to hear... on the days I'm lucky enough to hear it.

Who is this guy? And what's he doing with My Lulu?

Is this the 'friend' from the coffeehouse yesterday morning?

Hoisting her work bag and purse higher on her shoulder, she reaches into the truck, taking something from him. Waving, she walks away, and the guy reverses, pulling out of the parking lot. When she sees me staring, she just points to my truck, walking in that direction. I finally find my footing and hit the unlock button on my key fob, allowing her to jump in the truck before me.

I put the waters in the cupholders, toss my stuff in the back seat, and quickly reach for my sunglasses, hiding my eyes from view.

She seems completely oblivious to the turmoil surging through me right now. She flashes her green-flowered notebook in the air. "Sorry about that, I forgot my notebook. I need it for the interview." She shoves it down in her work bag and twists in her seat, depositing it all on the back floorboard. I try to avoid looking at her, but the contortion of her body makes her blouse fall open, gifting me a quick glance of her black bra.

"Forgot it? Where? A public place, like a restaurant or bar? The library?"

She doesn't follow my line of thinking. She thinks I'm actually concerned about her stupid notebook. "Oh no, I would never leave it out like that. It has confidential notes about Carrie's case. I just left it at home. I was looking over it in bed last night, re-reading the information from Tyler's interview, and I accidentally left it on the nightstand."

Holy hell. This guy has a key to her house? Was he in her house with her? Last night? In bed with her? "Who dropped it off?"

Now, she gets it. She blinks, pausing before answering. "Oh, nobody, just a friend."

"A friend? The same friend from the coffeehouse yesterday?"

She sighs. "Ry, don't put words in my mouth. I said he was a friend, and that's all you need to know, alright?"

Hell no, that's not alright.

Huffing out a breath, she crosses her legs and stares out the window. Damn this woman and her skirts. A woman with legs that long should be outlawed from wearing anything that falls above the knee.

We drive for twenty minutes straight without saying a word. But Lulu makes it known that she doesn't like my attitude. She huffs and puffs and grunts and groans every quarter mile of interstate. "So, help me, Lulu, if you sigh one more time, I'm gonna flip my shit."

She spins in her seat, reaching across the console to point in my face. "Then stop being an asshole."

I can't help it. Hearing Lulu call me an asshole from her pouty little mouth has me cracking up. I try not to laugh. Really, I do. But I can't help it. I burst out laughing, playfully slapping her finger away. At first, she looks like she's going to explode, but eventually, a smile turns up the corner of her lips. Refusing to laugh, she looks back out the window, forgetting I can see her hidden chuckle in the reflection of the glass.

Although I'm not done learning about this douchebag she calls a 'friend', I declare a truce for now and break the tension. "It's still crazy to see how Tyler put his life back together."

"Yeah, leaving Holly was the best thing he ever did."

Yesterday was the first time we could meet with him. He's been working a welding job in Nebraska for the past few months and just came home for two weeks on vacation. He's then going back to Nebraska for two more months. After that, he'll be sent to Alaska for six months. Besides being gainfully employed, he's completely sober. After the raid and Trey and Trash's arrests, he moved in with an aunt who helped him get clean. He broke up with Holly and began to focus on his work and health.

And you can see it. He looked healthy, happy, and stable. His fiancée is pregnant with their first child. His company provides family housing at all job sites so she and the baby will be moving to Alaska with him. He didn't tell us anything we didn't already know. He didn't specifically remember the night from the pictures. He was too wasted.

"How do you think things will go with Dakota today?"

She shrugs. "Not sure. I haven't seen any of Carrie's friends in years. I'm just glad that one of them still lives close by."

We small talk about nothing in particular as we finish the drive to the upscale Birmingham suburb. Following the directions from the GPS, we eventually pull into the driveway of the largest house on the block. This mansion makes Lulu's house look like a potter's cottage. "Shit," I mumble underneath my breath, "looks like Dakota's done well for herself."

"From what I saw, it looks like her husband has done well for himself."

"Surgeon?"

She nods, "Yeah, a very well-known and sought-after neurosurgeon. He's twenty-two years older than Dakota."

I put away my sunglasses and reach behind me for my vest. "A second marriage for him?"

Lulu scoffs. "You think?"

Handing her my file, I step out of the truck and get my vest secured on my chest. Surprisingly, she waits for me to open her door. She's actually responding to an email really quick, but I'd like to pretend she's waiting on me. I offer my hand, and she stares at me for a split second before sliding her fingertips against my palm. Using her notebook and my file folder to cover the exposed skin of her thighs, she climbs out of the truck. I wanna knock the papers out of her hand, just to see more of her.

"Thank you." She quickly pulls away from me.

Is that because she doesn't want to touch me? Or is it because she wants to touch me too much? Because I sure as hell know I wanna touch her *way* more than that.

The doorbell is quickly answered by a maid who ushers us past a lavishly decorated living room, through some kind of music room with a grand piano, and down a small hallway. "She's waiting in the reading room." The maid pauses at a closed doorway. "Would either of you like anything to drink?"

A beer would be incredible right about now.

We both politely decline, eager to start the interview.

The maid pushes open the heavy wooden door and announces our presence before excusing herself. One thing strikes me right off the bat. Dakota has had *way* more plastic surgery than anyone her age should have. She's only thirty-three, like me, and she's well on her way to having a permanently plastic face and permanently tucked stomach.

"Ella!" Dakota rushes forward, wrapping Lulu in a fake hug. Dakota keeps her at arm's length, before air kissing both of her cheeks. "I can't believe I'm actually seeing you again. It's been so long. Too long."

Lulu is completely stiff and frozen. A weak smile tweaks on her face.

I glance around the elaborate room. Two walls, including the one with the door we just walked through, are covered with floor-to-ceiling bookcases, filled with leather-bound books. The third wall is floor-to-ceiling glass windows and doors that lead outside to the manicured lawn and infinity pool. And the fourth wall has a huge gas fireplace, crackling with the sound of fake, burning wood.

They actually paid to have sound piped through the fireplace.

Ridiculous.

There's a wooden desk, a round table with six chairs, and set of four plush, cushioned reading chairs. Dakota points a red-painted nail at the puffy chairs. "Shall we get more comfortable?"

Lulu looks down at her notebook and my file folder in her hand. She wants to speak up and say she prefers to sit at the table so she has somewhere to take notes. But she doesn't say anything. Her jaw twitches, and she takes a step toward the floppy chairs.

I guess she's right—some old habits do die hard.

"Actually," I point to the table, "the table would work better for our visit today." My tone leaves no room for negotiation.

Dakota likes that. She likes the no-nonsense approach. Her cheeks flush and her eyes widen. She probably pays the pool boy to fuck her and bark orders. She swishes her hips, sashaying back and forth, obviously trying to draw my attention to her small waist and rounded ass.

Lulu rolls her eyes, grimacing in her anger. I hide my laugh, clearing my throat.

Before I have a chance to take charge of the conversation and get clearance for recording, Dakota homes in on Lulu. "You look like you're doing well, Ella. I was shocked to hear that you and Hudson divorced." She giggles, pushing a hair-sprayed curl behind her ear. "Actually, I was more shocked to hear that the two of you had married. So young, so quick. It must've been quite the whirlwind romance."

Lulu straightens her spine. "Oh, it was a whirlwind, alright."

"You never mentioned that the two of you were romantically involved. In fact, you gave the impression that you didn't quite care for his company."

"Impressions matter to you, don't they, Dakota?"

Hell yeah. Score one, Lulu.

Not giving Dakota time to absorb the dig, I interrupt, getting permission to record the interview.

"So, what's this visit all about? You're reopening Carrie's case?"

I sit forward in my seat. "Carrie's case was never closed. It's been open this whole time. I took over as head investigator from Lieutenant Marcum a couple of years ago. Some new information has recently come to light, so we are interviewing everyone again. Sometimes the fog of memory clears as the years pass."

"I'll be happy to help. Carrie was a wonderful girl, one of my dearest friends. Just tell me how I can be of assistance."

I lick my dry lips. Yeah, we'll see about that. "Why don't you give us a little information about yourself, just for reference. Give us the highlights of your life since graduating college."

She smiles brightly. She must love talking about herself. "Well, obviously, I'm married." She pretends to be shy about flashing the large diamond on her left hand. About as shy as a stripper spread eagle on the pole. "Edward and I met at a charity function for the hospital six years ago. He had just gotten out of a horrible marriage. She just didn't understand the caliber of man she was married to. Neither of us were looking for something serious. He's quite a bit older than me, you know? But we just fell in love." Her eyelashes flutter in fake desire. "What is it they say? The heart wants what the heart wants."

She stares at us, waiting on a response. Is she really wanting us to answer that rhetorical question?

Lulu's voice is cold and sterile. "Congratulations."

"Thank you, Ella. That's so sweet." She sighs. "Anyway, we married, and we have two beautiful children now. Our son, Elliot, is five, and our daughter, Marisol, is three."

"Where are your children now?"

"They're at preschool, a wonderful program at one of the private schools here in Birmingham. They tested in. My brilliant little babies."

I glance at the clock on the desk. "What time do you have to pick them up?"

"Oh, the nanny does that." She leans forward, raking her eyes across my body. "So I'm all yours, Sergeant."

Hell no, you're not.

Lulu's voice cuts through the innuendo, slicing it like a sword. "You don't work, Dakota? What about your degree? Marketing, wasn't it?"

Dakota's eyes turn to small little beads. "Ella, running a household like this *is* work. The kids have so many extracurricular activities—ballet, karate, swim team. And I have to make sure the staff does everything just to Edward's liking. He works so hard to provide for our family. Things should be exactly the way he wants them. The housekeepers, the gardeners, the handymen. You know how hard it is to find good help nowadays. Now that your parents have passed, you're responsible for running a large household yourself. I'm sorry about that, by the way. It must be hard to be all alone now."

She's not alone, bitch. I'm here.

Dakota has turned into the kind of woman Lulu hates. The kind of woman she spent her whole childhood resenting. Dakota has become Lulu's mother.

Lulu looks up from her notebook. Her knuckles turn white, holding her ink pen in a death grip. Palpable anger hums from her body, deafening the silence in the room. I can't speak aloud words to calm her, that would make her appear weak. And My Lulu is anything but weak.

Instead, I lower my hand beneath the table and quietly sneak it across her leg. Her bare skin is warm and smooth. Immediately, my dick stirs in my pants, making me widen my legs into a more comfortable position. I squeeze her knee. My throat clogs with emotion, taking me back to twelve years ago. Turning me into a young kid. A young kid who's madly in love with the girl—this woman—sitting next to him.

I always do what I shouldn't do. And touching Lulu? It makes me want things I have no right to want. I want the life I should've had. The life *we* should've had.

Lulu's face softens and she glances over at me. Her long black eyelashes fan against her face, slowly shading the chestnut and caramel swirls of her eyes. Nodding once, letting me know she's fine, I pull my hand away. Her body shivers when my calloused fingertips leave her thigh.

Our moment didn't go unnoticed by Dakota. Her brow furrows in confusion and her eyes dart between the two of us. "Is there something I should know about?"

I ignore her question and ask one of my own. "Let's go back, tell me what all happened when Carrie went missing."

She tells us all the information that we already know. That Carrie was supposed to show up at the girls' apartment for a Fourth of July party but never did.

"And do you think her drug activity had anything to do with her disappearance?"

That catches Dakota completely off guard. Her smile falters for one split second. "Excuse me?"

Lulu sits back, folding her arms across her chest. "We know about the drugs, Dakota."

Dakota clicks her long fingernails against the marble top of the table. "Pardon? I'm not sure I know what you're talking about."

"We know that Carrie was an addict and that she was selling drugs. To Catie. To Hannah." Lulu pauses for effect. "To you."

Dakota's lips purse into a thin line.

"Catie didn't tell you?" Lulu presses. "She didn't tell you that I knew? I confronted her. Threw her stash down the drain."

Dakota is thinking about lying. She's thinking about it real hard. I nip that shit in the bud. "There's no point in lying, Dakota. We know a lot more than you think we do. If we wanted to come after you for the drugs, we would've done it way before now."

Snorting, her face contorts into an ugly snarl. "No, she didn't tell me you knew about the drugs. Catie was probably worried that me and Hannah would make her stop. We were always the ones worried about getting caught. Not Catie." She pins Lulu with her stare. "Not Carrie."

Lulu pulls her shoulders back. "So, you're telling me if I check your purse right now, there won't be any pills inside of a breath mint box?"

"It was college, Ella. Normal people experiment in college. Alcohol, drugs, sex. I can't help it if you were some old married schoolmarm by the time you were eighteen." She pushes away from the table, making an elaborate show of crossing her legs. "Of course, there's nothing in my purse. I stopped my recreational drug use when I graduated college."

I tap my finger against the table, drawing her attention. "So, tell us what you know about the drug business. Did Carrie ever talk about it? Discuss how she obtained the pills? Anything?"

"Not much. It all started with her knee surgery, with the pain pills. We noticed that she kept taking pain medication. One night, at a party, she gave us each an Oxy. High dose. That's all it was for me and Hannah... party use. And Ritalin for studying. And the occasional sleeping pill when our schedules got off whack. For Carrie and Catie it was more. They used all the time. Basically, every day. But she never told us how she got the pills or who she got them from. She said she couldn't tell us, that it would put us in danger."

Lulu slams her pen down. "And did you even consider that this business would put my sister in danger? What about Carrie's well-being? You were one of her best friends."

"We paid for our product. Carrie said she was safe as long as she turned her money in and kept her mouth shut."

I toss my hands in the air. "Safe? She was selling drugs, and you thought she was safe?"

Dakota doesn't answer. She just raises her eyebrows, waiting for another question.

"She never talked about the supplier?"

"No, and I didn't ask any questions. I don't know where she got the pills, how she got the pills, or who she got the pills from."

"What about her other customers? Do you know anyone who would hurt Carrie to get to her supply?"

She shakes her head. "She only sold to people she knew. People she was sure would keep their mouth shut. She didn't want Caleb to find out."

"But he did?" I ask, confirming what we've known for twelve years.

"Yes, that's why he broke up with her."

"What about me?" Lulu sounds like a small, innocent child. She reaches back, rubbing her scar.

Dakota sighs, shaking her head. "She didn't want you to know, either. We weren't allowed to say anything about it to you."

Lulu's breath hitches in her chest, and it breaks my damn heart.

I reach for the file folder. "Did you notice anything unusual in the months leading up to her disappearance?"

"No, nothing sticks out. Everything was normal until that Fourth of July weekend. She wasn't answering our phone calls and texts as quickly as she normally did. And then she stopped altogether. When she didn't show up for the party, we knew something was wrong." She looks at Lulu. "That's when Hannah called your mom."

Opening the folder, I slide the pictures across the table, nodding for Dakota to pick them up. "Take a look at those pictures. Tell me if anyone looks familiar."

Straightening the diamond pendant dangling between her massively fake breasts, she scoots closer and picks up the small stack of pictures. I don't say anything; I let her study the images in silence.

"I don't know anyone in these pictures besides Carrie. They're not exactly the kind of friends I hung out with in college."

"Meaning?"

She tosses her head to the side. "Really, Detective? You're going to make me say it?"

You bet your ass I'm gonna make you say it, lady.

"Fine." She tosses her hair behind her shoulder. "Low class, trashy, poor. We didn't hang out with poor people. And I'm not being discriminatory. It's just the way things were. Right, Ella?" She raises her eyebrows, waiting on Lulu to agree with her. "You know what I mean, all of your friends were privileged."

Lulu stares at Dakota like she's a rotten piece of meat.

My voice growls loudly in the room, startling the smug look from her plastic face. "Not all of them." I point at the pictures. "Keep looking."

When she gets to the last image, she gasps. "Oh! Is that what I think it is?"

"Yes, Dakota," Lulu says, "that is a picture of my passed-out sister being raped."

Dakota looks from me to Lulu and then back at the picture. "I had no idea. She never said anything. Nothing at all." She turns the picture over, hiding the offending image.

I stuff them back in the file. "You have no idea who did that to her?"

"No, no idea at all."

I turn to Lulu. She nods, letting me know that she believes Dakota.

"And what about Hannah or Catie? Do you have any reason to believe they may know anyone in those pictures? Any reason to believe they know about the sexual assault?"

"I don't talk to them anymore. But, no, I don't think so."

Lulu closes her notebook. "You didn't stay in touch with them?"

"We tried. But it was too hard. I mean, Hannah and I are friends on social media, but that's about it. She lives in Los Angeles, works for a local news station. Her husband works for a movie studio."

"And what about Catie?"

She plants a look of empathy on her face. "Catie lost her way. She let the drugs control her life." She shrugs her shoulders. "I guess she just wasn't as strong as me and Hannah. Last I heard, she was a single mom, working at a diner, somewhere in Kentucky, where she's from. It's so sad, really. Her family owns race horses, you know? She really could've been something."

Dakota stands up, indicating she's done with the interview. "Well, the children will be home soon. I should make sure the cook has a snack prepared. Is there anything else?"

"No. We have all we need." I usher Lulu from the mansion, guiding her with a gentle hand on the small of her back. I'm determined to transfer the strength from my body to hers.

When we get to the front door, Dakota leans forward, whispering. "Edward doesn't know about the mistakes of my youth. I assume you'll use discretion and avoid tossing my name around when speaking to others about drug use. I was happy to talk with you today, but I'd hate to involve our attorneys in all of this."

Lulu stiffens. A slow defiance creeps across her face, letting me know she's had enough of Dakota and her pretentious ways. I quickly turn off the camera on my vest.

"Dakota, I have no idea how my sister counted you as a friend. You are a parasite, sucking the life out of everything around you, a maggot feeding on shit. Screw you." Lulu spins around, stomping toward the truck. Tossing her head over her shoulder, she leaves Dakota with one last parting sting. "And by the way, my tits are *way* better than yours, and I didn't spend thousands of dollars on them. Get your money back."

And... that's *My* Lulu.

Chapter 21

Crutch

The bar is crowded tonight. Will's had really good luck with lining up popular bands lately. I weave my way through the throngs of people. Some of the off-duty guys holler, asking me to join their table, but I point to the bar. Finding an empty barstool, I lean forward, waving a finger at Cullen.

He finishes with his line of customers, tosses a towel over his shoulder, and shakes my hand. "Hey, man, good to see you." He sets my normal beer bottle in front of me.

"You too. Crowded tonight."

"Yeah, the band's supposed to be good. I thought I might have to miss it. Now that spring has rolled around, the wedding scene is picking up. Dad had a catering order for a rehearsal dinner, but it got canceled because the venue had a burst pipe."

"That sucks. Did he lose out on the money?"

"The venue offered to pay the couple's cancellation fee. I keep telling Dad it's time for us to have our own event space. Something new and unusual and unique."

"What does he say about that?"

Cullen shrugs. "That he'll think about it. But I have enough great ideas to last for a lifetime." He pounds his fist against the bar top and moves on to help another group of customers.

Pulling my cell phone from my pocket, I check the home screen for any missed calls or texts messages. She still hasn't responded. And that pisses me off. And makes me pathetically sad. Like a lost little puppy.

"Something wrong?"

Will's voice catches me off guard. I didn't even see him walk up. "Huh?"

"You're frowning."

"I'm not frowning."

"I'm married. And I have a five-year-old. I know a frown when I see it."

I pick up my beer. "Is Lulu out of town?"

"No, why?"

"She hasn't been to the station the last couple of days. She finally texted me yesterday to say she wouldn't be back in until next week, but she didn't say why. Did she pick up a job out of town? Something from an attorney or one of the TV shows?"

Will tries to hide his smirk, but he's not very successful at it. "Missing her?"

There's no point in lying. "You already know the answer to that."

He doesn't make fun of me. I always knew Will was a smart man.

Nodding, he hands a couple of drinks to the people beside me. "She's sick."

My ears perk and my stomach drops. "Sick?"

"She's fine. It's just a bad cold."

I take one more glance around the bar. "Is that where Holt is? Taking care of her?"

"Holt's been in North Carolina since last Friday. He closed on the sale of his condo today. He has some meetings with his financial people and the NFL folks. He won't be back until Monday."

My brow furrows. "Well, who's taking care of her?"

Will laughs. "She's a thirty-year-old woman, Crutch. I think she can fight a cold all by herself."

I'm not even paying attention by this point. I'm tossing some money on the bar and rushing out the door.

"Crutch, wait! There's something you should—"

The door to the bar closes, keeping Will's parting words locked in with him.

I knock on the door, pounding a little harder in case she's back in her bedroom and can't hear as easily. Enjoying the warmer nights, bugs fly around the lightbulb hanging above the threshold. I'm about to pull out my phone and call her when the door opens wide.

And I lose my damn mind.

Standing in front of me is a half-naked man. The guy's dressed in jeans and is holding a T-shirt in his hands. He's a couple of inches shorter than me but still tall. I can't even focus on his face because his chest and dumbass man nipples are flashing in my face.

Seriously?

He couldn't take an extra five seconds and slide the shirt over his head *before* answering the door?

This has to be the guy—the 'friend' from the coffee shop, the 'friend' who dropped off her notebook. And he's walking around my woman's house.

Half-naked.

Anger runs ice cold through my body, freezing the worried thoughts in my brain.

What did I expect? I did this to myself. Nearly twelve years ago, I walked away, and I'm still paying the price. I'll be paying it until the day I die. Trapped in a purgatory of my own making.

I'm such an idiot.

She's doing exactly what I wanted her to do. She's found someone else. How can I be mad at her for that? It makes no sense.

It makes me hate her. And I have absolutely no right to do that.

And the really stupid thing? It makes me love her even more.

Turning on my heels, I walk away, muttering behind me. "Sorry, wrong house."

Wrong house. Wrong life. Wrong *me*.

Turning the ignition in my truck, I sit for a few minutes, trying to gather my scattered thoughts. Dragging my hands down my face, I lift my head and reach for my seat belt when I see the guy walking across the driveway.

Great.

Now, the douche wants to know the real reason I showed up at his girl's house. Does he even know who I am? Has she even mentioned me?

I can't see his face through the shine of my headlights, but at least he has a shirt on now. Sighing, I turn off the truck and climb out.

I barely have the door shut when his hand shoots out. "Been a long time. It's good to see you again, Crutch."

What? Stepping forward, I study his face for the first time. "Ridge?"

Laughing, he shakes my hand and leans against my truck. "I know I was a little scrawny back then, but surely, I'm not completely unrecognizable."

What the hell. Cullen's older brother? Holt's best friend? "*You're* the one dating Lulu?"

He frowns. "What? No, of course not. Ella's not dating anyone. Well, not that I know of, I mean."

"What are you doing here?"

"I just moved back to town. I'm staying here for a few days since Holt's out of town. My apartment will be ready next week."

I think back to everything Cullen told me. "You were living down at the beach, right?"

"Yeah, Gulf Shores."

"And you just moved back?"

"Yeah, my first day with the department is Monday."

"The fire department?"

He nods, stuffing his hands in his pockets.

"Let me ask you, did you and Lulu grab coffee the other morning?"

His brow furrows. "Yeah. Why?"

"And did you bring something to her at the station the other day?"

"Yeah, one of her notebooks about Carrie. She said she needed it for y'all's investigation." He pushes away from the hood of my truck, folding his arms across his chest. "What's going on, Crutch? Something I should know about?"

I chuckle. That damn little minx. She let me think she was seeing someone, dating someone. "No, everything is fine."

"Well, obviously you didn't come here to see me. You came to see Ella, right?"

"Yeah. Will said she was sick. I wanted to check on her."

Ridge whistles. "I have to warn you, man. Her piss-and-vinegar attitude is even more profound when she's sick."

I bite my lip, holding back my smile. "Good. That's what I like to hear."

"You know she was never like that when we were growing up. She held everything in. Never showed her emotions. Well, never showed them to anyone but us and Carrie. She always agreed with everything, never ruffled anyone's feathers. Like some kind of perfect little porcelain doll. Me and Holt used to joke that she was like a balloon, filling up and filling up. We said one day she would just explode. Pop. All of that changed, though, when she met you. She started speaking her mind. Finally stood up to her parents. It was freakin' amazing."

She changed me too. For the better.

He taps the watch on his wrist, checking the time. "I still see it some, though. The stiff back, the fake smile, the passive-aggressive politeness. Holt told me to call her out on it. Point it out whenever I see it. But it's hard to do sometimes. Sometimes, she deserves to be a bitch." He takes a step toward me, puffing out his broad chest. The smile falls from his face. "After everything she's been through, you know? Most women aren't as strong as Ella."

Are you shitting me? Is he challenging me? Calling me out? "What are you talking about, Ridge? If you have something to say, just say it."

Taking a deep breath, he takes a step back, shaking the tension from his neck. "Nothing to say. I always liked you, Crutch. I never saw two people better fitted for each other than you and Ella. I'm just saying that none of us wanna see her hurt again."

"I have no intention of hurting her." Deciding to bring honesty into the conversation, I add what we're both already thinking. "Again, I mean. I have no intention of ever hurting her again."

He judges the look on my face before smiling. "Good. I have to head out. I have a date."

I glance around. The only vehicles in the driveway are mine and Lulu's two cars—her old SUV and the newer one she drove up from Mobile. "Where'd you park?"

Ridge starts walking across the front yard. "I parked in the garage over on the Big House. Oh, by the way, she refused to eat. There's a can of chicken soup on the counter if you can force her."

I watch as he disappears into the curtain of the night sky. The relief that floods over me when I walk back to the door is almost humorous. Almost. I can't believe she let me think Ridge was a new man in her life. It's bad enough to know she has random one-night stands from the bar.

Well, it's more than bad. But I can't think about that right now.

I knock several times, chuckling when I hear her grunting and fussing on the other side of the door.

"Damn it, Ridge. How hard is it to remember a house key! You're a grown-ass man, for goodness' sake." She jerks the door open with so much force I worry she may rip it off the hinges. Her jaw drops when she sees me standing in front of her.

The sight of her nearly brings me to my knees.

Her face is makeup free, and her messy hair is piled high on her head. She looks even younger without her makeup on. Flawless skin, flawless face. Her cheeks are rosy with the flush of a fever. Her nose is bright red and raw from blowing it, and her lips are swollen and dry. Even sick, she's the epitome of beauty.

My voice catches in my throat when I see what she's wearing. The T-shirt is faded, having been washed and dried a thousand times, but there's no mistaking the emblem on the left breast of the blue shirt. *Harlan's Garage and Automotive.*

She's wearing *my* shirt. It's shorter now than it used to be, barely covering her ass and panties.

And she's not wearing any pants or shorts.

"What the hell, Lulu. You just go walking around the house without any clothes on? Ridge was just here. Did you let him see your ass?"

Her mouth closes, and she grinds her teeth. "I wasn't walking around the house. I was covered up. With a blanket. On my nice, comfortable couch. Until some jackass pounded on my front door. And no, Ridge doesn't check out my butt. Don't be gross."

"Me? You're the one who let me think Ridge was some guy you were dating."

She tries to hide her smile, but does a very poor job with it. "I don't know what you're talking about. I told you it was just a friend."

I lick my lips, trailing my eyes across her long, lean legs. "Oh, you know exactly what I'm talking about."

She shivers underneath the intensity of my gaze. Either that, or her fever is rising, giving her the chills.

She sniffles and then coughs. "Why are you here?"

"To take care of you. Will told me you were sick."

"I'm fine. I can take care of myself."

"I know you can. I'm here because I *wanna* take care of you, not because I *need* to take care of you." That's not really true. I need her, just like I need air to breathe.

She opens her mouth to tell me no, but I stop her. "I'm not leaving, Lulu. You know that. I know that. So save us both some trouble and let me in."

She growls. The extra effort makes her cough again. "Fine."

The second she turns to walk away, I do fall to my knees.

Literally.

Flashes of concern bounce through my mind like vicious lightning strikes. The pinkish-purple line doesn't belong on her beautiful skin. It's foreign. New. Wrong. Its home shouldn't be on her tanned and perfect body. Grabbing her waist, I pull her closer to me. Wrapping my fingers around her left thigh, I lift the hem of her shirt, searching for the starting point of her scar. She stumbles against me, placing her hands on my shoulders to stabilize herself.

"Ry! What are you doing?"

Ignoring her white cotton panties and the fact that my hands are agonizingly close to her crotch, I trace the long surgical scar with my finger. It feels flatter than it looks. It disappears underneath her panties. Not asking for permission, I grab the elastic band and push it up, out of my way. The scar starts at the crest of her pelvis bone and runs for at least eleven or twelve inches down her hip and thigh. There are two smaller scars on her thigh, closer to the round globe of her ass. Looks like she had stitches.

"Lulu, what the hell happened to you? Are you okay? Did you have surgery?"

"Ry."

I rub my thumb back and forth against her skin, like the scar is a smudge of dirt I can just wipe off. "Tell me what happened."

"Ry." Her voice breaks with emotion.

My head snaps back. Oh my god. My Lulu is about to cry. I whisper, scattering my breath across her bare skin. "Lulu?"

She closes her eyes and licks her lips. "You have to stop touching me. Please. Please stop touching me."

Lowering my head, I absorb the sight before me, taking in every small detail. Her scars. The chill bumps that flare across her skin with the caress of my finger. The thin white fabric that separates me from her most private part.

I can still taste her. I can still feel my body buried deep inside of her.

I've thought of nothing less every time I've closed my eyes. For twelve years, I've drifted off to sleep every single night thinking of her. Her body. The way her pussy was made for me. No two things have ever fit together more perfectly. My Lulu and me.

"Why? Why do I need to stop?"

She blinks her eyes open. "I can't think when you touch me."

"And?"

"And I don't want you to stop."

Holy. Shit. "And that's a bad thing?" The scent of her arousal floods around me, making my dick hard as a rock.

"Yes. Because that's not our reality. And reality reminds you where you belong, right?" Stepping out of my grasp, she leaves me empty and wanting.

I despise the fact that I allowed those words to rule my life—and hers—for so many years.

It's time to make my own reality. With Lulu.

Silently, she walks back over to the couch and crawls underneath a thick blanket. It takes a minute before I can stand without breaking my erection in half. Crossing the living room, I sit on the coffee table in front of her. There's some throat spray and cold medicine spread across the tabletop. There's a trash can on the floor next to her, filled to the brim with snotty, used tissues. Eyeing me, she pulls the blanket up to her chin.

Reaching across, I bend down, pressing the back of my hand across her forehead. "You have a fever."

"I just took some medicine right before you got here. It'll break soon."

"You plan on telling me what happened?"

"No."

"Well, I suggest you quickly modify your plans, then."

Despite herself, she smiles softly at our familiar game of words. "I had a hip replacement."

I shake my head in disbelief. "A hip replacement. When?"

"The fall after I left town. November."

"You had a hip replacement when you were eighteen? Why?"

"I was in a car accident. I was driving and someone hit me. My hip was basically crushed by the driver-side door."

I can't even wrap my head around the words coming from her mouth. I drag my hand across my face, scratching my facial hair. "Shit. But you're okay? You don't limp," I say, stating the obvious. "You're okay, right?"

Please say you're okay. Please. Please. Please.

"I'm fine. I had an excellent surgeon. It was a long recovery, but I'm all good. My hip doesn't hurt at all."

My woman nearly died. My Lulu nearly died. No wonder Ridge said she was strong.

I should've been there. But I wasn't.

Hudson was.

"It happened in Michigan? When you were with Hudson?"

She nods, holding out her hand for a fresh tissue. I pull one from the box on the coffee table and give it to her, waiting on her to blow her nose. "He wasn't in the car with me, no. But the wreck did happen when we were married, if that's what you're asking."

"I can't believe you didn't tell me. You freaked out when I didn't tell you about my injury. And then you keep something like this from me?"

"That's different, and you know it. A car accident is just that—an accident. Someone wasn't actively trying to kill me. I wasn't laying my life on the line to protect someone else. My body has healed, Ry. You still have pieces of metal coming out of your body."

It's a moot point to argue with her about that. So I choose something else to argue about instead. "Wanna tell me why you let me think Ridge was some new boyfriend?"

Poking her stubborn little chin in the air, she squints her eyes. "To make you jealous. Is that what you wanna hear?"

"Is that the truth? Because if it is, your plan succeeded."

She snorts, making herself cough. "Truth. That's always been a scary word around us, hasn't it?" She flops back against the couch pillow and flings her arm over her eyes. "And by the way, that's a rhetorical question, Ry. I don't have the energy for that fight tonight."

I don't think I have the energy for it, either. Even though I know damn well what the truth is.

I slap my hands against my thighs and stand up. "You need to eat. I'm fixing you some soup." I grab her empty water cup and head over to the kitchen, smiling when she whines.

Just a few minutes later, I return with chicken noodle soup, crackers, and a fresh glass of ice water. It's no use; she's passed out. Breathing deeply, her chest heaves up and down in her sleep, and I'm glad to see the red fever in her cheeks has dimmed. Setting everything on the table, I sit on the end of the couch. Lifting her lower legs, I hold her feet in my lap, making sure to keep my hands on top of the blanket. The last thing I need tonight is another raging boner from the feel of her bare skin.

I study the curve of her body, the peaceful look on her face, the lines of her collarbone peeking out from the collar of my old T-shirt. Like I said, I know the truth. The truth is she's the love of my life. Always has been, always will be.

I love her.

Tucking the blanket around her, I whisper into her dreams. "You're mine, Lulu. All mine. Never before and never after. There's only you. And now, I just have to make you realize it too."

I chuckle. "Game on."

Chapter 22

Ella

Today is going to be a shitty day.

I knew it when I went to sleep last night, and I knew it the second I woke up. This date is always a shitty day. Trust me, more difficult anniversaries are coming up, but this day still sucks. And despite the good times, rekindling friendship, and building sexual tension between me and Ry over the past few months, there's not going to be anything he can say or do to make this day any better.

He already tattooed this date into my memory. Twelve years ago, this date changed the events of my future. It set me on a completely different course from where I thought I would be.

And I hate him for it.

Regardless of the fact that I am completely and totally still in love with him... I hate him for this.

And I have no intentions of hiding my bad mood from him.

I pick up my cell phone the second I hear a work email ding. Punching out a response, I'm acutely aware of someone staring at me. "Why are you staring at me?"

"You're sitting at my desk. I'm allowed to stare at you." Marcum cocks his head to the side. "Are you in a bad mood today?"

"Of course not."

"Nancy says the exact same thing, using the exact same tone

when she's in a bad mood. Did something happen I should know about?"

"Don't be absurd. I'm just responding to an email. Since when does concentrating mean I'm in a bad mood."

Marcum holds his hands up like a hostage. "Point taken."

I'm clicking send when something hits my chest and bounces down onto my lap. Startled, I yelp, sitting up straight. I pick up the silver wrapped protein bar and turn it over in my hand. "Really?"

"Maybe you're hungry. That definitely makes me grumpy."

"Who's grumpy?" Ry's voice pours over my body like hot molasses.

Damn him and his seductive growl.

"Ella." Marcum's voice overlaps with mine.

"No one." Grunting, I toss the protein bar back in his face.

Ry walks around to the side of the desk. "You're in a bad mood?"

Stiffening my spine and squaring my shoulders, I purse my lips. "No. But if you guys don't stop your harping, I'm gonna show you exactly what kind of mood I can be in."

"Okay. Point taken." Ry winks at Marcum, making my blood boil.

I slap my hand on the desk, grabbing his attention. "Do you actually plan on working on my sister's case today? Or do you just wanna saunter around making useless small talk?"

Ry lifts his eyebrows and stares at me with his translucent green eyes, making me feel one split second of shame for my harshness.

"Alright." After drawing the simple word out over ten syllables, he waves a thumb drive in my face. "Finally received all of Trey's prison records—visitor logs, phone calls, everything." He licks his lips, making me quickly reach for the comfort of the scar on my neck. "That's why I called you in today. But if you have other projects you need to—"

I jump up from my seat, cutting him off. "Are you deranged? We've been waiting on these for months." I grab my work bags and snatch the thumb drive from his fingertips.

I don't even bother to say thank you because I am, in fact, grumpy.

The setting May sun burns the sky in brilliant hues of pink and orange. I can't believe how hot it is already. I bet this summer will be miserable.

His voice catches me off guard, making me stumble against a divot in the sidewalk. His muscular hand darts out, wrapping around my upper arm, helping me catch my balance.

As soon as I'm steady, I tear into him. "What's wrong with you?! You can't just walk up on someone like that! You scared me."

"I can't help it if you weren't paying attention to your surroundings, Lulu. It's not like I was being quiet. Don't blame me because you were daydreaming."

"I was *not* daydreaming." I turn and walk to the corner of the street, looking both ways before crossing to the bar. "Why are you following me?"

"Following you? I'm not following you. I'm going to the bar for a drink. Call me crazy, but for some reason, I'm stressed out after being trapped in a room with you all day."

Me? Stress him out? Please. My jaw falls open and I plant my hands on my hips. "Excuse me? I can't help it if you weren't being very observant today. Part of my job is to point out things that others may have missed."

He's changed out of his work polo and into a soft green T-shirt. The hem catches on his belt and gifts me with a small glimpse of his stomach when he tosses his hands in the air. "It's hard to find something when you don't even give me the opportunity to look. We make a great team, Lulu, but our jive was definitely off today. Something is wrong, and I just wish you would tell me what it is."

I debate saying it. For a minute I do debate it. Then I realize that this day changed the course of his life too. He should remember it. It was a pretty fucking momentous day.

Instead of answering, I just stand there, staring at him, willing him to grow a brain and remember. Wanting him to be the sensitive man I know he can be.

A group of guys cuts around our standoff in front of the bar. But not before one of the guys checks me out. He's not shy about it and even hisses a sound of appreciation between his teeth. I'm wearing a white blouse and a blue skirt, with nude wedges on my feet. I glance over at the guy and watch as his eyes trail slowly up every inch of my legs. He's fairly cute. Maybe a couple of years younger than me, if I had to guess.

Ry takes a step in his direction. "Hey, asshole, eyes to yourself."

Ignoring Ry, the guys walk into the bar, and I stomp my foot like a child throwing a tantrum. "What was that?"

Ry glances from the door to me and back again. "Are you being serious right now? That guy was checking you out."

"Yeah. So?"

"Oh, excuse me!" Ry bows like he's begging for an apology. "I didn't realize you needed affirmation from random strangers on how sexy you look. The Lulu I know is pretty damn confident without it."

"Shut up. It's not about that, and you know it. I have to deal with women fawning all over you all the time. I bought stock in four major condom companies because of you. And you can't even stand for one guy to *look* at me. Kind of a double standard, don't you think?"

I don't give him time to respond. I swing open the door and charge my way to the bar. Will's not working tonight, it's just Cullen and one of the other bartenders. I plop down at the edge of the bar and immediately order a Long Island Iced Tea. In frustrating fashion, the only other available barstool is caddy corner next to me, and I'm not lucky enough for him to sit at a table tonight. Oh, hell no, he'll sit next to me just to drive me crazy.

"Uhhh... everything okay, guys?" Cullen sets my drink in front of me and opens a beer for Ry.

We answer at the exact same time. "Yes" for me and "No" for him.

"So, which is it?"

Ry leans forward, pointing a finger at me. "She would have you believe everything is just fine, but it's not. And she refuses to tell anyone what's wrong." He guzzles his beer and scoffs. "Women."

"Like you know women." I lift the drink to my lips and sniff it before setting it back down. "The only thing you know about women are which holes make you happy. Fortunately for you, it's easy to figure out. One has lipstick, the other has pubic hair."

Ry leans over, invading my personal space. The scent of his soap mingles in the air. His whisper is ragged, like his voice is being dragged across glass. "If I recall correctly, *one* woman I know shaved bald. And *she* loved it when I touched her and tasted her smooth skin. It made her moan and scream."

Well, I walked right into that one.

Snatching my purse and drink off the counter, I hop down from the bar. "Cullen, I'm going in the back room. I have a work phone call I need to return."

I pace around the storeroom for a good ten minutes before finally calming down enough to come out. As soon as I open the door, I see Ry walking toward me. The expression on his face is easy to read—concern, worry, regret. He's coming to apologize. Except he's wanting to apologize for his behavior today, not his behavior from twelve years ago that he can't even remember.

Glancing around for an escape, I spot my admirer and his group of friends mingling around the pool tables. I make a beeline for them before I can change my mind. It's been a while since I've left the bar with someone. I think that's just what Ry needs to see right now.

Sliding next to the stranger, I gently squeeze his bicep with my free hand. "Hi. I just wanted to say I'm sorry for my friend's behavior. It was completely uncalled for."

Out the side of my eye, I watch as Ry freezes in his tracks. He definitely doesn't like what he sees. His jaw clenches and his hands ball into fists. When the guy wraps his arm around my waist, it takes literally all my strength to stay relaxed and not stiffen my spine. I must fake it pretty good because Ry drags his hand over his sexy three-day scruff and turns around, leaving me to my own destructive devices.

"Friend? Not a boyfriend?"

I shake my head. "No, I'm single."

He smiles. He has a dimple on his left cheek. In my wedges, I'm about an inch taller than him. He doesn't seem to mind though. "That's the best thing I've heard all day. I'm Alec."

"Ella. Nice to meet you."

"You play pool, Ella?"

I smile widely, flashing my white teeth. "I can hold my own, Alec." Setting my drink and purse on a shelf, I grab a cue and hand it to him, mentally buckling myself up for the night. I wouldn't give Ry the satisfaction of climbing out of this car if it were on fire and careening off a cliff.

Two hours of flirting, smiling, laughing, and fake drinking have worn me out. Fortunately, Alec's young—twenty-four—and he's horny. By nine, he's pulling me into full body hugs and whispering in my ear.

It doesn't feel like Ry. Ry's whispers are hot and dry, sending shivers from my neck down to the base of my spine. Alec's are loud and wet. They make me wanna clean my ears with a towel.

Alec kisses my cheek. "You wanna get out of here?"

About damn time. "Yes."

"Let me use the restroom and say goodbye to the guys. I'll meet you by the door."

Stepping to the side, out of Ry's piercing glare from his perch at the bar, I roll my shoulders and take several deep breaths. I've been holding my tension in check, and I'm about to explode. Sighing, I swing my purse around my shoulder and grab my tepid and smelly drink. Long Island Iced Teas smell even worse when they get hot.

Putting on a brave face, I make my way to the bar. Leaning across, I put my glass on the edge closest to Cullen. "Bye, C. See you later."

He grabs my hand, nearly causing me to knock over the glass.

"Seriously, Ella? You're doing this again? Raylee is gonna flip out."

"Then don't tell her."

Pulling from his grasp, I spin around and run smack dab into Ry. A very unhappy Ry. "What the hell, Lulu? You're going home with that asshole?"

"He's not an asshole. He's actually a nice guy. And what I do is none of your concern."

His eyes flash with anger, instantly coloring them five shades darker. "You're always my concern. Always."

The possessiveness in his voice makes my heart stop beating. I instantly reach around, running my fingertips across my scar. My voice is weak, almost invisible underneath the music pouring from the overhead speakers. "I shouldn't be, though, should I? I shouldn't be your concern."

He takes a step closer, pressing his body to mine, trying to erase the distance between us. "Why are you doing this? You're killing me. Luella Margaret Hill, you're killing me."

I lift my chin. My nose and lips graze against his cheek. He shivers, and it's then that I tell him what he should already know. "It's our anniversary."

He leans backward, studying my face. "Huh? What are you talking about?" He knows it's not the anniversary of when we met. He knows it's not the anniversary of our first kiss. Not the first time we had sex.

"It's our anniversary, Ryland Joseph Crutchfield. Exactly twelve years ago today, I received a letter telling me to hate you. So this is me, doing what you asked."

His face instantly shatters into a million pieces. I should feel good, but I don't. I feel just as shattered. But I couldn't be the only one suffering here. He deserves to bear some of this.

Stepping around his massive frame, I head to the front door, gasping when Alec squeezes my waist. Laughing, he holds the door open for me. "Sorry about that, didn't mean to scare you."

I walk out into the warm air, unable to look back at Ry. "That's fine."

He points to the side of the building. "So, I'm parked right around the corner. Wanna ride with me?"

"Where do you live?"

He names a large apartment complex that's about two miles away. I nod. "I know right where that is. It's probably best if I drive. I have an early morning. Give me ten minutes, and I'll meet you there. I drive a white sedan. What's your apartment number?"

"34B. But I really don't mind bringing you back to your car whenever you want. I can get up early. We can have breakfast together."

Oh Alec, you'll make someone very happy. That someone just isn't me.

"That's okay. Ten minutes." I kiss him on the cheek and walk away.

Twenty minutes later, I'm lying in my bed, crying into my pillow. Alone.

Just the same feeling I've had every night for the past twelve years.

Chapter 23

Ella

My lungs burn as I glide through the pool, enjoying a peaceful swim as the sun hangs low in the sky, begging to slip below the earth and sleep. Water splashes over my head, grabbing my attention. I pop to the surface, immediately wiping the water from my eyes.

And wouldn't you know it. There's Ry.

Standing on the side, he spreads his arms open wide. A bouquet of orange roses is in one hand and a large, greasy white paper bag is in the other.

I swim to the edge of the pool so we can talk. I don't have the strength to scream while treading water. "What are you doing?"

"So… I figured it's time to make a new anniversary."

"Really. And what's that? *'Breaking into Someone's Backyard'* Day?"

"I was hoping more for like *'Please Don't Hate Me'* Day."

Is this really happening? Is he trying to play coy and cute with something so serious?

Suddenly Holt's voice screams from the patio. "Agree to it! He brought me a cheesesteak too. I'm freakin' starving."

"Trying to buy off my family now?"

"Is it working?"

I snort. "Holt's a football player. He'll do anything for food."

Ry holds out the bag, and Holt races over to grab it. "I'll set the outside table," Holt says in excitement.

Once Holt's out of earshot, Ry crouches down next to me. He's wearing cargo shorts and they gape open, showing me the material of his black boxer briefs. "I'm sorry about yesterday. I'm sorry I didn't remember what day it was." He sighs, glancing around the backyard. "In all honesty, I've spent twelve years trying to forget the words I wrote in that letter."

"Why? Did our time together mean so little to you that you can't even bring yourself to have empathy for what I went through."

He smirks, driving me mad. "Don't play the stupid card with me, Lulu. You're the smartest person I know. And you know that our time together was the best part of my life. You *were my life*—the reason I wanted to live and breathe and survive." He reaches down in front of me, swirling water around his finger. "Breaking up with you was a mistake, and I've been fighting that shame. I'm tired of fighting it; I realize I'm not strong enough to win that battle. I honestly thought leaving was the best thing for you. I know you'll never believe that, but it's honestly what I thought. I had nothing to offer you, nothing to give you. I didn't want you to derail your future because of me. Somewhere along the way I realized I took the coward's way out. I'm so damn sorry. I don't expect you to forgive me, but I want you to know that I'm sorry. And I regret it every single second of every single day."

"Are you guys coming or not?" Holt hollers. "If not, I'm gonna eat your fries."

Ry chuckles. I can't help but notice that he seems a little lighter. Like a weight has been lifted from his shoulders. He told me some of his truth. Plus, he apologized.

Maybe I would feel lighter if I told him some of my truth.

The full truth.

He reaches down with both hands, urging me out of the water. "I don't know about you, but I'm hungry. And I really don't wanna fight your cousin for my French fries."

I push away from the side, getting ready to swim to the steps, when Ry reaches out and grabs my hands. I stare at him. "What are you doing? You can't pull me out of the water. I'm too heavy, you'll fall in."

"I remember hauling you into my arms on many occasions," Ry says with a playful wink.

"I was a teenager then," I say.

He wraps his hands around my wrists, so my wet hands don't slip from his, and pulls me from the water, like I'm light as a feather. Granted, I give myself a pretty good jump to help out, but still. My soaking wet body presses into his. The temperature change immediately causes my nipples to pebble and chill bumps break out across my skin. Ry's eyes scan my body, absorbing every small detail of my one-piece blue bathing suit. The high-cut leg showcases the contrasting colors in my skin tone. I've been laying out in a different swimsuit so my tan lines are lower. He traces his finger up my left thigh, charting the course of my surgery scar. At least the neck on this one isn't low cut, so he can't see how badly my breasts are heaving from his touch.

I stutter across my words. "T...Towel."

Ry grabs the large beach towel from the lounge chair and wraps it around me, rubbing his hands up and down my arms to warm me. His yellow T-shirt is soaked.

I nod at his chest. "I got you wet."

He smiles softly. "I don't mind." Stooping, he picks up the bouquet of roses and grabs my hand, leading me over to the table, holding my hand like he used to. His calloused fingertips tickle my skin.

Holt stares at our intertwined fingers but doesn't say anything. "I grabbed you a beer, Crutch."

"Thanks. Appreciate it."

Ry reaches across and twists the lid on my bottle of water, opening it for me, while Holt puts the most glorious sandwich I've ever seen on my plate. We stuff our faces and small talk about nothing important. When finished, we clear the table, and Holt discreetly heads inside, leaving me and Ry on the patio alone.

Ry leans back in his chair, splaying his legs and studying me. I wipe my face with my fingertips. "What? Do I have cheese on me again?"

"No, you sucked that thing down like a vacuum cleaner. No time to get anything on your face."

Laughing, I throw a leftover napkin at him.

"No, I was looking at your hair. Seriously, I can't get over how wavy it is now, when it used to be so straight. It's even curlier when it's wet."

I shrug, avoiding more of the conversation. "Thank you for the roses. They're beautiful." I nod at the house where Holt took my roses inside with him.

He sighs, rubbing his fingers back and forth across his lips. "So... my grandma passed away two years after I came back home."

I turn abruptly at the change of topic. "I know. I'm so very sorry."

"How do you know?"

I cock my head. "Excuse me?"

"How did you find out? If Marcum didn't talk to you about me and your family didn't talk to you about me, how did you find out?"

I shrug again, biting my lip. "I guess I just heard it somewhere."

He makes an interesting noise. "When I left for the Marines, I was worried about her. I couldn't even call to check on her for a long time. I finally got to where I could call once a week, and I was surprised to find out that someone was sending fresh, orange roses to Grandma every single week. When I asked about it, the staff told me they made a promise to keep the donor anonymous. After a couple of months, the donor started sending fresh flowers for the dining area too."

My heart thunders in my chest. I wipe my sweaty palms on the beach towel, underneath the table. "Huh. That's nice."

"It is, isn't it? Weekly fresh flowers can't be cheap. I mean, we're talking about five-and-a-half years' worth of flowers."

Stars twinkle above us. Cicadas and tree frogs chirp around us. It's nowhere near as loud as the homestead used to be, but it's still a nice noise. I stand up, pulling the damp towel closer around my body. "Thanks so much for the food and the flowers. I should head inside. I have a lot of work to do tomorrow, several web calls."

He doesn't let me take too many steps before he's crowding me, invading my space. He reaches out, hooking a finger around mine as I hold my towel closed. "Please tell me you didn't use that cheating asshat's money to buy flowers for Grandma."

There's no point in denying it; he knows I sent the orange roses to her. Every week, without fail, I sent them. "Of course not. Despite what you did to me, I would never disrespect you that way. I worked for spending money in college. I did online tutoring for some of Holt's friends and teammates—proofread their papers, helped with their homework, advised them on their college essays, and I did some transcribe work for some of the attorneys at Mr. Plott's firm. That's surprisingly good money."

"Your parents actually let you work?"

I lift my eyebrows. "Remember, I wasn't on the best of terms with them when I left town."

He nods. His finger moves from my hand to my shoulder, and he grabs a small curl, twirling it around and around. "Why? Why would you do that? Take care of her like that?"

"You didn't just leave me when you left. I didn't want to punish your grandma for our issues. Orange roses helped her remember your grandpa. I didn't want her to be alone. I didn't want her to feel the way I felt."

"Is that how you felt? Alone?"

I don't answer. And I don't like his question. I straighten my shoulders, and his hand falls to his side.

"But you weren't alone. You had Hudson, right?" His voice is strangled and worried. Worried of what answer he may receive.

"I need to go inside." This time he lets me walk away. He's too scared to make me stay. Too scared of the truth. Just like me. Before walking through the door, I turn back to him. "And thank you for the apology. It was nice to hear. Our time together was the best part of my life too."

I close the door before he sees the tears fall from my eyes.

I hate crying in front of people.

And I really hate crying over Ry. Again.

Chapter 24

Crutch

"What in the world does 'Girls' Night' actually mean?"

She laughs, closing the lid on her laptop. "Why in the world is this bothering you so much?"

"I know you, Lulu. You've never done the things that normal women do. That includes makeover parties and drinking Cosmos."

This time, she laughs so hard she snorts. "You're right. I'm definitely not meeting up with other women to do their makeup and drink frilly little drinks."

Leaning against the doorway, I cross one ankle over the other, staring at her. She glances up and I watch her eyes as they hungrily scan my body. She tries not to blush, but she does. Hiding her beautifully flushed face behind a curtain of hair, she packs her work bag. Sighing, I cross the room and tug the computer bag from her shoulder to mine. She used to fight me about that, but she doesn't now.

Little by little, our frozen past is thawing. And I'm not sure what to think about that.

I lock the conference room door and walk her to the parking lot. When we pass by Tara at the front desk, she rolls her eyes.

"Will there ever come a time when you don't roll your eyes when we walk past Tara?"

She leans against the door of her SUV. "Will there ever come a time we stop running into women you've seen naked?"

I hate it when she talks about me being with other women. I know I've been stupid. I don't need the constant reminder of what a piece of shit I am. "Maybe. When I settle down. Know anyone up to the job?"

I take a step forward, lightly pressing my body against hers. She stops breathing. Her nipples peak, shining through the thin fabric of her yellow blouse. At least she has on pants today. True, they are tight-ass pants that only come to her ankles, but still. That's better than a skirt. If she were showing me her nipples *and* her legs all at the same time, I would have to jack off the second I make it somewhere remotely private.

She licks her lips, making me instantly hard. "I'll be happy to check my contact list. Perhaps a nice, mild-mannered librarian?"

Chuckling, I take a step back. I have to. Being that close to her is pure, sweet torture.

Smiling like she won the game, she turns, opening the car door. I grab the frame, leaning against it as she climbs in. Eventually, she cocks her head. "Fine. It's just me, Raylee, and Aunt Teresa."

"What is?"

"The 'Girls' Night'. Raylee got a babysitter. We're going to dinner and to the movies. Afterward, we're going to the bar to hear the band. Will, Holt, and Uncle Ray will be there. We're making a whole night of it."

"Sounds like fun."

She grabs the steering wheel, turning her knuckles white. All of a sudden, a black car pulls up behind us, honking the horn. The passenger lowers the window, and Raylee leans half her body out the open hole.

"Ella, what the heck are you doing? Did you forget we were picking you up?"

I bend down and see Teresa behind the wheel. I give her a small wave before turning back to Lulu.

She frowns, mumbling to herself. "Oh, I forgot. I guess I got distracted." Grabbing her purse from the seat, she jumps out, and I slam the door behind her.

Raylee hollers again before raising her window. "Come on, I'm freakin' starving."

"I see it runs in the family," I tease.

"Yeah, sometimes, it's scary how much alike she and Holt are." For a second, Lulu fidgets with her fingers. Quickly releasing her hands, she stands straighter and lifts her chin in the air. "So, I guess I'll see you next week sometime. I'll let you know what my work schedule is."

I run my fingers across my belt in habit. "Go ahead and ask me. I know you want to."

"I don't know what you're talking about."

"Don't beat around the bush, Lulu. I like you when you get to the point."

She sighs. "Fine. Are you coming to the bar tonight? Will you be there?"

"Meaning, will I be there with you?"

She shrugs, trying to act nonchalant. "Well, sure. I just told you I would be there."

I take a step forward, crowding her once again with my body. Before she has time to react, I bend my head, whispering against the shell of her ear. She loves it when I do that. At least she used to, so I'm assuming I still have that effect on her. "Of course, I should always be where you are. Maybe that should be our new rule. We always had rules for our games, didn't we?"

Walking backward, I watch as her closed eyes open. Her entire face is relaxed, and her mouth is parted. What I wouldn't give to take her, right here, right now. Make her mine, *show* her she's mine.

Nodding her head, she turns and climbs into the back of her aunt's car.

Looks like I'm going to the bar tonight. Mowing the yard will have to wait until tomorrow.

I take a seat next to Ray, shaking his hand, and then I lean across the bar, grabbing Holt's attention. "Surprised to see you behind the bar. Everything okay?"

"Yeah, Cullen had to work an event for his father tonight so I told him I would fill in." He places a beer bottle in front of me. "Will has another bartender coming in to help too. The band will be starting in about an hour. They're good. You should stick around."

Ray chuckles underneath his breath. I can only assume he talked to Teresa and knows that I plan on sticking around until my woman gets here.

I tip my beer to Holt. "I told him before that he can always ask me for help when Cullen is out doing a catering thing with his dad. I don't know how to mix drinks, but I know how to use a bottle opener."

"It's fine, man. I was gonna be here anyway. Might as well earn my keep a little bit."

Ray and I spend the next forty-five minutes chatting. It's the most I've talked to him in twelve years, and I really enjoy it. Turns out, I missed him too. Maybe that's why my friendship with Will grew so much. I wasn't only looking for a connection to Lulu, but to Ray and Teresa as well.

Holt and Will are serving some customers right next to me and Ray when I feel that familiar shift in the air, the one that lets me know My Lulu is close by. Turning on my stool, I watch as Teresa, Raylee, and Lulu walk in the bar. And I watch as two different guys check out My Lulu, stirring jealousy deep in the pit of my stomach.

Ray and I immediately stand, offering our seats to the ladies. All the other barstools are occupied so Lulu opts to stand, giving her aunt and cousin the seats at the bar. Raylee stands on the footrests and leans over the bar, planting a long, sexy kiss on her husband. Will immediately starts laughing. "Well, someone tastes like vodka. Drinks at dinner, my little wife?"

"Yep! Shelly already agreed to spend the night so she can get up with the kids first thing tomorrow."

"So, this 'Girls' Night' also means I have to pay a babysitter double time to spend the night at my house? You're costing me a small fortune tonight, woman."

"Well, maybe you'll get lucky. I'd like to get lucky. Multiple times," Raylee says with a wink.

The look on Holt's face is priceless. "Dad, seriously, you're gonna let your little girl talk like that?"

"Son, your sister hasn't been a little girl since the day she could speak."

"I completely agree." The new addition to our group takes us by surprise.

"Ridge!" Raylee covers him in a hug.

Holt leans over, shaking his hand. "I thought you were helping your dad."

"I was," Ridge points to his white button-up and black slacks, "but Cullen has it all handled. You know that kid is like a powerhouse."

Lulu leans over, wrapping him in a hug. "Well, it's good you came out for the fun."

Fortunately, Ridge doesn't do anything that could get his ass kicked—like sniff her hair or hold her too close or fondle her backside. I'd hate to have to ruin this night before it even begins.

"Speaking of people coming out for fun," Will points toward the back of the bar. "Kristie's here. And I've already had to stop serving her."

When Lulu turns to peer over my shoulder, her hip brushes against my side. "She's already that drunk?"

"Yeah. She must've been drinking before she got here. I sold her one beer before I realized how intoxicated she was. I told her no more. But she's bad to send guys up here to buy her drinks."

"With promises of getting into her panties, no doubt," Raylee says, drinking the soda that Will set in front of her.

Lulu looks at me. "Maybe I should go say something to her, just to check on her."

I shrug. "That's up to you." I really hope she says no.

Right then, the band strikes up, blaring deafening music through all the nooks and crannies of the bar.

Raylee screams. "There's no time for that! It's time to dance, Ella! Honey, put our purses behind the counter." Raylee, Teresa, and Lulu stack their bags on the bar, and Raylee drags her mom and cousin clear across the bar to the music room. Without being asked, Holt sets out a fresh beer for me, Ray, and Ridge, and we follow the women.

The band's good, playing a mix of well-known cover songs for the first thirty minutes. All upbeat, dancing songs. Ray and Teresa huddle together in a corner, whispering, and watching the crowd. Ridge runs into a couple of friends he hasn't seen since he came back to town, so he's talking to them and their wives. I recognize one of the guys as a patrol deputy.

That leaves me. Standing here, slowly drinking, and watching every move Lulu makes. Her body bends and twists and jumps. It's so damn sexual. But more important than that... she looks happy. Happy and carefree. She looks like the Lulu who spent a whole week sleeping with me in a tent. She looks like the Lulu who would cuddle next to me watching hours upon hours of true crime documentaries. She looks like the Lulu who curled on my chest, tracing the lines of my ribs, while I read aloud to her. It feels so good to see her like that.

It also feels so bad. I hurt—physically hurt—to touch her.

Time moves slowly. When will she realize she's mine? I don't know how much more of the game I can play. Or what I need to do to show her that we can be good together again.

Will's standing next to the stage, surveying the crowd. He just brought the band some fresh beers and water. When the song finishes, they start to play a familiar, long-winded ballad, giving the audience time to cool down. I watch as Will parts through the people, searching for his wife. Wrapping his arms around Raylee, he pulls her to the back of the crowd, and they melt into one another, dancing.

Some random girl walks up to me and smiles. Her eyes widen in delight. She's about to ask me to dance, but I fend her off before she can even open her mouth. Politely smiling and shaking my head, I point at Lulu's back. The girl understands what I'm saying and moves off to the side, quickly homing in on Ridge. Sliding behind Lulu, I reach out, grabbing her waist with both hands. She jumps. But only for a split second. She knows it's me.

She smells me. Senses me. Feels me.

Nuzzling my head next to her face, I bend and whisper in her ear. "May I have this dance?" I take another step forward, molding the front of my body to her ass. Instead of tensing, instead of stiffening her back, she actually sighs, rolling her body against me even more.

It's pure ecstasy. If you were to ask me right now, I'd say it's the most erotic thing I've ever experienced. And that's saying a lot.

Taking that as my only answer, I spin her around and fold her into my arms. Together, we dance. I'm holding her so close you couldn't slide a piece of paper between the two of us. Without prodding, her arms snake around my neck and her fingers tangle in my hair.

I love it when she does that. It's been too many years since she's had those fingers entwined in my hair.

Pressing my hands against the small of her back, I crash her body against my massive erection. Her eyes dilate and her body hums with a wild energy. Energy so strong, it's tangible, pulsing like a magnetic field. I stand straight, pulling her to her tiptoes. She loves it when I hug her with my whole body, forcing her to seek shelter in my shadow.

Her whisper is soft, barely audible against the music. "Ry, what are you doing?"

"I'm dancing. With you. Do you remember the last time we danced?"

She smirks. "I remember the four-foot-long cheesesteak and ginormous bowl of cantaloupe."

I chuckle. "That's what you would remember, huh?"

Her smile fades, and her face grows serious. "I remember everything, Ry. Everything. Maybe that's why we shouldn't be doing this."

"Maybe it's why we *should*." I lean forward, grazing my nose against hers. "Maybe it's the only way we can fix what I broke. Make what's wrong, right."

She licks her lips in thought. The wetness shimmers, making me weak in the knees.

"Because it feels so right to me, Lulu. Everything about you feels so incredibly right."

"I'm scared."

I shake my head, never wanting to hear those words from My Lulu. "Why?"

"Because... maybe... I feel like it's right too."

Moving one of my hands, I cup the back of her neck, tracing my thumb over the ridge of her scar. I brush my lips against her cheek.

And then it happens.

She moans.

That all-encompassing little moan that tells me she's ready to be kissed. That sexy little moan I've played on repeat throughout my every fantasy for the past twelve years.

I thought I would never hear it again.

And here it is.

The best damn sound I've ever heard.

The second my mouth slants over hers, her lips part. She's ready, she's waiting. Except we don't kiss. I just need a minute to *feel* her. So... we breathe. Her hot and heavy breath pours from her lungs into mine, giving me the oxygen I've been living without. Moaning, breathing, panting.

And just as my tongue is about to taste her for the first time in over a decade, all hell breaks loose.

Several loud screams erupt through the crowd, followed by laughing and cheering. The band falters off key. Someone bumps into us and spills a beer down my back. Trying to gather my senses, I glance at my immediate surroundings. The crowd has pushed in front of us, blocking the stage.

"Crutch!"

I spin around as soon as I hear Will scream my name. He's at the back of the room, holding onto Raylee and pointing wildly at the stage. "Crutch! Get her!"

The crowd parts just enough for me and Lulu to see the culprit of the commotion.

Kristie.

She's standing on top of one of the huge amplifiers, dancing and flashing her tits to the entire bar. Her shirt is completely off, and her bra is pulled down, trussing her bare breasts in the air.

"Oh my god," Lulu's gasp rings in my ears.

Suddenly, the portion of the audience filled with young—slightly drunk—and super-horny guys start to mob the front of the stage. Someone knocks into Lulu, bouncing her around like a pinball. Catching Ridge's eye, I gently push Lulu toward him. Nodding, he races up to protect her. Off in the corner, I hear Ray yelling.

"Get the family in the back room," I order Ridge.

I barge my way through the people and jump on the stage. The second I block Kristie's bare chest from public view, men and women alike fuss and boo. One jackass throws a beer bottle, and it crashes in an explosion of shards against the back wall. Knowing better than to touch Kristie's naked body and force her bra back up, I order her to dress and come with me. She slaps me across the face. She's too drunk to put any real force behind it, but it still pisses me off.

By this time, Will's made his way to the stage. "Put your clothes back on and get down, Kristie! Are you fucking insane?"

She just laughs. A small bubble of spit flies from her mouth. She looks me in the eyes, and that's when I see her pupils. Yep. High as a damn kite.

Ripping the clothes from my own body, I toss my T-shirt over her chest, covering her. Several women in the crowd shriek in delight. Scooping down, I tuck my body underneath her waist and toss her over my shoulder. Scrambling from the stage, I follow Will through the bar to the back storage room.

Good thing Kristie's a woman. If she were a man, I'd strangle the last breath from her for ruining my kiss with Lulu.

And for leaving me with balls so blue they could be mistaken for Olympic-size blueberries.

Chapter 25

Ella

You know the saying 'tension so thick you could cut it with a knife'? Well, the sexual tension between Ry and me has been so thick you would need a chainsaw powered by jet fuel to slice through it.

I spent the remainder of Friday night and all day Saturday babysitting Kristie at my house. Holt had to stay with Ridge because I was afraid Kristie would hit on him. It wasn't hard to confirm Ry's suspicion that Kristie was high. I tried to stage a one-woman intervention, threatening to tell her father. Kristie swore up and down that she doesn't have a drug problem. She said she just started a new anti-anxiety medication and she had an adverse reaction when mixing the medicine with alcohol and her normal sleep medication.

I don't know if I believe her, but I've been out of her life for so long I don't know if it's my place to enforce rules on her. One rule did get enforced, though—Will has banned her from the bar. She's not allowed to set foot in there again.

By the time I drove Kristie to her house Saturday night, Ry had caught a big case. A missing thirteen-year-old girl, lured away from home by an older man she met in a chat room. All the detectives were overwhelmed, chasing lead after lead all week long. I tried to stay out of the way, knowing they would ask for my help if they needed it. We only saw each other for a few minutes here and there when

I was in the station working. But those few minutes were filled with unspoken passion, electricity, and desire. Stolen glances and passing touches gave me enough hope to dream about what our future may hold.

Am I really ready to dive back into a relationship with him? Are we really ready to try this again? I can't have my heart broken. Not again. There's no way I would survive it. Lying in a ditch and being run over by a train would be easier than living through that.

And now, on this Friday afternoon, I can't help but wish we weren't going to see Trash for a follow-up interview, but instead, tumbling into bed together. I daydream of pulling the covers over our heads and rediscovering all the different kisses and touches that make us each scream out in pleasure. Because it's been a long damn time since I've had some *pleasure*.

"You're blushing."

I cover my cheek with my hand, watching as Ry locks the conference room door. "What?"

He laughs, pocketing his keys. "You're blushing. What are you thinking about?"

I snort, pretending what he's saying isn't true. "Don't be silly. I'm not thinking about what you probably *hope* I'm thinking about."

"And what do I *hope* you're thinking about?"

I ignore him, holding the lobby door open for him. "What's the latest on the girl? Have they let her go home yet?"

"Yeah, she's been released from the hospital. That was more of a precaution than anything else. She'll definitely need some long-term counseling. I'm just glad we found her when we did. And from what it sounds like, the district attorney's office feels confident the guy will plead guilty. The evidence against him is overwhelming."

"So, you finally got some rest last night?"

Ry laughs, returning the favor and holding the outside door open for me. The sound of his raspy breath makes me dizzy, and I literally grow weak in the knees when his hand grazes the small of my back, guiding me out into the heated summer air. "Yeah, I slept for twelve hours straight. I don't think I've ever done that. At least not since I was injured."

"Marcum was the same way. I talked to Nancy last night, and he was already passed out by seven."

"Maybe I'm getting older than I realize."

I stop walking and turn to him. My hip bumps against his thigh. Squinting my eyes, I pretend to pluck at his hair. "Come to think of it, I thought I noticed a gray hair."

Smiling, he playfully slaps my hand away.

Switching topics, I ask about Trash. "So, does he know it's us coming today?"

"Yeah, I figured the novelty of a surprise visit would wear off by now. I told him we just needed to ask some questions about the visitor and phone call logs from when Trey was in prison."

We're right by the truck when someone catches our attention, yelling Ry's name. Turning, we see a woman with shoulder-length brown hair, wearing a black department-issue polo and khaki pants. The look on Ry's face doesn't give me much—no smile, no grimace. Nothing.

"Give me a minute?"

Nodding, I slowly walk around to the passenger's side and climb in. Ry opens the driver-side door, leans in, and turns the ignition, cooling the cab from the heat. He shuts the door except it doesn't latch all the way and the noise from his conversation floods though the vehicle despite the fact that he attempts to move out of earshot, near the back door.

"Hey, I'm so sorry to keep you."

I discreetly turn around, trying to get a glimpse of the woman. She's short, only coming up to his chest. Cute. Not gorgeous, but cute. Plain brown hair, not much makeup.

"It's fine. I'm just heading out on an interview. What's up?"

She sighs, nervously. "I can't believe I'm having to say this, but I just got a phone call from the summer camp. Laura broke her glasses."

"Her new glasses?"

"Yes. Not the lenses, just the frames. Apparently, she got hit in the face with a volleyball."

"Is she okay?" The worry in his voice is hard to ignore.

"She's fine. Just the broken glasses. I called the eye doctor, and they have another pair of the exact same frames in stock. But..." the woman stalls, twisting her fingers back and forth in a cat's cradle, "payday isn't until next Friday, and I—"

I watch as Ry reaches across, gently rubbing her arm. "Don't worry about it. You know I'm here for you and Laura. Always. Just tell me how much you need."

She sniffles, wiping away a tear. "I feel so bad. You just bought those glasses two months ago."

"Brooke, she's a kid. Stuff like this is gonna happen. You can't get this upset every time she breaks a pair of glasses or stains her new clothes or accidentally breaks a toy." He takes a step closer to her, bending his face closer to her height. "Now, tell me how much you need."

Bile swirls in my stomach, rising up against the back of my throat. The sour taste consumes my senses. Something deep in my heart tells me this conversation is about more than just charity.

"The frames are $89."

"I don't have cash on me right now. I'm gonna write you a check. Just swing by the bank and cash it before going to the eye doctor's office, okay?"

Opening the door, he leans in, grabbing a checkbook and ink pen from the center console. He doesn't look me in the eyes. He doesn't say anything.

And that makes my heart thunder against my chest. Powerfully. Hard and wild, like a rabid animal is chasing me through the dark night.

"I didn't even ask...do you need me to get her from camp and take her to the doctor? You're on shift, aren't you?"

"It's slow right now. Stinson said I can take the afternoon on sick pay."

"You sure?" He tears the check and hands it over to her.

She nods and turns the check over in her hand. "Crutch, I only need $89. This check is for $200."

"I know," he says, simply. "It's been a while since Laura's come over to my house. You know she loves it there. Let me come get her... I'll pick her up tomorrow morning and she can stay the night. I promise to have her back Sunday evening before bath time. You need a break, some alone time. Use the extra money and go get a manicure or a pedicure or what-the-hell-ever you women like. It's on me."

Brooke stutters over her words. "Are...are you sure?"

"Of course, I'm sure. She's family." He tucks a finger underneath her chin, lifting her eyes to his. "You both are."

The world stops spinning. I stop breathing. Panic doesn't even come close to describing it. Life as I thought I knew it ceases to exist.

I always do what I shouldn't do.

I knew I shouldn't have allowed myself to fall for him again.

Ry—the man I'm in love with—has a child with another women.

Chapter 26

Crutch

"Do you plan on telling me what's wrong? Or do I just have to sit here and keep guessing?"

She shrugs, staring out the passenger-side window. "Nothing's wrong."

"Bullshit, Lulu. You barely said two words during the interview. Something is obviously wrong." I narrow my eyes, thinking. "Did Trash say anything to you? Something inappropriate? When I went to the bathroom?"

Turning to me, she scowls. "You think I don't know how to protect myself from your stupid brother and his come-ons?"

"I didn't say that. I asked if he said something inappropriate."

"No, he's not the inappropriate one."

"What's that supposed to mean? Who's been inappropriate to you? Someone at the station?"

"Nothing. No one." Pulling out her phone, she pretends to answer work emails.

"Lulu, I'm not done talking to you."

Raising her eyebrows, she glowers at me with menace in her eyes. "Do you mind? I'm trying to do some work."

There's no point in trying to talk to her when she's like this. I'll just have to wait until we get parked, and I can force her to look me in the eyes.

Turns out, that's wishful thinking. She jumps out of the truck the second we park. Grabbing her purse and work bag, she flees to her vehicle, tossing the large bag in the back seat and locking the doors. She's already walking down the sidewalk when I race up next to her. "What are you doing? Are you going to the bar?"

"Yes."

I step in front of her, forcing her to stop. I reach out and wrap my fingers around her waist, tugging her closer to me. I choose to ignore her stiffening spine and straight shoulders. "I thought we could talk, grab some dinner. We haven't had any time alone since last Friday night."

"You mean since you kissed me?"

I'm not really liking this look in her eyes. Not one damn bit. Ella's fighting My Lulu, the war clearly visible across her face. "Since I *nearly* kissed you. Because trust me, that was not the kiss I was hoping for. I had so much more in store."

She takes a step back, forcing my hands to fall from her body. Despite the lift to her chin, her voice trembles. It's not noticeable to the untrained person, but I'm well-trained and well-versed in all things Lulu. "It was just a kiss, Ry. Nothing more. There's no point in trying to read between the lines." She sidesteps me. "I think it's best if we just focus on our job—finding out what happened to my sister. You haven't forgotten about Carrie, have you?"

I grab her arm, not allowing her to escape. "What the hell is wrong with you? Are you serious right now?"

Her eyes flare.

Before she can respond with her fire and brimstone, my cell phone rings. I grab it with my free hand, barking into it.

It's Colson. "Hey, Crutch, don't forget about our meeting. Marcum wants to talk with everyone before we go home for the night. Are you back from the interview yet?"

"Yeah. I'll be inside in just a second."

Hanging up, I invade Lulu's personal space, being careful not to hurt her arm or pull too hard. "Now, you plan on telling me what has you so damn fired up?"

"No." Her hot breath tickles my face.

"Well, I suggest you quickly modify your plans, then."

Grunting, she wriggles from my grasp.

I let her go. But it won't be for long. Because I'm never letting her go again.

Turning on my heels, I head into the station.

"So, what did you do this time?" Cullen opens a beer, setting it in front of me.

"What makes you say that?"

He leans against the bar, lifting his eyebrows.

Chuckling, I down half my beer. "Point taken. But hell if I know what I did."

"Well, it must've been something big."

His voice has a tone to it that I don't like. Serious. Worried. "Why? What's happened?" Turning on my barstool, I rake my eyes across the crowd, searching for Lulu.

Will's voice catches me off guard. "She's drinking."

"You mean she's *holding* a Long Island Iced Tea."

"No, I mean, she's *drinking* a Long Island Iced Tea. Swallowing it, drinking it, consuming it."

I slam my hands against the bar. "You're letting her drink?!"

Will throws his hands in the air. "Letting her? Have you met Ella? And by the way, she's a thirty-year-old-woman. I've had Cullen diluting them since the day she first ordered one, just preparing for the time she actually decided to drink."

"How many has she had?"

Cullen serves another customer beside me. "Just one. Well, she was nearly done with it when I last checked on her. She knows we limit customers to two Long Islands, so maybe she won't ask for another one."

I pinch the bridge of my nose. "Why the hell did she pick that drink anyway? It's like a fourteen-year-old trying to get drunk at their aunt's third wedding."

Cullen shakes his head. "She thinks it looks pretty. She likes the glass we use, and she likes the cherry and the orange."

I can't even dignify that with a response. "Where is she?"

Will grimaces, pointing toward the tables in the back. "You're not going to like that, either."

I stand, grabbing my beer. Anger grips my heart in a vise, squashing it like a bug. "What?"

"She's with a guy."

Over. My. Dead. Body.

Weaving through the crowd, I nearly flip my shit when I see Lulu and some random guy sitting at the exact same table we sat at when we talked about my injuries. She doesn't see me at first, but she must sense me. She stops talking and looks around. Spotting me, her plump lips fall into a thin line. She immediately reaches across the table, running her fingernails up and down the length of the guy's arm. Fake laughing, she reaches for her drink, sucking the last of the alcohol from her straw.

I stop right beside their table. "We weren't finished talking."

"I think we were."

The guy looks up, studying me. "Uhh, can I help you, man?"

His hair is spiked with gel, and he's got a gold chain around his neck with a fake diamond cheetah charm on it. What a tool. I ignore him. "Well, we weren't. Let's go in the back."

She turns to the tool bag. "Aaron, this is Ryland, my work colleague. Please forgive him. Apparently, he checked whatever manners he has at the door."

Work colleague? Is she trying to kill me?

Aaron pushes back from the table. I nearly laugh when he stands. He's a squirmy little thing compared to me. I'd be surprised if he were taller than Lulu. "Hey, man. I think she wants you to leave."

"I would keep out of this, if you know what's good for you."

His face turns beet red. "Don't make me—"

I dare you to finish that sentence, asshole.

Lulu wisely interrupts him. "Aaron, why don't you get me another drink. Be sure to tell them it's for Ella. They'll give you a discount."

Grabbing her empty glass, he heads off for the bar.

Pulling his chair back, I sit down across from her. Grabbing my ballcap, I turn it around backward on my head so I can see her better. She's really drinking. I can't believe it. Her cheeks are rosy and her eyes are glassy. Trying to calm myself before I say something I'll regret, I take a few seconds and finish my beer.

She sits back, pouting and folding her arms across her plump chest. "Why do you have to wear baseball hats?"

I lean forward. "You used to love it when I wore baseball hats. You thought they made me look sexy. Is that no longer the case?"

She leans forward. The scent of her alcohol burns my nose. "Nothing is sexy about you."

"You're lying."

"No. I'm not."

"Yes, you are, Lulu." I lick my lips. "Are you telling me if I reach under this table right now and push my fingers inside you, you won't be wet? Dripping? Ready for me?"

Her pupils immediately dilate and her breathing turns shallow. When she sits up, I see her nipples pressing against the thin fabric of her shirt. "I might be wet. But it wasn't you sitting at this table a moment ago, was it?"

Possessive fury courses through my blood. "Why are you trying to piss me off? Why are you sitting here, flirting with a man you just met?"

"What's it to you? We're not together, Ry. We haven't been together in a long time."

"What about last Friday night?"

She reaches into her purse and pulls out a lipstick. "What about it?" She paints her mouth in a pink sheen before tossing it back in her purse.

"You wanted me to kiss you."

"That was all in your head."

"The hell it was. You moaned, Lulu."

"I don't know what you're talking about."

"The hell you do. You moaned. The same moan you gave me the very first time we kissed. The same moan you gave me every single time you wanted me to kiss you. The very same moan I've heard every single night in my dreams for the past twelve years."

"You have a funny way of showing that you missed those so-called moans. Did you ask all those other women to moan like me when sticking your dick inside them?"

I don't even have a chance to answer. The tool is back.

He sets a fresh drink in front of Lulu. And it doesn't go unnoticed by me that he's drinking a beer seltzer. He just reduced himself from *tool* to *pussy*.

"Ry, I appreciate the chitchat. But I'd like to get back to my conversation with Aaron now, please."

Reluctantly, I stand. Before I leave the table, I lean down, rubbing my lips against the shell of her ear. "I've seen you leave this bar with a stranger for the last time. It's not happening again."

Her laugh is demented. "Wanna bet? Game on."

I don't go far. I make sure to stay within view of her at all times. I should be given a medal for keeping my cool, for not breaking the guy's nose. When they move from the table to the dance floor and she stumbles, I growl at Cullen. "I thought you made her drinks weak!"

She's drunk. Not just buzzed, but drunk.

It's easy to see.

Music pumps through the speakers from the satellite radio. She's letting him grind against her and she's not even stiff. She's relaxed. Limp, like a wet noodle.

The bar gets really crowded right as the band for tonight starts warming up. I wave, getting Will's attention. "I'm running to the bathroom, keep an eye on her."

Peeing in record time, I panic when I can't find her. "Where did they go?" Will and Cullen are both buried, taking care of customers. Jumping on the foot hold of the bar, I grab Will's shoulder, shaking him. "Where the hell did she go?"

Will nods at the dance floor. "She's still there."

Scanning the crowd, dread sinks deep in my stomach.

Will looks around my shoulder. "Wait, where'd she go?" His eyes grow wide with fear. "Shit. Where'd she go?"

Pushing through the people, I race to the front door. Relief floods over me when I see the two of them standing outside the bar, tucked against the shadows.

Her voice is higher than normal, showcasing the alcohol coursing through her system. "I told you I'll just follow you to your place. I drive the white sedan. Wait here, I'll pull around."

Huh? She doesn't drive a white sedan. And she would never drive drunk, she knows better than that. *I* taught her better than that.

He steps closer to her. "Just ride with me. I'll bring you back to your car."

"I have an early meeting. I told you I'll just follow you. Give me a few minutes to pull around."

He grabs her arm. "Don't be a tease. Come on." He jerks her behind him.

"Ouch!"

My voice is low but easily carries across the distance, traveling on the wings of my rage. "Take your hands off her."

He slowly turns around. "Mind your own business."

"She *is* my business."

He drops her arm and takes a step in my direction. Not having patience for this idiot, I pull my badge out of my back pocket. The second he sees it, he takes a step backward, lifting his hands in the air.

Turning to Lulu, he hisses through his teeth. "You didn't tell me he was a cop. Are you a cop too?"

I don't give her a chance to respond. "This is a cop bar, douchebag. I suggest you leave. And if I were you, I wouldn't come back. Ever."

Cursing under his breath, he turns and walks down the sidewalk, disappearing around the corner.

She plants her hands on her hips. "Well, what do you have to say for yourself?"

"What the fuck was that, Lulu! Are you kidding me with that guy? You can't tell me you really wanted to leave with him. Why do you keep doing this?"

"Doing what?"

"Sleeping with strange men."

She blows a raspberry like she's a horse. Spit flies all over her chin. "Oh, please. You're so obtuse."

"What is that supposed to mean?"

"I haven't slept with anyone."

I close the distance between us. "What are you talking about?"

She attempts to stand on her tiptoes, trying to see eye to eye with me. After losing her balance, she gives up. "The only dick that's been inside of me in over four years has been purple and needed C batteries."

What? My heart skips a beat. "But you've gone home with all these guys?"

"Not much of a detective, are you? You didn't see me go *home* with men. You saw me leave the bar with men. The last time I saw them was right here," she points at her feet, "on this very sidewalk."

The puzzle pieces slowly fall into place. That's why she told him she would follow him. That's why she told him she drove a white sedan.

She ditches them.

I shake my head. "Why? Why would you let me think you were sleeping with random men?"

"To make you jealous! I want you to feel the way I feel every time I run into one of your whores!"

They weren't all whores. But I definitely don't think now is the time to bring that up. "But why tonight? I thought last Friday night was the start of something for us? A chance to rewrite our story, change our ending."

Tears immediately start pouring from her eyes. Makeup runs down her cheeks in large black streaks. Her fists curl into angry balls.

She hates crying in front of people.

"We can't start over, Ry. Our ending has already been written. You took *our* future and made it *your* future."

She stumbles, and my arm snatches around her waist, steadying her. Hair falls into her eyes, sticking against her tears. I gently push it out of the way. I kiss her cheeks. The salt stings my lips. "What's wrong, Lulu? Talk to me."

"How could you? How could you do this to me?"

She's ripping the air from my lungs. I can't stand to see her like this. It hurts. Physically aches. "What did I do?"

Loaded question, I know.

"I can't believe you have a kid. How could you have a child with another woman?" She pounds her fist against my chest, but I don't even feel it. The pain in my heart takes precedence. "You made a baby. With her. It was supposed to be me." She looks up at me with more love and heartbreak than I ever thought possible. "Didn't you want it to be me?"

Fighting against her own emotions, she eventually lays her head against my shoulder, crying herself into a drunken sleep.

Chapter 27

Ella

O^{w.}

My head hurts. My body hurts. Even my teeth hurt.

I quickly—and painfully—remember why I don't actually drink. From now on, I'll stick with just carrying the drink around with me. Rolling over, I sink into the plush mattress. Sniffing the pillow, Ry's scent fills my nose.

And the scent of lavender.

Lavender sheet spray?

So... I'm at his place.

I can't remember exactly what all happened last night, but I remember enough to know that I'm not proud of my behavior. And I remember enough to know that Ry has a child. Rubbing my breastbone, I try to ease the heartache consuming my hungover body.

Slowly, I open my eyes. The blinds are drawn tight, but the small amount of sunlight that breaks through lets me know it's midday. Once my head stops spinning, I sit up and glance around the room, taking in my surroundings. King-size bed, two nightstands, a dresser, and a plush wingback chair and ottoman. My blouse and skirt from the night before are draped across the back of the chair. Looking down, I rub my hands across the blue *Harlan's* T-shirt covering my body. I don't remember changing clothes last night, so I can only assume Ry changed them for me.

Despite the curdled feeling in my stomach, this room makes me smile. Color is everywhere. Cherry-colored wood furniture with reds, browns, creams, taupes, blues, grays, and golds. It's the complete and total opposite of the room I grew up in—the room I live in now. It does, however, remind me of my own bedroom at my house on the coast. The room I specifically decorated to carry no resemblance to the room—and the wing of the house—that my mother made for me.

Something on the nightstand catches my attention. Rolling over, I see a plate with two pieces of dry toast, a large sports drink, and a bottle of over-the-counter pain relievers. I pick up a torn piece of paper, eagerly reading his words.

Take 3 pills. Eat both pieces of toast.
Drink the whole bottle.
Shower. A fresh toothbrush and towel
are on the counter. (Hangover stink is the worst.)
Whatever you do, don't go back
to sleep after you wake up.
Come find me.

Taking his advice, I slowly climb out of bed when finished eating. Running my hands across my clothes from yesterday, I find them damp. Well, that can't be a good sign.

Peeking through the blinds, I'm rendered speechless. Completely and totally speechless. Clambering for the string, I yank the blind open, pulling so hard, the faux wood slaps against the window frame.

The pond.

His pond.

Our pond.

There's no mistaking it. Some of the trees have been cut, showcasing a bright green, manicured lawn. The small wooden dock has been rebuilt; it's longer, stronger, sturdier. The concrete pad is still there, but the furniture surrounding the fancy firepit all matches now. No mismatched pieces of junk. Despite all the changes, there's no question in my mind.

I'm at the homestead.

I can't believe I never asked him where he lives. We've worked side by side all these months, and I never asked him where he lives. It never even occurred to me that he would live here. In a house. In what feels like a very big house, as a matter of fact. I just filed the homestead away in a closed and locked cabinet. A figment of my past, a figment of the happy time before Ry left me. Before his reality pulled him away.

I stare out the window for so long, my eyes actually start to water from the bright sun. With a shaky hand, I close the blind and head into the bathroom. I can't help but laugh when I flip on the light. Ry always said that one day he would have the largest shower known to mankind, and I think his goal has been achieved. The bathroom is massive for just one person, and I realize that I'm naïve to think no one has ever lived here with him before. He has a child. There's a very good possibility he and his ex-girlfriend shared this bathroom at some point.

A new green toothbrush and a plush gray towel sit in the middle of the double vanity. The marbled counter is a swirl of grays, browns, creams, and blues. The gray and cream tiled shower looks like it belongs in my parents' mansion and not here, in the very place where I slept in a tent and brushed my teeth with water from gallon jugs.

I take my time showering, using his soap, shampoo, and conditioner. His scent overwhelms me. It fills the empty cavern of my soul. Pretending I don't know what I know, I sit on the shower bench and let my fingers roam over my body. Touching myself, I dream of Ry... the Ry I used to know, the Ry I know now.

Well, the one I knew before yesterday afternoon. Before I found out he's a father.

The moment I set foot outside this room, my life will change forever. He'll tell me about having a child. He'll tell me about how he met the girl's mother. How he made love to her, how he watched her give birth, how he promised her they would always be a family.

Knowing all of this, I do the only thing I can think of doing. Removing the shower head from its perch, I let the water pour over my engorged clit. My eyes squint closed so hard, they hurt. Imagining his body sliding in and out of mine, his baby growing inside of me, I come all over his expensive shower tile.

And I don't even bother to rinse my juices down the drain.

When I leave, I want to leave a part of me behind.

As soon as I'm clean, I slip back into my bra and panties and T-shirt. My clothes are still damp, so I unabashedly pilfer through his dresser. The second drawer I open holds his underwear. I tug a pair of black boxer briefs over my panties. Quickly making his bed, I grab my dress clothes and tiptoe out of the bedroom. I'm on the second floor of the home so I would assume Ry is downstairs or outside.

Turns out, the upstairs has four bedrooms—the master and three others. One bedroom is basically empty. One bedroom has a modest double-size bed and a dresser; a guest room, I'm guessing. The other bedroom is fit for a little princess. Decorated in pink and white and silver, there's a canopy queen-size bed, a bookshelf filled with dozens of books, and a dollhouse filled with miniature furniture and a miniature little family.

I check my pulse, making sure I'm still alive because seeing this almost stops my heart.

Walking down the steps, an uneasy feeling pools low in my stomach, like I'm forgetting something. Like something not's quite right. Anxiety gnaws at my brain, even worse than the hangover headache. Like a zombie, I walk from room to room. Open floorplan. Living room. Half bath. Ry's office. A large rec room with a connected full bathroom. Laundry room. Mud room. And a huge kitchen with oversized appliances and an island running nearly the entire length.

He built our house.

Ry built our house.

The one I designed all those years ago.

Tossing my clothes on the kitchen table, I stumble to the five-gallon water jug in the corner and fill up a glass of water. I down two glasses before the thick cotton strangling my throat starts to dissolve.

Why didn't he say anything?

Why didn't I ask?

The hardwood floors creak underneath my bare feet. The heavy wooden front door stands wide open, and a glass storm door is my only protection from what waits for me on the outside. Hanging on the wall, framed and preserved, are my sketches of the house. I don't even remember him taking those. I also can't believe he saved them.

I drag my fingers through my damp hair, pushing the waves from my face. I don't even know if I have the strength to take a step out onto the front porch. All I want to do is collapse. Go back in time—twelve years, to be exact—and live the life I was meant to live. Here, with him.

But then I remember who I am. Holding my head high, I open the door.

The slats of the front porch are polished smooth and painted white. Right next to the door is a pair of black rubber rain boots. Slipping my feet into them, they slap loudly against the floor and knock back and forth against my shins as I walk.

They obviously belong to Ry; they're huge.

Holding onto the rail so I don't face plant, I clamber down the stairs and race into the yard. Turning around, I shield my eyes against the glare of the sun and take a good long look at *my* house.

White siding. Green shutters. Stone veneer. Wraparound porch. Rocking chairs. Porch swing. Huge dining table. The connected garage is to the left. Farther to the left is a separate building. It looks like another garage. Workshop, maybe? I stare at the house until my body aches from being in the same position. When I finally turn back toward the pond, I see Ry standing there, watching me.

He's on the dock. And he's not alone. Patting the little girl on the shoulder, he says something to her. She nods, but is otherwise completely engrossed in casting her rod and reel.

In a foggy haze, I somehow find enough coordination to put one foot in front of the other. We meet mid-way, on the concrete patio, next to the firepit. The place we always talked, the place we watched documentary after documentary on my computer, the hub of our homestead for all those wonderful months.

And if my brain fog wasn't thick enough between the lingering effects of the Long Island Iced Teas and the knowledge that my former lover built me a house, Ry adds more confusion to the pot by not wearing a shirt. Sweat glistens on every single inch of his deliciously sculpted body. His cargo shorts hang low at the waist. My mouth waters involuntarily when his hands land on his hips, showcasing the firm cut of his pelvic muscles and the band of his boxer briefs that match the ones I'm wearing. His tennis shoes are covered in mud from the edge of the pond. A baseball cap shades his face from view.

"Damn, Lulu. I expected many things from you today, but seeing you in my clothes was not one of them." I look down at the boxer briefs I'm wearing like shorts and the rain boots. He chuckles, low and heady. "You're fucking torturing me." Unashamed, he grabs his crotch and quickly adjusts the growing erection in his shorts.

I try not to blush. Really, I do. But it's hard not to when I know exactly what those cargo shorts are hiding. I quickly reach behind my neck and rub my scar. "You're the one without a shirt on."

He lifts the ballcap from his head and turns it around, giving me a chance to study his face. When his arms raise, my fingers twitch to touch the contours of his ribs.

He licks his lips. "Maybe a part of me wanted to play our game. What would you think of that?"

I toss a hand at the house. "Is that what this was, Ry? A game?"

His jaw clenches. "You have to be more specific. Are you talking about the house itself? Or the fact that I brought you here? Because it should be pretty self-explanatory why I brought you here. You were drunk off your ass and getting yourself into trouble by pretending to go home with a strange man."

I lower my head in shame. Then, I remember who I am and why I'm mad and hold my head high once again. "I apologize for the trouble I put you through. Thank you for your hospitality, but I should give you some alone time with your daughter. I don't want to intrude. I'll call Holt or Raylee for a ride. I saw my purse and cell phone in the kitchen."

I turn around but don't make it far before his arm grabs my waist, spinning me around and pinning me to his side. The movement makes my head swim, and a quick fire of nausea flames in my stomach. Ughh. Hangover.

"There's someone I want you to meet." He lifts his hand in the air and whistles, drawing the little's girl's attention. He yells to her, "Laura, come here!"

I push against his sweaty and massive frame. The salty smell of his body makes it hard to think. "Ry, I don't think this is the best time to—"

He interrupts me, completely ignoring my protest. "I've told her a million times that she needs to wait until dusk to go fishing, but she insists that the fish want lunch, just like people."

I've never seen him look at someone with such innocent and pure love. Not me. Not anyone. And it breaks my heart into a million pieces, imagining what could have been.

She skips up to us in a bundle of energy. Her brown hair is in a ponytail and she's wearing a purple shirt with small white flowers on it. She's pretty. She doesn't really look like Ry, but she's pretty. And that's when I see it. Her head turns up and she pushes the small pair of glasses up on her nose.

Her eyes. The same translucent green as Ry's. The exact same. And just as gorgeous.

"Laura, this is Lulu."

Her little hand sticks up in my face, waiting on an introduction. "Hello, my name is Laura Margaret Crutchfield. Pleasure to meet you, ma'am."

He has a child. He made a baby. With someone else. And he gave that child *my* middle name.

What the hell is this guy doing to me?

I stand there, frozen like a statue, unable to flap one single syllable out of my stupid mouth.

Finally, she grunts. "Are you okay?" She flips her hand over and looks at it. "It's just a little dirt. Uncle Ry says that a confident, mature woman always introduces herself with a firm handshake."

Swallowing past the lump in my throat, I shake my head and quickly wrap my hand around hers. "I'm sorry, sweetie, I just—"

Wait. What did she just say?

"Wait. What did you just say?"

Ry's hand snakes around my back. His fingers massage against my hip. Bending, he brushes his lips against my cheek. "Lulu, I'd like you to meet Laura. My niece."

Chapter 28

Ella

Niece. Niece. Niece.

I keep repeating the word in my head.

He leans across the chair, rubbing his hand across my thigh. "Can you talk now? Or are you still in shock?" He nods at Laura as she swings from a tire swing hanging underneath one of the trees. She's holding a baby doll in her hand and mumbling under her breath, her imagination fueling a conversation between the two of them. "Because I can tell you from experience, we only have about fifteen more minutes before she gets tired of swinging with the baby and wants to do something different."

"I thought she was your daughter."

Sitting back in his chair, he rubs his fingers across his stubble. "I gathered as much from our conversation last night. I assume you heard what I said to Brooke yesterday? I really wish you would've just talked to me when I kept asking what was wrong." He cocks his head to the side. "Why didn't you?"

I start to shrug and say I don't know, but I decide against it, however wise or unwise that decision may be. "Because I was scared."

"Scared of what?"

"Scared of the answer. Of what you'd admit to me."

"What if she were my child? We've been apart for twelve years. We lived our lives. You were married to someone else. What was so upsetting about the thought that I may be a father?" He narrows his eyes when I don't immediately answer. "And so help me, Lulu, if you lie, I'm gonna flip my shit."

"Because that was literally the very thing that I wanted. I wanted to marry you, have a life with you." I look at the beautiful house behind us. "Fill our home with babies. For so long, that's what I wanted."

He stares at me, swallowing hard. I watch as a small bead of sweat rolls down his temple. "And now? What do you want now?"

I watch Laura swing back and forth. She's singing. "I've done some amazing things with my life. So many things I'm proud of. My education, my career." Sensing my stare, Laura looks up and waves. "So many things didn't turn out the way I thought they would, though. When you met me, my life was black and white. And filled with sadness. Grief over Carrie, anger at my parents. And then, you made me see color... all of these bright and wonderful and sparkling colors. I dreamed of a life together. With you. After you left, I told myself it was just the foolish wishes of a young girl's first love. I learned to live with that. Embrace it. Make it fact." I stare into his eyes. "But then I see something like that." I nod at the house. "And it makes me question everything I thought I knew. Question everything that could have been."

He follows my eyes, appreciating the homestead before him. "The hydrangeas will look better next year. I just planted them this spring. I had decided to do green shrubbery instead," he smiles, "but then you came home, decided to stay for a while. Back then, you told me you wanted hydrangeas in the front flowerbeds. That's what you said, anyway, so I tossed the green shrubbery idea out the window."

I cough, trying to dislodge the words from my dry and scratchy throat. "You saved my sketches."

"Of course, I did."

I nod, biting my lip.

"Go ahead and ask me. I know you want to."

"What?"

"Don't beat around the bush, Lulu. I like you when you get to the point."

My words stutter. "Did… did you build this house for me?"

"Of course, I did."

My heart drums against my ribcage, stealing the breath from my lungs. "But that's crazy. How could you know I would be here to see it one day?"

He leans forward. "I've never been without you. You've always been here with me. Every single second of every single day. All I had to do was close my eyes and I could see you." His thumb grazes the side of my leg. "I'm selfish. I kept you. I never let you go."

I don't have an opportunity to digest those words and formulate a response because Laura jumps down from the swing and races over to us. "Uncle Ry! Let's show Miss Lulu our special place. Pleeee-aassse!"

Ry grins as the little girl crawls onto his lap. "Little Girl, it's a hundred degrees out here. Why do you have to crawl on me like a monkey?"

Laughing, she squeals like a monkey and scratches her armpits.

"Fine, little monkey. We can show her." She jumps off his lap and starts to run across the yard. "But not until that fishing stuff is put back where it belongs."

Turning on her heels, she dramatically moans with attitude.

"Laura," Ry scolds.

Her behavior quickly changes. "Yes, sir." She holds out her baby doll to me. "Will you hold her, please? I have to get my stuff."

"Sure." I squeeze the toy in my arms.

Ry laughs. "Be right back." He calls over his shoulder, "Baby's name is Felicia Stinkbottoms, by the way."

Well, that's a suspicious name.

After a second, Ry and Laura return from the pond. She's carrying her pink rod and reel and Ry's carrying his rod and reel and the tackle box. I fall in step with them.

"Miss Lulu?"

"Yes, sweetie?"

"Why are you wearing Uncle Ry's panties?"

My mouth falls open, and Ry bursts out laughing. I don't think I've ever heard him laugh so hard in my life. Despite my embarrassment, I giggle.

He pats her on the head. "I've told you before. Guys don't call their underwear *panties*. It's just underwear. Got it?"

She nods. "So why are you wearing Uncle Ry's underwear?"

"Well, I wasn't feeling too good last night. I drank some bad medicine. He let me stay here, but all I had was my fancy work clothes. He didn't know I was gonna wear his underwear. I took them out of his drawer without asking." I wink at Ry. "I hope he's not mad."

She shakes her head. "Oh no, that won't make him mad. He doesn't really get mad as long as you use your manners and do your chores and don't talk back."

Smirking, Ry plucks the pink fishing pole from her shoulder. "Miss Lulu has a master's degree in talking back."

Laura giggles. "You mean the college degree? That's funny."

"Haha. Your uncle is stretching the truth, Laura."

She reaches up, grabbing Felicia Stinkbottoms from my hands. "Yeah, he does that sometimes."

Ry narrows his eyes. "Snitch. Make yourself useful and go open the door."

Skipping ahead, she pulls open the large side door of the huge outbuilding. It takes a few seconds for my eyes to adjust, but when they do, I nearly collapse in delight.

"Your truck! I mean, your grandfather's truck! You still have it?"

"Hell yeah. That thing will probably run forever."

I trace my fingers down the side and circle around to the tailgate. Vivid memories flash alive, pouring intense heat throughout my body. Ry sneaks behind me. Grabbing my waist, he tugs my ass against him as he whispers in my ear. "A lot of good times were had in the bed of that truck. I can still hear you screaming, feel you writhing with every lick of my tongue." His cock jumps with every syllable he speaks.

Laura peeks around the corner, catching us. She smiles widely. "Come on, I'll show you where Uncle Ry used to live."

My T-shirt clings to my chest and my hair sticks to my neck. And I don't think the summer heat has anything to do with it.

Untangling from his arms, I follow Laura, flopping my way through the garage workshop in the huge rain boots. The front of the garage holds the truck, some kind of all-terrain utility vehicle, a small tractor, and a riding lawnmower. Tools and yard equipment line the walls. At the back of the garage, there's a door. Laura steps through it and turns on the light.

There's a kitchenette, a small dining table, a couch, a twin-size bed, a dresser, and a TV. I lean inside another door, catching a glimpse of the shower, sink, and toilet.

In true Ry fashion, it's neat as a pin.

"Uncle Ry lets me watch cartoons in here if he's having to work in the garage and it's too cold for me to play outside. I'm not allowed to have a TV in my big room at the house until I'm a teenager, and Uncle Ry doesn't wanna be with me all the time because I'm moody and mean and want to kiss boys. Then, he says, I can hide in my room and watch TV."

He chuckles. Bending down, he tickles her side. "Little Girl, you make me sound like a mean, old ogre."

She races away, jumping on the couch and tossing her doll in the air.

"You lived here?" I ask.

"Yeah. It's the Taj Mahal compared to my room at Harlan's." He nods for me to follow him. "Laura, we're gonna fill up the side-by-side with gas. Be sure to use the bathroom before we leave."

I watch Ry as he piddles around the garage, getting the all-terrain vehicle ready for me to see whatever Laura wants me to see. "You built this place first? Before the house?"

"Remember I mentioned that Harlan bought the land all those years ago? So Harlan left the land to me when he died. I tried to give it back to his son. Told him I would find a way to buy it from him, but he refused to go against Harlan's wishes. After my injury, I stayed with Marcum and Nancy for about six months while my discharge and VA disability pay was getting sorted out. After that, I rented a small apartment. I sold ten acres, then used that money to start building this garage. It took a year for me to finish because I saved money and paid cash as I went. I moved into the garage here and started saving the rest of the money to build the house. It took three years to save and get all the workers and materials cost lined up. Found a bank willing to do a construction loan for me. It took eighteen months for me to finish the house. Fortunately, a lot of the cops and firefighters around here do construction jobs on the side, so I had a lot of help. This fall will be three years that I've been in the house. There's still a ton of work that I wanna do, though."

He places the gas can back on a shelf. Turning to me, he leans against a cabinet. The muscles in his forearms flex, calling to me, singing sweetly. "I hope it meets the high standards of the architect," he says with a wink.

"Definitely. It's amazing."

"You checked it out before coming outside?"

"I just did a quick walk-through. Saw Laura's room."

He lifts his eyebrows. "Never thought I would paint a room pink. The color was called *Baby's Breath Blush*. Can you imagine? But that's the color she wanted. She was three, at the time."

"How old is she now?"

"Six."

"Close to Anna's age." Raylee's daughter will turn six at the end of July. "Does Laura stay here with you often?"

He shrugs. "Not as much as I would like. Sometimes the job makes it hard for me to plan in advance, make arrangements with Brooke for Laura to come here. But Brooke's a good mom. She's attentive and loving. I just really want Laura to have a positive male influence in her life. That's why it's important for us to spend time together. She's an amazing kid."

"I can't believe Trash didn't even mention her to me," I say. "We've talked about everything under the sun over the past few months during those interviews. I can't believe he didn't say anything about being a father."

"That's because he's not. Not legally, anyway." Ry's jaw tightens and his mood shifts. He hates talking about his brother. "Brooke made the horrible mistake of tagging along with a friend to a party that someone had for Trash when he was released from prison. She was young, stupid, vulnerable. Looking for something forbidden. Her family life was crap. She started hooking up with Trash. Wasn't long before she wound up pregnant. That's when she realized things had to change. She showed up at the station one day, doctor's report in hand, terrified and scared. I rented her a small, one-bedroom loft. Helped her get a janitor job at the station. I told Trash if he signed over all of his parental rights, then Brooke wouldn't come after him for child support. He couldn't get his hands on an ink pen damn quick enough."

I knew Trash was an asshole, but this is a whole new level of being a dick. "I can't believe he gave up his child, just like that. Does he ever see her?"

"Of course not. And I won't let him. Brooke won't either. Not that it matters, he hasn't even tried to contact her. He wasn't at the hospital when she was born. Just me. He doesn't take her to dentist appointments, doesn't go to school functions. Just me." He looks back at the open door where Laura plays contently on the couch. "It's my job to fill that void. I never want her to feel inadequate because her father isn't in the picture. I refuse to have her grow up in a situation like I had with my parents."

"How did Brooke care for a baby all on her own?"

Shaking his head, he clears his thoughts. "I helped Brooke get some public assistance for daycare after Laura was born. The university actually has a childcare center, and they offer scholarships to needy individuals. It's open for the whole community, and not just enrolled students. Laura went there until she could attend Pre-K at public school. And I help out any way I can. Anything they need, I'm there for them. But Brooke's doing okay financially. When Laura was a year old, Brooke got a new job as a dispatcher. It came with a good raise. She's a super hard worker and is next in line for a new promotion at work."

"And the glasses?"

He chuckles. "Well, glasses are expensive. Even though Brooke is doing good, flying volleyball hazards aren't really in her budget."

He walks over to me. I'm too absorbed in his story to move. Too engrossed in the movement of his predatory body. Taking my face in both hands, he caresses my jaw line, tracing his fingers down my neck, grazing my collarbone. "I'd better go get her. I highly doubt she has used the bathroom like I told her to do. Like someone I know, she has a mind of her own and can be a little defiant," he teases with a wink. "I'll grab us some waters too."

My throat constricts. Lust boils in the pit of my stomach and tender affection circles my heart. I can't let him walk away without telling him this. "Ry, you're a good man. Laura's lucky to have you."

He smiles softly. "I'm the lucky one. She's like a daughter to me."

He turns and walks away.

A torrent of emotion is running though me. Equal parts love and hate at the same time. But how can I hate him? Look at what he's doing for his niece, for this innocent child? All Brooke did was *show up*. She showed up and he did all these wonderful things for her and Laura. What if I had been given the chance to *show up*?

That's all I needed—the chance.

But Ry didn't give me that.

He took away my chance when he left me.

Chapter 29

Crutch

"Uncle Ry, when can we have pizza?"

"Are you starting to get hungry?"

Laura looks down at her stomach and pokes her belly button through her shirt. "I'm starving."

I look over at Lulu. She lifts her eyebrows. "I'm starting to get pretty hungry too."

"So, the effects of the Long Island Iced Teas have finally worn off?"

"I like sweet tea," Laura chimes in.

Lulu laughs, rubbing Laura's shoulder. "Oh sweetie, you wouldn't have liked this tea."

Getting up from the dining table on the front porch, I rake all of the *Go Fish* cards in a pile. "Alright, but we have to go get it. You know no one delivers out this far. Go inside and grab your shoes."

"Can't me and Miss Lulu stay here?"

I glance back and forth between Laura and Lulu. I hate to put Lulu on the spot. "Oh. Well, I—"

Lulu interrupts, quickly putting herself on the spot. "I think that's a good idea. I mean, if you don't mind, Ry? We'll clean up the games and set the table."

Laura folds her little hands together. "I can do that! I set the table every night for me and my mom."

Lulu smiles brightly. "See? My job's already gotten easier."

It's good to see Lulu smile again, to hear her laugh. I'm not sure where she went mentally when Laura and I drove her out to the creek, but she went somewhere deep and isolated. She always loved the creek, and now, it's Laura's favorite spot too.

After I moved back to the homestead, I cleared out a wide path, running all the way from the big garage to the creek. I was surprised to find that the wildflowers had quadrupled in number. They come back each year, blooming from spring to fall. Every single color under the sun. Thousands upon thousands.

Lulu smiled politely at Laura's endless chatter and quietly giggled at Laura's jokes, but when Laura and I took off our shoes to wade and splash in the creek, Lulu walked away. Leaving us, she hid beneath the shade of a large tree. She sat and sat and sat. At one point, I thought I heard her crying. Normally, I would've raced to her side to see what was wrong, but the moment seemed too intimate, too personal. Instead, I gave her some space. Eventually, she walked back out into the sunshine, joining me and Laura at our game of skipping rocks.

The creek was always Lulu's favorite spot. We watched the sun set there. We made love there. We read books and talked about our hopes and dreams. It was our secret spot. Maybe being here... there's just too many memories.

Laura tugs on my shorts, drawing my attention. "And cheese bread too, please."

"I guess I can make that happen." Kissing the top of her head, I grab my T-shirt and pull it on. I nudge Lulu with my shoulder, rubbing my body against hers. "Any special requests from you?"

Biting her lip, she playfully winks. "Surprise me."

By the time I get back from town, the girls have cleaned up the porch, set the inside kitchen table, and baked some brownies with some mix they found in the cabinet—I forgot it was even in there. Chitchatting over dinner, we stuff ourselves silly.

Pushing my chair underneath the table, I tug on Laura's hair. "It's bath time, Little Girl."

"Woo-hoo!" She watches as Lulu loads the dirty plates in the dishwasher. "My bathtub here is huge, much bigger than my bathtub at our apartment. I love the water. Uncle Ry said, maybe, one day, he'll build a swimming pool for me."

"I love swimming too," Lulu says. "The house I live in has a pool. Maybe Ry can bring you swimming one day."

Laura jumps in the air, clapping her hands. "Yes!"

"I have a little cousin, Anna, who turns six at the end of next month. Maybe the two of you can have a swimming playdate."

Laura spins around in excitement. "Can we, Uncle Ry? Can we have a playdate and swim?"

Lulu just made my niece's day. "Sure. But right now, you need to swim in that tub. You're damn filthy."

"Ry!" Lulu scolds me for my choice of words.

Laura grabs my hand. "It's okay, Miss Lulu. Uncle Ry cusses all the time. I'm used to it."

I furrow my brow, faking insult. "Not *all* the time. It's just hard to stop my habits just because little ears are around to hear."

Lulu laughs. Laura and I start up the stairs when her voice stops us in our tracks. "I'll go ahead and call Holt for a ride; it's getting late."

I don't have time to argue. Laura does it for me. "What! It just got dark outside. Uncle Ry always lets me watch a movie after bath. Don't you wanna watch a movie with us? I'll even let you pick."

Lulu reaches behind her neck, rubbing her scar.

"Stay." My plea is calm. Controlled. "Stay the night. I'll take you home when I take Laura home tomorrow. Holt already took your car back to your place. You don't have to worry about that."

She takes a deep breath, thinking. "I have to be in Jackson for that medical malpractice suit by lunch on Monday. I was gonna leave tomorrow afternoon, but I guess I can just get an early start on Monday."

A small weight lifts from my chest, and I realize the thought of her leaving nearly choked the life from my heart. "Good. It's settled."

After filling Laura's bath water, I leave her to play with her bath toys. I'm about to head back downstairs when I hear the shower turn on in my bathroom. Walking through the bedroom, I see that Lulu made the bed from this morning. Leaning my ear against the closed bathroom door, I hear the water displace the second she steps into the shower.

Lulu's naked. In my house. In my shower.

The thought alone makes my dick painfully jump to life. I think back to last night when I was undressing her. I wouldn't have undressed her. Really, I wouldn't have. But... she kind of threw up on herself when I was driving her home—to her place. That quickly changed my mind and had me driving the country roads to my house instead of the city roads to hers.

She was so upset at the thought of me having a child that she drank herself into a sick stupor. I knew it was time to show her more of my life, show her my house. *Our house.* Show her what I built for us, not knowing if I would ever get the opportunity to have her in my life again. Show her that I was an uncle. Not a father.

When I saw her in her bra and panties last night, I nearly lost my shit. Nearly came in my pants like some young teenager watching porno for the first time.

And my first impression in the police station was right. Her breasts have grown over the years. She's at least one full cup size bigger. The combination of her soft curves and long, lean legs was nearly too much. And although I'm a dick, I'm not *that* kind of dick. So, I quickly covered her gorgeous body in my T-shirt, put her clothes in the washer, and slept downstairs on the couch. I couldn't even trust myself to sleep in the guest room upstairs. But I did check on her multiple times throughout the night. And each time, the sight of her body curled in my bed, nestled among the sheets and blankets, cut its way into my dead heart, making it beat and thunder with vibrant new life.

I love her. I love her so damn much it hurts.

I stand there for so long that it scares me when I hear the shower cut off. Jumping, I quickly walk from the room. I'm halfway down the stairs when Laura yells for me. "Uncle Ry! You help me wash my hair?"

After I clean up the bathroom and Laura dresses in her unicorn nightgown, we race downstairs. Lulu's sitting on the couch, typing on her phone. Her towel-dried hair is a mass of wavy curls. She's wearing a fresh T-shirt and a fresh pair of my boxer briefs. She's the most beautiful thing I've ever seen. The most beautiful thing I will *ever* see. Laura plops down on the couch next to her, turning on the TV, and flicking through the movies available for streaming.

"Sorry." Lulu leans forward, putting her phone on the coffee table. "Raylee had texted me." When she sits back, the T-shirt tugs against her body and her peaked nipples make me weak in the knees. She's no longer wearing a bra.

I clear my throat, "Laura, go into the mud room, look on the shelf. I put a surprise there when I came home." Jumping up, she races from the room.

Lulu stares at me. Her caramel-coated eyes trail down my body, widening in surprise when they get to my crotch. She swallows. Hard.

"No bra, Lulu? Seriously? You're wearing my shirt. My underwear. And now, you're not wearing a bra." My hand grabs my crotch, adjusting my dick. "Are you trying to kill me?"

Wickedly smiling, she winks. "Game on."

"Sour gummy worms!" Laura bounces back into the room. Pouncing on the couch, she holds the bag in front of Lulu's face. "Do you like gummy worms too, Miss Lulu?"

"I sure do."

"Will you open the bag, please?"

Lulu opens the bag and gives Laura first pick. Then she picks a blue and green one for herself, slides it deep into her mouth, and slowly pulls it from her lips, licking the sugar from it.

Fuck me.

"Miss Lulu, what movie do you wanna watch?"

"You pick."

"I have the perfect one." Laura starts the movie and reaches for another piece of candy. "Uncle Ry? Aren't you gonna sit down?"

"Y'all start without me. I need a quick shower." I walk up the stairs, mumbling under my breath. "A cold shower."

Lulu's giggle follows me up the stairs and into the bathroom. It plays on repeat in my ears... the whole time I jack off in the shower.

Once showered and relieved to where I can somewhat function like a normal human being, I head back downstairs to my girls.

Lulu and Laura are snuggled into a pile of arms and legs beneath a large blanket, watching a musical about a princess. Great. She just had to pick a princess movie. I like it much better when Little Girl chooses *Star Wars* or *Indiana Jones* movies. The second I sit next to her she offers me some of the blanket. My niece really is the sweetest little girl.

I wrap my arm around the back of the couch, using it as an excuse to trace my thumb across Lulu's shoulder. The air thickens, sending tangible energy from her body to mine. It's completely unexpected when Laura grabs my hand and Lulu's hand, joining them together across her lap. Gently she wraps her little fingers around ours, so that all three of us are holding hands.

Like I said, she really is the sweetest little girl.

I watch Lulu as she studies our intertwined fingers. Slowly lifting her head, she smiles at me. Softly. Sweetly. Her smile is like the first ray of sunshine after a week of storm clouds.

By the end of the movie, Laura's yawning so much I'm afraid she's going to dislocate her jaw. I flip off the TV. "Come on, Little Girl, time for bed."

"Can Miss Lulu tuck me in too?"

I shrug, tipping my chin at Lulu.

"Sure, I'd love to." When she stands from the couch, the boxer briefs she's wearing tangle against her thighs and the round globe of her ass cheek hangs out. She quickly covers herself.

Kill me now.

A few months ago, she told me she couldn't even stand to be in the same zip code with me, and now, here she is, wearing my clothes, sleeping in my bed, playing with the child I consider to be my own little girl.

"You girls go turn the bed down. I'll get your glass of water. And don't forget to brush your teeth, Laura. I'm going to smell your breath."

Laura grabs Lulu's hand and tugs her up the stairs. When I join them, Lulu's reading a children's book to Laura—I don't point out the fact that my niece is smart as a whip and outgrew that book two years ago. I stand in the doorway, watching them. An unfamiliar feeling cascades through my body. I don't know how to describe it. It's... weird. Odd. For the first time in my life, I feel like a grown man. A patriarch. A provider.

It's literally the best feeling in the world.

Well, next to my memories of being inside of Lulu.

When they finish, I put the glass of water on Laura's nightstand and bend down next to her face. "Let me smell."

Giggling, she blows in my face. "See? Minty fresh."

I make a fake gagging sound and pretend to pass out. "Alright, get some sleep, Little Girl. You've been a thorn in my side all day. Time to give me some peace and quiet."

Ignoring my teasing, she wraps her arms around me and gives me a kiss. "No adult book tonight?" She frowns. "That's just plain wrong."

"Not tonight. It's late."

I pause, waiting for Lulu and Laura to hug goodnight before I turn out the light. Instead of pulling away, Laura plants both hands on Lulu's face, pressing so hard, she smashes Lulu's lips together into a pucker. Her little eyes grow wide and she whispers into Lulu's face, "Tell me something. Something no one else knows."

Oh my god.

Instantly, all the air is sucked from the room. The three of us are left in a void. In a vacuum. In a shell.

Laura, in her innocence, doesn't know anything is wrong. Folding her hands in her lap, she patiently waits for Lulu's answer.

I can't believe this is happening to me.

I have no idea how My Lulu is going to react. And that scares the shit out of me.

I've just started getting her back. I can't lose her again.

I won't lose her again. I refuse to.

I'm about to scold Laura for playing our secret game when Lulu makes a noise.

She clears her throat and quickly wipes her eye before a tear spills from the corner. "Well, let's see. It's been a very long time since anyone has asked me that question."

"Who asked you last? Uncle Ry?"

She nods, tossing me a glance. "Yes. It was him."

"But you haven't seen each other in a really long time, right? So, there must be lots of things that no one else knows."

Lulu nods, sniffling and clearing her throat again. "Well, I learned something new today."

Learning is an immediate trigger word for Laura. Her eyes widen again, and she grows very serious. "You did? What did you learn?"

"I learned that you must be very special to Ry."

"Why am I special?"

"Because of the creek. For a very long time, only two people knew about the creek. Me and him. He showed it to me. A long time ago, when we were much younger, it was our secret place. And now, it's your secret place too. That makes you very special."

Laura nods eagerly. "And I learned that you're special too, Miss Lulu."

Lulu mimics Laura. "Why am I special?"

"Because you call Uncle Ry '*Ry*'. He told me that the only people who are allowed to call him '*Ry*' are the girls he loves. He said that was me and someone else. He never told me who, but now I know. It's you. He loves you."

I can't breathe. I turn away, hiding my emotion from the two girls on the bed. Raking my hand across my face, I take a second to compose myself before turning back. "Time for bed. Goodnight."

Laura flops backward, hugging Felicia Stinkbottoms to her side. I wait for Lulu to leave the room, before I turn out the light.

"Night-night, Uncle Ry. I love you."

"I love you too."

Pulling her door closed, I watch as Lulu silently walks down the hallway and turns into my bedroom. I follow behind her like a dog on a leash. I shut the door and stare at her.

She's so damn beautiful.

Her face is free of makeup, innocent and fresh. Her breasts tug against the fabric of my T-shirt. Her fingers twist the hem in worried thought.

"When did you start doing that with her? Asking her that question?"

"The first time she stayed the night here at the house. It was so big compared to her apartment. She kept hearing noises and couldn't go to sleep."

She nods, not saying anything.

The anticipation is killing me.

"Are you angry with me?"

She snorts. "Isn't part of me always angry with you?"

Good point. "Let me rephrase, are you angry with me for sharing that game with Laura?"

Her hand circles around her neck. "Of course not. I think Carrie would be happy to see someone carrying on the tradition."

I take a step in her direction. And then another. And then another. My growl is harsher than I intend for it to be, but I can't help it. I'm on edge. "Tell me something. Something no one else knows."

Her chest swells, her nipples immediately bud, and she discreetly rubs her thighs together. Because she's My Lulu, she tilts her chin in the air, staring straight at me. "I've been fighting my feelings, pushing you away. Letting my anger control me. For twelve long years, I've been drowning in my silent rage. I can't keep doing it. I wanna let go. I want happiness. I want your mouth on mine. Now."

Sweeter words have never been spoken.

I cross the distance between us and take her in my arms. I don't even give her the chance to moan before my tongue slides into her hot mouth.

Holy. Shit.

My memories of her don't do her justice. Kissing her is the pinnacle of erotic desire. She gives it back, she takes it from me, she makes me into her own. Our tongues tangle. Tasting, remembering.

She's making a new heart in the dead hollow of my chest.

Just like the very first time I kissed her, life as I know it ceases to exist.

My right hand tangles in her soft, honey-colored waves, and my left hand traces the beads of her spine, running lower and lower until I find that sweet curve where her back meets her ass. Pulling her against me, my body seeks the smallest friction against my throbbing cock. Nothing has ever felt so good—or so painful—in my entire thirty-three years.

Her fingers tug at my T-shirt, eagerly searching for my skin. She quickly finds what she's looking for. Her fingertips slide across the lines of my stomach, tenderly tracing the outline of my ribs. Her touch is feather-light, until I deepen our kiss, forcing the breath from her body. Her grip tightens, digging into the muscles of my hips.

Ready for more, she pushes the fabric up my torso. She whispers against my lips. "Take it off."

Yanking the T-shirt over my head, my dick throbs when I see her eagerly devouring my body with her eyes.

That look alone is more fulfilling than ninety percent of the sexual encounters I've had in the past decade.

And kissing her? Well, hell, that's better than any fuck from any other girl on the planet.

My Lulu jumps forward, crashing into my body, moaning for me to kiss her, to ravish her. Wrapping my arms around her, I pull her into a hug, forcing her to her tiptoes. She loves it when I do that.

I can't help but smile.

She wipes the smile from my mouth with the trace of her tongue.

She's making me weak in the knees.

I kiss her. I kiss her until my soul is about to explode.

I step forward, walking her backward to the bed.

I'm gonna bury myself in her if it's the last thing I do.

"Uncle Ry!"

Lulu gasps, jerking her mouth away from mine. We both perk up, like wild animals listening for a hunter.

Please be a false alarm. Oh, please. Please. Please.

"Uncle Ry! I had a bad dream and spilled my water."

Lulu stumbles from my arms. Taking a step back, I swipe my hand across my face so hard my stubble burns my palm. Her eyes are wide and her chest is heaving like she just ran a marathon. Her lips are swollen and red. She's dazed. And horny. And completely gorgeous. And all mine.

Sighing, I look at the ceiling, grunting in frustration. "I can't believe this is happening." Rolling my shoulders, I try to ease the tension coursing through my body.

I turn my head, shouting to my niece. "I'm coming. Be there in just a second."

Lulu giggles, nodding at my crotch. "It doesn't look like you're coming."

I'm glad she finds the situation humorous. Because I don't.

Not. One. Bit.

My hand cups my erection, forcefully trying to make myself limp. "I can't believe I'm being cock blocked by a six-year-old."

Lulu smiles, planting her hand on her hip. The movement causes her breasts to sway. "Who said you were getting any tonight?"

I lift my eyebrows. "That kiss spoke volumes."

"Maybe it's just been too long since you've kissed anyone."

On my way out of the room, I pour my hot breath across the shell of her ear. "It's been too long since I've kissed you, Lulu."

Chapter 30

Crutch

Twelve Days.

I haven't seen her in twelve days. I'm like a damn giddy school-girl counting down the minutes.

When I finally made it back to the bedroom on that Saturday night, she was passed out. Dead asleep. I wanted nothing more than to crawl into the bed next to her. To slide my throbbing dick deep inside her, to wake her with a mind-blowing orgasm, to cover her body from head to toe in love.

But that wouldn't have been the right thing to do. So I slept downstairs on the couch. Once again, I couldn't even trust myself to sleep in the guest bedroom upstairs. I mean, her scent carried down the hallway. How could I ignore that?

We spent the whole next day together—Laura, Lulu, and me. And when I dropped Lulu off that night, Holt was home. Call me old fashioned, but I don't really want to make passionate love to Lulu while her protective, football-playing cousin is one wall away. Plus, she had to leave early the next morning for the trial in Jackson.

We spent the days calling and texting. She didn't have much free time between the trial and meetings, but I eagerly took every second I could get.

She actually got back in town yesterday afternoon. I had every intention of seeing her last night after work, but her body had other plans. After she didn't return my phone calls or texts, I called Holt. He told me she unpacked and was asleep by four p.m. She hates sleeping in a hotel room—never actually sleeps well—and was exhausted.

Now, I would give nothing more than to call in sick and spend the entire day making Lulu come all over my face. But...alas, it's our interview day with Caleb.

So, instead, I'll have to settle for a three-hour drive to Atlanta.

I knock on the door, impatiently waiting for her to answer. The second she swings it open, my voice catches in my throat.

I made it nearly twelve whole years without seeing her. Sure, they were miserable years in many ways, but I still made it. Now, here it is, just twelve days and I feel like falling to my knees and begging her to never leave me again. Not even for one minute.

Her smile is happy. Genuine. Perfect.

Not able to stand it for one more second, I sweep her into my arms and cover her mouth with mine. Her lips part and her tongue darts out to taste me. Her fingertips trail up my forearms, tickling my skin.

"Ahem." Holt clears his throat. Loudly.

Laughing, I pull my face away from Lulu's. Not ready to let go of her just yet, I possessively hold her hip. "Sorry, man, didn't see you."

"Yeah, I can see that." Holt holds up a carton of orange juice from his perch at the kitchen counter. "Want something?"

"No, I'm good."

Lulu blushes. She tries not to, but she can't help it. "Let me pack my work bag, and we can head out."

Holt watches in amusement as Lulu tosses her laptop and notebook into her bag. "So, it's safe to assume you two don't hate each other anymore?"

"Holt!" Lulu throws an ink pen at him.

He easily dodges it. "What? It's a valid question."

I lean across the counter, grabbing a grape from his breakfast plate and popping it in my mouth. "Well, if this is *hate*, I'm damn excited to see what *like* brings to the table."

"Ry!"

∝

We're walking through the parking deck, heading toward the lobby, at the downtown building where Caleb's office is, when Lulu's question catches me off guard.

"I never did ask you what happened to my clothes."

"Huh?"

"At your house? My clothes were wet. And I woke up in your T-shirt, wearing my bra and panties. Did you undress me?"

"I did. But really, I had no choice."

"What do you mean?"

I chuckle, running my hand through my hair. "Well, you kind of threw up on yourself."

Lulu freezes mid-stride and her jaw falls open. "What? Are you kidding me? Please say you're joking."

She's horrified.

I try not to laugh. "Sorry. Not joking."

"Where did I throw up?"

"In the truck when we were leaving the bar."

She covers her face with her hands. "Holy shit. How mortifying."

I tug at her hand, teasing her. "So, it's not the right time to tell you that you threw up on me too?"

"What!"

"Down my shoulder."

Squaring her shoulders, she lifts her pouty little chin in the air. "No, Ry, it's not the right time to tell me that."

I can't help it. I burst out laughing.

She tries not to giggle. Really, she does. But she's not successful. "Well, that solves the mystery about why my clothes were washed."

I punch the button on the lobby elevator, straightening the badge and weapon on my belt.

Lulu tilts her head, studying me. "And what about the T-shirt? You saw me in my bra and panties?"

"I did. But don't worry, I didn't look." I smirk. "Much."

We step into the elevator, and at the last minute a pretty blonde woman races in. She's putting her phone in her purse and nods at the keypad. "Ten, please."

I press the buttons for the nineteenth floor and the tenth floor and take a step back. Finally getting her cell phone where she wants it, she sighs deeply and glances over at me and Lulu.

And comes back for a second glance at me.

And a third.

Well, this ought to be interesting.

She runs her manicured hand through her hair and smiles. "Thanks."

I nod.

"I haven't seen you in the building before, officer. Here for business or pleasure?"

It's a thirty-story building filled with offices. What kind of pleasure would I find in that?

Lulu dramatically rolls her eyes. When she catches me watching her, she turns to the side, using her shoulder to block my view.

The lady takes a step in my direction, garnering my attention. Before Lulu came back into my life, I'd really consider finding a secluded corner restroom with this girl and banging out a quickie. That is, assuming one of us had a condom. And of course, I would be picturing Lulu in my mind the entire time. Every woman on the face of the planet pales in comparison to My Lulu.

"In town today for business."

"Well, if you have any time for pleasure, I'm free for lunch."

Holy crap. I have to say this woman has brass balls. It's impressive. "Thanks for the offer, but my lunch plans have already been made." I slide behind Lulu. Dipping my head, I brush her hair out of the way and kiss the scar on the back of her neck. Her body immediately relaxes into mine, and her ass grinds against my crotch. I don't even think she realizes that she does it. Taking advantage of her lapse in composure, I wrap my hand around her waist, hugging her from behind.

The bell dings and the doors open to the tenth floor. The blonde tsks our public display of affection and races out of the elevator with her high heels clicking the whole way. Lulu giggles.

I whisper against her ear. "There. Wasn't that more effective than just rolling your eyes."

"I do not roll my eyes."

"You most certainly do."

Lulu pulls out of my grasp, and furrows her brow in playful irritation. "Well, stop looking so damn hot, and women wouldn't hit on you left and right."

I wink. "You love the way I look. And if you keep up that cussing, I'm gonna wash your mouth out with soap."

Her face flushes and her eyes widen in delight.

Fortunately, the elevator opens on the nineteenth floor, saving her from more banter. Caleb's employer takes up the whole floor, so the receptionist's desk is right out front. I inform the woman we have an appointment with Caleb, and she calls back to his office. After a minute, his secretary meets us and walks us back through the winding halls. I can tell Lulu is nervous. She's rubbing her scar and glancing out the windows we pass by, watching the traffic on the streets far below us.

We're barely past the threshold to Caleb's office when he's racing around the desk and engulfing Lulu in a hug. "Ella!" He holds her at arm's length to look at her and then hugs her again. "I can't believe you're really standing here. It's so good to see you."

She clears her throat, trying to wipe away the emotion, but I still hear a slight tremble in her voice. "You too. It's great to see you, Caleb."

He holds out a hand to me, introducing himself.

"Sergeant Ryland Crutchfield. Thank you for taking the time to speak with us today. I know your schedule must be busy."

He studies my bulletproof vest and glances down at my weapon, before turning back to Lulu. "The police, Ella?" His eyes grow wide with horror. "Oh my god, did you find her? Did you find Carrie?"

"No, we haven't found her." Lulu reaches out, rubbing Caleb's arm. The familiarity between the two of them stings a little bit.

He reaches up and rubs his sternum. "Good." He furrows his brow. "Well, I don't know if *good* is the right word. At this point, I honestly don't know if I want her to be found or not. If we don't know what happened, then I can still imagine her alive. Alive and happy and living on a deserted island somewhere, you know?"

Lulu smiles sadly. "It's time to be realistic, Caleb. I haven't felt Carrie's presence in a really long time. We need to find out what happened and bring those people to justice."

Solemnly nodding, he waves us over to his desk. "Please, sit. Can I get either of you anything? Water? Coffee?"

I pull the chair for Lulu and set her work bag beside her. "We're fine, thank you." While Lulu's pulling out her notebook and my file, I get permission to record the interview.

Caleb fiddles with an ink pen on his desk. "Why do I get the feeling this has nothing to do with a book?"

"There may be a book one day, but right now, there's no ending for it. That's what we're searching for, Caleb." Lulu takes a deep breath. "When I came home for my parents' funeral, I found some new evidence. So we are re-interviewing everyone."

"I'm so sorry about that, Ella. After my secretary told me you called, I did an internet search on you. I read about Robert and Susan's plane crash. I'm sorry you had to go through that."

She licks her lips and picks at a fake piece of lint on her shirt. "Thanks."

Somehow, I get the picture that he knows her relationship with her parents wasn't the best. I can only assume Carrie shared some of the same feelings and thoughts with him that Lulu shared with me.

He nods. "So, new evidence? What did you find?"

I jump in, taking the lead. "First, why don't you go ahead and tell me about your relationship with Carrie? I took the case over about two-and-a-half years ago, and I would love to gain more insight on Carrie's life at the time of her disappearance. As her boyfriend, you knew her better than most people."

Caleb is easy to talk to. He openly answers all of my questions about his and Carrie's past. He even discusses the drug activity, confirming that it's the reason he broke up with her. Lulu listens intently, taking notes. When it's time to show Caleb the pictures, I nod to her.

"After my parents' funeral, I was finally moving some stuff out of Carrie's room and I found some pictures."

"Pictures? What kind of pictures?"

Lulu slides the stack—except for the last picture—across the desk. Before lifting her hand, she warns Caleb. "They're not easy to look at, Caleb. Take your time. Tell us if you recognize anyone in the photos."

I notice that his hands are trembling when he picks up the pictures. He shakes his head. "I nearly forgot how beautiful she was. I still can't believe she even agreed to go out with me." He slowly flips through the pictures. Silent tears roll from his eyes when he sees Carrie passed out cold. Tossing the stack back across the desk, he wipes his face with the back of his hand. "No, the only person I recognize is Carrie." He shakes his head.

Lulu sits straighter in her chair. "I found something else." She takes a deep breath, inhaling in small spurts. "A pregnancy test."

"Excuse me?"

"A pregnancy test. It was positive. There's reason to believe that Carrie was pregnant when she went missing."

Caleb had no idea. The shock is written all over his face. In fact, he would probably be less shocked if Carrie walked through the door right now and sat on his lap.

He's stuttering so badly, he can't even form a word. "Wh...what? I mean, huh? N...no. Are you sure?"

"We are still waiting on the DNA test to confirm that it's Carrie's DNA on the pregnancy test, but it's safe to assume it was hers."

"Who? Who got her pregnant?"

Lulu squares her shoulders and stares into his eyes. "Well, I was hoping you could tell me."

"Me? You think it was me?" His eyebrows lift so high, they disappear into his hairline.

"Carrie didn't share the intimate details of y'all's relationship with me all that much. She thought I was too young. But I do know that y'all were sexually active. Very, very active from what I remember."

"Of course, we were. We were young and in love. But we broke up months before she disappeared. And we always used protection. Always. She said your parents would go completely ballistic if she ever came home pregnant, said they would disown her."

Lulu stirs uncomfortably in her chair and accidentally knocks her notebook and pen to the floor. She nervously fumbles to pick them up.

I press on, not wanting to lose the momentum. "And you didn't share any time together after the breakup? A lonely night? A drunken party?"

"No, of course not. I was staying firm to my ultimatum that she had to stop selling and get clean before we could get back together. It hurt not being with her. It hurt like hell, but I wanted her to know how serious I was."

Lulu discreetly reaches across and gives my knee a little squeeze, letting me know she's back in the right mindset. "What if the pregnancy test was old? Did y'all ever experience a pregnancy scare during y'all's relationship?"

Caleb sits back in his chair, rubbing his fingers across his chin in thought. Spinning around, he grabs a framed photo from the windowsill behind him. He hands it over to Lulu. It's a framed picture of him with his wife and children standing on a rocky beach. "That's my wife, Amelia, and our children."

Lulu smiles, nodding. "You have a beautiful family, Caleb. You look happy."

"I am happy. Trust me, after Carrie went missing, I didn't think I would ever be happy again. I met Amelia during my very first week in Atlanta. Falling in love with her came as a surprise. I always thought there was one person for everyone on this earth. I knew without a doubt that Carrie was mine. She was my forever. And just like that, she was gone. I couldn't believe how lucky I was to find love like that twice in my life. Amelia knows all about Carrie. She knows how much I loved your sister. She's never asked me to choose. Not once. She's never asked me to pick who I love more—her or Carrie. Amelia has this," he chuckles, trying to grasp the right word, "amazing grace about her. She knows that love isn't linear. It's not a straight line. It's a circle. And she knows that she and Carrie fit into the exact same circle."

Lulu lowers her voice, whispering. "That's great, Caleb. It doesn't answer my question, though." She gently places the frame on his desk.

He points to the image of his family. "We adopted our son when he was two years old. We adopted our daughter when she was just five weeks old."

She cocks her head to the side, thinking. "Caleb? What are you saying?"

"I can't have biological children, Ella. I have an autoimmune disease that makes me infertile. I didn't know it when Carrie and I were together, but the doctors say I've most likely been infertile since puberty."

Shit. I wasn't expecting that.

"Oh, Caleb, I'm so sorry."

He shrugs, clearly having come to terms with his situation long ago. "Don't be. I couldn't imagine my family being any different. My children are amazing." He leans forward, wrapping his hand around Lulu's. "But if Carrie was pregnant when she went missing, it wasn't because of me. And I know without a doubt that she wouldn't have been pregnant before our breakup. Carrie would have never cheated on me. Never. We loved each other. Plus, she never wanted to be like your father."

Lulu nods. Turning to me, she holds out the last picture. She can't do it. She can't show it to him. She wants me to do it.

Of course, I will. I'd crawl through fire for this woman.

"We have one last picture to show you, Caleb," I say. "Now that we know about your medical condition and your history with Carrie, it may provide some context to support the idea that Carrie was pregnant at the time of her disappearance."

Caleb glances back and forth between me and Lulu. "Okay." The trepidation in his voice is palpable.

"It's disturbing and graphic. It's hard to look at, but I need you to focus on the man in the picture. Tell us if anything about him is familiar." Not giving him the chance to reconsider, I put the photograph in Caleb's hands.

He loses it. Completely loses it.

He's seeing the woman he loved—still loves—getting raped. If it were me? Well, let's just say that hell itself wouldn't even be a competition for my anger if something like that happened to My Lulu.

He cries. He screams. He paces.

It's one of the most intimate and intense experiences I've ever been forced to watch. I turn off the camera on my vest, giving him some modicum of privacy.

His secretary rushes in to check on him. Not once, not twice, but three times. Each time, quietly closing the door without saying anything. By the third time, she's even crying with him—for him—even though, she has no clue what's happening.

Eventually, he calms enough for us to finish the interview. He has no idea who the guy is.

With red eyes, he walks us to the office door. He shakes my hand and hugs Lulu tightly in his arms. As we're walking out, he calls after her. "Ella?"

My hand finds the small of her back, holding her close, when she turns to him. "Yeah?"

"My son's name is Jackson. My daughter's name is Caroline Olive. We call her Ollie."

Lulu gasps and her hand flies to her heart. "Oh, Caleb." She sniffles, "I'm honored. And I know she would be too. Thank you, thank you for loving my sister the way you did."

Chapter 31

Ella

He's waiting on me when I come out of the restroom. "I'm gonna finish filling up. Grab me a bottle of water?"

"Sure."

Ry turns to walk out the gas station door, but stops in his tracks. I'm about to ask him what he's doing when he plants a soft kiss on my temple and smiles.

He's done everything possible to cheer me up since we left the interview with Caleb. He thinks he's being sly about it, but he's not. It's pretty obvious what he's doing, and it's making me fall even more in love with him.

As if that's possible.

He drove forty minutes out of the way, through Atlanta traffic, to take me to a late lunch at a sandwich spot he read about that has mind-blowing Philly cheesesteak sandwiches. Instead of listening to his normal rock music, he downloaded a new crime podcast and has been patiently listening to that during our drive back home. He's held my hand, caressed my back, and now, gently kissed my temple.

I grab a bottle of water from the cooler and search for something to drink for myself. I'm completely taken aback when my eyes settle on something familiar—Slayton's Southern Blackberry Tea. I didn't even know they still made it. Snatching it up, I quickly pay for the drinks and head back out to the gas pumps. Ry's leaned against the bed of his truck, pumping gas. Sensing my presence, he turns around. I stop on the sidewalk and hold up my hand, waving the drink around in the air. He flicks the ballcap higher on his head to get a better look. I love it when he does that. Even from here, I can see the arch of his eyebrows.

Laughing, I take a step off the curb when something catches my attention from the corner of my eye. There's a large SUV with a mom trying to pay for gas at the pump. A young girl, about ten or eleven, is talking to her. It sounds like she's asking about going to a friend's house. A little boy, about six or seven, is next to them, trying to interrupt. He's wanting to go inside the station to get a snack and is asking for money. The mom is trying to listen to them both, but the machine keeps beeping at her, warning her that her credit card isn't working. Right then, the back passenger-side door opens and a small little boy, about three or four, jumps out of his booster seat. For a split second, he wobbles and then takes off running toward the front door of the gas station.

Running toward me.

The plumber's van reversing out of the parking spot in front of the store can't see him.

There's no way they can see him.

Everything else happens in slow motion. It feels like I'm moving in water, like my limbs aren't moving as quickly as my brain tells them to. It's frustrating. It makes me angry. I feel like I'm trying to run a marathon in a dream, drugged and sluggish.

I throw the drinks and my wallet on the ground and race across the asphalt. Panicked and determined. Scared.

I think Ry shouts my name, but I'm not sure.

My arms wrap around the little boy. I feel the air whoosh from his lungs in surprise. I don't even have time to turn around. I basically jerk his body to the side, placing myself between him and the van, and run sideways, trying to gain clearance from the vehicle. It slams on the brakes and stops right when my foot trips over the curb. I fall flat on my back with the little boy on top of me.

He immediately starts screaming and crying. I sit up, searching his body for injuries. He's okay.

He's absolutely perfect.

I lie back down on the sidewalk as everyone rushes to my side.

And I watch in silence as my blood pools against the steaming hot sidewalk.

I bite my lip, trying not to laugh. "How much longer can you pace around? You've probably walked five miles back and forth across this room."

Ry grabs his ballcap and turns it around backward on his head. I love it when he does that too. "They should've come back by now to check your head."

"They already told you that I don't have a concussion. That bump was nothing. I've hit my head harder than that on a headboard."

Wrong time to joke.

He rakes his hand across his stubble. "Do I look amused, Lulu? Shit, I'm covered in your blood."

I study the blood covering his shirt and pants and then look down at my own clothes. I knew the arm could bleed a lot, but it's different seeing it in person. I make a mental note to learn more about blood evidence. Some new studies came out recently, and I should really familiarize myself with them.

"What's that look for? What are you thinking about?"

I shake my head. "Nothing." I smile, changing subjects. "Hey, look at the bright side. We're across the Alabama state line, so I don't have any out-of-state insurance co-pays to worry about."

Again, he's not amused.

It's true, I did bump my head on the sidewalk when I fell, but it wasn't bad at all. What did hurt was the fact that I fell onto the busted glass from the Slayton's Southern Blackberry Tea bottle. A large piece of jagged glass sliced my right forearm. That and a scrape on my ankle are my only injuries. More importantly, the little boy is safe and sound.

The hospital has already stitched my wound. The numbing shot and tetanus shot were not pleasant at all. We're just waiting on the nurse to finish dressing my wound and give me the after-care instructions. And of course, they need to finish my paperwork. They were more concerned with the blood gushing from my arm when I got here than with my Social Security number and employer address.

My arm is propped on a pillow, and I count the nine small stitches. I was really lucky in the fact that a plastic surgeon was working in the hospital tonight. The emergency department doctor called him to do the sutures. My scar should be minimal.

Ry sighs and walks over to the side of the hospital bed. His fingers tenderly graze over mine. He's washed his hands three times already, but I can still see my blood caked in the corners of his cuticles. "Can you feel that? Is the numbing shot starting to wear off?"

"I feel everything you do," I whisper.

His eyes dart to mine. That color will captivate me forever. Translucent and green. The eyes I loved to hate every single day for nearly twelve years. The eyes I now want to love. Every. Single. Day. "Tell me something. Something no one else knows."

He lovingly tucks my hair behind my ear. "I'm so damn proud of what you did today. Saving that kid. You were amazing. I'm also so damn mad at you. What if that van hadn't stopped when it did? What if..." His voice trails off. He can't finish his thought. Instead, he leans down and kisses me. Softly and slowly, he pours devotion from his body into mine.

"Ahem."

Ry quickly pulls away when the nurse makes her presence known. Smirking, he winks at me and heads back over to stand against the wall. "Sorry, ma'am."

Nurse Dorothy chuckles. "Never say you're sorry for kissing the one you love. That's good advice to heed. My forty-third wedding anniversary is tomorrow." Something about her completely puts me at ease. She reminds me of Harlan.

"Happy anniversary."

She smiles, patting me on the good arm. "Thanks, hon. What do you say we get this wound dressed, finish this paperwork, and get you lovebirds on the way?"

She runs through everything with us. I have to change the dressing daily, wrap my arm in cellophane and tape to shower, watch for infections, and go somewhere local in fourteen days to get the stiches removed. She tells me the doctor will give me a prescription for pain pills to take as needed, but I politely decline, telling her that addiction runs in my family, and I would prefer to make do with over-the-counter medicine.

"Alright, hon, now time for the fun part. We have to finish this paperwork." She grabs her electronic tablet and starts typing. She looks over at Ry and then back at me. "Would you like some privacy for this?"

Ry takes a protective step in my direction. "Over my dead body. I'm not leaving her. Ever."

I snort on a chuckle. "It's fine. He can stay."

Dorothy leans forward, pretending to whisper-shout, and jerks her thumb in Ry's direction. "Is the handsome officer always so serious?"

I scrunch my nose, playing along. "He's been known to cut loose. Once or twice, that is. He has a thing for the ladies."

"Lulu!"

By now me and Dorothy are laughing like crazy. Ry opens his mouth to say something, but instead pouts, folding his arms across his broad chest.

We settle down and she runs through all my personal data—name, Social, address, date of birth, and so on and so on. She lifts an eyebrow when I say I'm unmarried and makes a tsking sound in Ry's direction. I have to bite my lip to keep from laughing. We go through the medical history of my immediate family. Cancer, diabetes, high blood pressure, etc.

And then we get to the questions I hate.

The questions I always forget about.

The questions I block from my memory on purpose.

I am screwed. Completely and totally fucked.

Why did I let Ry stay in this room? Why, oh why, oh why?

"Number of children?"

My heart thunders in my chest. "Zero."

"Number of pregnancies?"

My body breaks out in a cold sweat knowing the answer I'm about to give. "One."

Ry's head snaps up in my direction, faster than a bolt of lightning.

In a split second, tension floods the room. All the oxygen is sucked out of the area, leaving me panting and gasping for air.

Dorothy notices something is off. She asks the next question slowly, as if saying the sentence one syllable at a time will magically diffuse the situation. "Number of live births?"

I can't do this. I can't do this. Tears spring to my eyes. I bite my lip, trying to keep my untamed reaction buried. Ry's eyes widen and his mouth falls open. He thinks I had a child with Hudson. He thinks I lied to him, omitted a major fact.

I did lie to him. I omitted a major fact. But he gave me no other choice.

Lifting my face and squaring my shoulders, I firmly answer the question. "One. A daughter. I had an umbilical cord prolapse. She died six hours after her birth."

"Oh hon, I'm so very sorry you went through that." Dorothy reaches out and wraps her fingers around mine. "How long ago was it?"

My eyes bore into Ry, drilling a hole directly into his soul. "Eleven years and seven months ago. I was thirty-four weeks pregnant when it happened."

He stumbles backward, reaching out and gripping the doorframe for support. His eyes dart around the room, mentally counting our time together and our time apart, trying to determine if his first thought was wrong. But he knows he's right. He knows it's him. He knows that he's the father.

After all these years, he knows I was pregnant with his child when he left me. When he turned his back and walked away, I was carrying his baby.

He finally knows.

He coughs, drowning in his own emotions. He grabs the collar of his shirt and yanks on it, like it's a vise, choking the life from him.

His episode is so disturbing and traumatic to watch, Dorothy stands up. "Officer? Are you okay?"

Spinning on his heels, Ry slams his fist so hard into the wall that a framed picture of the digestive tract falls to the ground and shatters into a million pieces. His bellowed moan is dragged directly from the pits of hell, filled with so much sorrow and pain, I don't know if he'll ever be okay. His voice is so broken, I can barely make out the words. "I need some air."

He walks out the door, leaving me crying on the hospital bed.

Chapter 32

Crutch

No wonder she hated me.

I abandoned her and our unborn child. The child who died before I even knew she existed. For six hours, I was a father.

A father.

I was Dad. To a daughter. A little baby girl.

And she was a mother.

And My Lulu had to do it all without me. No wonder she was so devastated when she thought Laura was my child.

I can't believe this is my life. I can't believe this is happening to me. *To us.*

The initial shock slowly seeps from my body, leaving me savagely broken. And I cry. For the first time in years, I cry. I sit on a bench, bury my head in my hands and watch as my tears soak the sidewalk.

What did she look like? Did she have a name? Was she in pain? Did she feed from Lulu's breast? Did she fight for her little life?

It sounded like something went wrong with the pregnancy. Does that mean Lulu was in pain? How much suffering did she endure? Did she know she was pregnant when she married Hudson?

How could she keep this from me? How could she not tell me about the baby? Why did she do this to me? Did she want to hurt me because I left?

Things could've been so different.

It's not like I could've left the Marines, but we could've made things work, made a life together. I would've married her, made it right. Hell, it's what I really wanted. I wanted to marry her and have a family with her. I just thought she was giving up a chance at a great future to be with me. I didn't want her to give up anything for me.

And in running away, I forced her to give up the greatest future of all—our daughter's future.

I'm not sure how long I sit there, but eventually, my tears dry. My face stings from the salt and my lips are cracked and chapped. All of a sudden, I'm bone-tired. Weary and exhausted. Angry, frustrated, and miserable.

My head jerks up the second I hear her voice. "Well, you certainly know how to make a dramatic exit."

Even through the dark, I can see her red and swollen eyes. She's been crying. That thought fucking rips my heart out.

But empathy for Lulu isn't the only feeling I have right now. My spirit is in turmoil, and the raging war inside is splitting my soul in two.

Despite my love for her, a devious snake of anger slithers its way through my blood. It tries to freeze me, tries to harden me, tries to consume me.

"You're finished in there?" I nod my head at the brick hospital building.

"Yes. Discharged."

I stand up. My back is so tight and tense, it feels like all my muscles are ripping. A single drop of rainwater falls on my head. "I'll be back in a minute. I need to settle up for the damage I caused."

She doesn't look at me. She just stares straight ahead at the parking lot. "I already took care of it. I explained the delicacy of the situation. They were very understanding. They refused to let me pay for the glass frame. I made a donation to the cancer center instead."

A few more rain droplets fall. "I didn't ask you to do that. I could've handled it. It was my mess to clean up."

She tries to reach behind her neck with her good hand, but her purse and a bag of hospital stuff is weighing her arm down. Giving up, she sighs, "And you always take care of your messes, don't you, Ry?"

What the hell is that supposed to mean? "You plan on telling me what you mean by that comment?"

"No."

"Well, I suggest you quickly modify your plans, then."

The rain is starting to fall at a faster pace, so she takes off walking toward the truck, ignoring me and leaving me standing like a dumbass on the sidewalk. I click the fob to unlock the door for her and take my sweet time walking across the parking lot. I need time to gather my thoughts. How are we supposed to even talk about this? About what happened? About our child?

I climb into the truck and toss my ballcap in the back seat. I shake the rainwater from my hair and drag my hands down my face. She shifts in her seat, trying to get comfortable.

"Is your arm hurting?"

"It's fine. I took some ibuprofen a few minutes ago. It'll kick in soon."

"What's in the bag?"

She shrugs. "Some extra bandages. Paperwork."

I nod, not saying anything.

She points at the armrest and dashboard, where streaks of her dried blood mar the leather. "I'll pay to have it have cleaned."

"I don't care about my damn truck."

"Hmm."

I can't stand it, enough with the small talk. "Why didn't you tell me, Lulu?"

She turns to study me. Her jaw works back and forth. "Why didn't I tell you then? Or why didn't I tell you now?" Her voice raises an octave. She's really starting to get pissed off.

Welcome to the club.

I shake my head. "Now. Then. Both." All of it. Why is she asking such a ridiculous question?

"I wanted to tell you. I tried to tell you."

"Oh really? It's not that hard to do. *I'm pregnant. We're having a baby.'* See, less than twelve seconds. So, how come it took twelve years for me to find out?"

She shoves her finger in my face. "It wasn't that simple, asshole!"

I toss my hands in the air. "Enlighten me. Please."

"You didn't wanna be found, Ry. Your goal was to leave me, to cut ties, and you did a damn good job of it. You left your cell phone. You deleted your email account. I went to the recruiting office, I begged the recruiter for your information, for anything—a phone number, a mailing address, an email address. He couldn't give me anything because you designated your file as 'no contact'. He was forced to honor your request. I even tracked down your mom, drove her to the office, and had her ask. You had it marked that your mailing address couldn't even be given out to family."

Shit. I did do that. I did it because I was afraid Lulu would write while I was in MCRT, and I knew her letters would distract me. "You met with my mom after I left town?"

Lulu snorts. "Yeah, and she was a real pleasure as always. I had to pay her $200 to even get her to go to the recruitment office."

Now, that sounds like dear old Mom.

"I begged the recruiter to call you himself. I told a complete stranger I was pregnant and begged him to get in touch with you. He couldn't, of course."

She sits forward, watching the rain slap against the windshield. "I didn't tell Harlan I was pregnant. I didn't want him to worry. I just told him that he had to make you call me. But that was a moot point too. You called him when you arrived at MCRT, but that was while I was in Puerto Rico. Harlan told me you wouldn't be able to call back until MCRT was finished. Thirteen weeks, Ry. You had that boot camp for a full thirteen weeks. We kept waiting on you to call. *I* kept waiting on you to reach out to one of us. But you didn't. You left Harlan a coward's voicemail a few weeks before MCRT ended, telling him you weren't taking your ten-day leave before SOI, but instead going straight there. You didn't even leave a contact number on the voicemail so we could call you."

She shakes her head, fighting her anger. She's losing the battle. "Guess how pregnant I was gonna be at the end of SOI? Six months! I couldn't just sit around and not have a plan. I had a baby to prepare for."

She reaches behind her neck and rubs her scar. "You left Harlan that voicemail on August 4th, saying you weren't coming home for your ten-day leave. I left town one week later."

That piques my interest. And not in a good way. "*What you mean is* you married Hudson, and left town one week later with your new husband."

Her eyes narrow and her spine stiffens. "That's exactly what I mean."

"Why the hell would you marry someone you don't love while you're carrying *my* baby?"

She spins in her seat, pulls her seat belt around her, and stares out the side window. "I can't talk about this anymore tonight. Drive. Take me home."

I want to ask about my daughter. I want to know every single thing there is to know. But talking to her now will be like talking to a brick wall. Growling under my breath, I pull out of the hospital parking lot and navigate my way back to the interstate. We travel in silence.

And the silence is scary.

Terrifying, actually.

I'm losing her. I'm losing My Lulu.

Her spine stiffens, her shoulders square, her chin points in the air. The gleam in her eyes disappears. The fight in her soul dies.

With each and every mile I drive, I lose My Lulu to Ella.

She flies out of the truck the second I pull into her driveway. Not a goodbye. Not a fuck you. Nothing.

Screaming a swear, I yank the truck in reverse. She thinks she's the only one who can be angry? She thinks she's the only one who can hurt? Well, I lost a child too; I just didn't know it until a couple of hours ago.

I slam on the brakes.

What the hell am I doing?

I drag my hands through my hair. I'm breathing so hard my chest hurts. I'm starting to hyperventilate. I grip the steering wheel so hard my knuckles turn white, and I think I'm about to break my fingers.

I force myself to take slow, deep breaths. Eventually, my blood pressure equalizes.

I can't do this. I can't leave. Leaving is what got me into this trouble in the first place. She's the love of my life. Nothing will ever change that. Nothing.

She's mine. Never before. Never after. Only her.

She's my forever.

And now, I have to make her realize that too.

Yes, we're hurting, but we need to hurt *together*. I want to support her, heal her, make her whole. If that's even possible. If it's not? It doesn't matter; I'm never leaving her side again.

I jump out of the truck and slam through the front door. She's standing in the middle of the living room, crying in Holt's arms. They stare at me like I'm an escaped lunatic.

"Ry?"

"I told you I would never leave again. I meant it."

Holt takes a step in my direction. For a second, it looks like he might attack me.

I've always liked the guy; it'd be a shame to kick his ass.

Using his better judgment, he simply nods and plants a soft kiss on Lulu's temple before retreating to his bedroom. "I'll give y'all some privacy."

She wipes her eyes and sniffles. "What do you want, Ry?"

I don't see the need for any answer but the simple truth. "You. I want you, Lulu." I cross the distance between us and sink to my knees. Gathering her body against mine, I rub my face against her stomach. The stomach that carried our child, the stomach that's been through more than I could ever imagine. I pepper kisses all over her blouse. It smells like dried blood and her coconut lotion.

She doesn't move. She stands like a statue. Unmoved, unfeeling.

Come back to me. Please come back to me, Lulu.

I squeeze her tighter, wrapping my arms around her waist, her ass, her hips. "Come back to me, Lulu. Please don't leave me. I'm here." I nuzzle myself against her, murmuring over and over. "I'm here. I'm here. I'm here."

When her fingers finally thread through my hair, I nearly collapse in relief.

Standing, I gently kiss her lips and wipe the moisture from her rosy cheeks.

"I can't talk about it anymore tonight," she says. "My heart is all plugged up."

Mine too.

Grabbing her good hand, I pull her behind me, wordlessly leading her down the hall. I shut her bedroom door, and she stands next to the bed, watching in curiosity as I shed my clothes, stripping down to my boxer briefs. I turn down the sheets and grab one of my old Harlan T-shirts from her dresser. They're still in the exact same place they were all of those years ago. I point to her heels. She kicks them off her feet. She doesn't shy away when I grab her blouse and gently pull it over her head, taking extra care with her hurt arm. The plump skin of her breasts spills from the top of her satin and lace bra. She shudders when my fingers hook in the elastic waistband of her ankle pants. I push them down her legs, and my dick jumps when I feel the silkiness of her smooth skin.

Her hand covers her stomach, hiding something. I can't help but wonder if she had a C-section. I didn't notice a scar the other night, but I was too preoccupied in keeping my libido in control while changing her clothes.

I don't want to upset her, so I don't stare.

I help her step out of her pants and then trace a finger up the scar from her hip surgery. I can't see the whole thing. It disappears underneath the edge of her pink flowered panties. With a trembling hand, she reaches up to my shoulder and rubs my own scar, following its jagged path around to my shoulder blade. She sucks in a breath, shocked by the divots, bumps, and unevenness of my skin—the particles left behind from the explosion. Her eyes never leave mine.

When she drops her hand, I motion for her to spin around. Unhooking the clasp of her bra, I watch as it falls to the floor. Her back is so smooth, the curve of her spine so alluring. What I wouldn't give to see her. To touch her. To graze my teeth across her brown nipples.

But I don't.

I pull the T-shirt over her head, covering her before she can turn around and drive me to the brink of devastation with the temptation of her half-naked body.

I turn out the light and climb into bed. When I hold back the covers, welcoming her to bed, she smiles weakly. Her body relaxes the second she sinks onto the plush mattress, and I fold my body around hers.

We fit together perfectly.

I think we fit better now than we did.

"Let me know if I hurt your arm."

She sighs and then yawns. "I think we're done hurting each other."

Truer words have never been spoken.

Chapter 33

Ella

I park on the driveway, right beside the front porch. I'm halfway up the stairs when he comes outside. The late afternoon sun covers him in shadowed streaks of yellow and white. He's freshly showered with wet hair. His shirt is slung across his shoulder. His cargo shorts hang low on his muscular hips, showing me the band of his boxer briefs. I watch as one lone droplet of water races down the middle line of his six pack. It makes my stomach flutter and makes my body feel thick and heated.

"Lulu?"

Focusing my attention on his face, I see the amusement in his eyes. He likes it when I look at him like this. Like he's a mouth-watering piece of meat. Like he's the sexiest man on the face of the planet.

He was. And he still is. He also knows it.

"Hi."

He takes a sip from a glass of ice water. "I was just about to drive back into town to see you. You were still sleeping when I left. I told Holt to tell you that I would come back. I had to get home and do all of the yardwork; it's supposed to rain tomorrow."

I nod. "He told me. I just thought talking here might be better. Less chance of interruptions." I walk up the rest of the steps. "I mean, if you're ready to talk."

He sniffs and looks past me to the pond. Stepping in front of me, he grazes a thumb across my jaw. "Forget about what *I* want. Are *you* ready to talk about it? Because when you're ready, I need to know everything. Every single thing that happened, every small detail. But only when you're ready. I'll wait forever if I have to, if that's what you want. I'm yours and I'm not going anywhere. I'm never leaving your side again."

I reach up and rub my scar, drawing strength from it. "All these years, a boulder has been sitting on my chest, crushing me. Making it hard to function, making it hard to even breathe. I've been trapped and I'm ready to be free."

Together, we sit on the porch swing. I carefully prop my purse next to me. He tosses his T-shirt on the table and holds his water glass out in front of me. I take a sip, trying to douse the flaming anxiety in my stomach, before I set it on the porch railing.

"I got your letter the day after I got back from the graduation trip. I was mad that you hadn't called me or come to see me yet so I went to the garage and Harlan gave it to me."

He shakes his head in disgust. "I was such a damn coward. I should have never left the way I did... without telling you. I never wanted to break up with you. I know it sounds like a cop out, but I honestly thought I was doing the right thing for you at the time."

I trace my fingers across the bandage on my arm. "I know that now. It took me all this time to realize it. You didn't value yourself at the time, Ry. You thought you weren't worthy of my love. You honestly thought you were destroying my picture-perfect future. I know that now. But at the time... it was hard to see past the blinding pain. You were the love of my life, and it felt like you tossed me away like some one-night stand, like one of your other girls. My sorrow was so profound, I literally thought I was gonna die."

"I can't believe I put you through that. I just wanted to make myself into the man you deserved. I wanted to be someone you could be proud of. And I couldn't do that if I stayed here."

A piece of dandelion fuzz carries in the breeze and catches on his facial hair. I pluck it away. "Do you regret joining the Marines?"

He thinks for a minute. "I regret leaving you. I regret that decision every single second of my life. But I don't regret joining the Marines, no. I did a lot of good things in the service. I'm proud of what I accomplished for my country and my fellow brothers. It led me to a career in law enforcement, and it helped make me the man I am today."

"Good, I'm glad to hear it. I'm tired of me and you having all these regrets. I'm ready to be done with that." I take another drink of water and clear my throat. "I found out I was pregnant a week after I got back. I was sick on the graduation trip, but I thought it was just a stomach virus. And then I was sick after I got back, but I figured it was just because I was experiencing so much devastation with the breakup.

"I had run out of tissues and was grabbing some from the bathroom closet when I knocked over a box of tampons. They fell out all over the floor, and that's when I realized I hadn't had my period in a really long time. I immediately ran to the store and bought a test." I reach down beside me and pull the small plastic baggie from my purse.

He furrows his brow and grabs it. It doesn't take long for him to recognize what's inside. Just like Carrie's pregnancy test, the image is still clear to see, even after all these years. A bright pink plus sign stares back at him. "Your pregnancy test?" Awe is etched across his face. He rubs the plus sign through the clear plastic. "You kept it?"

I shrug. "Carrie keeping her pregnancy test wasn't unique. Lots of women keep them as a memento. I mean, it's a pretty momentous occasion when you find out you're pregnant."

He smiles and waves the stick back and forth. "Thank you. Thank you for showing me this."

I pluck it from his hand and stuff it back in my purse, chuckling, "You do realize this stick is covered in twelve-year-old pee."

He laughs. "Hell, I'd frame the damn thing if you'd let me."

He would've made such a good father.

"Anyway, after having a gigantic panic attack, that's when I tried tracking you down. I got online and read everything about the

Marines that I could find. That's how I ended up at the recruiting office." A slice of anger carves its way into my healing heart, and I do my best to stifle its sting. "Why did you refuse to give out your mailing address and contact information?"

He bites his lip, drawing my attention to the perfect curve of his mouth. "Because I was afraid you would write me. I knew you would track me down, and I was afraid of what you might say. Part of me was terrified that you would tell me to go fuck myself, tell me you had never even loved me. And the other part of me was terrified to know how much pain I caused you. I was afraid I'd go AWOL running back to you." He scratches his chin. "Did you tell my mom you were pregnant?"

"Of course not, I knew you would never want your parents or your brother in our child's life. I just told her that I needed to get in touch with you. She didn't ask any other questions except what was in it for her."

"I like it when you say that."

I furrow my brow. "Say what."

His palm slides across my thigh. "Our child."

I watch as his thumb rubs back and forth across my sensitive skin.

"And you didn't tell Harlan?" he asks.

I shake my head. "He was already worried about you. He loved you so much. I didn't want to make him worry even more." I take a few deep breaths. "So I turned to my parents. I thought Dad could possibly wield some influence in some shape, form, or fashion to get your contact information."

He sucks air between his teeth. "And how did that go?"

Resentment and bitterness coat my mouth, making me want to gag. "Mom cried, she screamed, she called me a whore. Told me I had ruined my life, told me I had ruined her life. Dad was surprisingly calm. I thought he was gonna stand by me, put my mother in line. He immediately made me an appointment for the next day with one of the best Ob/Gyns in the Southeast, a doctor over in Atlanta. He said they specialized in teen and young adult pregnancies." I close my eyes, thinking back. "We got up early. He even stopped at this pancake spot, and we had the best breakfast. Really good cantaloupe. When we finally got there, he rushed me straight into one of the back rooms. I thought I was getting special treatment because I was the daughter of a surgeon. Then, the doctor came in to discuss the procedure and get my signature on the consent form. It was an abortion clinic."

I turn to Ry, watching as his eyes grow wide in fury. His hand grips my thigh tighter. "My dad tricked me. He made an appointment for me to get an abortion. He didn't even talk to me about it. He thought I wouldn't fight it once I got there. I was always so good at going along with everything they said. Be perfect, don't rock the boat, be good little 'Ella'." I smile at him. "But someone had been teaching me to fight, to stand up for myself. So that's what I did."

"I can't believe he did that to you. What a bastard."

"That night they threw me out of the house."

Ry sits up straight, rocking the swing sideways. "What! They did what?"

"They told me that, as the remaining daughter, I had a certain image to uphold for the family. Carrie was gone, so it all fell on my shoulders. They said they wouldn't allow me to tarnish the family name and everything they had worked for. They said they refused to spend their money on, and I quote, 'a stupid slut who was deceived by some piece of white trash with a big dick'. I had two options: get an abortion or be disowned. I chose the latter. I had to give them my cash, my credit cards, my car keys, my house keys. Everything. They let me pack a bag with some clothes and toiletries. That's it. Well, I did steal my laptop and my cell phone. I put those in the bag when they weren't looking." I shrug my shoulders. "In all honesty, I'm surprised they never changed the will—I thought they wrote me out of it when they kicked me out."

Ironically, I have ended up with my parents' extreme wealth. When all I really wanted was their love.

Ry jumps up from the swing and starts pacing, hands on his hips. "Holy shit. This is all my fault. I made you homeless! What... what did you do?"

"I walked out the door without even looking back. I called Uncle Ray and immediately moved in with him."

I grab Ry's hand, relishing the feel of his calloused fingers. I tug him back down on the swing. "That night was actually a gift."

"Huh?"

"The night I was disowned, the night I was thrown away like a piece of trash, the night my heart was broken even more by the very people who gave me life is also the very same night that I've never felt more loved, more part of a family. Ray and Teresa opened their home to me. Holt held my hand. Raylee drove through the night just to be by my side when I woke up the next morning. They told me how much they loved me, how they would always be there for me and the baby, and how they would do anything in their power to give me and my child a wonderful life. Our child."

He leans forward, cupping his head in his hands. Leaning back up, he shakes his head in disbelief. "I can't believe they've been keeping this from me, all of these years. They were standoffish, sure, but they always treated me with respect. Why? They should've been treating me like dirt. I was scum. Ray should've knocked me flat on my ass." His hand finds its way back to my thigh, like my body has a homing beacon and he can't function without being tethered to me. "How can I ever repay them? How can I thank them for what they did for you?"

I shrug. "You don't have to. It's what real family does for one another." I reach back, rubbing my scar. "But... it started getting complicated."

"What do you mean?"

"My queasiness and nausea took a turn for the worse. I couldn't keep anything down, not even water. I would go for days without being able to eat or drink anything. I got so dehydrated, they had to hospitalize me to give me fluids. It's called hyperemesis gravidarum.

I was in the hospital for ten days. Fortunately, my condition got better once I hit week fourteen of my pregnancy."

"Oh, Lulu." He leans forward and nuzzles my neck, inhaling my scent and kissing the sweet spot of skin under my ear.

I keep on. "But the doctor had another concern. Most women with hyperemesis gravidarum have low blood pressure because they are dehydrated, but my blood pressure stayed slightly elevated above normal. He was worried that was an indicator I may develop preeclampsia, which is high blood pressure during pregnancy. If not treated properly, it can be really, really bad. Seizures, premature labor, even death.

"All of a sudden, I had these hospital bills to worry about. My parents dropped me from their insurance the week after they kicked me out. I owed a small fortune. Uncle Ray and Aunt Teresa told me not worry about it. They set up a payment plan with the hospital and started sending in $50 a week. Can you imagine! It would have taken them five-hundred years to pay off my bills."

I toss my hands up in the air. "And what if the doctor was right and I developed preeclampsia? That could mean more hospital stays, more specialists, more intensive care. Maybe even full bed rest. Sure, they were financially stable, but they definitely weren't counting on having to pay for their niece's medical bills—let alone her food and shelter and pregnancy clothes and baby stuff. I felt like a huge burden."

His jaw tenses and his pale green eyes cloud with fury. "Is this heading where I think it's heading?"

"Hudson." My throat makes a weird noise when I swallow. "I told him I was pregnant. He knew something was going on. My parents told his parents that I had become rebellious and moved out on my own. I needed someone to talk to, so I told him about my fears. I was worried about everything all the time. The baby, my health, bills, college. *You.*" The next words taste sour as they leave my mouth. "He offered to marry me and say the baby was his. As his wife, I would have really good health insurance. His parents could claim me on their policy."

I shake my head. "But it wasn't just that. As his wife, his parents would pay for a nanny so I could still attend college. I wouldn't have to worry about how to pay for diapers or formula or medicine."

Ry closes his eyes and takes a deep breath. It's ragged and rattles in his chest.

"But I told him no. I told him that as soon as you came home for leave after MCRT, we would figure it all out. I told him everything would be fine once I talked to you. *I just needed to talk to you.*" I clear my throat, trying to rid myself of the deep-seated hatred I've held onto for so many years. "And then you left Harlan that voicemail, saying you weren't coming home, and you were disappearing to SOI for another two months. I had a doctor's appointment that very same day. He told me my blood pressure was still elevated." I shrug my shoulders. "I was left with no other solution to my problem. I called Hudson and told him I would marry him."

Ry doesn't say anything. We sit in silence, watching the sun sink low in the sky. The pond shimmers in vibrant, reflective streaks of white and gold. I'm lost in my own consuming and overwhelming thoughts about the past when Ry's voice startles me.

"Go ahead and ask me. I know you want to."

"What?"

"Don't beat around the bush, Lulu. I like you when you get to the point."

Shit. He knows me so well.

It's disturbing. And infuriating.

"Fine. Do you think I'm a whore? I basically sold myself to Hudson for food, shelter, and clothing."

He grabs my chin, forcing me to stare into his eyes. He leans in so close I can smell his toothpaste. "Lulu, you're the smartest person I know, but that's the dumbest thing you've ever said. I know I jumped your ass last night about you marrying Hudson, but I was being an insensitive douchebag. I didn't know the whole story, and if I made you feel that way, I'm so incredibly sorry. You did what you thought was best. For you and our child. I would never, ever think poorly of you for fighting for survival. I'm the one who pushed you to make that decision. I'm the one who forced all this on you. It falls on my shoulders, not yours." Laying his forehead against mine, he sighs. "You weren't being a whore, Lulu. You were being a *mother*."

Sitting back, he wraps a protective arm around my shoulder, pulling me closer to his side. "So, you married him and moved to Michigan?"

"Yes."

"And did you have the really high blood pressure? Is that what happened to our daughter?"

When he says 'our daughter', I nearly lose it. The tenderness in his voice is so loving, it makes me ache for what all we could've been.

"No. Fortunately, I never developed full-blown preeclampsia. My blood pressure did stay slightly elevated throughout the entire pregnancy, but it never crossed that threshold."

"So, what happened?"

"It was the car accident. It happened the Saturday after Thanksgiving. After my hyperemesis gravidarum got better, and I could eat again, I developed a craving for frozen yogurt. You know, the soft serve kind from frozen yogurt shops? When I was still here, I used to make Holt and Ridge run out at all hours of the day and night to get me frozen yogurt. I couldn't get enough of the stuff. Well, that craving lasted my whole pregnancy. That night, I just had to have some. I couldn't stop thinking about it, even though it was late."

My heart starts beating fast and my vision blurs around the edges. Does it ever get easier? Thinking about it? Feeling it?

"I was in the turn lane when a truck came speeding across the center line. He T-boned me right behind my driver's door."

Ry's growl is low and primal. "A drunk? Someone texting?"

I loop my fingers through his. "No, Ry. He was driving and had a massive brain aneurysm. Died instantly. He was married, and they had four little kids. He was a deacon at his church. Just..." I sigh, "a dad driving home from work."

He curses underneath his breath.

I open my mouth, but just a squeak comes out.

Give me strength. I can't do this.

Help me. Help me.

Ry squeezes my hand tightly. His thumb rubs against me, tracing a circle pattern on the back of my hand, trying to calm me. The automatic porch light comes on as night falls, and I watch as the thick band of muscle in his forearm flexes each time he makes that circle.

"The door caved in on me." I point to my left hip snuggled up against his thigh. "Broke my hip. But the worst part was... the impact was so severe, it sent me into premature labor and my water broke. When my water broke, the baby's umbilical cord dropped past my cervix, into my vagina. Her head immediately started to descend, and it trapped the cord, blocking her flow of oxygen and blood. The pressure from her own body was," I choke on a strangled sob, "killing her."

By now, there's no point in stopping the tears. Yes, I still hate crying in front of people, but it seems to be all I do lately.

"Emergency crews couldn't get me out of the car. The whole side was basically caved in around me. The dashboard was squashed down. I couldn't even get my hands all the way underneath me to feel what was going on. I couldn't take my pants off." I lick the salt from my lips. "At the time, I just thought I was in labor. Very, very painful labor. I didn't know the umbilical cord prolapse was happening. All I knew was I was wet. Soaked in blood and fluid." I snort, cry-laughing, "I remember being terrified she was gonna suffocate on my panties. I asked the paramedic to give me scissors so I could try to cut the clothes from my body because my panties were gonna strangle my baby."

The tears cascading down Ry's handsome face break my heart. Shatters it. Grinds it to a fine powder.

Moisture catches in his scruff and he wipes it away.

"When they finally got me out, I realized just how serious it was. I could see it on their faces. They rushed me to the hospital, and

I had an emergency C-section. She was alive, but she had lost too much blood and oxygen. She passed away six hours after her birth. Her oxygen levels were too low, and she had a seizure."

He stands from the swing and walks over to the porch railing. Gripping it with white knuckles, he lowers his head and sobs. Wild and manic. Frenzied and frantic. His own pain supersedes mine for the moment. It's so intense, I can feel it in my bone marrow. I've had nearly twelve years to process the pain of losing a child; he's had only twenty-four hours. I wrap my body around his. I lay my head between his shoulder blades and kiss the burning hot skin of his back. His devastation is raising his body temperature. He feels like a furnace. My fingertips trace every hard muscle, and I'm careful to use a softer stroke on his injured left side.

"She was beautiful. Small, but beautiful. She was five pounds, one ounce, and she was nineteen-and-a-half inches long. The doctor said if I had gone to full term, she probably would have been one of the longest babies he had ever delivered. She had a full head of brown hair, long eyelashes, and her eyes were a gray/hazel color. I really think they may have turned translucent green like yours, in the end."

In the end. She didn't really get an end, though.

"Would you like to see a picture?"

He raises his head, wiping his eyes and spitting across the yard to clear his throat. "You have a picture?"

Reaching into my purse, I dig out my phone and pull up the saved album of electronic pictures. I lean beside him against the railing. I accidentally bump my stitched arm and wince.

"Are you okay?"

I smile at the man I love. "I'm fine." I flick to the first picture. "This was the first ultrasound I had. You see that circle? That's her."

"That's it? That's how it looks in the beginning?"

"You didn't see any ultrasound pictures of Laura?"

He shakes his head. "Brooke had one with her when she showed up at the station that day to tell me she was pregnant, but I didn't really study it; it seemed too personal. I went with her to some of her appointments, but I always stayed in the waiting room."

I hand the phone to Ry and let him scroll through the different pictures. "I had an ultrasound at nearly every single doctor's appointment since I was considered high risk." Mingled in the album are different pictures of me, holding my belly, documenting the growth of my body, month after month.

He pauses at the picture of me when I was about six months pregnant. Raylee had come to Michigan to visit me. She snapped the picture of me standing by the window, laughing at something she said. He stares at the picture for so long, I start to worry. "Ry?"

"You're so damn beautiful. Glowing. I thought people just used that word to be nice, but it's true. And your hair is wavy here."

"I was huge," I say with a laugh. "And yeah, about that time is when my hair started changing."

"You weren't huge." He touches my stomach on the screen. "Our baby is in there. A whole person. A human being." He looks over at me. "That's amazing, Lulu." His gaze falls to my lips. Swallowing deeply, he turns back to my phone.

After another couple of pictures, he comes to the last one. The only picture I have of our daughter. My purse and phone were left behind in the wreckage, so I didn't have a way to take her picture. I was so focused on being present with her during the time she had left on this earth, that I don't think I would've remembered to take pictures, even if I had my phone with me. Plus, I was in extreme pain with my hip. The surgeons stabilized me and agreed to wait about doing the hip replacement until we knew more about my child's health.

One of the nurses took this picture with her phone. The doctors had done everything for our baby that could be done. It made no sense for our daughter to spend her last few hours isolated in an incubator or hooked up to one-thousand machines. I'm sitting in a hospital bed with my hospital gown folded down to my waist. I'm holding her small body tightly against my naked breast. She wouldn't and couldn't breast feed. Her head is snuggled underneath my chin, and I'm kissing the top of her perfect little head. Blood stains my hair.

I didn't have any injury to my head. The blood was from my hands—where I felt around my bottom half in the car and then ran my fingers through my hair in despair.

Ry gasps in loving disbelief. "Oh, shit."

Chapter 34

Crutch

Oh, shit.

I have a kid. *I had a kid.*

Lulu's eyes are closed in this picture, as she's kissing the top of our daughter's head. It looks like she's praying. Praying for our daughter to live? Praying for the pain to stop? Praying for me to be there? The sight of blood all over her makes my soul plummet to the depths of hell.

And that baby? Our baby? She's the most perfect thing I've ever seen. Lulu was right, she's beautiful. *She was beautiful.*

"She doesn't look sick."

"No. At first, I didn't believe them when they told me how sick she was. She looked like a perfectly healthy baby to me. Ten fingers. Ten toes. Eyes that looked at me. But the lack of oxygen and blood flow damaged her organs. They called it fetal hypoxia and fetal respiratory acidosis. I promise they did everything they could. They just couldn't get me out of the car quick enough."

My throat feels raw and swollen, like I just guzzled a cocktail of screws and nails. I can't even swallow. I reach for the glass of water and down the rest of it in one gulp. Unable to fight the despair growing in my heart, I throw the glass as hard as I can off the porch. It hits the side of a tree and shatters into a million pieces. The jagged shards shimmer underneath the moonlight. Tears stream down my face, burning me, scalding me.

I'm such a pussy. I should be comforting Lulu, but all I've done tonight is cry.

I should close my eyes, but I can't stop looking at the picture of my baby girl. Every time the screen starts to grow dark, Lulu reaches around, tapping it and making it light up again.

Minutes. Hours. I'm not sure, but eventually, enough time passes that my tears dry and my body stops shaking.

Standing tall, I stretch my back and roll my shoulders, trying to ease the tension. I hand the phone back to Lulu. "She's beautiful. And you're beautiful. I should have been there. I fucking ruined our lives, and I can't begin to tell you how sorry I am, Lulu. I'm not even gonna ask for your forgiveness, I don't deserve it. And I can't believe I'm saying this, but no matter how much I've always hated Hudson, I'm glad you didn't have to go through all of that alone. I'm grateful that he was by your side."

Lulu bites her lip, slowly walking back over to the swing. She sits down and tosses her phone back into her purse.

She's not telling me something. "Lulu?"

She sighs, crossing her legs and lifting her chin. "I was alone. He wasn't there."

"Excuse me?"

"I was alone. Hudson wasn't there."

"What do you mean, he wasn't there? He was your husband, wasn't he?" I ask.

"He went on a ski trip with a bunch of friends over Thanksgiving break. He didn't fly back in until Monday night."

"And the wreck was on Saturday night?"

She nods. "Yes."

That bastard. I rub my eyes so hard they nearly pop out of my eye sockets. "He shouldn't have left his pregnant wife—his high-risk pregnant wife—home by herself to go on a ski trip with his buddies. And he should've been on the very first plane back."

She shrugs. "Monday was his normal return flight."

A murderous rage courses through my blood. "Are you kidding me right now? I'm gonna kill him."

She raises her eyebrows, looking at me like I'm a child who's throwing an unwarranted temper tantrum.

"Don't look at me like that, Lulu. He was your husband. I don't care if it was a marriage of necessity. He should've been there. I can't believe he was a jackass for the entire time you were married. Beginning to end."

"He tried in the beginning. Well, he tried the best he knew how. He was still a kid. He was nice, he tried to please me. In all fairness, I set the bar pretty high for him." She pins me with a stare. "He wasn't you. And I resented him because of that. He was my husband, and I wouldn't even let him touch me. I told him that I couldn't have sex with him while I was pregnant. I told him the doctor said it was too much of a risk." She reaches around and rubs her scar in thought. "Not to be graphic, but I just couldn't fathom the idea of him being inside me, pouring himself into me, into the same place where your baby was growing."

She watches as a bug flies around the flickering front porch light. "Anyway, he tried in the beginning, but he stopped trying after the baby was born."

I pace back and forth across the porch. "Why? Why did he stop trying? Was he grieving her loss? Was he angry?"

"He was angry, alright, but not because she didn't make it."

"Then why?"

She smiles weakly. "Because I refused to list his name on the birth certificate or death certificate. I put your name on everything."

I stop pacing and stare at her. My heart beats against my ribcage. "She's mine?" I shake my head, rewording my question, "I mean, legally, she's mine? On the paperwork?"

"Yes. She's yours."

An unusual and unique sense of pride swells in my chest. I clear my throat, "So, why was that so upsetting to him?"

She chuckles on a dry laugh, "He was worried that if he ever ran for public office, someone would dig up the certificates and see that he wasn't the father of his wife's child."

"And he's not worried about the five-thousand affairs he's had?"

She cocks her head. "Women can be paid off with no trace."

I sit back down next to her. The porch swing creaks as we rock back and forth. I slide my hand across her smooth as silk thigh.

I need to be touching her.

"What happened after that? Between y'all? With you? How long were you in the hospital?"

"They did my hip replacement just a few hours after our daughter passed away. They waited as long as they could. Even though they stabilized me enough for the C-section, it was still an emergency. I wasn't alone, though. Uncle Ray, Aunt Teresa, and Holt had just gotten to the hospital. I asked one of the responding paramedics to call them when I was trapped in the car. Holt said from the time they got the phone call until the time they hit the interstate, was only thirty-one minutes." She giggles, "I guess that's how Uncle Ray ended up with a suitcase full of T-shirts and shorts when it was already below freezing and snowing in Michigan." She sighs, a serious memory overpowering her humor. "I wanted to see them before surgery in case I didn't make it."

Oh my god. "They were afraid you wouldn't make it?"

She just shrugs. "My body had gone through a lot of shock and trauma."

I can't believe I nearly lost her too.

She gives my hand a comforting squeeze. "I was in the hospital for five days. Uncle Ray had called Marcum from the car when they were driving up. He immediately caught a flight. After six days, Uncle Ray, Holt, and Marcum drove back home. Aunt Teresa took a six-week leave of absence from work to stay with me and help me. Hudson had class so he was gone a lot. She took me to physical therapy, held me when I cried, talked to me when I was so depressed, I thought I would die. I don't know what I would've done without her.

She even got an extension for me from my online professors so I could take all of my finals after the Christmas holiday."

I kiss Lulu's knuckles. "She's an amazing woman. Just like you." I brush a hair from her forehead. "Did you tell your parents?"

"When he got back to town, Uncle Ray went and saw Dad. He never told me what my dad said, and I never asked. He just told me that I was his now, that I belonged to him and Aunt Teresa and that it didn't matter what anyone else thought or what anyone else said. I was their daughter."

I knew I always liked Ray.

Shifting in my seat, I ask, "And what happened with Hudson?"

"You know what happened with Hudson. We stayed married for nine years. He had his life, and I had my life."

"Why did you stay married to him for that long?"

"I know it doesn't make sense, but we just grew complacent. Lazy. He had his freedom, and it's not like I needed my freedom to date other people. Dating was the last thing on my mind."

"So, what finally led to the divorce?"

She debates not telling me. She debates lying. I can see it in her eyes. "So, help me, Lulu, if you lie to me, I'm gonna flip my shit."

She growls. "Fine. After the accident, Hudson wasn't always the friendliest. He'd say mean things. Degrade me, try to make me feel worthless."

"He what?!"

"Don't worry; it didn't work. In the beginning, I was too dead to feel anything at all. By the time I came back to life, I'd already had enough criminology classes to see through his façade. It was his veiled attempt at asserting his masculinity over me. I'd chosen someone else over him, and he wanted me to think that no one else would ever choose *me*. I just ignored him. He was like a peacock strutting around with his feathers splayed out. It got much easier once we moved to Mobile since we lived separately. We'd always been in separate bedrooms, but separate houses made things much better. Anyway, he came over one night to tell me that his office's charity ball was the next weekend. I told him I wasn't going. He didn't like that answer. He tried to lunge at me."

Anger clouds my vision. My jaw starts to twitch and my foot bounces against the floor in nervous energy. I. Am. Going. To. Kill. Him.

Lulu reaches over. Placing a hand on my knee, she urges my leg to stop moving. "He'd been drinking, he was slow. I jumped out of the way. He stumbled and fell into the coffee table." She smirks. "Busted his lip. It bled all over his suit."

Well, that makes things a little better.

"I told him it was time for a divorce. That was four years ago. Even though it was a simple divorce—no alimony, no child support, no assets or liabilities to split—it took him nearly a year to finalize it. He wanted to drag it out so he could play the shocked and grieving husband card."

"You didn't tell anyone what he did to you?"

She shakes her head. "His father had lined up some initial clients for me when I was starting my business. He still had a relationship with them. He threatened to ruin my reputation if I said anything negative against Hudson. As twisted as it sounds, I felt like I owed them some small portion of gratitude. I mean, they paid for my health insurance, paid off my hospital bills, paid for my college, financially supported me when my own parents disowned me. I did some due diligence, though, before agreeing to that. I knew several of his mistresses. I checked with them, and he had never been violent or mean with any of them. He treated them like princesses. All of the affairs ended amicably. It was only me. He only treated me that way because he knew I would always choose you over him. And he didn't like that."

I would always choose you over him.

And yet, I drove her into his arms.

We sit in silence for a while, listening to the summer noises of the cicadas and crickets and tree frogs. It's a lot of information to absorb. A ton. Happy news, devastating news, unbelievably remarkable news.

Even though I had planned to reach out to Lulu someday, I never thought all of *this* would happen. A few short months ago, that first night in the bar, she was driving me bat-shit crazy, and now? Now, she's still driving me bat-shit crazy. But for all the same wonderful reasons she drove me crazy twelve years ago.

Suddenly, a crushing pain chokes me, making me stutter over my words. "Did you... Is she... What happened to..." I struggle to take a breath. "What I mean is, is there a place I can visit her? Did you bury her in Michigan?"

Her whisper is low. I lean closer to hear her. "I asked that she be cremated. I spread her ashes."

Oh. "Where?"

Lulu points behind her head, toward the darkened woods. "Here."

"Huh?"

"I came here during Spring Break that following spring. Hiked through the woods, spread her ashes at the creek."

Holy. Shit. "She's here? She's been here with me this whole time?"

"Yes."

"That's why you were so upset when we went to the creek with Laura," I say, suddenly making sense of Lulu's reaction that day.

"I wasn't upset. I was in awe. All of those wildflowers? There were never that many flowers there before. When you told me you didn't plant them, I knew it was her. She's been telling you, year after year, that she's okay."

My daughter. My little baby. My angel.

I bite the inside of my cheek. I refuse to cry again tonight. I've had enough of that to last me for a lifetime. "What's her name? Did you name her?"

"Of course, I named her. Our daughter's name is Reality."

Reality reminds you where you belong.

Hell yeah, it does.

Chapter 35

Ella

I strum my fingers on the dashboard of Ry's old truck—his grandfather's truck. It's always the vehicle we take for surprises.

After absorbing the massive heap of information I just threw his way, Ry checked his watch, jumped up, and asked if I felt like a surprise. What did I say? I said yes.

Of course, I said yes.

We drove into town, stopped at the store, and bought a bunch of random items—toiletries, food products, socks, books, school supplies, unisex sweatshirts, blankets. He bought a gigantic storage container to put everything in. He had me pack it all. It was a tight fit. I had to arrange everything like a puzzle and, even now, the lid won't close. Items are spilling from the top. It's so heavy, I don't even know how he can carry it.

Well, I've seen his muscles so technically, I know *how* he can carry it.

We've been sitting across the road from a small one-story house for about ten minutes now. The outside is trimmed and neat, but you can tell it's in need of some maintenance. The front columns and windowsills have peeling paint, the side wooden gate is broken, and the roof is missing a few shingles.

"So, do you ever plan on telling me what we're doing here? And why we have to wait until midnight to do whatever it is we're gonna do?" I ask.

"A single mom and her two kids live here. Her oldest was brought into the station for shoplifting. He's fourteen. He was let go with a warning."

"What did he steal?" I fully expect him to say a video game or a phone or an expensive pair of tennis shoes.

"Deodorant."

"Deodorant?"

He rubs his fingers across his lips. "Yeah. His little brother just turned twelve. His hormones have changed, and he was starting to get body odor. He needed some deodorant to carry to gym class. His mom didn't have the money to buy extra toiletries until her next payday. The little guy was terrified of smelling after gym class, so his big brother tried to steal some deodorant for him."

My heart skips a beat. How awful. I think I have three different sticks of deodorant at my house right now, simply because I like to change the scent each day. A fog of shame drapes across my shoulders like a cloak. "That family lives here?"

"Yeah. The mom works full time as a receptionist at a small insurance company. Still, her salary alone isn't enough to pay for all the bills and buy two growing kids everything they need."

"Do you do this often? Buy things for needy families you meet at the station?"

"I want to, but I force myself to only do it a couple of times a year. If I didn't limit myself, I would probably go broke."

The moonlight bounces through the truck, shading him in a pale white light. He's so handsome. After all these years, he's done nothing but grow sexier. Edgier. I glance away before my desire becomes too much to bear. "When do you normally do it? Christmastime?"

"I'll usually deliver one at Christmas, one at Easter, and one tonight."

I furrow my brow. "Why tonight?"

"Well, I always wait until 12:01 to drop it off, so I guess you can call it tomorrow."

"Why?"

He smirks. "Don't you know what tomorrow is?"

I cock my head. "Sunday."

"No, the date. What's tomorrow's date, Lulu?"

My eyes roll back in my head while I think about the actual date. It only takes two seconds for it to click. My hand flies to my mouth, covering my gasp. "Carrie's birthday."

He doesn't say anything, he just reaches across the bench seat and runs his hand across my thigh, leaving tingles in his wake.

"You do this each year for my sister's birthday?"

"A long time ago, you said you wanted to do something special to remember Carrie each year. And you said you didn't want it to be on the anniversary of her disappearance, you said that wasn't something to celebrate. I agree; it isn't. So I do this each year. On her birthday."

"Thirty-three. Carrie's turning thirty-three." Moisture collects in the corner of my eyes. I can't believe he does this. I can't believe he does this for me.

And her.

He picks up his cell phone from the seat and lights up the home screen, showing me the time. 12:00 midnight. I hold my breath, counting the seconds until it turns to 12:01. Wordlessly, he climbs from the truck and pulls the large container from the truck bed. I spin in my seat, watching him. He tries to balance the lid on top and then tosses it to the side when he gets frustrated with it. My giggle is cut off when he grunts loudly under the weight of the heavy box. He walks across the street, up the chipped sidewalk, and gently sets the container on the small front porch. He rings the doorbell—just one time—walks back down the sidewalk, and jumps in the truck. He doesn't wait for anyone to come to the door. He just drives away.

"You don't watch them open it?"

He studies the road in front of him. "Of course not, that's a private moment. Giving a hand-out is one thing. Having people witness it is a completely different thing. Before my grandparents took me, I had some teachers who would try to give me things. They weren't very good at hiding their efforts, though, and the other kids would make fun of me for being poor. I never want to make anyone feel that way. That's why I do this in the middle of the night. By the time they get out of bed and make it to the door, I'm gone."

I always knew Ry was a good person. Even when I hated him, I knew his heart was filled with nothing but pure intentions. But this? Remembering my sister's birthday? Celebrating it like this? This is something on a whole new level.

With every mile he drives, my nerves and anxiety build. By the time he parks the truck in his driveway in front of my SUV, I'm so on-edge, I feel like either throwing up or passing out. I know he feels the tension, feels the electricity. There's no way to avoid it. It's like walking through a minefield, holding your breath, and waiting for an explosion.

How much longer can I fight this? Fight my attraction?

Before Laura called out that night, I was ready to give myself to him. Ready to break down the fortress I built around me so long ago. And he wanted it too.

He wanted to take from me. He wanted to give to me.

He wanted *me*.

And then... he found out about Reality.

I honestly have no idea where that leaves us. I lied to him. For years. I have no idea if he'll ever forgive me.

Does he want me? He's touched my thigh, he's kissed my temple, he's let me caress his back.

Was that all just comfort? Or attraction?

History? Or future?

He opens my door and offers his hand. When my skin touches his, my stomach twists in knots. I shut the door, but he doesn't move out of my way. I lean back against the truck. I'm wearing a tank top, and my bare shoulders stick against the window. Stepping forward, he traps me, eclipsing my body with his. He lifts his arms, gripping the roof of the truck. My eyes run the length of his body, charting every thick band of muscle.

Just like this.

We were standing just like this the very first time he kissed me. The very first time his lips found mine.

But he doesn't kiss me now.

He's not doing anything.

My eyes grow wide and I blink. The silence feels heavy, like a weighted blanket, suffocating me. I need to fill the silence. "Tell me something. Something no one else knows."

His gaze darts down my body and back up, pausing at my breasts, pausing at my lips, before finally settling on my eyes. "I'm an asshole. You've been through so much. I made your life hell. I wanted to do the right thing, but instead, I did the wrong thing. After all you've been through, you should hate me. But I don't want you to hate me. I want you to wrap your arms around me, I want you to kiss me, I want you to spread your legs for me."

My breath quickens, spurting from my chest in short, shallow convulsions.

He licks his lips. "I want you to spread your legs so I can bury myself deep inside you. I wanna feel your hot pussy around me. I wanna hear you scream. I wanna make you come so hard you completely forget the pain I caused you."

He takes a step closer, rubbing his hard erection across my body. I shudder in delight.

"I've waited twelve long years to be inside of you, and I don't think I can wait another second. I'm dying." He leans down, brushing his lips across the shell of my ear. "So, see, like I said, I'm an asshole."

He slowly leans back, giving me some space. He's still looming over me, but he's given me enough space to make my own decision.

But my decision was already made. A long time ago. On the back porch of a drug dealer's trailer.

I reach for him, grabbing wildly, blinded by my own crushing desire. The moan leaving my lips is feral, animalistic. I need him. I need him more than I need air to breathe.

And he doesn't need more of an invitation than that.

He grabs the back of my head and crashes his mouth against mine. Instantly, the stress, pain, and grief of last night and tonight drain from my body. He absorbs it, takes it from me, shoulders the burden himself. The sensation of his tongue in my mouth sends waves of carnal pleasure shooting low in my stomach. My panties dampen and my clit throbs.

My hands slide underneath his shirt, roaming over every inch of his taut skin. When my fingers wrap around the firm V-shaped muscles of his hips, I tug his groin against me. I rise to my tiptoes.

Friction.

I need friction.

A low growl purrs from his throat. Grabbing my ass, he effortlessly lifts me from the ground, spinning me around as he turns. I hook my ankles around him. Pulling his lips from mine, he peers over my shoulder and starts walking to the house.

My mind races with excitement. This is happening. This is *actually* happening.

Concern immediately floods my mind, and I scramble down from his arms. "Stop. Let me down. Ry. Stop."

It takes a few seconds for my words to sink in. His jaw slacks open. Even in the dark, I can see the flush of his face, the puffiness of his swollen lips. He carefully places my feet back on the ground. His voice is soaked in agony, coated in pure suffering. He rakes his hands through his hair. "Fuck. I'm so sorry, Lulu. I shouldn't have done that. You've been through too much tonight. I'm sorry," he repeats.

"Do you have sex with women here?"

He shakes his head in confusion. "What?"

"You've slept with a lot of women. Did you have sex with them here? In your bedroom?"

He looks like I just slapped him across the face. That wasn't my intention. I just worded my question poorly. But in my defense, I'm not thinking properly, all of my blood flow has been diverted to my crotch.

"Of course not. This is *your* house. I built this for you, for the memory of us. I would never defile it. I would never bring another woman here."

Skirting past him, I race back to the truck. Sure, I haven't looked in the glove box of his grandfather's truck lately, but if it's like his other truck, it's stocked with condoms. Sure enough, a pile of loose condoms is scattered throughout the glove box. I grab a handful of the foil packets and slam the door. "Then we'll need these. You won't have condoms in your bedroom."

His laugh catches me off guard. It's pure and light and sexy as hell. He holds out his arms and I eagerly jump into them. He quickly punches a code into the keypad by the front door, unlocking it, and races up the stairs two at a time. I take the opportunity to kiss his neck. I take no prisoners, branding him and marking him with hickeys. He bursts through the bedroom door like a tornado.

I shimmy down his body and toss the condoms on the nightstand. I'm simultaneously kicking off my shoes and pulling my tank top over my head. Clothes fly left and right, and Ry's so distracted when I remove my bra, he trips over the bedroom rug and has to lean against the dresser to stop himself from face planting on the floor. By this point, we're both standing in just our underwear.

There's a small lamp on in the corner of the room, and I'm so glad that there's some light in here. I'm so glad that I'm able to see him. I flick my head in his direction. "You first."

He's breathing so fast, the muscles of his six-pack undulate like an alien is trying to rip through his body. Grabbing the band of his boxer briefs, he shoves his underwear to the ground, freeing his massive erection. His body is epic perfection. Better than my memories, better than my dreams, better than my fantasies. It's like the sexy man of my youth was just a tiny precursor for what he would become. The velvet hardness of his cock makes my mouth water. It's thick and engorged, tinted with the most wonderful reddish-purple hue from the blood coursing within.

I can't take it anymore. I'm a fidgety mess. I should be worried about my love handles, about my stretch marks, about my thighs.

But I'm not. My only worry is satisfying this need that is scorching me from the inside out. My palm covers my mound, pressing firmly against the fabric of my panties. I need pressure. It's the only way I can function.

He grabs himself, pumping over the length of his shaft. "What are you doing, Lulu?"

I lift my head, staring deeply into his pale green eyes. "I'm throbbing. I need the pressure. I can't make it even one more minute."

"Take off your panties."

I smirk. "Make me."

In one split second, he crosses the room and tosses me backward on the bed. I laugh and squirm, choking on my giggle when his fingers drag the soaking wet fabric down my legs. He studies the white cream covering the gusset. He closes his eyes and inhales deeply. Before tossing them away, his tongue reaches out and licks the moisture from the cotton.

Holy hell. It was hot then. And it's just as hot now. "I remember the first time you did that."

"Well, do you remember the first time I did this?" He immediately pushes two fingers inside of me, instantly finding the sweet spots he spent hours mapping in the years of our youth. I scream. Loudly. His fingers pull out and when they gently graze my clit, I nearly come unglued.

I can't take it. I slap his hand away. Hard.

"Ow."

I didn't hurt him. I just shocked him. "Enough of that. We can do that later. I need you. Now." I lean up on my elbows, trying to enforce my threat. "Now!"

Fumbling for a condom, he knocks two of them to the ground. Tearing the foil, he rolls the latex over his dick. He barely has it in position when I'm pulling him on top of me.

"Impatient little minx, aren't we?"

I can't joke. I can't laugh. It's real now. It's completely real. I can't make light of this situation. I can do nothing but pant his name. "Ry."

He gently wipes the hair from my sweaty brow, studying me with pure adoration. "I'm here, Lulu. I'm here."

And with that, he slides into me so deeply, I don't know how we'll ever be separated.

Chapter 36

Crutch

She moans.

Rolling over, she stretches her arm across my side of the bed, searching for me. "Ry?"

It's not even seven in the morning. It's raining outside so the gray morning light casts her swollen and well-loved body in the most beautiful of shadows. Gorgeous. My Lulu is gorgeous.

"I'm right here."

Her voice is thick with sleep. "What are you doing?"

I pull on my boots, walk over to the bed, and sit next to her. I trace my finger up the curve of her spine. Something catches my eye. The bandage on her arm has some blood on it. Shit. We were pretty wild last night. Well, this morning, I guess you would call it. I hope she didn't bust a stitch.

She tries to open her eyes, but they're too heavy. She looks like a little kid trying to stay awake in church. It makes me laugh. "Go back to sleep. It's early."

"Come back to bed."

"I can't. I got called in. There was a gas station robbery, I have to work."

"What time is it?"

"Close to seven."

She pats my thigh. "We didn't go to sleep until after three. Come back to bed."

"I'll be back as soon as I can. Keep the bed warm for me." I lean forward and kiss her temple. She doesn't budge. She's already fallen back asleep.

Walking into the bathroom, I grab the first-aid box and then set it on the nightstand. I open the drawer, push my latest book aside, and grab a notepad and pen.

I'm sorry I had to leave for work. I'll be home as soon as humanly possible.

Do not move. Not a single inch. I expect to find you in my bed. Naked. Wet. And waiting for me.

Last night was nothing. I have so much more to give. It was just the beginning.

GAME ON.

PS-I'm sorry about your arm.

I can't believe I had to work all day. All damn day.

But there were some positives to it. Like when Lulu texted me asking what time I would be home.

Home. To our home.

It made my heart feel like melted butter.

I could get used to that. Hell, one text, and I'm already used to it.

Marcum was waiting at the gas station for me when I pulled up this morning. He saw the hickeys all over my neck. He also saw the shit-eating grin plastered all over my face.

He grunted. "She's like a daughter to me. Besides that, you show up to a crime scene parading yourself around like that? You look like you just left a strip club. Not very professional, son."

I nodded, respecting the chastising from my mentor. "Yes, sir. It won't happen again." I shook my head, not meaning what I literally said. *Because you better believe it will happen again.* "What I mean is, I won't show up in a physical state like this again."

He nodded, but when he turned around, I caught his reflection in the side mirror of his truck. He smiled. Smugly, proudly.

It was something small. It probably meant nothing to him, but it made me feel like I just had a talk with my dad. Well, not *my* father, obviously, but it felt like what a fatherly talk should be like. So, I enjoyed the moment.

Oh yeah, and we caught the bad guy.

All in all, it was a damn good day.

And now, I get to see My Lulu.

I can tell she's been somewhere. The position of her SUV has changed in the driveway. I park my truck in the garage and walk through the mudroom. Hanging my hat and keys on a hook, I shake the rain from my hair and toss my wallet on a small table before turning the corner into the kitchen.

Oh, hell yeah.

Melted butter again.

The kitchen table is set for two. There's some kind of salad, bread, and chicken. And cantaloupe. The washed frying pan is drying next to the sink. Over on the kitchen counter, her work is all spread out—her laptop, her notebooks, her day planner. In the distance, I hear the toilet flush in the hall bathroom, followed by the running water of her washing her hands. The noise of her bare feet padding across the floor gives me a hard-on.

When she rounds the staircase, she literally steals the breath from my body. She's wearing a white shirt and, courtesy of the bright lights of the kitchen, I can see her black bra underneath. Her short, gray cotton skirt showcases the brown tan of her skin. Her honey and caramel waves are pinned out of her face with a small barrette, and her face is free of makeup.

But the best thing?

Her smile. Wide and beautiful and happy.

"There you are. I was wondering when you would get home. I'm starving."

I lick my lips. "Me too. But not for food."

She laughs, holding her stomach. "Well, tough shit. Because I'm hungry for food. I did some pan-fried pretzel-covered chicken. It's great."

I stare at her, trying to use my non-existent powers of telekinesis to make her drop her panties.

It's not working.

She sits down and nods at the seat next to her. Pouting, I grab a seat as she plates my food. She studies me from the corner of her eye. "You can pout all you want, but we're eating supper."

I concede with a grunt. As soon as I start eating, I realize how hungry I am. "The chicken is great, Lulu, thank you. Did I have this stuff in the fridge?"

"No. I ran home to get a few things. I really needed to catch up on some work today, so I needed my laptop and paperwork. I stopped at the store on my way back."

"Did you get a lot of work done?"

"I did. It's been raining all day, so I set up outside on the porch and worked. It was so peaceful."

"You could've used your office." I nod down the hall. "That's what it's there for."

She tries not to blush. Really, she does. It's the cutest thing ever.

"Thanks. But you know I love watching the rain droplets bounce off the pond."

And I love you, Lulu.

I finish before she does. She's eating so painstakingly slow. I think she knows what she's doing; I think she's teasing me on purpose. Finally, she sits back, declaring. "That was so good."

I jump up from the table and pull her against me. "It was. Now, let's go work it off."

Giggling, she pushes back. "I need to clear the table. I made dessert too."

"I don't want dessert. I want you."

She leans forward, poking my chest with her finger. "I made it. And you're gonna eat it. Sit."

Are you kidding me right now?

Flopping back down in my chair, I splay my legs wide in front of me and watch as she clears the table. I should help her. It would be the nice thing to do. But she's not being nice to me. She knows I need more. More of her.

I've never seen someone rinse dishes and load the dishwasher so damn slow. A sloth could move at a faster pace than this. Not to mention, every time she bends over, flashing the back of her thighs to me, my erection grows harder. I mean, I could knock down concrete pillars over here.

She's playing our game. And she's not playing fair.

After an eternity, she closes the dishwasher and makes her way back over to the table. Stepping between my legs, she grabs the hem of her skirt and lifts it to her waist.

Kill. Me. Now.

She's not wearing any panties.

"Your dessert is served. Game on, Ry."

My eyes dart to hers. It's the best thing I've ever heard.

Wrapping my hand around the back of her head—so I won't give her a concussion—I fling her across the kitchen table and make up for twelve long years.

Starting with eating that dessert.

I wish I could say that coming home Monday night was as pleasant as coming home Sunday night, but it wasn't.

She wasn't there.

I didn't have a chance to call or text her until about four and she didn't respond. When I pulled in my driveway, her SUV wasn't there. I raced through the house calling her name. Like a fool, I even checked the closets. I immediately jumped in the truck and raced back into town.

And here I stand, pounding on her front door. "Open the damn door, Lulu."

After just a second, Holt opens the door. He takes one look at me and starts laughing. I'm about to punch him in the face when he steps to the side, letting me pass. Lulu's sitting at the counter, laptop open, and earbuds in her ears. Smiling brightly, she waves and motions that she's on a web call.

Looks like I'm waiting.

Holt takes a long sip of a sports drink. He's drenched in sweat. He's obviously been working out, doing his physical therapy. "I see, after all this time, she's still driving you crazy," he says.

"I want her to drive me crazy until the day that I die." Whoa, I didn't mean to get that serious with Holt.

The humor fades from his face and his brow furrows. "You never moved past her, did you, man? It was always her."

I lean against the back of the loveseat, watching as she furiously scribbles notes in a green notebook with purple polka dots. "She was my one and only. She'll always be my one and only." I turn and study him. "Just wait. Just wait until it happens to you. You'll know exactly what I'm talking about."

He shrugs, fiddling with the wrapper on his bottle. "Hey, I'm ready." Lightening the mood, he nudges my shoulder, "Got any hot female relatives you wanna set me up with?"

"The only female relative I have is my mother. And she's currently in jail."

Holt's eyebrows lift into his hairline. "Uhhh. Hard pass." He walks back to his room, hollering over his shoulder. "Nice hickeys, by the way."

I pace around the living room, waiting on Lulu to end her work call. When she finally does, she yanks the earbuds from her ears and races over to me. Throwing her arms around my neck, she kisses one of the healing hickeys. "Hi."

"You left."

Pulling away, she studies my face, smirking like she can't believe I'm actually upset. "Of course, I left. It was a regular workday today. You had work, I had work."

I toss my hands in the air. "So?"

"Plus, I only packed enough for one night."

"So, pack more shit this time." I look down the hall and point to her bedroom. "In fact, pack all your shit."

She squints her eyes. "What? What are you talking about?"

I spin in a circle, looking at the living room. "This isn't you, Lulu. Can't you see that? You don't belong here. You belong with me. At *our* house. The house you designed and I built. It's ours."

She walks over into the kitchen and grabs a diet soda from the fridge. "What are you saying? You want me to move in? You wanna live together?"

I grab the soda from her hand and put it down on the counter. Scooping her into my arms, I hug her, holding her body tightly against mine, forcing her to her tiptoes. She loves it when I do that. Bending my head, I slowly lick the shell of her ear and whisper, "Hell yeah, I do."

She loves it when I do that too.

And having her in our house, I'll be able to do all the things she loves whenever I want.

Ella

Fourteen days.

Twenty-three times.

I've had sex with Ryland Joseph Crutchfield twenty-three times over the past fourteen days, and I'm ready for a million more. I never wanna stop making love to him.

Never. Ever. Ever.

And that's what I'm thinking about when Marcum tosses a box of tissues in my face. The box bounces off my chest and lands on the edge of his desk.

"Ow. What was that for?"

"A Kleenex, for you to wipe that smile off your face."

I lean forward, splaying my hand across the form he's been trying to read for the past twenty minutes, the twenty minutes I've been sitting here pestering him. "You like it when I smile."

He tries to camouflage his chuckle with a cough. Leaning back in his chair, he gives me the evil eye. "So, living together now, are we?"

I'm not a rocket scientist, but I *am* a pretty good detective, and I know the 'we' he is referring to is not me and him.

"Well, not technically speaking. I still have my parents' house. And I still have my house in Mobile. I mean, I'm still making a mortgage payment on that one for goodness' sake."

The air around me sparks to life. I feel the connection of his presence even before he rounds the corner and walks into the office. Standing behind me, his fingertips trail underneath my hair, searching for my scar. His calloused thumb gently strokes the raised skin.

The timbre of his voice sends chills up my spine. "Technically, the answer is yes. And I told her to put the Mobile house on the market."

Marcum pokes out his bottom lip, glancing between me and Ry. I can't decide if he's happy or angry. I fully expect him to say that we're moving too fast; instead, he folds his hands behind his head and says, "I hear the market is really hot down there right now. Might not be a bad time to sell."

Well, that was unexpected.

Shifting in my seat, I look up at Ry. "Did you come in here just to make Marcum worry about my finances?"

He looks to Marcum and back at me. "Nope. I've got the DNA results." He doesn't wait for us to respond; he simply walks out of the office and heads into the conference room.

I jump out my chair so fast, I nearly knock the thing over. Marcum flings his ink pen across the desk. We race into the conference room, trailing behind Ry.

Waiting on him to pull out his laptop and sign into the secure portal for the private lab is agony. Pure slow death. I tap my foot impatiently on the floor. When I hear the ding, telling me he's entered an incorrect password, I reach for the computer. "Here, let me do it."

He cocks his head and twists out of my grasp.

"Ella, settle down. You're gonna give yourself a heart attack." Marcum pulls a protein bar out of his interior jacket pocket. "Here, have a protein bar."

I pick it up off the table and study the mangled bar. "How long has this been in your jacket?"

"I'm not exactly sure. But it's a protein bar. It doesn't expire."

"It most certainly does. And your armpit sweat probably speeds up the rotting process."

"Okay, I'm in."

Ry's voice makes me jerk, and I loudly drop the bar on the table. I toss it across the room, ringing the trash can. "What does it say?"

He holds up a finger. I watch as his eyes flicker back and forth. It's like watching a typewriter. He mumbles to himself while scrolling through the screens. Scrolling back to the top of the page, he clears his throat and starts. "Okay, here we go. Tape: Carrie, you, and Unknown Female (1). Envelope body: Carrie, you, and Unknown Female (1). Envelope flap: Carrie and Unknown Female (1). All six pictures: Carrie and Unknown Female (1). Pregnancy test: Carrie. And trace amounts of DNA in the urine are a match for Carrie as well." He sighs, "No hits. Unknown Female (1) is not in any system."

I shake my head back and forth. It's not enough. I need more. This was supposed to give us answers. This *wasn't* supposed to give me 'Unknown Female (1)'. I hold out my hands, and Ry slides the open laptop across the table. I read and re-read the words. Over and over and over.

Marcum reaches out, squeezing my shoulder. "Ella?"

I bite my lip, refusing to cry. Instead, I shift in my seat, squaring my shoulders and stiffening my spine. "This is what I paid for? This bullshit? This lab is supposed to be the best." I slap the offensive computer away from me. "We're never gonna find out what happened to her. This was pointless! The evidence died with that piece of crap, Trey!"

Ry sits back, folding his arms across his chest. I can see it in his eyes. He's not going to coddle me on this one. He's not going to let me play the woe-is-me card. "Lulu, this isn't your first investigation. You do this for a living, it's your job. One, I might add, that you're damn good at. You knew the likelihood of having a hit come back on the DNA was not very probable unless the offender was in the system. We know more now than we did. And that always equates to good news in this world."

He leans forward, staring deeply into my eyes. He enunciates each word slowly, like I'm hard of hearing. "Now. Tell me what you see."

My lips flatten into a small line. "I see the death of this case, Ry. That's what I see. Dead. Just like my sister."

His growl is angry, demon possessed. "So, help me, Lulu, if you don't tell me what you see, I'm gonna flip my shit."

"Fine!" I close my eyes and rub my temples, thinking. "Well, there's no doubt now; Carrie was pregnant. It's safe to assume she was pregnant at the time she went missing. It's safe to assume she kept it a secret. At least, she didn't show anyone else the pregnancy test. Someone else would've picked it up to look at it. The only DNA on it was hers."

I blow a raspberry, thinking. "The pictures all came from the same person, a female. If anyone else was involved in sending those pictures to Carrie, they kept their distance. They didn't touch anything. A female? I believe what Christina said. I don't think she stayed at the trailer that night to take the pictures. If the only people who knew about the rape pictures were the people present that night, then that means our camera person was a female." I tick through the list on my fingers, "Carrie, rapist, Trey, and Unknown Female (1)."

My fingers leave my temple and tap against the table. "If we still operate on the theory that the rapist and supplier are one in the same, then we have Unknown Female (1) in the mix. She sent the photos to Carrie. Why?"

I try to think of all the reasons someone would send the pictures to my sister. "Jealousy? Maybe the supplier was her boyfriend. But if the pictures were meant to be a threat, a 'stay away from my man' warning, you'd think there would be a note in the envelope saying just as much. There wasn't a note. Carrie kept everything else, I can't imagine she threw away a threatening letter.

"So, if not for jealousy, then maybe… empathy? Unknown Female felt sorry for Carrie. She didn't like keeping this secret from her. She wanted her to know the truth. Why? Either Unknown Female had been a victim of sexual assault herself, or Unknown Female actually knew my sister."

My eyes fly open. "She knew Carrie. Before that night, she knew her. Knew her well enough to feel bad for her. The envelope wasn't addressed. Unknown Female knew where we lived. She dropped it off. Or she put it on Carrie's car. Or put it somewhere where Carrie would specifically find it. None of the normal people from Trash's parties knew that much about Carrie. This was someone else."

Anger beats against my heart like a drum. "Someone who knew my sister showed up that night and watched her get raped."

Marcum whispers a curse word. Ry's eyes leave mine, and he winks at Marcum. Standing up from the table, he kisses the top of my head on his way out. "I told you she was good. That's My Lulu."

Will leans across the bar, handing a drink to the guy behind me. "Well, I guess it was wishful thinking to believe the DNA report would give all the answers, just like that." He snaps his fingers.

Ridge takes a deep pull from his beer. "Still doesn't make it easy." He nudges me with his shoulder. "I'm sorry, Ella."

"Thanks." I lean forward, sipping on my cocktail.

"You made us watch all those crime documentaries after Carrie went missing. I guess we all got our hopes up, that this would be one of the stories that had an immediate ending. DNA test, bad guy, jail. Boom." Ridge slaps his hand on the bar.

I shake my head. "We just have to keep digging."

I catch Cullen nodding to the door, and I spin on my barstool. Ry stalks across the room. It's a good thing I'm sitting because he's making me weak in the knees. His gray T-shirt is sticking to his sculpted chest, courtesy of the mid-July heat. He just came from the station, so he's still wearing cargo pants and boots. Cargo pants, might I add, that are the perfect fit across the rounded globes of his ass. Lifting his arm, he raises and repositions the ballcap on his head. He smirks when he sees me watching him. It's a teasing smirk that only lifts one side of his luscious mouth.

Right before he's about to reach me, a small brunette spins around and accidentally bumps into him. She's thrown off balance, so he reaches around, grabbing her upper arms to steady her. Once she's back on stable feet, she looks up to thank him. "Than— Oh." She's immediately struck mute by the gorgeous man standing in front of her.

She flips her hair and quickly recovers. Obviously, hair flipping is where she gathers her strength.

"Thank you. I'm such a klutz." She places a hand in the middle of his firm stomach. "Buy you a drink?"

Ry looks over her head, studying my reaction. Growling, I spin back around on my barstool. Will, Cullen, and Ridge are all laughing.

Jackasses.

"Thanks for the offer, but I don't think my live-in girlfriend would appreciate that. Have a good night."

Well, that's new. And unexpected.

And quite frankly, music to my ears.

Sitting beside me, his large hand circles around my hip, and he tugs my barstool closer. It screeches across the floor. "I was worried about you for a minute."

I snort. "Oh, yeah?"

"Your eyes rolled so far back in your head I thought you were having a stroke."

"I did not roll my eyes."

Cullen puts a beer in front of Ry. "You totally rolled your eyes."

My mouth falls open. "Cullen!"

He holds his hands up in surrender and disappears to help the next customer.

"Well, if I rolled my eyes, it was only because you couldn't keep your hands to yourself."

He chuckles. "She was about to fall."

I sip on my cocktail, talking around my straw. "She probably fell into you on purpose."

Ry nods at my drink. "I see you're drinking again."

I spin the glass, watching the pretty blue liquid swirl around against the ice cubes. After my incident with the Long Island Iced

Teas, Will and Cullen decided to have me taste-test a sampler plat-ter of non-alcoholic mocktails. Knowing I wanted something pretty, Cullen plied me with all sorts of concoctions in hues of pink, red, purple, and green. The winner was a non-alcoholic version of a Blue Lagoon. Cullen garnishes it with a stick of oranges, cherries, and mangoes.

"Yep. And who knows, I may get shit-faced tonight."

He leans forward, playfully nibbling on my ear. "Good thing you're coming home with me tonight. I can take care of you." He sits back, taking a long drink from his bottle. "As long as you keep your throw up to yourself."

Will leans against the bar, tossing a rag over his shoulder. "Eww. Raylee told me you threw up on him. I forgot about that. Gross."

Ry laughs, squinting his eyes in good humor.

I open my mouth to make a catty comment, but really, there's no defense. I did throw up on him.

Ridge points at his brother. "Cullen threw up all over me once. Remember, C, on that road trip to the Grand Canyon?"

"Shit. I completely forgot about that. You're the one who paid me five bucks to eat five hotdogs."

"Okay! As intriguing as this conversation is, me and my woman have somewhere to be." Ry tosses some money down on the bar and grabs my hand.

"We do?"

He leans in and almost growls, as if I didn't know what he meant. "Yes. Bed."

Chapter 38

Crutch

I'm glad we live out in the middle of nowhere.

She's even more vocal than I remember.

Moaning, screaming, panting.

It's fucking amazing.

I slowly pull my head from between her legs. Trailing my tongue up her stomach, I lick the mound of her large breast. Maturity has settled in her curves. Her breasts are heavier now, hanging from her body at a different angle.

They're perfect. She's perfect.

She bucks against me when I playfully bite her pebbled nipple. The dark brown skin is too perfect to ignore.

Reaching for a condom, I sit back on my knees and roll the latex over my throbbing erection. Lulu watches my every move. Her eyes widen in delight. Instead of pulling me down on top of her, though, she sits up, scrambling to her knees, mimicking my stance.

"Lulu?"

"You've had sex with a lot of women."

I definitely don't like the start of this conversation, but there's no point in lying. "Yes."

She tries to hide the pain, but I can still see it written all over her face. Plain as day. Like a flashing neon sign.

She swallows. "How many times have you had sex without a condom? I mean, with how many women? I'm not actually asking you to remember the exact number of times."

But that's an easy number to remember. "None."

"None? Never? You've never had sex without a condom?"

"No. Never."

She takes a deep breath. Her breasts bounce with the movement. "You and I always used a condom. And, still, I ended up pregnant."

Visions of Reality pierce my soul, filling me with longing for my daughter. "Yes."

She shifts on the mattress, firming up her stance. When her legs move, the scent of her arousal wafts through the air. "Have any other women come to you with pregnancy scares?"

"No. Never."

She purses her lips, letting the information sink in. "I'm on birth control now. I take a pill every morning."

Is this conversation going where I think it's going? My heart stops beating, my vision blurs, my dick hardens even more. "I know. I see you take your birth control pill every morning."

Her gaze travels down my body. Her fists curl, slowly scratching the sides of her thighs. "I want to feel you inside of me. Just you. Nothing between us. No barriers." Her caramel eyes are swirled with ribbons of black passion. "Do you want that too? Do you wanna have me like that, Ry?"

I open my mouth, but I choke on the words. Nothing comes out. All I can do is nod.

She leans forward, carefully taking possession of my cock. With tender fingers, she rolls the condom from my body and tosses it on the floor. Flames of excitement ignite in my stomach, tightening my muscles. She swirls her thumb around, coating me with a drop of my own pre-cum.

Pressing on my shoulders, she rolls me over on my back and straddles me. Her fingertips dig into my pectorals. Getting into just the right position, she slowly lowers her body onto mine.

One delicious inch at a time.

Kill. Me. Now.

The bastard who said wearing the thinnest condom is just like wearing nothing at all, is a liar. It's a lie. A complete and total fabrication. Because nothing has ever felt this good in my entire thirty-three years.

The second her body is flush with mine, she presses down even farther, wanting more. And I give it to her. Grabbing her hips, I thrust as deep as I can. Lulu's head rolls back and she screams. Needing a moment to gain my composure, I lie back against the pillow, close my eyes, and breathe. It's taking all of my strength not to blow my load this very minute.

Her heat. Her moisture. The ridges of her wall.

I'm lost in my own bliss when I realize that she's not moving. She's panting like she's run a marathon, but she's not moving.

"Lulu?" My hands shift up, from her hips to her neck. "Are you okay?"

She nods, thrashing her hair across her face. Her whisper is low and gravelly, her sentence coming out in small bursts. "You. Feel. So. Good."

Every time she talks her body clenches around mine. She shifts higher on my pelvis, making my body shudder.

"Never. Felt. So. Good."

I press my hand on her breastbone. She has to stop wiggling, or I'm gonna come in two seconds. "Wait. Lulu, you never had sex with your husband without a condom?"

She shakes her head. Her breasts slap against my hand. "Never. Hudson cheated on me. I protected myself." She swallows. The noise echoes through my own body. "You. You're always my first. Never before. Never after."

This woman will be the death of me.

Wrapping my hand around her neck, I pull her mouth to mine. My tongue meets hers. Taking, tasting, tangling. She quickly tires of kissing and wants more.

My Lulu always wants more.

She sits back up, and I grab her hips. She tries to start slow, but I won't let her. I meet her every thrust with one of my own. Claiming her, marking her as mine. Our momentum is frenzied and frantic, each of us racing to the bliss we crave.

But I want to make it last. We'll only have one *first* time together.

Every time I feel her about to explode, I force her to stop.

Stop moving. Stop grinding.

I pull her into kisses, dragging out the release we both know will come sooner rather than later. This goes on, and the fourth time I stop pumping into her and grab her for a kiss, she knocks my hand away.

And she keeps moving.

Moving without my permission.

"Stop. I need it. Now." Her lips are swollen. Her face is flushed. Sweat glistens on her brow. She's the sexiest creature I've ever seen.

How can I deny her?

Reaching up, I wrap my hands around her back and over her shoulders. I tilt my ass off the bed and thrust as hard as I can while pressing down on her shoulders, forcing myself so deep, it doesn't even seem humanly possible.

Please come, Lulu. Please come. Because this is it for me.

I lose my vision. My legs tremble. The blood stops circulating in my body. The split second my orgasm starts, I feel Lulu's walls crash around me. She screams and stops moving, lost in the throes of her own passion. She milks me dry, dragging every last bit of desire from my body.

I collapse against the bed and Lulu collapses against me.

Incredible. Flawless. Magnificent. No words can do it justice. So, I keep my mouth shut.

But because she's My Lulu, her dirty little mouth has other plans. "I feel your cum inside of my pussy." She leans up and kisses my lips. "Aren't those the best words you've ever heard."

"Hell yeah, they are."

Chapter 39

Ella

I turn in my seat, smiling when I see Laura bouncing in excitement. She doesn't see me watching her. She's too busy staring out the window as we pass by the gigantic houses in my neighborhood.

"I'm so very excited. I hope she likes my present."

"I know she'll love it, but your mom didn't have to buy Anna a present. I told you that."

"Mommy didn't buy it. Uncle Ry did. Mommy helped me make the card. She put the glue on the paper and I did the glitter." She gives me a knowing look, "I could've done it myself, but I didn't wanna hurt her feelings."

I steal a glance at Ry. "You enjoy shopping for dolls?"

He shrugs. "It wasn't all that bad."

Laura pipes up from the back seat. "He threw a football in the store and broke a display of blocks. You're not supposed to play inside of the store."

I burst out laughing. Ry looks at his niece in the rearview mirror. "Snitch," he snarls.

"Miss Lulu? You really have a big house like this?"

"I do. It was my parents' house. I grew up there."

She pushes her glasses up on her nose. "But I thought you lived at Uncle Ry's now?"

I open my mouth. I'm not exactly sure how to respond to that. Laura is going to stay the night at Ry's house tonight, and we haven't decided exactly what to do. Last time Laura was there, Ry slept on the couch. "Well, uhh... what makes you say that?"

Smirking, she folds her arms across her chest. "I'm six. I'm not stupid." Smiling proudly, she ticks off the evidence on her tiny fingers. "I saw your makeup in the bathroom, I saw your clothes in the laundry basket, and I saw your flip flops on the patio by the firepit." Her eyes immediately light up. "Hey! Can we sit by the firepit tonight?"

Ry answers, "We'll see. I guess I should start calling you Little Detective instead of Little Girl, huh?"

I grab the water bottle from the console and take a sip. "Well, that was certainly impressive. She's observant." I give him a teasing smile, "Gunning for your job one day?"

He holds out his hand for the bottle and takes a drink after me. "Sounds like she's going after both of our jobs." He hands the water back to me and turns up the volume on the stereo a notch so Laura can't eavesdrop as easy. "By the way, I spoke to Brooke. I let her know the status of our relationship. She's completely fine with us sharing our bed as normal tonight. She trusts us. And she trusts us with Laura."

I inhale so deeply my ribcage hurts. "And what's the status of our relationship?"

"We're in it, Lulu. There's no point in hiding our involvement from Laura. In fact, I think it will do her some good to see adults engaged in a healthy, caring relationship." He turns into the driveway and throws the truck into park. His hand covers mine. "There's no running away anymore. For either of us. You're mine."

I lean forward, eager to taste his lips on mine.

"What are we waiting for?" Laura whispers, looking from Ry to me. She's escaped her seat belt and pushed her way onto the middle console between the two of us.

For once, Ry's the one rolling his eyes. "Nothing. Let's go."

We walk around the back gate where everybody is already by the pool. You can tell Laura is just a little bit nervous to see so many people. She takes a step closer to Ry's leg.

Anna runs across to meet us. "Hi!"

Ry guides Laura forward with a soft hand on her shoulder.

She immediately sticks her hand in front of her, introducing herself. "Hello, I'm Laura Margaret Crutchfield."

The formality doesn't faze Anna one bit. She grins, shaking Laura's hand. "Hi, I'm Anna Ruth Beachum. Thank you for coming to my birthday party."

"Here, I made you a card."

Anna studies the card. "Ohh, it's so pretty. I love the glitter. I have a bulletin board in my room. I can hang it on that." Anna holds the card out to me. "Look at it, Smelly Ellie. Isn't it beautiful?"

I nod. "It's very beautiful."

"Smelly Ellie? That's a funny name. Does Miss Lulu fart a lot?"

"Laura!" My yell is louder than I intend for it to be.

Ry's laughing so damn hard I think about knocking him into the pool.

Our reaction makes the girls giggle uncontrollably. "No, I just started calling her that when I was really little because it rhymed."

Holt walks up, scooping Anna into his arms. The two of them have quite the special bond. "What's going on? What did I miss?"

Anna kisses his cheek. "We're talking about Smelly Ellie's poots."

He scrunches his nose, sniffing. "Ella farted?"

Ry doubles over, clutching his stomach. My face turns beet red. Despite my best efforts not to laugh, I can't help it. "No one farted! We are not talking about me and bodily functions."

Holt holds up his hands in surrender. "Hey, we all do it."

Anna shoves the card in front of his face. "Look at my beautiful card, Uncle Holt. Laura made it for me."

Laura holds out her hand, introducing herself again. Holt sets Anna on the ground and kisses Laura's outstretched hand. "The pleasure is all mine, milady. Holt Hill, at your service."

Laura's eyes grow wide. "Like a knight. And so handsome too." She turns to Ry. "Like *King Arthur and His Knights of the Round-table.*"

I rub Laura's head. "You've already read that book?"

"Uncle Ry read it to me. Every time I stay with him, before bedtime we read from a really old, really important adult book."

Anna looks at Ry. "Can I show Laura my cake before we go swimming?"

He nods and the girls race off.

Holt kisses me on the cheek and shakes Ry's hand. "I'm running out to get another bag of ice for the cooler. Y'all need anything?"

Ry shakes his head. "No, man, we're good." He places a hand on my back and traces the curve of my spine, settling right above my ass. He holds me tight as we walk over to join everyone else.

"I didn't know you still did that. Read classic literature before bed? Why haven't you been doing it?"

He leans over, nuzzling his lips against the shell of my ear. His hot breath makes me shiver. "In case you haven't noticed, we've been pretty busy each night before bed. There's been a lot of time to make up for. The games have been keeping my mind more than occupied."

I stop walking and pull him around so he's facing me. His back is toward everyone, and his body eclipses mine, so they can't see what we're doing. Under the guise of a cuddle, I lean in and fondle his groin. It immediately jumps to life in my hand. Standing on my tiptoes, I bite his lip. "Game on."

I immediately dart to the side and roll from his embrace. "Hi!" I wave at my family and friends and start dispensing hugs. I can't help but laugh when it takes a good minute before Ry can turn around and join us.

We're all lounging around the patio after gorging ourselves on amazing food and birthday cake. The girls have been playing with Anna's

new toys for the past hour. We convinced them to eat and do presents first because we knew that we'd never be able to get them out of the pool once they jumped in.

"Can we please go swimming now?"

Ry nods to Raylee, deferring to her for an answer.

"Yes, you can go swimming now."

The words are barely out of her mouth when the girls strip off their cover-ups and race to the side of the pool.

"Little Girl," Ry hollers, "aren't you forgetting something?" He points to his eyes.

"Oh! Right." Laura skips back over and hands her glasses to Ry.

We watch, as both Laura and Anna jump into the pool, holding hands.

"They're really getting along," Aunt Teresa says. "That's great."

Ridge and Cullen's mom, Dana, laughs. "They definitely play well together. Reminds me of all you kids when you were younger."

Cullen snorts. "Are you serious? Ridge and Holt made my life miserable."

Holt takes a swig of his beer. "I resent that. I think we treated you quite fairly."

Cullen squints his eyes. "Forcing me to eat worms does not constitute treating me fairly."

Ridge pushes the ballcap up on his forehead. "We did not *force* you. You did that all on your own. I can't help it if you'd eat anything for money."

Cullen *would* eat anything for money. I was there the night he ate a grasshopper.

"Speaking of friends," I say, changing the subject, "why didn't Anna invite any of her other friends or classmates? I told you it was fine to invite as many people as you want to the house, I trust you."

Raylee shrugs. "It was Anna's idea. She didn't want Laura to feel like the odd man out."

Ry shifts in his chair and rubs his fingers across his chin. "Oh, wow." He clears his throat, trying to mask his emotion. "That was really nice of her. Thank you."

Raylee smiles, watching the girls. "She gets that from Will," she says with a wink at her husband. "Laura goes to Parkside?"

"Yeah, Brooke's apartment is zoned for there."

Raylee nods. "That's a good school."

"It is, but their testing scores have been on the decline for the past couple of years, so that's a little concerning. Anna goes to Rockdale, right? That's an awesome school."

Test scores? Ry has time to study the test scores of our county's public schools?

"You know, I'm on the board for the Parent Teacher Organization. Last I heard, there were still a few out-of-zoning spots open. There's only two-and-a-half weeks before school starts back, but I could get you an application if you'd like."

Ry leans forward, engrossed in the conversation like Raylee just told him she knows the real identity of D.B. Cooper. "Really?"

"Sure."

"Thank you, Raylee." Ry adjusts the ballcap on his head, pulling it down closer to his eyes so I can't read his expression, but I know he's happy. He sits back in his chair and possessively wraps a hand around my crossed legs. His fingers trace up and down my thigh. I can't help but notice that all of the men in my life eagle eye his actions—Uncle Ray, Marcum, Holt, Will, Ridge, Cullen, and their dad, Jeff. If Ry's intimidated by their stare, he doesn't let on. Aunt Teresa discreetly pokes Uncle Ray in the stomach, making Nancy laugh.

The baby monitor crackles to life, and we all listen as Ty grunts and wiggles. You can hear the sound of his diaper scrunching as his butt bounces around in the playpen. "Uh-oh, someone's missing the party." Raylee scoots her chair back to stand up.

Nancy reaches across Marcum and shoos her hand in Raylee's face. "Let me. I always loved getting the kids up from naptime."

Raylee flips off the baby monitor as Nancy heads into the house. "You don't have to ask me twice, Nancy."

We spend the next two hours talking and relaxing. We laugh at the girls' antics in the swimming pool and their very elaborate game of mermaid. Holt has to throw some plastic cups and bowls in the pool for their pretend mermaid brunch. We videotape Ty eating Anna's birthday cake with his fist. It's an absolutely perfect day.

Until it isn't.

I'm in the middle of a story about one of my recent TV jobs when Marcum interrupts me, nodding his head in the direction of the gate. "Ella."

Turning around, I'm shocked to see Kristie standing there. She's dressed in shorts and a tank top and a baggy cardigan. She looks embarrassed to be intruding on our party, but not too embarrassed to turn around and leave. Sheepishly, she puts one foot in front of the other, walking in our direction. We haven't seen her since her little striptease at the bar, and you can tell Will's still not happy about it. He curses underneath his breath.

I push away from the table, but Ry doesn't let me go too far by myself. He's walking next to me, with his finger hooked in the back waistband of my shorts.

Kristie picks at her fingernails. "Hi."

"Hey, Kristie."

She looks past me to everyone gathered around the table. "Barbeque?"

I study her eyes. They seem clear and focused. I don't think she's drunk. "We're celebrating Anna's birthday."

"Oh. I'm sorry for barging in."

She may be sorry, but she doesn't make any move to leave.

Ry angles his body so the girls can't hear him talking above their game of Marco Polo. "Kristie, what are you doing here?"

His tone is harsh, and she takes a step back in shock. Cocking my head, I scold him with my eyes. I try a nicer approach. "Are you okay? Did you need something?"

She reaches out, grabbing both my hands. My spine immediately stiffens and my breath traps inside of my body. I still don't like people I don't know touching me. And I don't really know, Kristie. Not anymore. I didn't see her for nearly twelve years, and when I did finally come home, I found out she's a drunk who flashes her tits to the random public. In fact, I'm surprised Phillip didn't fire her after that stunt. I mean, she is the front-office face for his practice. Not to mention, I think there's a real possibility that she might have a drug problem.

I can't have that around Laura or Anna or Ty.

I mean, Ry won't even let Laura see her biological father for the exact same reason. Well, that and the fact that he's a felon. A felon who is most likely still doing felonious things, despite his probation.

"I was hoping we could talk for a minute, Ella. Is that okay?"

The look in her eyes is heartbreaking. She looks like a long lost puppy at the pound, just waiting for the right owner to come along and point at her cage—*'I'll take that one.'*

I nod. "Sure." I wave my hand at the sliding glass door, and she heads inside. I turn to Ry, "I'll be back in a few minutes."

His eyes flare. "Lulu," he warns.

"It'll be fine. What are you worried about? That she'll flash me? That she'll hit on me? That's all her destructive behavior consists of."

"Not funny."

"Just keep Holt out of the house. You know she's always had a thing for him."

Holt's voice startles me from behind. "You don't have to worry about that. We all know I don't mind a woman who's been around the block, but she's been to more neighborhoods than a census taker."

I slap Holt across the chest. "Y'all shut up and wait here."

I find Kristie waiting inside my bedroom. She's sitting on the bed, hugging a pillow to her chest. I sit down next to her. "Kristie, is something wrong? Are you okay?"

"I can't imagine what you must think of me."

I open my mouth to politely lie, but fortunately, she stops me.

"You don't have to say anything. I know my past behavior at the bar was unacceptable." She looks around my room, taking in the décor that hasn't changed since my mother had it professionally decorated all those years ago. "I miss the way things used to be. With me, you, and Carrie. It was so much simpler when we were younger. I loved coming here. I used to wish y'all were my sisters. I would lie awake at night and think about what my life could have been like... you had a mom."

I shake my head. "Our lives were far from perfect, Kristie. You're viewing the past through rose-colored glasses. Our nanny, Janine, was more of a mother figure to us than my mom ever was. You know that."

She sighs. "Maybe you're right."

"I know I'm right."

She fiddles with the fringe on the pillow. "I know what they all say about me, that I'm a slut who goes home with tons of men."

"Who cares what anyone says about you. You're a grown woman. You can go home with whomever you want. My only hope is that you're smart about it." I bend my head, catching her eye. "But from what I've seen, you're not being smart about it. The times I've seen you at the bar, you've been drunk. Too drunk to decide if you really wanna hop in bed with someone. Plus, you have your professional reputation to think about. You see a lot of patients at the practice."

She narrows her eyes. "Crutch sleeps with women all the time. From what I hear, his reputation is nearly as big as his dick. Have you given him this same speech?"

Excuse me? For someone who wanted to talk to me, she's rolling in here uninvited and being a bitch.

Anger vibrates so deep in my body that it rattles my teeth. "I am well aware of his reputation, thank you. And that is something we'll work through together. Our relationship is far more complicated than you know. If you want to have some tit-for-tat comparison of the indiscretions you and he have both experienced over the past decade, you need to find somewhere else to do it. And someone else to do it with. Because I won't listen to it."

Her eyes well up with tears. "I'm sorry, Ella. I shouldn't have said that. I'm glad things seem to be working out for the two of you. You deserve to be happy."

"And you deserve that too."

She wipes her runny nose. "I got into a fight with my dad."

"About what?" I ask.

"I told him that I wanted to move out."

"And he didn't take the news well?"

She rolls her eyes. "That's putting it mildly."

"Kristie, you're thirty-two years old. You don't need permission from your father to move out and start your own life. It's definitely time." I bite my lip in thought. "It might be just what he needs too. He's not had any long-term relationships since your mom passed away. I think y'all's dependency on one another has become a burden instead of a benefit."

She nods, but doesn't say anything.

"I have to meet with Dad's lawyers and financial advisors next week to close out the estate. We're meeting in the boardroom at the office. Your dad will be there. I could speak to him, if you'd like?"

"Really? You'd do that?"

"Sure." I stand up.

She nibbles on her bottom lip. "Dad's wanting to buy out Robert's share of the medical practice and building."

It's true. The lawyers presented me with Phillip's offer a while ago. It's completely generous. More than generous, actually. I just don't know if giving one person so much control is the wisest decision. The general surgeon they temporarily brought in to take Dad's place has made an offer as well. It's not as lucrative, but she seems to love what she does, and she seems to really care about her patients. I've done some digging on her, and from what I can find, she's honest and sincere. She's got two children—one in middle school and one in elementary school.

"Yeah. He does."

"Are you gonna sell to him?"

I furrow my brow. I can't decide if she sounds worried or hopeful. "No decisions have been made yet. I've got to do what I think is best for the practice in the long run." I walk Kristie through the house.

"I'll go out this door so I don't interrupt the party," Kristie says.

She's probably fishing for an invitation to stay, but I don't give her one.

She leans in for a hug, but stops when she sees me take a small step backward. "Sorry, I forget you don't like to be hugged." Smiling, she closes the door behind her.

But I do. I love to be hugged—only by everyone sitting on my back patio right now.

Chapter 40

Crutch

How can something so small hurt so bad.

Even to this day, I'm amazed at the pain.

I twist my arm, trying to decide the best angle to cut. The angry scar on my shoulder has been even angrier the past week. What started as a small, tender bump now looks like a bright red volcano. I open the first-aid kit and pull out the small black medical bag where I keep the sealed disposable scalpels.

I freeze the second I hear her feet padding down the stairs. I was hoping she wouldn't wake up. That's why I waited until the middle of the night. "Ry?"

"In here. In the kitchen."

The second she walks into the room, my heart melts. I swear this woman makes me feel like I've grown a vagina. I'm so damn mushy all the time. I can't even think straight when I'm around her.

Her wavy hair is pointing in a thousand different directions and her *Harlan's* T-shirt grazes the tops of her thighs, drawing attention to every inch of those mile-long legs that I love so much. She rubs her sleep-swollen eyes. "What are you doing?"

"Nothing. I'll be up in a minute."

She takes a step closer, peeking around at the makeshift hospital I set up on the kitchen bar. "What's wrong? Are you hurt?" She scurries over in front of me, scanning her eyes across my face and bare chest, searching for an injury. Her eyes widen and a blush covers her cheeks. It happens every time she studies my body.

Forget the vagina. That definitely makes me feel like a man.

When she finally eyes my shoulder, she jumps back. "Holy shit!"

"Language, language," I tsk.

"That's why you've been wearing a shirt?"

"I always wear a shirt."

She cocks her hands on her hips. "Not around here you don't."

I smile. "And why do you think that is?"

She smirks, pointing her little chin in the air. "Because you love it when I ogle you like you're some kind of male stripper. I'm just waiting on you to put a tip jar on the counter so I have to start filling it with dollar bills."

I laugh, rubbing my hand across my stubble. "That's not a bad idea."

She takes a step closer and points at the jagged red bump protruding from my skin. "Something's working its way out, isn't it? What is it?"

"Plastic, metal, glass." I shrug. "I don't know."

"Is it infected?"

"No. But it could get infected if I don't get it out. It's ready. It hurts like a son of a bitch."

"Why aren't you going to the hospital for this?"

"I can't go to the hospital every time this happens. It's not feasible, Lulu."

She swallows loudly. "Okay. Tell me what to do."

"Are you sure you wanna be here for this? Based on your reaction when you first saw my injury, it might not be the best thing."

"It wasn't the scar that upset me. It was the thought of losing you." She reaches out, gently brushing her fingers across my collarbone. "Am I in danger of losing you?"

Grabbing her hand, I kiss her fingertips. "Never."

"Well, then, we have nothing to worry about it." She sighs and looks at all of the supplies. "Sounds like this will be a part of my life now. I need to know what happens."

I lick my lips. "Alright." I point to a small bag of needles. "Grab that shot of lidocaine. You need to inject it very slowly all around the bump."

We give the medicine a few minutes to take effect, and she cleans the area with antiseptic wipes. "We need to cut with a scalpel. Can you do that?"

She shakes her head. "I don't think so. What if I cut too deep?" She chuckles, trying to lighten the mood. "I've researched too many medical malpractice suits. I don't wanna be on the receiving end."

"It's fine, I can do the cutting." Hell, I'm an old pro by now. Looking over my shoulder, I make a small incision with steady hand. I guess if part of me had to get blown up, I'm glad it was my left side. I'm right-handed. I can't imagine having to cut with my left hand. I tell Lulu to hold the gauze over the wound until the bleeding settles down.

By the third pile of gauze, the blood flow has slowed. "Won't you need stitches?" she asks.

"I have some alternative suture kits. It's kind of like butterfly tape except there are little brackets that you pull together to keep the skin closed." I check the wound. Whatever it is, it's green. I can see the edge of it already peeking through my filleted skin. "Grab the forceps."

She picks them up, her fingers stained with my blood. "Okay, now what?"

"Dig it out."

Her eyes widen and she holds her breath.

Laughing, I try to wrangle the instrument from her hand. "Here, I'll do it."

She yanks away. "No, I'll do it." Pushing my knees apart, she steps between my spread legs to get a better angle. "I just grab it?"

"Grab it and pull it out." I wink. "And then get the shit out of my arm."

She lifts an eyebrow, not amused.

She bends her head and investigates my shoulder. Unable to help myself, my free arm snakes around her waist and my hand travels to her ass, cupping it. All I feel is T-shirt. I don't think she's wearing any panties.

"Ry," she warns.

"Sorry. I'll stop."

She bites her lip. "Okay. Here goes." The second the forceps pierce inside my arm, she asks if I'm okay. She's so nervous she actually yells the question, nearly bursting my eardrum.

"I'm fine. That's what the lidocaine was for."

Nodding, I watch as she grabs the very edge of the object and tries to pull it out.

Well, that's never gonna work.

Sure enough, my blood makes it too slippery, and the shrapnel slips from the forceps and dives back into my skin, making her gasp in horror.

"It's okay. Try again. You have to dig deeper."

For a split second she looks upset, but because she's My Lulu, that doesn't last long. Stiffening her spine, she squares her shoulders and narrows her eyes into small little beads. She's gripping the forceps so tightly her knuckles are turning white. She finds the edge of the debris and slides farther down into my body. My flesh makes a sickening squishy sound, like someone's kneading ground beef through their fingers. She goes a little deeper than the lidocaine went, and I clench my teeth, fighting through the pain, trying not to move. She yanks the remnant from my body, and the wound actually makes a large popping sound, celebrating the expulsion of the foreign object. A large dollop of blood pours from the cut and rolls down my arm, pooling in the crevice of my elbow.

Her mouth falls open as we stare it.

Green glass. Like an old-fashioned soda bottle. About three quarters the size of my thumbnail.

"Glass," she whispers. "You have glass inside of your body." Her lip quivers. "Someone tried to kill you."

Grabbing the forceps from her, I toss them down on the counter. Drops of my blood mar the surface. Wrapping my good hand around her neck, I graze her puffy little scar with my thumb. "Hey. Look at me. I'm fine. Completely fine. We'll clean me up and throw that shrapnel right in the trash, right where it belongs. It's not coming between you and me. Nothing is."

Taking a deep breath, she nods, forcing her emotions in check. "Now what?"

I show her how to flush the wound, pack it with some antibiotic ointment, and close it with the suture alternative. Finally, we cover it with some fresh gauze and a large waterproof bandage. The lidocaine is starting to wear off, so I pop an over-the-counter pain reliver and watch as she cleans up the mess. When everything is tidy, she comes back over to check on her handiwork.

I tug her back between my legs. "How's it look?"

She nods. "Good."

"Good?" I snort. "Most of the time, I don't even think about it. But every once in a while, I'll pass by a mirror and it catches my attention. It looks like my shoulder went through a meat grinder."

Cocking her head, she watches me with those mesmerizing eyes. Honey and caramel and maple syrup all swirled into one. Lifting my right hand, she moves my fingertips across the fresh scar on her forearm from her fall at the gas station on our way back from Atlanta. She then moves my hand to her left thigh and forces me to trace the entire length of her hip surgery scar.

She's definitely not wearing any panties.

Grabbing the hem of her shirt, she yanks it overhead and tosses it across the kitchen counter. Her large tits swing in front of my face, causing my mouth to go dry and my dick to go hard. Her nipples immediately peak and the milky skin of her breasts breaks out in chill bumps. My eyes travel down the firm lines and soft curves of her body. Her shaved little pussy is like a magnet. I can't stay away from it. I couldn't then, and I sure as hell can't stay away from it now.

She reaches back out, grabbing my hand again, and places it on her pelvis, right across the soft skin above her pubic bone. Together, we trace the thin white line. It's barely visible, but I know it's there. In our time together, I've mapped every inch of her perfect body.

"My C-section scar." Twisting to the left, she moves her head to the side so the glow from the kitchen light illuminates the shadows of her stomach. She points to the small pink lines on either side of her hip bones. "Stretch marks." She looks up at me. "Sometimes, I see all these things and I think I'm not beautiful."

Kill. Me. Now.

This woman is mine. She's all mine. She's my everything. She's the epitome of beauty.

And it's my job to make her feel beautiful every single second of every single day. *For the rest of our lives.*

"Those scars are proof of your battles, Lulu. You've fought war after war, and you're still standing." I touch her forearm. "Some mother tucked her little boy into bed tonight because of you." I caress the vertical lines of her stretch marks. "Our daughter lived inside of this body." I shake my head in awe. "You grew a human being inside of you. Words can't describe how amazing that is." My fingers move over to her C-section scar. "We didn't get the time with Reality that we wanted, but it doesn't make it any less real. It doesn't make *her* any less real. These scars gave me a child, and they make your body even more remarkable than it was twelve years ago. That seventeen-year-old I met was gorgeous, but this thirty-year-old? She's absolutely breathtaking."

Lulu smiles softly. Her hands wrap around my thighs.

I lean forward, whispering to her. "Tell me something. Something no one else knows."

I can see the wheels spinning in her head and a flash of brilliance sparkles in her eyes when she settles on something. "LMC Forensic Consulting doesn't stand for Love My Career. LMC stands for Luella Margaret Crutchfield."

Kill. Me. Again.

Damn... That is one sweet sounding name.

I can't hold it in any longer. I'm so tired of not saying it. "I love you."

She gasps. Her hand flies to her chest. Knowing My Lulu, she's probably checking herself for a heartbeat.

My fingers dig into her hips, and I possessively tug her against me. "I love you, Lulu. I always have. I never stopped, not for one single minute. I will love you until the day I take my last breath. You're mine. Never before. Never after."

Her eyes hood with desire, and her face flushes pink with passion. "I lo—"

I cover her mouth with my hand. "I don't think so," I scold her. "Remember, we can't say it at the same time. Your rule."

She playfully bites my finger. "Well then, how about I just show you."

Sweeter words have never been spoken.

Chapter 41

Ella

I don't mind having all-day meetings on a Friday.

But these meetings just plain suck.

My phone buzzes with an incoming text message from Ry. Smiling, I answer his question asking if my meetings are done. I answer with very colorful language.

"Ella, did you hear me?"

Sighing, I lay my phone back on the conference room table. "I'm sorry. I had to respond to that. Would you mind repeating?"

"Your parents had pledged $50,000 to North and Camden for building the new wing on the library. Will you be honoring that donation?"

"No."

The attorney's eyes nearly bug out of his head. "No?"

"Correct, Mr. Coppock, I have no plans to honor that pledge." I write a reminder note in my notebook. "Instead, I will be giving that money to the Wounded Warrior Project."

The room is filled with five men and one woman, each dressed in suits that cost more than most people's monthly income. They glance at each other, not hiding their displeasure. "The charity for veterans?"

"That's the one, Mr. Coppock."

"Ella, that's a noble gesture, and I would definitely encourage you to donate funds to the organization as you see fit, but the school is really counting on that money. The construction work has already started."

I square my shoulders and fold my hands in front of me on the table. "From what I understand, Mr. Coppock, your own children attend that school. In fact, last I heard, you were on the school board. If the new library wing is that instrumental to the education of the young minds at North and Camden Academy, then I suggest *you* make the donation. I am well aware of the money that will be in your pocket after today, and I know you will be more than capable of making, and even exceeding, my parents' pledge."

The scowl on his face is almost comical. I stare at him until he finally wearies of my gaze and turns his head.

I gather my notebook and all my papers. "I assume our business is concluded?" When no one immediately answers, I stand up and pull my work bag and purse over my shoulder. The men in the room suddenly remember their fake manners and politely stand, acknowledging my exit.

One of the other attorneys taps his ink pen on a leather portfolio. "We'll draft the documents for the sale of Robert's share of the business and building and send them to you for your review next week."

I nod and walk out the door. "Have a good weekend."

Waiting for the elevator, I stare out the window, watching the bright August sun sink lower in the sky. Heat rises from the black asphalt, dissecting the air in wavy, invisible lines.

"I was hoping I would get to see you before you left."

Spinning around, I prop myself against the window ledge. "Hi, Phillip. I was actually gonna stop by your office on my way out. What brings you up to this floor?"

He's wearing scrubs and his white coat. After all these years, he's still attractive. And still a good actor. His emotions are strategically hidden underneath a fake smile, expensive hair gel, and a spray tan. "Like I said, I wanted to see you." Walking over, he leans next to me. "You've been in town for over seven months now, and I've barely seen you."

"Work keeps me busy."

"That crime helper thing?" He waves a hand in the air and chuckles, indicating he can't believe my career consists of such fodder.

Asshole.

"It's a little more complicated than that, Phillip."

"You could have been a great architect, Ella. Your father always displayed the drawings you did—buildings, houses. You had great attention to detail."

He did not. Not once did I ever walk into my father's office and see anything that me or Carrie made. No painted handprints, no stick-figure family drawings, no coloring book masterpieces. The only thing he had in his office were professionally painted family portraits where we looked like little glass dolls.

"Well, that wasn't for me." I shrug. "Sometimes parents have to let their children carve their own paths in life."

"You used to be such a good girl, always going along with whatever your parents asked of you. So polite and charming. I always told Kristie she should be more like you." He shakes his head. "I must say I'm still shocked that Robert and Susan let you marry that Plott boy at such a young age." He turns to me, giving me a once over. "I still say there's more to that story. Your parents refused to talk about it." He winks. "Care to share? I mean, we are old friends here."

His gaze lingers on my face for a couple of seconds too long. It weirds me out, makes me feel like cockroaches are sprinting across my spine.

I stare back at him, refusing to look away. "I think I've done enough traveling down memory lane today."

"Ahh, yes. Speaking of, how did your meetings go? Attorneys, financial advisors. I heard you were meeting with them all."

"I did. There's a couple of more documents to finalize, and then the estate will be closed."

His jaw clenches. "So, you reviewed my offer then?"

I take a deep breath. "I did. It was a very generous offer, Phillip."

He stands straight, crossing his arms over his chest. "But?"

"But... that would give you majority control over the practice and the building. I don't think that's the best decision for the longevity of the business. Dr. Bussman has done a remarkable job since taking over for Dad. Y'all all decided that she was the best fit for the practice. Sure, at the time, it was a temporary move, but everyone had to assume that it would become permanent if things went well. I've done my research on her; I've met with some of her patients and the staff, including all of the staff that stayed with the practice after Dad's death. Everyone loves her. She's competent, engaging, and passionate about what she does. Her children are still young, and she's looking to build a life here, in this town. I've decided to sell to her."

He already knew what I was going to say, but he definitely doesn't like it. His eyes grow cold and blank. He cocks his head to the side, popping his neck. "Well, you can't do anything without the approval of the other partners."

I lift my chin in the air. "Seriously, Phillip, you really wanna stonewall this? Why?"

He doesn't answer.

Gathering my bags, I press the button for the elevator again. "It's a moot point anyway, the others have already consented." Well, not our pharmacist. But I don't tell that to Phillip. "The paperwork will be finalized next week. You can expect something on your desk by next Friday. I told Dr. Bussman we can make it public and celebrate at the Annual Appreciation Gala next month."

The elevator doors start to close, but I suddenly remember why I needed to talk to him. I slap my hand against the closing metal and it springs open. "And by the way, your daughter? She's a grown-ass woman. She needs her own life and her own space. It's time for her to move out. I think you'll be able to function just fine having her as an office manager and a daughter. You don't need her to be your roommate and surrogate companion anymore." The elevator starts to buzz, annoyed that I'm keeping it from its very important job of delivering me to the bottom floor. I point my finger in his face. "You're fucking her all up in the head. Stop being a selfish weirdo."

His eyes flare with anger and he takes a step in my direction. The elevator is faster than him, though.

Man, that felt good.

I shouldn't laugh. But I can't help it. I always do what I shouldn't.

I laugh so hard I nearly pee my pants.

Chapter 42

Ella

So, this is why he didn't want to go to the bar tonight.

I jump out of the vehicle, unable to contain my excitement.

The second my door slams, Ry and Laura hold out their arms and yell, "Surprise!"

My heart flutters against my ribcage like a thousand butterflies are trying to escape. They're standing on the patio where the firepit rages, sending gorgeous blue flames into the dusk sky. There's a big tent set up, right where *our* tent used to be. This one is slightly larger and looks a little nicer. On the other side of the patio is a large table overflowing with food. I could be wrong, but that looks like a four-foot-long Philly cheesesteak sandwich.

I'm still taking it all in when Laura races up to me. I immediately scoop her into a hug. "What's all this?"

She pushes her glasses up on her nose. "It's a campout. Just like you and Uncle Ry used to do all the time. Except I get to camp out too!"

I watch Ry as he walks over to us. Stalks would be the more appropriate term. He's wearing a T-shirt, cargo shorts, and flip flops. His ballcap is pulled down low on his head. Every muscle in his body flexes. He's pure danger and power. And when he lovingly ruffles Laura's hair, he's never looked sexier.

"Y'all did this for me?"

Laura nods wildly. "Uncle Ry said you had a really bad day and that we needed to do something to cheer you up. He picked me up from summer camp and we planned the whole thing. He said that we're gonna start camping out once a month. He said we're *going back to our stump*'."

I furrow my brow. "Huh?"

Ry laughs. "Going back to *our roots*, not going back to *our stump*."

She scowls, mumbling under her breath that she liked her saying better.

I smile. "It's even better now." I nod at the house. "We have a working bathroom this time."

Laura runs back down to the patio. We watch as she grabs Felicia Stinkbottoms and skips to the tire swing.

Taking the opportunity, Ry wraps his fingers around my waist and pulls me against his hard body. I react. Instantly growing wet.

Flipping his ballcap around backward, he nuzzles his lips against my ear. "Hi."

"I can't believe you did this for me. It's wonderful. Thank you."

He pulls back and bends his head. He's so close that his lips rub against mine when he talks, driving me to the brink of insanity. "I was worried you might not like it. We spent all those nights sitting outside, sleeping in a tent. But we were kids then. You haven't grown too accustomed to indoor living, have you?"

I open my mouth, breathing his air, becoming part of him, renewing my soul. "Never. That tent is a sight for sore eyes." My tongue dart outs, licking his. I couldn't stop myself from moaning even if I wanted to.

But he doesn't give me what I want.

Instead, he steps away and smirks. "Good. Then go change out of those work clothes so we can eat. My Philly cheesesteak is getting cold."

After we eat, Ry and Laura fish while I clean up the food. I take the leftovers inside and store them in the fridge. That's definitely an upgrade from our past as well—no more coolers filled with ice. Laura catches a fish and proudly poses next to Ry as I take their picture. By the time we play a few card games, Laura starts to yawn.

Ry hands his cell phone to her. "Little Girl, why don't you call your mom and say goodnight before it gets too late."

I snuggle next to Ry on a loveseat, watching the blue flames dance in the fire. Hearing Laura's sweet and excited words to her mother stirs a longing deep in my heart. I reach around my neck, rubbing my scar in thought.

"She'll jabber for twenty minutes if you let her," he jokes.

"She's got a lot to say."

He snorts. "Little Girl always has a lot to say." Noticing my mood, he gently kisses the top of my head. "Are you thinking about Reality?"

"I always think about Reality."

I feel him nodding. "I was thinking we should do something special at the creek, a memorial of sorts. I was thinking about a rock garden, maybe? I did some research, and they make these fake rocks now that are eco-friendly and solar powered. They glow blue and green at night. We can build a really nice wooden glider out there. I was even thinking of lining the path I cut with lights and a cedar log railing. Instead of driving the side-by-side up there, we could walk. Enjoy the creek at night."

I shift in my seat, studying him. "Really?"

"Yeah. Everyone said they would help me—Marcum, Ray, Holt, Will, Ridge, Cullen, and Jeff. I told them I just had to run it by you first."

I blink several times, willing my tears not to fall. This man. I can't believe this is my life right now. I never thought in my sadness that I could be this happy. The words of his letter haunt me. *Hate me.* How could I ever hate him? "I think that's a beautiful idea. Thank you."

Leaning back, I chew on my lip in thought.

He bumps me with his shoulder. "Go ahead and ask me. I know you want to."

"What are you talking about?"

"Don't beat around the bush, Lulu. I like you when you get to the point."

I grunt. "Fine." I twist in the seat, allowing him to pull my legs into his lap. He lazily traces a finger up and down my shin. "Why ask me? It's your house, Ry. Your property. You don't need my permission to build or upgrade or change."

He yanks the cap from his head and tosses it on another chair. He rakes his hand back and forth through his light brown hair. "For someone so smart, you can still be so stupid sometimes. I've told you before and I'll tell you again, this house is just as much yours as it is mine. I built it for you. It's the only way I could live my life, knowing that I made your vision come true. But it's not just this house, Lulu. It's everything. Everything you see and hear and touch and think. There is no you. There is no me. Not anymore. There's only *us*."

"And there's me."

We turn and see Laura standing right next to us. She slaps the cell phone into Ry's hand. "Can I go inside and get the book now?"

"Sure. But brush your teeth while you're inside."

"Okay. Come on, Miss Lulu, you need to brush your teeth too."

I raise my eyebrows. "I do?"

"Yep. Because I know you and Uncle Ry will wanna kiss after I fall asleep."

Ry bursts out laughing. "How'd you get to be so smart?"

She smiles and pushes her glasses up on her nose. "I'm six. I know these things."

Taking her hand in mine, we walk up to the house.

She falls sound asleep after two chapters in *Little Women*.

Ry carries her into the tent, laying her to sleep on the air mattress. Before sitting back down, he grabs a fresh beer for himself and a bottle of water for me from the small cooler he packed and brought down to the concrete patio. I swing my legs onto his lap, and his hand possessively holds my thigh.

"So, how bad was it today?"

"Bad." I shrug. "My parents. What can I say? They had their secrets, even after all these years. Dad had secret bank accounts so he could buy things for his mistresses. Mom hid money to keep it away from Dad so he didn't spend it on his mistresses.

"Apparently, Mom had several secret plastic surgeries over the past few years. The last disbursement checks I approved today included a balance of $42,000 to some plastic surgeon in Miami."

I reach out and run my fingertips across the bones in his wrist. I trace the muscular cord of his arm up to his elbow and back again. His calloused thumb works the sensitive skin of my inner thigh.

"I don't ever want that." I watch as the flames of the firepit dance across his pale green eyes. "We've already been through that. We hid things from each other. We kept our distance; we kept our secrets. And it nearly ruined my life. I don't ever wanna fall into that trap again. Promise me we won't."

He takes a deep breath, studying my face. "We won't. Because I'm never letting you go again."

I snuggle against his side, and we soak in the comforting noises of the night. Eventually, I nod at the tent. "It's hard to believe school is already starting again. Is she excited about her new school?"

He chuckles. "She's more excited about being in the same class as Anna." He sighs, "Raylee didn't have to do what she did. I'll be forever indebted to her. I'd crawl across glass to make sure Laura has all the opportunities that Trash and I never had. I know it's only elementary school, but she's too smart to be in a struggling school that doesn't challenge her." He kisses the top of my head. "I'm also glad Holt accepted that coaching job. I know he's on the other side of the campus in the high school building, but it's still nice to know he's close in case anything happens."

"I'm sure she wishes Ridge were that close. Laura has a major crush on him. And did you see her with Nate the other day, when she met him? She couldn't stop staring at him," I say, talking about Marcum and Nancy's thirteen-year-old grandson.

Ry snorts and shakes his head. "Let's hope that's not an indicator of what's to come in her teenage years."

"At least she has good taste in men."

He pulls back, studying my face. Good humor and jealousy color his features in equal parts. "Something I should worry about? You carrying a torch for your old pal, Ridge?"

I lick my lips. "The only man I've ever carried a torch for has been you." I kiss his jaw, running my tongue across the sexy stubble shading his face. "I love you, Ry." He loves it when I say that. When I speak the truth.

His eyes grow heavy with desire. His head lowers and his hot breath tickles the sensitive skin below my ear. "Fuck yeah, you do."

His body presses against mine, making me forget every dirty detail I trudged through today regarding the strangers I once called Mom and Dad.

Chapter 43

Crutch

The weather matches my mood.

It was supposed to be a beautiful, sunny, blazing-hot September day, but it's not. Storm clouds rumble in the distance, blocking the sun. At least the temperature is bearable, especially when combined with the whipping wind. My ringing cell phone breaks the scowl on my face.

Marcum.

I only left him twenty minutes ago. I guess he wasn't kidding when he said he was going to call and check on me. "Hey."

"How you doing, son?"

All these years later, I still fill with warmth when I hear him call me that. It always makes me think of my grandpa. And Harlan. "I'm fine." Considering I haven't slept in thirty-one hours, I count not falling asleep behind the wheel as doing pretty damn good.

He grunts through the phone. "I highly doubt that." He sighs, trying to grasp the right words. "Days like today are part of the reason we want to be a cop. But they're also part of the reason we want to be anything *but* a cop."

I swipe my hand over my face, thinking about the consuming relief that flooded my body when we found the little boy. And then I think about the overwhelming despair that engulfed my soul when I found out what all he'd been through. He was missing for just over twenty-four hours.

One day.

That's all it took.

One day, and he'll be fighting this trauma for the rest of his life.

"Crutch, I know you've been by yourself for a long time now. We've had tough calls like this before, and you've been able to go home and deal with it privately. You've been able to wallow in your fear and pity and anger all by yourself—for days, weeks. You've haven't had to answer to anyone. That's not the case now. You have Ella.

"Trust me, in the beginning, you won't want to talk to her about the job, about the tough things. You'll think it'll be easier to keep it all inside. You think you'll be sparing her feelings. But don't. Don't keep it inside. I've been married long enough to tell you that sharing your thoughts and emotions with your soulmate is the best kind of medicine for this kind of stuff. Don't bottle it up." He clears his throat. "If you keep it bottled up, it will kill you. A slow and agonizing death. You'll lose her. Again. And I should know, back when I was your age, I bricked myself off from the world, and Nancy nearly left me. You don't want that. I think we both know that neither of you would survive another breakup."

He's right. I wouldn't make it. If Lulu left me, I would cease to exist.

I nod, eventually agreeing. "Okay, you're right. I know you're right." I turn onto my driveway, counting down the seconds until our house comes into view. My voice lowers to a whisper. I'm ashamed to even say the words I've been thinking. "I wanted to kill him. I was praying he would do something stupid so I could kill him—fight, run, make one wrong move." I blink, forcing images of the vile man to the back of my mind. "Fuck shooting him, I wanted to kill him with my bare hands, wrap my fingers around his throat and squeeze until his windpipe popped and his eyes bled." I take a deep breath, trying to rid myself of the violent thoughts. "I just kept thinking about Reality. If my daughter had survived, is this the kind of world I would be raising her in? Could the same thing have happened to her? What about Laura? How am I supposed to keep her safe?"

"You keep her safe by being you. By doing the best you can. That's all any of us can do."

I end the call, pull the truck into the garage, and head into the house. In the mudroom, I remove my utility belt and put everything in its proper place while Lulu's angelic voice floats through air. She must be in the kitchen. When I round the corner, the sight of her takes my breath away. If I were more of a puss, I'd break down into a pile of tears right now.

She's standing at the kitchen bar, kneading dough with both hands. She must be on a conference call because her earbuds dangle from her ears, and her phone is close enough to touch but out of danger from any flying flour. On cue, she talks into the air. "I would agree with that assessment." Sensing my presence, she turns to me and breaks into a huge grin. Her caramel eyes glitter in the morning sun, pouring from the window. She grabs the box of biscuit mix and shakes it in my direction, proudly showing off her attempt to make biscuits for breakfast.

She's barefoot, wearing one of those short simple cotton skirts that she traipses around the house in. Her pink tank top and blue bra straps showcase the golden glow from her tanned shoulders. Despite the melancholy coursing through my veins, my body instantly responds to hers. My balls vibrate and my dick swells. It's always that way. It *will* always be that way. Even when we're eighty, with gray hair, and covered in wrinkles.

I circle my arms around her. Her hair is piled high on top of her head in a lopsided ponytail, giving me free reign of her neck. I gently kiss the puffy scar given to her by her sister. She sighs and leans against me, rubbing her tight ass in all the right places. My fingertips graze against her thighs. Pulling her skirt up around her waist, I grab her panties and pull them down in one swift movement. She freezes. I can feel her body swell beneath mine. The air charges with tangible electricity, filled with love and lust. It's only been two seconds, but the smell of her desire fills my nostrils, making it hard to form a cohesive thought.

I fondle the perfect globes of her ass and plant my palm on the small of her back, bending her forward. She bites back a gasp, quickly pushing the half-kneaded dough out of the way. The box of biscuit mix clatters to the ground and a puff of flour dust covers the bottom of the cabinets.

"Mmm-hmm. That's right, Michael."

I chuckle. She'll figure out the best way to get off the call. She won't be able to stay on it, given the things I plan on doing to her. My Lulu likes to make noise. Lots and lots of noise.

I trace the scar from her hip replacement and snake my hand across her mound. When my finger rakes across her engorged clit, her body bucks, driving me wild. I slide my fingers through her slit, spread the wetness over her sensitive bud, and massage my woman into a damn frenzy. With my other hand, from behind, I plunge two fingers deep inside her tight pussy. With unforgiving abandon, I fuck her with my fingers, bringing her to the brink of orgasm. Her back arches and her body sways back and forth against mine. She clutches the lip of the countertop so tightly, I worry she'll break her own fingers.

I need her.

I need her so badly I'm shaking.

I pull my shirt over my head and toss it across the room. I work my belt buckle, quickly unzipping my pants and lowering them and my boxer briefs to my knees. Grabbing my cock, I fold her across the kitchen island and position my throbbing head at her entrance.

"Gentleman, I hate to interrupt, but I have an urgent meeting that I must attend. We'll touch base again next week. Hopefully, I'll have all of the responses compiled by then. Good day." She ends the call and flings the earbuds across the countertop. She barely has time to take a breath before I'm driving balls deep inside of her.

Her scream nearly shatters my eardrum.

I love it.

I pump into her, releasing all of my love. All of my fear. All of my worry. I need her. I need her to help me fight this world. I need her to help me live in this world.

Lulu reaches back, wrapping her hand behind my neck and pulling me down. Turning her head, she nips at my ear. "Did you think about me, Ry? All those years? With all of those other women? Did you think about me?"

I growl. "I couldn't get off unless I closed my eyes and pictured you." I playfully tug on her ponytail, snapping her head back. My words are breathless. "What about you, Lulu? Did you think about me? When you touched yourself? Did you think about me?"

Panting syllables fly through the air, timed perfectly with the motion of our bodies. "I thought about you every time my fingers were buried deep inside me. I always thought about you. It's the only way I could come. Make me come, Ry. Make me come all over you." Her whisper sends an electric shock through my body.

Sweeter words have never been spoken.

Needing to touch even more of her, I slide my hands underneath her tank top, reach inside her bra, and fondle her breasts. Her nipples grate against my hot skin, putting my already nervous body on edge. Together, we chase our release. She pushes back against me, wanting more of me. Wanting all of me. And I give it to her. I pray she finds her satisfaction soon because mine is about to erupt.

Mid-stroke, she screams. Her body stiffens with the surging euphoria of her orgasm. Her insides tighten, driving me out of my mind. Then, her body loosens and relaxes, giving me free reign to let myself go. My cock is covered in the thick heat of her moisture.

Sweat rolls down my face.

I lose my vision. I lose my voice. I lose my hearing.

I lose myself.

I give her everything. I give her my all.

How did I ever think I could live my life without her? There is *nothing* without her.

My Lulu is my heart.

Once our breathing returns to normal, I pull out of her and haphazardly pull up my pants, leaving my belt undone. I don't even care that white jizz stains my gray boxer briefs. I won't be in them long.

I spin My Lulu around and she immediately presses her lips to mine. I hug her tightly, pulling her against me and up to her tiptoes. I tap her thigh, telling her to hop up, and I haul her into my arms. Her legs hook around my waist. I can feel our juices leaking from her body, wetting my stomach.

It's so damn hot.

I walk away, leaving her panties on the kitchen floor.

"Wait!" She squeezes my shoulder. "Turn off the oven."

Growling, I spin around and hit the off button before heading upstairs.

"What are we doing?"

"I'm exhausted. I need sleep. And I need you beside me."

Even though it's nine in the morning, even though she's in the throes of her workday, even though she probably has a million other things to do, she simply says okay and kisses that sweet spot of skin underneath my ear. In the bedroom, she pulls the blinds closed as I strip down naked. I don't even bother with fresh boxers; I'm too tired. She shrugs out of her own clothes and climbs into bed with me. Our bodies tangle together.

She knows I had a bad day. She doesn't have to ask. She knows. When a man doesn't come home from work for thirty-one hours, it's a bad day.

Her whisper is sweet, like candy. "You'll tell me about it later? You'll talk to me?"

"Yes."

She doesn't press. She knows I'm telling the truth.

Sleep is about to drag me under when she asks me one last thing. "Tell me something. Something no one else knows."

My brain is fogged, completely frazzled and sleep deprived. "What if I'm a bad father? What if I can't protect our child from this shitty world? I couldn't protect you. I couldn't protect Reality."

I'm not playing by the rules. I basically had the same conversation with Marcum just a few minutes ago. So, technically, someone else *does* know those thoughts.

Oh well.

I always do what I shouldn't do.

Breaking the rules isn't a first for me.

If she answers, I don't hear her as I fall into a troubled sleep.

My throat is dry and thick when my eyes finally squint open. Lulu's still beside me, except she isn't sleeping. Wearing an old *Harlan's* T-shirt, she's propped against the headboard, working on her computer. I open my mouth to talk, but only a squeak comes out. Giggling, she grabs a glass of water from her nightstand and hands it to me. I drink two-thirds of it in one swallow. She grabs it back from me and finishes it off.

I stretch my body, grunting, "What time is it?"

"A little after three." Closing her laptop, she sets it down on the floor and snuggles into bed, facing me. "You snored."

"I do not snore."

She smirks. "You most definitely snore."

I stare at her beautiful face. I'm mesmerized by the small freckle above the right side of her mouth. I noticed that freckle the very first night I met her—that very first night on the porch.

"Go ahead and ask me. I know you want to."

She smiles gently, playing our game. "I don't know what you're talking about."

"Don't beat around the bush, Lulu. I like you when you get to the point."

Her smile fades, and she reaches out, softly tracing my furrowed eyebrows with her fingertips. "What happened on your call?"

Night before last, we were woken up from a dead sleep by my ringing phone. It was two in the morning, and a six-year-old boy was just reported as missing. That's all Lulu knows. I pick up from there, giving her the highlights of the case.

"A neighbor in a duplex downtown heard screaming and yelling a little before two in the morning. She called the police. When patrol units arrived, they found a deceased woman in the kitchen. She'd been stabbed multiple times in the neck with a pair of scissors. It didn't take long for them to figure out she was a single mother with a child. And the boy was nowhere to be found."

Lulu knows where this conversation is heading. Her eyes widen and she bites her lip. I reach across and tug the bedsheet higher around her body, planting my hand on her hip in the process.

"Fortunately, her phone was at the scene and it wasn't locked. We found a series of threatening texts and social media messages from a guy. We talked to the neighbor and found out that the victim and this guy had gone out on a couple of casual dates. She broke it off, but he wasn't taking no for an answer. He showed up at the house a couple of times. The vic and the neighbor both threatened to call the cops. He went away. Or so they thought."

Lulu traces the vein in my arm, running her fingers from my elbow to my wrist. She's been in the business long enough, she's not shocked, she's heard it all. She's even interviewed victims like this, once they've become grown adults, I mean. That's the sad thing. Shit like this happens all the time. To everyone, everywhere. No one is immune.

Just look at Carrie.

"It wasn't long after we landed on him as a suspect that we were able to get the security camera feed from the landlord. Fortunately, he had cameras installed in the parking area because of some car theft that's been going on downtown. We caught them on video. His car—after murdering the mom, he tossed the little boy in the trunk and took off."

Her eyes flicker with activity. She's thinking. My Lulu's one damn smart woman. "You got his home address from the tag registration? Or his license? Or public records?"

"Yeah, all of the above, but they weren't there. We put out a BOLO at all of the hotels and motels in the state. We pulled up ownership records for his known relatives. He has an uncle in Indiana who owns a hunting cabin and acreage in the county next to us. We called him, and he confirmed that the nephew has a key to the place and does upkeep on it. Immediately, he gave permission for us to search his property."

She nods, staring into my eyes. "You found them there?"

"Yeah."

"And?"

I shake my head, not wanting to say more.

"You have to talk about it, Ry. This stuff will eat you up if you don't. We've been through hell and back. I don't wanna risk our future by keeping things hidden away. Do you?"

I swallow against the lump in my throat. It feels like I've got a concrete ball lodged in my windpipe. "The zip ties were so tight on his hands and feet that his fingers and toes were purple. His wrists and ankles were coated in blood. The guy had made him strip down to his underwear. They were soaking wet. He was so scared he peed and defecated all over himself."

Lulu lifts her stubborn chin in the air, steeling her face. She knows there's more. There's more, and she refuses to be anything but strong for me. "And?"

"And the fucker burnt him. All over. Hundreds of cigarette burns. Slapped him. Hit him. Made him kneel on a broom handle. His knees were already too bruised to even be touched."

"What about the guy?"

"I nearly killed him," I say matter-of-factly. "I was praying he would resist, praying he would run. I wanted to pull the trigger so bad." I shake my head. "He wasn't putting up a fight. He wasn't resisting. But it didn't matter. I nearly did it."

"But you didn't. And that's what makes you the good guy."

Am I the good guy? I left her alone to deal with the death of Reality.

I sigh. "I held him—the little boy. He wrapped his arms around me, and I told him to close his eyes, and I carried him out the front door. I wish I could make him forget every bad thing that has happened to him."

"Does he have family? Or will he go into foster care?"

"His grandparents live in Texas. We called them as soon as we knew what we were dealing with. We had to tell them that their daughter was dead and their grandson was missing. They left right after getting our phone call. They were so relieved when we found him. They're still completely devastated, but they have this beacon of hope now."

I don't tell her that their reunion was so emotional I had to leave the room. I couldn't even stand to watch it.

She brushes her hand across my cheek, lovingly stroking my face. She wants to comfort me, but she doesn't want to fill the distance between us with mere words. Scooting closer, her hand falls to my scarred shoulder. Leaning forward, she kisses my pebbled and marred skin. Her fingers brush across my chest, where her fingernails scrape against my nipples. She traces the lines of my muscles, gliding down the center of my stomach. I love it when her hands are on me.

And she knows that.

I press my mouth against hers. But I don't kiss her. I breathe her in. I draw strength from her. I replenish myself. I give myself reason to fight another day, a purpose to go back to the job, a determination to solve the cold case that still haunts us both, even to this day.

The vibrating of a silenced cell phone breaks our trance. She nods her head at her nightstand. "It's yours. It rang a few times while you were sleeping. I don't recognize the number, and they aren't leaving a voicemail."

"I'll take it." Grunting, I sit up against the headboard while Lulu hands me my phone. "Sergeant Crutchfield," I answer.

"Crutch? Hey, it's Mike Malone. From State."

He means the state penitentiary.

He nervously clears his throat. "I'm not sure how to say this."

I grit my teeth. "Then just say it."

"Your dad OD'd. I'm sorry; he didn't make it."

I knew this day would come. I knew the asshole would do this one day. "Okay."

My one-word response throws Mike for a loop, and it takes him a few seconds to recover. "As you know, an autopsy will have to be done since he died in custody. We're still investigating, but it looks like he's been buying some of the other inmates' pills and making his own concoction for snorting. Allergy medication, blood pressure pills, vitamins, motion sickness medication—really anything and everything. Anyway, we'll let you know the results of the investigation as soon as we complete it. I promise, we'll try to round up anyone who sold their pills to your dad and file new charges against them." He sighs, relieved he got through the worst of it. "I'll call you when his body is ready for release."

"I don't want it."

"Excuse me?"

I think twice about it. I really don't plan on having a burial or memorial service for him, but the state shouldn't have to deal with the financial burden of taking care of the body. Plus, it's not like Mom is around to take care of anything. Last I heard, she left for Florida after getting released from the city jail, and Dad got sent to the pen for the credit card skimming. I'll have him cremated. Trash can have the remains if he wants. If not, I'll take them to the county dump. "Sorry, that's fine. Just let me know when his body is ready and I will coordinate with a funeral home."

"Okay. Sorry to be the bearer of bad news today, Crutch."

"It's fine, Mike. It was just a matter of time."

I put the phone on my nightstand. Lulu's face is etched with worry. She sits up straight on the bed, with a stiff back and squared shoulders. She knows someone died, simply based on my funeral home comment, but she knows it's not someone either of us consider family. If it were Marcum or Ray, I would be completely devastated.

She can see… I'm not devastated.

"Ry?"

"My father's dead. Overdosed in prison."

Her mouth falls open. "Oh." She rapidly blinks, thinking. "That must hurt. No matter what happened, he still made you."

I shake my head. "He didn't make me. Grandpa and Grandma made me. Harlan made me. Marcum." I lean forward, wrapping my hand around the back of her neck. I pull her across the bed, onto my lap. "You, Lulu. You made me."

She leans her forehead against mine. "And *you* made *me*."

Chapter 44

Ella

"Ry?" I lean up on my elbows and watch him as he sleeps. The tortured, cute, sexy boy I once knew has evolved into the masculine, sexy man before me.

Still tortured, but not devastatingly so.

It's the middle of September and hard to believe that he's only been back in my life for a little over eight months. I've gone from hating him to loving him. Although, I think we all know that I never actually hated him. I loved him, wildly and passionately and whole-heartedly, even when I was supposed to hate him.

Our past doesn't haunt me anymore. It doesn't toss me overboard and drown me. It's there, don't get me wrong. And the pain of him leaving me, leaving *us*, will never fully go away, but I can see the big picture. I can see it brought us to this place.

And this place? Well, it's pretty damn good.

The strong lines of his chiseled jaw are highlighted in the moonlight. My fingers reach out, rubbing against the growth of his five-day beard. I lean forward, breathing my hot breath against the curve of his neck. "Ry, wake up."

He sighs, fighting against sleep.

I suckle the soft skin underneath his earlobe and then whisper against the shell of his ear. "Ryland Joseph Crutchfield, it's time to wake up."

He moans. I watch as his eyelids slant open. He automatically pulls my body against his, kissing the top of my head. "What's wrong? Bad dream?"

"Happy Birthday."

"Hmm?"

"Happy Birthday, Ry."

Grunting, he reaches over and his hand blindly fumbles across the top of the nightstand. Grabbing his phone, he checks the time. "Lulu, it's been my birthday for exactly one minute. This couldn't wait until six in the morning?"

"Absolutely not. I've never been with you on your birthday before. Thirty-four. Getting a little old. Maybe I should trade you in for a newer model." I playfully bite his muscled chest, right above his nipple.

He chuckles. "I'm a good vintage, classic, even. I'd think twice before doing that."

I look at his face, wishing I could see the pale green of his eyes, but it's too dark. "What do you want for your birthday?"

He grabs a strand of my hair and wraps the golden-brown wave around his finger. "What are you willing to give?"

"Anything. Everything."

After a second, his lips curl into a slow, seductive smile. The kind of smile that still has women everywhere fawning all over him. And the smug little bastard knows it too. "Good. I was hoping you would say that." He abruptly sits up against the headboard and flicks on the lamp on the nightstand.

My eyes barely have time to adjust before he's wrapping his hands around my waist and ass and hauling me onto his lap so I'm straddling him. I squirm, getting comfortable, and immediately smirk when I feel his hard erection bob against me. Reaching over into the drawer of his nightstand, he grabs something, hiding it in his hand. I'm about to ask what's he's hiding, when his palm opens wide, and he flips the lid on a black ring box.

"Marry me. Marry me, Lulu. Let's fill our house with love. And babies. Lots and lots of babies."

I study the beautiful piece of jewelry before me. "It's a wedding band."

He licks his lips and shrugs. "I know most women expect a big engagement ring. And that's totally fine, I'll buy you whatever you want. We'll go shopping together and you can pick one out. I just couldn't bring myself to buy an engagement ring the other day. I don't want to be engaged to you; I want to be married to you. Right now, right this second. I feel like we had a twelve-year long engagement. That's damn long enough."

I try not to smile, but I can't help it. I'm grinning ear to ear. My finger hovers over the ring, but he beats me to the punch, grabbing it and tossing the box to the floor. It's wider than most. Not as wide as a man's band, but definitely wider than a normal woman's wedding band. One half of the white gold is adorned with three large circular diamonds, set almost flat. The other half of the ring is engraved. In a beautiful script is our daughter's name.

Reality

I gently touch her name.

"They thought I was crazy. They said that inscriptions are supposed to be on the inside of the ring. They're the ones who are crazy. Why would you want something inscribed on the inside? You can't see it there. It should be where you can see it, every time you look down."

I still hate crying in front of people. But that doesn't stop the silent tears from spilling down my cheeks. I hold out my hand, watching in awe as he slides the wedding band onto my ring finger.

I don't even have a chance to admire how perfect it looks. His mouth is on me. His tongue slides against mine, stirring passion and love into an intoxicating concoction, making me drunk. Emotion explodes in my chest and butterflies swarm in my stomach.

I can't believe this is happening. It might've taken us longer than my eighteen-year-old-self thought it would, but we finally made it here. I'm going to marry the man I love. I get to grow old with him, build my life with him, have a family with him. It's so unusual to think—this will actually be my second marriage.

I look at my finger. The ring is gorgeous. This is all I want. I don't want or need an engagement ring. Hell, I married Ry the second he slid this ring on my finger. "What about you? You need a ring."

He cocks an eyebrow. "I do?"

Much to my surprise, he rumbles around in the nightstand drawer again and comes out with another jewelry box. I nudge my face closer, watching in awe as he pulls a man's black wedding band from the velvet and slides it on his own calloused finger.

I nearly lose it.

That is, without a doubt, the sexiest thing I've ever seen.

He knows it too. He can sense my arousal in the air.

Laughing, he says, "You never answered my question."

I cock my head to the side, staring at him. "You never actually asked me a question."

He opens his mouth and then closes. "Huh. Guess I didn't, did I?" He brings my hand to his mouth and kisses my knuckles. "Luella Margaret Hill, will you marry me?"

"Damn straight, I will."

Growling, he leans forward, whispering his hot breath against the sensitive skin of my ear, just the way I like. "I don't know if I will ever get used to hearing you cuss."

"And I don't know if I will ever get used to sleeping in a bed with you instead of a tent."

His eyes flash with good humor. "We should do that tonight. Sit by the fire, sleep in the tent."

"Tonight? It'll be late when we get home. Did you forget about the Annual Appreciation Gala?"

He snorts. "Are you sure we have to go?"

I squeeze my thighs, making his erection bounce against me again. "Yes. And after tonight, everything will be settled with my father's practice."

"Well, then, what better way to celebrate? It'll be a double celebration." Grabbing the sides of my face, he softly kisses me, slowly sucking my bottom lip into his mouth. "There's nothing better than watching your naked body, as I pound into you, underneath the stars and moon."

And there's really nothing like watching *him* watch *me* as we make love outside.

I take a deep breath. My chest heaves, grating my swollen breasts against his rock-hard body. "What about the other part?"

"What other part?"

"The making babies part?"

"Oh, I fully plan on tossing your birth control pills into the trash can as soon as the sun rises."

I raise my eyebrows. "Oh, really?"

"Yep. Any objections from you?"

I grab the hem of my shirt and pull it over my head. Before he can fully appreciate the sight before him, I tug his face down to my cleavage. Knowing what I want, he immediately takes my puckered nipple in his mouth. I buck against him, tangling my fingers into his light brown hair.

I whisper. Two sweet words.

"Game on."

Chapter 45

Crutch

I never really understood the suggestive meaning of 'little black dress' until Lulu walked down the stairs tonight. She's wearing this sleeveless thing that subtly showcases her plump cleavage and blatantly showcases her mile-long longs. Her waves are piled high on top of her head, and her dangling pearl earrings draw attention to her neck, calling to me, making me want to mark her with a thousand hickeys to tell everyone she's mine.

But I don't have to do that.

I know she's mine.

She's wearing my ring.

But there is one thing I hate about tonight—she's not fully *My Lulu.*

She's the one I met on the back porch all those years ago. The one with the stiff back, squared shoulders, and nose poked high in the air. The Lulu who blandly talks about the weather and the stock market. The Lulu who fake-smiles and nods once when asked a question. That damn single nod used to drive me ape-shit crazy.

I ignore the mindless chatter of the buxom blonde in front of me and scan the crowd, searching for Lulu. My heart skips a beat when I see her in the corner of the room, chatting with a small group of people. Sensing me, she turns her head and immediately catches my eye. The gorgeous smile on her face fades the second the blonde reaches over and whispers in my ear. Lulu's jaw tenses in anger, and her eye roll is so dramatic I fear she might faint. Good thing she isn't close enough to actually hear what this woman just asked me.

There's a very good possibility I could be arrested in at least ten states if I actually perform the action this stranger just suggested.

Lifting my eyebrows, I hold my left hand in front of her face, wiggling my ring finger. The black wedding band catches the light in just the right way. "Sorry. Married."

Actually, I'm not sorry at all.

Biting her lip, the blonde shrugs and bats her fake eyelashes. I keep waiting for one to fall off and land in her champagne. "Doesn't bother me if it doesn't bother you."

"It bothers his wife." Lulu wraps a possessive hand around my bicep.

Sneaky little minx.

Scowling, the woman turns on her heels and walks away, searching for her next prey.

Chuckling under my breath, I slide my arms around her waist. "How long have you been waiting to say that line?"

She smirks. "Since I was seventeen and met you on a porch." She shakes her head. "These women act like we're at a bachelorette party." She pulls away, slowly looking up and down my body, studying me. Her simple gaze makes me feel like a damn sexual warrior.

Snorting, she frowns. "And you."

I throw my hands in the air, laughing. "What about me?"

"Do you have to look like that? Why couldn't you dress like all the other men? You're egging it on."

"What are you talking about? You mean because I'm not wearing a suit jacket and tie? You know I hate those things." I'm dressed in black slacks and white button-up shirt. Of course, the neck is unbuttoned, and I rolled the sleeves up to my elbows. It's hot in here. What other choice did I have?

She plants her hands on her hips. "You know exactly what I'm talking about, *Mr. Let-Me-Show-You-My-Sex-Bucket-Forearms.*"

"You like my forearms?"

She tries not to blush. Really, she does. "You know I do."

It's true. I do.

I can't stand it. I gather her in my arms again, taking the opportunity to dance with her as the band plays a slow song from the stage. I kiss the soft line of her jaw. "My wife loves my forearms."

She molds her body against mine, sighing contently. In her heels, we're nearly eye to eye. Smiling, she lifts her hand from my shoulder and admires her wedding band. "I love it when you call me your wife."

"That's good. Because I love calling you my wife." I look at my watch. "Best twenty hours of my life."

"When can we make it official?" she asks.

It's already official in my book. "As soon as you want. You just have to decide what kind of wedding you want."

"Can we go to the courthouse on Monday?"

Hell yeah, we can. Instead of blurting that response, I just cock an eyebrow. "Seriously?"

Her lips pucker in thought. "Of course. Why?"

I shrug. "Not to drag up the past, but your wedding to Hudson was a quick courthouse thing. I wasn't sure if you'd want the big, fancy, once-in-a-lifetime event."

She immediately bursts out laughing. "Really? You want me to throw some huge, elaborate wedding and invite strangers? You think I want that?"

I shake my head. "No, actually I don't. You never struck me as the bride-zilla type. I just didn't wanna rob you of the choice. Because this will be the last wedding you will ever have, Lulu. I'm never letting you go." I lean down and press my lips against hers. "You're mine. For-fucking-ever."

She licks her lips, licking mine in the process. "Never before. Never after."

The song ends and another one immediately starts up. In the middle of the instrumental ballad, she starts giggling, piquing my interest. "What?"

"They're gonna kill me. I never even called Aunt Teresa and Raylee to tell them you proposed."

"They know."

Her head lobs to the side. "Huh? You called them?"

"Well, I didn't call to tell them I asked you today, but they knew it was coming. I asked Ray for his permission."

Her eyes widen. "You did? You asked my uncle for my hand in marriage?"

"Of course, I did. Both him and Marcum."

"What did they say?"

"They said no."

Her mouth falls open in shock. "What?!"

I pinch her waist, teasing her. "I'm just kidding. Of course, they said yes."

She smiles brightly. Whatever she is going to say is cut off by a young college-aged girl. "Excuse me, Ms. Hill?"

Lulu stops dancing and straightens her shoulders. "Yes."

"We haven't officially met. I'm Marissa, Dr. Bussman's new receptionist. I'm sorry to bother you, but there's a little situation in the restroom." She nods at a darkened hallway. "The servers' restroom."

"What situation?" I ask, not caring that she wasn't speaking to me.

The girl steps closer, whispering. "It's Kristie Vann. She's asking for you."

Lulu blinks. "What's wrong? Is she injured?"

Marissa thins her lips and nervously rings her hands in front of her.

I growl in anger. "Is she drunk? High?"

Marissa looks down at the floor. "I... I really can't say, sir."

Well, that answers that.

Lulu does that singular nod. "Thank you for coming to me. We'll promptly handle the issue. Perhaps it will be best if we keep this between us." She awards Marissa with a fake smile.

Marissa nods, relief washing across her face. She's clearly happy to pass the baton to someone else.

Placing my hand on Lulu's back, we walk across the elaborate ballroom, making our way to the bathroom nestled in the back, next to the kitchen. At least Kristie isn't making an ass of herself in the main restrooms where all of the guests are coming and going.

Lulu knocks on the closed door. "Kristie? It's Ella." She twists the handle, finding the door locked. "Open the door."

Nothing happens.

I take a step back, fully prepared to shoulder my way through. Lulu gently lays a hand on my chest. "Kristie, I need for you to open the door. Otherwise, we'll have to break it down. That will create a commotion, and Phillip will know about it. Is that what you want? Do you want your dad to know about whatever is happening here?"

After a few seconds, the handle jiggles and the door cracks open. I don't give Lulu a chance to sneak in front of me; I walk in first. Who the hell knows what's happening in this room, and I'll be damned if I send my woman into harm's way.

Well, this certainly is a shit storm.

The bathroom is a complete wreck. The paper towel dispenser has been ripped from the wall; pieces of drywall hang like cheese from a cheese grater. Her purse has been overturned, and the vanity is covered with her credit cards, dollar bills, lipsticks, and what looks like small, decorative pill cases. Apparently, she threw a flower vase in the corner of the room. Fresh flowers lay in a crumpled mess, and jagged shards of the blue pottery are scattered across the floor. It looks like Kristie cut her hand. Blood coats her knuckles and some of it is spread across the front of her yellow party dress—the yellow party dress that's a little too much *party* for a function like this. The only thing still intact is the toilet and the martini glass sitting on the back of the toilet tank.

Lulu's face crumples as she looks around the room. Her hand immediately flies to the back of her neck, rubbing her scar in worry. "Oh, Kristie. What did you do? What happened in here?"

For the first time, Kristie looks up. Her eyes are glassy and half-closed. She wobbles from side to side. "Nothing. I was just looking for something."

I clench my jaw. "What? Your damn sanity?"

Lulu glares at me.

Kristie sighs and starts scratching the side of her face, smearing blood on her cheek. "I'm fine. I just had one too many martinis. The bartender is making them too strong. He thinks I'm cute, he's just trying to get in my pants."

Oh, please. Now it's time for me to roll my eyes.

Lulu crosses the distance and pulls Kristie's hands down to her side, trying to save her from looking like she got into a fight with a panther. Turning her hand over, she finds the bleeding cut and pulls her over to the sink, rinsing the blood down the drain. I grab some paper towels and Lulu wraps them tightly around Kristie's hand, ordering her to hold them in place.

The ring on Lulu's finger quickly catches Kristie's attention. She grabs Lulu's hand and holds it so close to her face it looks like she's about to poke her own eye out. "Y'all got married?"

"Yes," I quickly answer. Technically, no, but that's just semantics.

She sniffles, wiping her runny nose with her free hand. "Good. That's good."

"Kristie," Lulu says softly and sternly, drawing her attention, "why did you tear this room apart? What's going on?"

"Nothing, I told you I was looking for something."

"For what?"

Kristie just shrugs.

Fuck this shit. I've seen it too many times. With my parents. With Trash. With all of his friends.

With Carrie.

I run my fingers across my belt, wishing I was wearing my normal utility belt. "What are you on?" She turns to me, trying to open her eyes wide, but she's definitely unsuccessful. "Oxy? Kickers? Fluff?"

Kristie reaches over and grabs a tube of lipstick from the countertop. Spinning it in her hand, she wobbles on her feet and opens her mouth to lie. "I hurt my back exercising last week. I wasn't thinking and took a pain pill before coming tonight."

I fold my arms across my chest. "Bullshit."

Kristie starts crying. "I just wanna go home. I'm not feeling well." She turns to Lulu, playing the sympathy card. "Ella, please don't tell Dad. I wasn't thinking. I shouldn't have been drinking. I'm sorry."

Sighing, Lulu turns and starts shoving all the stuff back into Kristie's purse.

I clear my throat. "You're not buying this, are you? She's lying. She's been on this stuff forever. She's an addict." I don't bother lowering my voice. I could not care less if I hurt Kristie's feelings.

"Of course, I'm not buying it." She looks over my shoulder, watching as Kristie tries to apply the lipstick. Tries and fails. "But she can't stay here. Not in the shape she's in. I'm ready to be done with this. I don't want anything derailing tonight."

I lean against the counter. "This has to be addressed. She needs to get help. She's an addict," I say again.

Lulu nods. "I know. And I'll make sure she talks to Phillip first thing tomorrow and gets help...just...not tonight. I'm ready to move on and live my life." She leans her head against my shoulder. "Live *our* life."

I kiss the top of her head. Her shampoo smells like coconut and strawberries. "So, what do you wanna do?"

"I can't leave, it's nearly time for me to give the announcement about Dr. Bussman permanently taking over Dad's practice. Can you take her home?"

Kristie reaches out, taking her purse from Lulu. She looks like a clown version of a street hooker. Smeared eye makeup, lipstick on her teeth, stained dress. She's given up on the paper towel. Fortunately, it looks like her hand has stopped bleeding. "I don't wanna go to my house, Ella. Can't I go to your house? I'll just sleep on the couch. You know I've always loved it there."

Sneaky bitch. "No. Holt lives there, and you know it," I say.

Lulu runs her fingertips up my spine. "Holt's visiting friends this weekend, remember?"

I side glance at her. "It's still not a good idea, Lulu."

"Please, Ella. Please," Kristie begs.

Lulu reaches around and fondles her scar. In the middle of her train of thought, there's a soft knock on the door. "Ms. Hill? It's me, Marissa. They're ready for you."

"Thank you, Marissa. Please tell them I'll be right there." Scowling, she caves to Kristie's pathetic plea. "Fine. You can sleep in my bed; I don't live there now. But do not touch one single thing in Holt's room. Do you understand?"

"Yes!"

I grab Lulu's elbow. "This isn't a good idea."

She bites her lip, thinking. "It'll be fine. It's just for one night."

Happy with her win, Kristie grabs the martini glass from the toilet and finishes off her drink. "Kristie! Are you kidding me right now?" I toss my hands in the air.

"You have to stay with her. She doesn't need to be by herself."

I whip my head toward Lulu so fast I nearly give myself whiplash. "I know you did not just suggest that. I may be a cop, but I'm not a babysitter. Especially for addicts. I did that enough with my parents and my brother. You know that."

She frowns. "I do know that. But look at her. She can't even keep her eyes open or walk straight. It's just for a little while. I'll be there as soon as I can."

"We rode together. You want me to leave you stranded here?" I nod at her hand. "I'm pretty sure that ring on your finger means I can't do that."

Kristie pulls her keys from her purse. "Here, take my keys. I drove Dad here. You can drop him off before you come home. Tomorrow morning I'll drive my car home from your house. Problem solved."

Her words are slurred, and I'm surprised she had enough brain power to come up with a plan.

Lulu plucks the keys from her hand. Smiling, she tries to ease the tension coursing through my body. "See, it'll be fine. I'll take Phillip home as soon as the gala ends. I promise, I won't be long."

"If you don't walk through the door the second this party is done, I'm gonna flip my shit."

My Lulu brushes her lips against mine, breathing her life into me. "We definitely don't want that. *Husband*."

So much for our date with the firepit and tent.

Chapter 46

Ella

I breathe a sigh of relief when I pull into Phillip's driveway. The announcement of Dr. Bussman's buyout of Dad's practice and share of the building went better than expected, with Phillip graciously toasting her at the end of my speech. Despite his public acceptance of her, I know he's still pissed, so I wasn't looking forward to being alone with him in the car.

He didn't even seem really concerned when I told him that Kristie fell ill and was resting at my house.

"Kristie will be back home tomorrow morning. Will you be here?" I want to make sure she discusses her addiction with him as soon as possible. Once I know he's getting her the help she needs, I'm washing my hands of the whole situation. I can't have her in my life.

Addiction took my sister from me. Addiction ripped Ry's family from him. I refuse to let it ruin my life anymore. I refuse to let it ruin my husband. Our children. Our world.

"Yes, I should be home? Why?"

I nod once, not giving an answer.

"Why don't you come inside?"

"It's late, I should get going. Check on Kristie."

His hand pauses on the door handle. "I have something of your father's I want to give you." He nods at the ignition, urging me to turn the car off. "It won't take long."

I'm not sure why I say yes, but I do. I guess I don't want to be rude. I guess I want to soften the blow for the news I know he'll get tomorrow about his daughter. I guess I want to thank him for not being a butthole at the gala.

Oh well, I always do what I shouldn't. Tonight should be no different.

I've been in this house more times than I can count. It's just as large as my parents' house. Just as grand, just as glamorous. Phillip definitely had a different decorator, though. Mom wanted our house to be on the cover of every home décor magazine south of the Mason Dixon line. Phillip's house, however, is the stereotypical bachelor pad of a man with too much money and too little self-esteem. The furniture is modern and uncomfortable, the floor is decorated in bear skin rugs, and the kitchen looks completely un-cooked in. In all honesty, it's always given me the willies to be here. Even Kristie's room always looked more like a hotel bedroom than the bedroom of a little girl. Maybe that's part of the reason she always came to our house instead of us coming to hers.

Phillip stops at the wet bar in the living room and pours himself a drink. He makes an elaborate show of swirling the brown liquid around in the crystal tumbler. "Can I get you a drink?"

He knows I don't drink. "No, thank you. I'm fine."

He reaches out and touches my left hand. My jaw tenses and my spine locks in place. I shift away from his touch, clasping my hands in front of me.

He takes a sip of his drink. "Sorry, I always forget that you don't like to be touched." He puts his glass down. It clinks loudly against the marble of the bar. "That always bothered your father, you know? Not being able to hug you and kiss you, like a normal child?"

That's the thing, though. If my mother and father hugged and kissed me like a 'normal child', then I wouldn't mind being touched.

My hugs came from my sister. From my aunt and uncle. Hell, even from my nanny.

He shrugs when I don't answer, nodding at my hand. "I noticed the ring on your finger. It looks like a wedding ring."

I swallow, trying to politely smile. Some habits die hard. "It is."

"You're married?"

"Yes." Semantics, I think to myself.

"That garage kid? The one who's a cop now?" Shaking his head, he picks up his drink and downs it. "Well, I suppose congratulations are in order. I wasn't invited to a wedding. I assume it was an intimate event?"

I ignore his comment. "You said you had something to give me?"

He snaps his fingers like he just remembered. "Yes. I went to a medical conference back in May. They presented me with a posthumous award on your father's behalf. I wanted to give it to you. It's just in the office." He extends an arm down the hallway. "Shall we?"

"I'll just wait here."

Furrowing his brow, he shrugs again. "Suit yourself," he says, as he wanders off down the darkened hall.

I glance around the living room, which doesn't look lived in at all. No throw pillows tossed on the couch. No blankets draped over the chair. No dog-eared book sitting on the coffee table. Even the framed pictures on the fireplace mantel look fake. My eyes immediately dart to the picture of me, Carrie, and Kristie from a garden party.

I always hated that picture.

I was so mad at Carrie that day. I was in middle school and she was in high school. She was supposed to take me to the movies that night, but she met a boy at the party and decided to go on a date with him instead. I hated that picture because every time I saw it, it made me think about how angry I was at my sister that day. Carrie and I always got along so well that being mad at her felt wrong.

And it feels wrong now.

Growling, I turn the offensive picture around. I look at the other pictures. There's one of Phillip and Kristie's mom on their wedding day. One of Kristie at kindergarten graduation. One of my parents and Phillip at a black-tie charity event. And one of Phillip, my dad, and Carrie at a bicycle race. They're dressed in their matching jerseys and tight shorts, posing next to their bikes, holding their medals high in the air.

It must have been one hell of a race. My father looks like he's about to pass out. My sister has a scrape on her elbow. A small trickle of blood is running in a line, like red rainwater, down her arm. And Phillip's bloodied shorts are torn, showcasing the majority of his left leg, like he's some kind of deranged pantyhose model.

My hand drifts to the back of my neck and I rub my scar, thinking about my sister. She's so beautiful. She really could've been a model. Strands of her blonde hair blow in the breeze. Her skin glistens with sweat from the race. Her brilliant smile makes my soul feel light and airy. I'm about to step away from the vivid memory when my eyes lock on something unexpected in the photograph.

Phillip.

More importantly, Phillip's leg.

There, on his upper left thigh, is a cut. A bloody, yet unmistakable cut. A cut shaped like the letter *J*. A cut like that leaves a scar. A scar just like the one I've spent the past eight-and-a-half months staring at on a daily basis.

I can't breathe.

I don't think my heart is beating.

I think I'm dying.

Immediately, my palm flies to my chest. Rubbing my breastbone, I try to pump life back into my lifeless body.

All this time. It's been right under my nose all this time. And I refused to see it.

My throat constricts. I try to gulp air into my lungs, but all I can manage are short, painful gasps. My vision blurs, forming a black tunnel. My ears start ringing, driving my swirling brain to the brink of psychosis.

Phillip's voice cuts through the room. "Here you go. Something to add to the collection of your father's lasting notoriety."

Bastard. Fucking bastard. "It was you," I whisper in disbelief.

"What?"

"It was you."

"What was me?"

I spin around to face him, the devil incarnate. "It was you. You raped my sister."

A flash of recognition burns across his face, but he quickly replaces it with shock and abhorrence. Placing my dead father's acrylic plaque on the table, he folds his arms across his chest. "What are you talking about? Are you feeling okay?"

"You raped Carrie."

"How can you say such a thing? Carrie was like a daughter to me. Just like you."

Vomit coats the inside of my mouth. "There's no point in denying it. There's a photograph."

His eyes widen, before narrowing in anger. He clenches his teeth and snarls, "Really? You have a picture? Of what?" He points to his chin. "Of my face?"

"I don't need to see your face to know it's you."

"Look, Ella, I don't know what you think you saw, but you're mistaken."

"I'm not!" I yell. "It's you!" I grab the frame from the mantel and tap the glass. "This. It shows your cut. A cut that turns into a scar. Not too many people have a scar like this on their leg. Carrie is passed out, and you are raping her. On the couch. At Trey's mobile home."

"Who's Trey?"

I have to give the asshole credit. He didn't even flinch at the name.

"You know damn well who Trey was. Apparently, you were his supplier."

"Supplier of what?"

"You tell me, Phillip. What drugs did you give him? How much money did he make you? Was the whole gas station operation your idea?"

Phillip takes a deep breath. Calmly, he walks back over to the bar and pours himself another two fingers. Fury courses through my veins, making me nauseous and dizzy. I quickly tire of his games and throw the race photograph at his head. He darts to the side and it shatters against the wall, sending glass scattering across the Italian marble floor.

Shaking his head, he chuckles. Cynically. Maniacally. "You know, Ella, you never used to cause problems like this when you were a little girl. You always did what you were told." He walks over to a hutch in the corner, opens a drawer, and pulls out a pack of cigarettes. "I remember once, when you had just started high school..." His voice trails off as he lights a cigarette and takes a drag.

I've never seen him smoke before.

He blows smoke in the air. "Well, anyway, you went to the gynecologist. Do you remember that?"

Of course, I remember it. It was traumatic. Mom said I needed to go because I was fourteen and hadn't started my period yet. I was a young, teenage girl and completely overwhelmed and embarrassed to have a doctor look at me and touch me. It didn't matter that the doctor was a woman. I was even more embarrassed when she confirmed for my mother that I was a virgin.

But my mother insisted I go. I listened to her. I obeyed her. Just like I always did.

Before Carrie went missing. Before I met Ry. Before I found my voice.

He laughs, "Of course, you remember that. I see it on your face. You know that doctor was having an affair with your father. That's why your mother wanted to meet her. She wanted to size up her latest competition. And you, my dear, were the perfect excuse. Sweet little Ella always making her mommy and daddy happy. You let someone touch your pussy just because you couldn't say no to that conniving bitch of a mother. Anything to try and gain her love, right?"

I wish I didn't have to hear his words. My eyes burn with the salt of unshed tears. The muscles in my throat hurt from holding in my sobs. "At least my parents weren't drug dealers."

"You think you have it all figured out? That little sleuth business of yours paying off?"

"I know that the surgery you did on my sister's knee turned her into an addict. I know she turned to Trey and Trash and that gas station for her fix. I know she started selling. She was selling your drugs, wasn't she? What happened? Did she find out you were the supplier? Did she confront you about the rape?" I take a step forward, closing some of the distance between us. "What did you do to my sister?"

He tosses the cigarette on the floor and grinds it out with his foot. "She brought all this on herself!"

"What happened to Carrie, you asshole!"

In two seconds flat, he rushes me. I'm completely unprepared. I should've been more prepared. Hell, this is what I do for a living. I interview people all the time who have lived through situations like this. And what do I do? I freeze.

He flings me down on the stiff, white leather couch. His hand wraps around my throat, squeezing. Squeezing hard. I immediately panic when I can't breathe. I claw at his hands, coughing and sputtering for air.

"I can't believe that filthy little bitch made a copy of the picture. She showed up here with a memory card, said she didn't make any copies. I guess that's my fault for believing her."

I buck against him, trying to knee him in the stomach or groin, but my position isn't right. My vision grows foggy, clouding with small spots of green and purple. He leans down, pressing his lips against the rim of my ear. "She was pregnant. Did you know that? She knew it was me in the picture. Same as you, she saw the scar. She told me I had to get her clean, pay for her to go to rehab. I told her to go ask Robert and Susan for the money. You know what she said? She said they would cut her off when they found out she was pregnant. Said they would disown her. I told her I would give her the money for an abortion."

He sits back a little bit, slightly loosening his grip. My greedy body hungers for the extra oxygen. I swallow as much air as I can.

His teeth grind. "She said no. She actually wanted to get clean and have the baby. Can you imagine that? What a stupid cunt. Did she actually think I was gonna let her have my kid? She would've ruined me. Completely ruined me. I've worked too hard; I've come too far."

My whisper is barely audible. "What did you do?"

He doesn't like that I'm talking. He grips me with renewed fervor. His eyes turn black as night. His face glows red like the coat of Satan. "I did what I had to do."

Chapter 47

Crutch

I'm miserable.

I just got engaged/married to the love of my life this morning, and she's not even around. I'm in her childhood home, surrounded by Holt's dirty laundry and babysitting her crazy-ass, former friend.

Kristie leans in the doorway to Holt's room.

I sit down on the couch and rub my eyes. "Kristie, don't even think about going in there. You promised not to touch any of Holt's things."

"This used to be Carrie's room, you know?"

Of course, I know that. I don't even respond to her.

"Carrie's disappearance was good in some ways, wasn't it?"

What the hell? "What are you talking about?"

She wobbles back over and tries to sit next to me on the couch. I clear my throat and point to the loveseat instead. Scowling and hiccupping at the same time, she flops over on the loveseat. Her blood-stained dress rides up, revealing purple panties. I shudder in disgust. She doesn't even notice when I toss a blanket over her legs.

"What I mean is, you and Ella wouldn't have met if it weren't for Carrie's disappearance. And y'all meeting was a good thing. I mean, look at you, you're married now." She starts scratching at invisible bugs on her face.

"Lulu and I were meant to be together. We would've met one way or another. Somewhere, sometime. She was meant to be mine."

"But you got together because Ella went to that gas station looking for Carrie." Kristie's head lobs back. "So that's good. Something good came from it. It makes it better. It makes it a little better." She makes a weird snorting noise, and I can't tell if she's about to laugh or sob. "Remember, y'all told me that you met in a coffee shop. That story was so lame. I knew she'd been to the gas station."

The tone in her voice sends chills down my spine. The hairs on the back of my neck stand. My brain starts churning.

Being a good detective means listening to your intuition. Intuition can lead you down the unseen road. It can lead you to the hidden pot of gold—the evidence. People always say, *follow the evidence'*. Well, guess what? Intuition is the compass that puts you there.

"Kristie, what are you talking about? Do you know something about Carrie's disappearance?"

She moans.

"Kristie!"

Her head bobbles forward and she stares at me. "What?"

"I asked if you know something about Carrie's case. Do you know what happened to Carrie?"

She covers her face with her hands and makes an unusual sobbing noise. I can't tell if she's really crying or just fake crying. With Kristie, either is a real possibility. Eventually, her hands drop. Her smeared makeup has smeared even more, giving her large raccoon eyes. Clear snot shines on her upper lip. Looking down at the floor, she tries to stand up. "I'm going to bed."

Hell no, she's not. I grab her arm. Probably a little too hard. "So, help me, Kristie, if you don't tell me what you're talking about, I'm gonna flip my shit and haul you into the drunk tank right this second."

I let her pull from my grasp. Taking a large gulp of air, she swallows. The sound is eerily loud, bouncing off the corners of the room.

"I thought giving her the pictures would help. She needed to know what happened to her. I thought it would scare her, scare her into getting help. I thought she would get clean and get back together with Caleb. I was trying to be a good friend."

My heart races. "It was you? You gave Carrie the pictures? The pictures of her sexual assault?"

She nods. "I printed the pictures and gave her the memory card too."

Theory after theory swirl in my brain, churning like a hurricane in the sea, a typhoon of fucking epic proportions. "Why didn't you speak up? I know Lulu told you we found the pictures. She told you we were interviewing everyone about them."

Her lip trembles. "I was scared."

"Scared of what?" I growl in frustration, rubbing my jaw. "Not of what. Of *who*, right?" I continue thinking aloud. "If you gave Carrie the pictures, that means you were there that night. You were hooked on pills all the way back then? You hung out with the same people as Carrie? Not only did you know Trey, and most likely my brother, you knew the supplier. He was the person who assaulted, Carrie, right?"

I question my own memory. Has it been trapped in my brain this whole time? Did I see Kristie at my brother's parties? Did I know her before I actually met her? I wade through my memories, trying not to drown in the sewage of my past.

I can't produce one single memory of Kristie.

Somehow, that doesn't make me feel any better.

When she doesn't answer, I press on, raising my voice. "Who was the supplier, Kristie?"

She sniffles, shaking her head. Her eyes are lazy and droopy again. I pray she doesn't pass out. "I didn't know she was pregnant, not until you and Ella started investigating everything again. I promise. He told me to never ask any questions, so I didn't. But it would've been different if I had known she was pregnant. I swear, it would've been different."

A sense of doom travels through my body, pinning me to the couch. I'm afraid. Fucking terrified. I'm afraid to breathe. I'm afraid to even blink. I feel like one wrong move could cause my whole world to come crashing down around me. "Who was the fucking supplier?!"

Her whisper rips terror through my heart. "My father."

I know that I've never really deserved this happiness. Lulu coming back into my life? It's more than I deserve. I left her. I forced her into the arms of another man. I abandoned Reality.

I built a life for her. A house for her. I always said that I would reach back out to her, at some point. But is that the truth? If she hadn't walked into the station that day, would I have searched for her? Or would I have just lived my miserable life, screwing faceless woman after faceless woman, trying to claim some portion of intimacy, all the while feeding my soul on the memories of my love for her?

I know I don't deserve this happiness, but the thought of having it ripped away from me now? It crushes me to dust.

I can't live without *My Lulu*.

I refuse to.

I pull out my phone for the hundredth time, trying her cell number again. Just as with the other hundred times, it goes unanswered. I called the venue and they said that everyone had left. So that means she's with him.

Phillip. The supplier. The rapist.

The man who murdered Carrie.

At least that's what I assume. I didn't stick around to find out. I ran from the house the second Kristie muttered the word *'father'*. I've already called a patrol unit to Lulu's house to take Kristie into custody, and I've called Marcum for backup. He's on his way and was calling Leary, Colson, and Wilson for additional support.

He told me to wait. He told me to be rational.

When it comes to My Lulu, I'm anything but rational.

Kristie's vehicle is parked in the back of the driveway when I pull up. Fortunately, Lulu and I took my truck tonight instead of her SUV, and I always have an off-duty weapon in my vehicle. It's secured in a lock box, tucked away in a hidden console behind my back seat. It's also where I store my extra vest when I'm not on duty. I try to keep a weapon on my person when I'm off-duty, but who the hell thought I would need a weapon at a gala for doctors. Grabbing my vest from the back of the truck, I quickly slide it over my head and activate the camera. I'm going in by myself, so I have to do this right.

Well, somewhat right. Going in alone breaks all normal protocol.

Drawing my weapon, I look through the driver-side window of Kristie's car. I see Lulu's handbag and phone on the console. Nothing seems out of the ordinary in the way of a struggle. I don't know why she would've gone into his house, though. Lulu can't stand Phillip. I can't imagine her even going inside to use his restroom. She would've rather peed in the street.

The garage is open and Phillip's collection of expensive sports cars glisten underneath the fluorescent lights. Nothing seems to be amiss, so I quickly head for the door leading into his house. Carefully twisting the knob, I hold my breath, praying the door is unlocked and that it doesn't squeak.

The door opens into a small hallway. I stand and listen, trying to gauge what's happening in the house. It's hard to hear past the beating heart echoing in my ears. I begin to quickly sweep through the house, clearing a laundry room, pantry, and storage room. It's then I hear things I shouldn't be hearing. Things I wish I weren't hearing. Loud voices, screams, grunts, a scuffle. I take off in a sprint, passing a huge kitchen, before entering the living room.

And what I see scares the shit out of me.

I'm trained for this. I've been through just about every scenario possible. Between the Marines and the sheriff's department, I've seen a lot of bad things. Things that haunt you, things that give you nightmares. Hell, I nearly had my arm blown off.

Still, I've never been more terrified than I am right now.

Lulu is sprawled on the floor, trying to scramble away from the maniac grabbing at her ankles and legs, trying to pull her underneath his body. Her eyes are drawn wide in fear. Her beautiful honey and caramel-colored hair is a tangled mess. Her neck is red and spotted with trapped blood, looming just under the surface of her bronzed skin. Did he cover her in hickeys? A coffee table has been turned over and shards of glass litter the shiny floor.

Phillip's face contorts in anger. His face is covered in scratches. One is bleeding. The crisp white collar of his suit is marred with crimson. "Why couldn't you just move on?" he screams.

"Because she's my sister!" Lulu's shrill scream shatters my fear.

And I get angry.

Very, very angry.

"Get the fuck away from her!" I level my service weapon right at his head. "I will shoot!"

And I'm a damn good shot.

For the first time, Phillip notices me. His head slowly turns. His eyes are glazed, not even focusing. He looks possessed. Demented. Inhuman. Lulu uses the opportunity to shuffle her right leg free, and before I can bark another order at the son of a bitch, she hauls back, kicking him right in the sternum with the heel of her foot.

And *My Lulu* kicks hard.

He grunts in pain and rolls to his side, fully freeing her. I rush him, quickly securing my weapon in my back waistband. Right before I reach him, he scrambles to his knees and violently lunges for my legs, trying to sweep me off my feet.

Hell yeah, motherfucker. Bring it on.

Kicking him backward, I kneel across his chest and fucking punch the shit out of him. One punch. A fucking glorious punch. Good enough to make me all warm and fuzzy on cold winter nights for years to come. Bones crunch, blood flies out of his mouth, and his eyes roll back in his head.

Turning him to his stomach—none too gently, I might add—I

grab the zip ties from the pocket of my vest and work at securing his hands.

I have to yell at Lulu to be heard over Phillip's painful moans and garbled words of protest. "Are you okay?"

Lulu's in shock, scanning the room from one corner to the next. Her body is poised to strike, ready to defend herself against anyone else who tries to harm her.

She's a fighter. A hellcat. The strongest woman I know.

I shift my head, begging her to make eye contact with me. "Are you okay?"

She looks at me. Looks at Phillip. And nods. Just one time.

Once Phillip is cuffed, I sit him up, leaning him against the couch. It's more than he deserves. I want to toss him out the window. I want to beat him until the life vanishes from his eyes. I want to break every bone in his body, make him pay for laying one single finger on My Lulu.

My body hums. I'm shaking with anger.

I can't control myself.

My fist curls into a ball, and I'm about to pummel his bloody face even more when I hear the coordinated scatter of feet. The tell-tale click of weapons, readying for a fight. Having Marcum as my partner, as my mentor, has given me a connection with him, an untethered umbilical. I don't need to see him to know he's here. I quickly call out, giving him the all-clear. I'm just standing up when everyone charges the room. Marcum makes it to Lulu first, bending to her level, his eyes and hands scan her body, asking if she's okay. He yells for Colson to call a medic.

"I'm fine. Help me up," she answers. I can't help but notice the scratchy timbre of her voice.

Phillip's house is in the city limits, so there's both city police and sheriff's deputies here. The patrol officers take charge of Phillip, and I give them the ten-second rundown of events. Anything more, and they'll have to wait. I need to see my wife.

Now.

Lulu's standing in the corner of the room, watching everyone. She's investigating. She's thinking. She's marking everything to memory. Marcum is patting her shoulder, and Leary is urging her to take a few sips of a sports drink. I'm not sure where he got it. He must've raided the kitchen.

Marcum narrows his eyes. "We'll talk about you making entry by yourself another time."

I snort. "You can talk until you're blue in the face. I'd do it a hundred times over to save my woman."

He slaps me on the back as he walks away, trying to hide a small smile. "I know. And we'll never be able to thank you for it."

I long to wrap my arms around Lulu. I need to feel her. I need to kiss her. But she's still in a stupor.

My adrenaline is starting to fall. My vision is blurry, and my racing heart feels like it's skipping a beat or two as it tries to slow down. If I feel this crazed, I can only imagine what she's feeling. This trauma could break her.

God, help me, I plead. I don't want to break her. Not again.

They teach us how to deal with victims.

But not when the victim is our wife.

I take a tentative step toward her. We're so close I can feel her breath dance across my skin. It's silent but labored, like she's about to start hyperventilating. "Lulu?"

Her hand plays with the scar on the back of her neck and her eyes keep darting to the officers as they work with Phillip.

Slowly, I reach around. Gently knocking her hand away, I replace it with my own. I rub my calloused fingers over her scar. Back and forth, just the way she likes. "Lulu?"

She blinks, trying to focus. Licking her lips, she swallows. The movement draws my attention to the petechia and red marks on her neck. It's undeniably fingerprints. He tried to strangle her. She'll be covered in bruises tomorrow. Fury ignites my anxiety, making my heart thunder against my ribcage like a freight train.

She coughs, trying to clear the pathway for her voice. Her strained whisper breaks my heart. "He killed my sister."

I nod. "I know."

"And her baby."

My shredded heart breaks even more. "I know."

Finally, her eyes find mine. "He tried to kill me."

I nearly collapse.

I need her. Holy shit, I need her like I need air to breathe. I was nearly too late. This is all my fault. I should've put the pieces together before now. I can't believe I let this happen to her.

How can she ever forgive me?

Again.

She can't stop the tears as they flow down her face. She wipes her eyes, smearing her expensive eye makeup down her cheeks.

And then...

She smiles.

One soft smile. Just for me.

"I hate crying in front of people."

That's the only invitation I need.

Hauling her into my arms, I sweep her from her feet and carry her from the room. With every step I take, her sobs grow louder and louder. She wraps her arms around my neck, struggling to grip me tighter and tighter. If she could crawl inside my body right now, she would.

And I would do the same fucking thing.

Racing from the house, I breathe a sigh of relief when we step into the night air. The sky is a fireworks display of swirling red and blue lights. Dozens of people mill around. Radio chatter drowns the symphony of the once-calm night.

Pulling down my tailgate, I carefully set Lulu on the back of my truck. She doesn't even get one single inch away from me before I'm crashing my mouth to hers. Her lips are dry and hot. Grabbing the sides of her face, I drive my tongue into her mouth. She immediately kisses me back. As always, she gives just as much as she takes. Her fingers grab my waist, pulling me between her legs. She wildly grabs at my shirt. I carefully take the gun from my back waistband and lay it out of harm's way on the truck, never breaking my connection with her. When she finally untucks my shirt from my slacks and her fingers slide across the muscles of my abdomen, she sighs in relief and her body relaxes.

Eventually, we both need to breathe. We stop kissing, but I don't let her go. I wrap her in a hug. Her fingers tangle in my hair. Tucking my lips against the shell of her ear, I tell her I love her. She buries her face in the crook of my neck, soaking me with her tears. I can't be sure, but I may be crying too.

"I love you. I love you so much. I'm so sorry, Lulu. I'm so sorry I didn't get here sooner. I love you."

"I love you. Ry, I love you."

She's breaking the rules.

I'm caught off guard when Marcum clears his throat. Pulling my head away from Lulu, I see him standing right beside us. By the looks of it, I would assume he's been standing there a while.

But he's not embarrassed. And neither am I.

His eyes look bloodshot, and I realize that this must've been a nightmare for him too. He thinks of Lulu as a daughter. She reaches out, tenderly touching his face. He bites his lip and nods. "The ambulance is here, sweetie. They need to take you to the hospital. We have to make sure you're okay." He nods to two paramedics standing behind him with a stretcher. "We, uh," he's so emotional, he can barely get the words out, "need to document all of your injuries."

Her eyes widen and she looks back and forth between the two of us. "You'll both go with me, won't you?"

I squeeze her thigh. "Of course, we will. The other guys can stay while the scene is processed."

Right at that moment, Colson walks up, holding an evidence bag. "Speaking of, I need to collect your weapon, Crutch."

I double-check the chamber and safety and drop my gun into the evidence bag. "It wasn't fired, of course. Lulu beat me to the punch. Or kicked me to the punch, I should say."

Colson hugs Lulu. "I'm glad you're okay, kid."

She laughs, making herself hiccup through her tears. "That's right. Who will wreak havoc on your desk if I'm not here?"

He shakes his head and holds out his hands for my vest. Turning the camera off, I pull it over my head. I hope the brass doesn't hound me for making out with the victim. Hopefully, they'll be a little understanding considering it's the night of our engagement and all.

A young city officer peeks around my shoulder. I recognize him. He's a regular at Will's bar. "Excuse me, Sergeant Crutchfield, would you like to read the rights?"

We all watch as Phillip rounds the side of my truck, being led to the waiting patrol car by Leary and Wilson. I look at Lulu, gauging her reaction. True to fashion, she straightens her shoulders and lifts that stubborn little nose of hers in the air. She holds out her hands, wanting me to help her down from the truck. Carefully, I lift her and set her on the ground.

"Marcum," I grip his shoulder, "you started this. You need to finish it. It's what Carrie would want."

Marcum walks over to Phillip. Standing right in front of his face, he starts to recite the Miranda rights. Cutting around me, Lulu immediately joins them. Her fingers wrap around Marcum's, tightly.

We all watch in awe as he delivers the warning to Phillip, hand in hand with the woman who brought him down.

Nearly One Year Later

Crutch

I finally make it out of the meeting. I check the conference room to see if Lulu's still there; she's not.

The department has once again hired my wife, proving to me that I married the world's smartest woman.

When I get to my desk, there's a sticky note stuck to my laptop screen.

I finished and walked over to the bar.
Come pick me up there. We don't want to be late.
PS- I have a surprise for you.

I wiggle the note in the air. "You know what this is about?" I ask Marcum.

He lifts his eyebrows. They look like furry caterpillars on his face. "Maybe."

I snort. "But you're not gonna tell me."

"She'll kill me if I tell you. She wants to be the one to tell you."

I shut down the computer and gather my things. "Are you coming tonight?"

"Yeah, we've got to pick up Nathan from a friend's house. He's coming with us. Stephanie and Brent left on their anniversary trip today."

"That'll be good. Laura will be happy," I say begrudgingly. "Her crush on Nate is really giving Ridge a run for his money." I say good-bye to Marcum and start my walk over to the bar.

I can't believe so much has happened over the past eleven months.

The depth of Phillip's drug ring and crimes was unfathomable. Using his position as an orthopedic surgeon, he basically forced people into an opioid addiction. He over-prescribed to those who actually needed pain relief, and he also prescribed to those who *didn't* really need it. He was the epitome of everything wrong with the health system.

How he handled them after getting them hooked was an evil story in and of itself.

For the good-looking young women, he exchanged prescriptions for sex. A hand job yielded a refill script for a certain number of pills. A blowjob? Even more. And sex? Even more. If the girls didn't comply, then they wouldn't get anything. It was then they had to fall into the ranks with the men... and the women Phillip deemed too ugly or too old or too undesirable for sex.

And how did those undesirables find dealer locations?

Kristie.

Her job was to pinpoint the thirsty and lead them to the fountain.

And one of those fountains was the gas station across from Harlan's. The fountain my brother swam in every single day. After I turned him and Trey in for drug distribution, Phillip shifted gears. He still needed businesses with lots of foot traffic and lots of cash coming in and out. He used a bakery in one location and a cigarette and tobacco store in another location.

You would think he would have trouble keeping up with the demand, but he didn't. Come to find out, he wasn't acting alone. He was working with four different pharmacies in the area. One of them was his legit business partner—the same pharmacist Lulu knew the whole time she was growing up, the same pharmacist who filled her bubble-gum flavored amoxicillin when she had strep throat, the same pharmacist located in the medical building with her father.

Sometimes Phillip would write prescriptions for fake patients. Sometimes he would write scripts for real patients—who never even knew about them. The pharmacists wouldn't run it through insurance, they would issue the scripts as a cash payment. Other times, he would write real scripts for real patients who actually thought they were getting the pain medicine they needed. In reality, the pharmacists were switching the pills with over-the-counter meds and pocketing the narcotic.

This was all going on when Carrie injured herself. She trusted Phillip. Not only was he her doctor, but he was her family friend. He prescribed too much. It didn't take long for her to get hooked. When she turned down his sexual advances, he wasn't happy. Apparently, he always had an unhealthy fascination with Carrie. If he couldn't take Carrie's body, he could at least take her money. Or her parents' money, I should say.

Kristie said she tried to keep Carrie 'safe' at first. She said she shared her own stash with Carrie. When that didn't work, she sent her to some of the low-level pushers on campus—fraternity guys. That didn't work because Carrie got caught by Caleb. Finally, Kristie led her to my brother and Trey. Her habit grew quickly, and she started pushing, trying to inflate her cache of spending money so Lulu wouldn't notice. It was Carrie, after all, who was trying to teach her little sister how to balance the checkbook and monitor credit card statements.

According to Kristie, it was just happenstance that Carrie was passed out at Trey's house the night she and Phillip showed up to make a delivery. It was that night that he decided to take what he always wanted—Carrie. Kristie said neither him nor Trey even noticed when she picked up Christina's camera and took the pictures. She took the memory card with her that night. In the throes of a growing addiction herself, she was afraid to tell anyone. She printed the pictures from her home computer and anonymously left them and the memory card for Carrie.

When Carrie went missing, she asked Phillip about it. He told her to never speak about Carrie again, never ask any questions. And she didn't. She tried to live with the guilt, drowning her sorrows in booze and more pills, wrecking her already ruined life.

Kristie was fucked up from day one. Phillip started giving her pills when she was just sixteen. By nineteen, she was regularly giving her own dad blowjobs for The Holy Trinity concoction.

She says they never had actual intercourse, though.

I don't know how many of us believe that.

The hardest part for all of us was finding out exactly what happened to Carrie.

From what we gather, she took a pregnancy test after receiving the photographs. She went to Phillip, telling him that he had to pay for her to go to rehab because her parents would disown her when she told them she was pregnant.

Carrie was perceptive. And she was right. Just look what they did to Lulu.

When Phillip realized that she wanted to keep the child, he snapped. They were standing in his kitchen and he stabbed her with a bread knife in the neck. He called it a crime of passion. Tried to say he was temporarily insane. Fortunately, no one believed him.

He wrapped her body in plastic, loaded her into the back of one of his many cars, and drove her to Trey's mobile home. They took her out into the woods and buried her. He then had Trey drive her SUV out to the place where it was abandoned, deliberately trying to draw attention away from both Phillip's part of town and Trey's part of town.

When we discovered that Phillip still owned the same car, we couldn't believe it. And when traces of Carrie's blood were found underneath the carpet in the trunk, we *really* couldn't believe it.

The day we searched the woods behind Trey's old, burned-down trailer was one of the worst days of my life. But it was also one of the best days. Despite her bitching and moaning, we refused to let Lulu go. The entire family gathered with her at our house. They kept her company as she waited for the news from me and Marcum.

That night, when we drove up to the house, I found everyone sitting by the firepit. At Lulu's request, Holt and Ridge soaked wood in copper chloride, making a blue-flamed fire. The entire pond was covered in floating water lanterns. More lanterns than I've ever seen in my entire life. More lanterns than her birthday and prom combined.

When we told everyone that Carrie's body had been found, it was like a collective weight was lifted from everyone's shoulders. There were tears, but there was also laughter. Joy. Fondness.

Peace.

Carrie and her child could finally have peace. They could finally get the justice they deserved.

The remains were cremated, and we scattered them at the creek, among the blooming wildflowers.

Reality isn't alone anymore. Her aunt and cousin are with her.

All three of their names are etched on the stone memorial we built. Lulu couldn't stand the thought of just putting the word "Baby" on the memorial for her niece or nephew. She'd been tossing and turning, thinking about what to do for days when Laura crawled into bed with us one morning after spending the night.

"Ask me," she said.

Lulu wrapped her arms around Laura. "Tell me something. Something no one else knows."

"I had a dream last night. A really good dream. I saw a little girl angel with blonde hair. She told me that I'm gonna live a really long time. She told me I'll be pretty and happy, and I'll marry a really handsome boy." She leaned over, so close, her nose nearly touched Lulu's, and she whispered, "I think she might've been talking about Nate."

We both laughed, and I winked at my wife over Little Girl's head. "Oh, yeah?"

"Yes, and she told me her name was Evie and she was my cousin. She told me that she plays with Reality." She propped up on her elbows and pushed her glasses up on her nose. "Do I have a cousin named Evie?"

Lulu grew too emotional to talk.

I kissed Laura's head and said, "You do now."

Ella

He's smiling when he walks into the bar. Sexy, masculine, dangerous, and… smiling. It's no wonder the two ladies in the corner immediately start eye-humping him. Trying to tamp down my jealousy, I do my best not to roll my eyes.

But based on Ry's laugh, I don't think I'm successful.

He kisses my cheek. "Someone in a mood today?"

"I'm not in a mood."

Cullen leans across the bar. "She's most definitely in a mood."

"There is no mood!" I protest.

Cullen's eyes dart to the man playing pool. "That guy hit on her. He didn't see her ring." He clucks his tongue against his teeth. "She chewed his ass up and down."

"Come on, guys. He hit on me," I pout. "What a sicko."

Laughing, Ry turns sideways on his barstool. Using his foot, he kicks my chair, turning me to face him. "And why is he a sicko?" He glances around the bar. "You're the most beautiful woman here."

I scowl. "Why'd you glance around?"

"Uh-oh." Cullen walks away to quickly grab a drink for another customer, smartly avoiding this conversation.

He laughs even harder. "Because if I didn't glance around, you'd accuse me of not being truthful when I say you're the most beautiful woman in the bar."

He's probably right. I pick up my blue drink and take a sip, finishing it off. "Well, he *is* a sicko. Who hits on a pregnant woman?"

Ry grabs the edge of my seat and pulls me close. The wooden barstool legs scrape across the floor. His calloused hands cup my large, round stomach. "You had this hidden underneath the bar. How was he supposed to know you were pregnant?" He brushes his lips against my ear. "And this pregnancy has done nothing but make you more beautiful. Why do you think I had to wake up in the middle of the night last night just to get a taste of you? I can't get enough of you. Being inside of you? It's all I can think about." He sits back, rubbing his jaw and studying me. "And every guy who lays his eyes on you is thinking the exact same thing."

Cullen takes my empty glass. "What's every guy thinking?"

Ry narrows his eyes, studying our friend. "Well, maybe not *every* guy," he says a little too seriously.

Cullen's brow furrows in confusion, making me giggle. I check the time on my phone and slide it into my purse. "We better get going. We don't wanna be late. Holt seems pretty serious about this girl."

Cullen nods. "Yeah, he does. And she's really nice. Sweet. Charming. Totally hot."

"You met her already?" Ry asks.

"He brought her in the bar. She's actually pretty funny. She reminds me a lot of you," he says, nodding at me. "I think she acts one way in front of people—serious and everything—but once you get to know her, she's completely different."

I cock my head to the side. "What do you mean, she's different?"

He chews on his lip, thinking. "Lucille Ball-like."

"She has bright red hair?"

"No, it seems like clumsy trouble follows her."

Ry stands up and holds out his hand, helping me. "Well, let's go meet this lady. Raylee texted, she and the girls are already there, and Will is picking Ty up from daycare."

Laura went home after school today with Anna. They've decided to form a book club. Ry has completely sparked Laura's love of reading. Today was the first official club meeting. How this differs from their other one-thousand playdates, I don't know, but Laura is taking it very seriously.

Cullen chats with the other bartender, reminding him that he'll be back in about nine tonight, after our family dinner. It'll be busy since it's a Friday night. "I'm parked out back. I'll see you guys there."

On our way out, I can't help but flamboyantly rub my large belly as we pass the two women who were ogling my man. Seven months. I'm seven months pregnant and growing larger every day. Playing along, Ry caresses his hand down the small of my back and gives my butt a squeeze.

What a good husband.

We walk hand in hand back down the block to his truck. "So, you plan on telling me what this big surprise is?"

I'm dying to tell him, but I pretend to be coy, just so I can hear his familiar words. "No."

"Well, I suggest you quickly modify your plans, then."

Smiling to myself, I whisper. "I finished."

He immediately stops walking and stares at me in awe. "You finished?"

I nod. Just once.

That's all it takes.

He pulls me into his arms, squeezing me tight—well, as tight as he can with a basketball between us—and forcing me to my tiptoes. I still love it when he does that.

His mouth slants over mine. Sliding his tongue against mine, a heated lava courses through my body.

"I can't believe you finished. I'm so proud of you." He shakes his head. "A book. A whole damn book. A novel! Carrie would be so proud."

I bite my lip. "Thanks."

After everything came out, it was just too much information for my brain to process. I not only had to deal with the complicated drug ring that had been operating since I was in middle school, but I had to process everything that happened to Carrie and her baby. Even myself. I started writing mainly to organize my thoughts for all of the trials and hearings, but then it became something more.

A release. A therapy. A way to grieve. A way to tell my sister's story.

Hell, a way to tell *my* story.

Phillip's sentencing was just last week. It gave the story what it needed—an ending. He'll never be a free man. He'll die in jail.

Alone and penniless and disgraced.

Just what he deserves.

Of course, I shudder to think about what he did to his own daughter. Much to my family's chagrin, I advocated for Kristie and wrote letters to the court pleading for a light sentence for her myriad of crimes. She was the ultimate victim—the patient zero—in all of this. She's serving her five-year term in a minimum security psychiatric and rehab facility.

All of a sudden, the baby starts kicking like crazy, bouncing against my sides like a pole-vault jumper. Grabbing Ry's hand, I place it on my stretched stomach. His pale green eyes grow wide, and he immediately smiles. A soft breeze blows, lifting his light brown hair, tousling it around. He looks just like the boy I met on the back porch when I was seventeen.

Only better.

So much better.

Love and desire cover his face like a shroud. "Amazing. Absolutely amazing. It gets me every time."

I smirk. "I know."

"You know, huh? Well, then, tell me something. Something no one else knows."

"Your son has a strong kick. He's a fighter. Just like his dad."

Ry stops breathing. His jaw falls open. He looks at my stomach, examining me like he has X-ray vision. "A boy? We're having a boy?"

"Yes."

He tosses his hands in the air, screaming. He screams so loud that two deputies walking out of the station look over, checking to see if they're needed. I've seen them both around. Laughing, I wave them away.

Finding out the sex of our baby has been a hotly contested topic. I wanted it to be a surprise; Ry wanted to know. This morning, when I woke up, I decided I couldn't stand it anymore. I called the doctor's office right when they opened to find out just *who* our love had made.

Wrapping his hand around the back of my neck, Ry kisses me. He steals my thoughts from my brain and my life from my soul. This kiss is everything I love. The taste of his tongue. The scratch of his five-day stubble. The press of his body against mine. It's my home.

He's my home.

He's my reality.

And Reality reminds you where you belong.

Not ready to say goodbye to Crutch and Ella?
Good... you don't have to. Follow the rest of
their journey in the next installment of The Hill Family.
It's time for Holt Hill, former football star,
to get his happy-ever-after.

Gratitude

Welp... I guess it happened. I wrote words (a lot of words) and put them out in the world for everyone to see. For everyone to love or hate. For everyone to laugh or cry. For everyone to share or hide.

I never saw myself as a writer. True, I did win two major awards in middle school. That's right, ladies and gentlemen—two, not just one. My first was in the sixth grade for an essay on the ramifications of drunk driving via the D.A.R.E program. (And if you don't know what that is, just search for "This is your brain on drugs.") The second award was in the seventh grade for a scary short story. Well, after those major accolades, who would need more, right?

Well, somewhere along the way, I guess *I* needed more.

So here we are.

No matter what happens, I crossed something off my Bucket List, and that's pretty amazing. I fell into my own world and found myself madly in love with Ella and Crutch. I can only hope you love them as much as I do.

I'd like to thank all of my sweet (and patient) family and friends who helped me throughout the process—voting on logos, voting on covers, giving me words of encouragement, beta reading, answering social media questions, testing the website and newsletter, spreading the word, and just being all-around cheerleaders and champions. Kuntry, Boo, Dandy, Big, Tonia P, Cassidy P, Aunt Karla, Kaleen G, Yolanda C, Ashley C.S., Adrienne C.E., Karisa B, Courtney W, Tanja E, Ashley R, Amy D, Misty M, Heather S.S., Casey Y, Amber M, Dani J, and Brooklyn W. And if I forgot anyone, please don't be mad!

A huge shout-out to all of my new followers on social media! Believe it or not, I was a social media virgin until I had to start marketing The Reality Duet. Why? As a self-proclaimed Nosy Nate, I was worried about the ramifications of social media on my psyche. Fortunately, I've been able to maintain a somewhat healthy balance—so far. If you see me slipping into a social media coma, please pick me up and throw me out!

Thank you to Tony B for looking at everything for me. And remember what I said about your art and romance novels. It could be a match made in heaven.

Thank you to Stacey Blake for accepting me as a client and designing beautiful covers for both novels. I appreciate you.

Thank you to the wonderful teams at Grey's Promotions (Jen and Olivia) and Give Me Books Promotions (Jo) for accepting me as a client and helping me with the ARC and promotional process. These two companies are on point!

Thank you to my new friend, mentor, and super-amazing author, Kelly Elliott. You have been sweeter than a candied apple, and I appreciate all your help—the phone conversations, the texts, the advice, and well... everything.

To Elaine York with Allusion Publishing... Holy freakin' cow, what can I say? I went looking for an editor, and I found an amazing friend. When I started the process of bringing The Reality Duet to publication, I was as lost as a Christmas goose. You have guided me the entire way. And by the entire way, I mean *the entire way*. When I was a hair's breadth away from posting to social media that I was backing out and publication would not happen, you talked me down from the ledge. You blessed me with the validation that I didn't even know I needed. You've filled a space in my writer's head and heart that I didn't even know was empty, and I will be forever in your gratitude for accepting me as a client. And a friend.

To Dandy and Big, the most amazing parents ever... Thank you for *almost* always buying me the Barbie doll. Like Dandy said, "I could entertain myself for hours with my imagination and a Barbie doll." Who knew that make-believe play would be a precursor to this? And thank you for always (not *almost* always, but *always* always) buying me the book to read. Considering I refused to check-out library books, you spent a small fortune on my book addiction. Books I voraciously—and quickly—devoured. Thank you for encouraging me to publish The Reality Duet. Thank you for loving me unconditionally, supporting me wholeheartedly, and singing my praises to anyone who will listen. I would be nothing without the two of you. I am beyond blessed that you are our best friends and that I have the privilege of seeing you every day. Thank you for loving my husband. Thank you for loving my son. Thank you for loving me.

To my Boo Boo Bear... I love you more than words can say. I've told you before and I'll tell you again—you are my heart. You are an amazing young man, and I'm beyond lucky to be your mom. You're filled to the brim with intelligence, empathy, and the best text-one liners known to mankind. I pray every single second of every single day for your happiness as you grow into the man you are meant to be. When I close my eyes, I see nothing but amazing things for your future, and I'm so excited for all the possibilities spread out before you. The love you give makes me a better person. Thank you for your hugs. Thank you for being my scary movie buddy. Thank you for being *you*—handsome, funny, smart, kind, and level-headed. And more importantly, thank you for making me a momma nearly eighteen years ago.

To Kuntry, my husband and my best friend... Thank you isn't enough. One party, and I was a goner. One look at that wonderful big butt of yours, and I knew you would be mine. We might've taken a little longer route to get back to each other, but the Lord knew what He was doing. If Boo is my heart, you are my soul. The way you love me brings me to my knees. You think I'm beautiful, funny, smart, crazy, and talented. You always treat me like I'm the only woman in the world. Literally. You only have eyes for me, and you have no idea how special that makes me feel. Not only that, you actually *like* me. Your favorite pastime is just being with us—me, Boo, Dandy, and Big. In a world where married people don't actually *like* each other half the time, you *like* me. That speaks volumes. You are the best husband, father, brother, son-in-law, friend, cousin, teacher... and the list goes on and on. Thank you for loving our son. Thank you for loving my parents. Thank you for loving me. You're stuck with me, baby.

To the Lord my God, my Almighty Savior Jesus Christ... Thank you. I am unworthy, but made worthy in Your eyes. You have blessed me beyond measure—with a family, with a home, with food in my (chubby) stomach, and with good health. I know it might seem crazy to some that I am thanking the Lord above when these novels are a little... 'unchurch-like'. But God gave me this imagination, and I am happy when I embrace it. Whether I sell one copy, one-hundred copies, or one-million copies, I am rich beyond my wildest dreams because I have an Eternal Home. My Granny went Home a few months ago. She's with You and Papa and her sons. I hear her. I feel her. And I miss her. Take care of her until I'm there.

About the Author

HALCIE DAWN is a happy and blessed wife and mother. She attended the University of Alabama where she graduated with a bachelor's degree in Business Management. A lifelong avid reader, her love affair with books started with the original *The Babysitter's Club* series when she was in the third grade and morphed into a love of all things romantic. After years of thought, she finally placed finger to keyboard and penned her first contemporary romance. When not writing or reading by the swimming pool, she can be found watching true crime documentaries or *Psych* (for the millionth time). Halcie lives in Alabama with her amazingly wonderful, funny, kind, and handsome husband and son. And she lives next door to her parents, whose antics often have her laughing so hard she pees her pants. But without a doubt, the star of the home is the family morkiepoo, Princess Doodle Fluffybutt.

Connect with me:
Website: www.halciedawn.com
Instagram: halciedawnromance
Facebook: www.facebook.com/halciedawn